THE TWO LIES OF FAVEN SYTHE

"Please." Faven's voice was unsteady with the necessity of begging, something the navi didn't have much practice at. "Take me with you. Do as Red was going to do—kidnap me for ransom. They'll pay handsomely."

"We're not that stupid." Amandine started to peel the woman's hand off her arm. Faven tightened her grip, digging her nails in.

"Navigators are being sent to the *Black Celeste* and aren't heard from again," Faven said, rapid-fire, her voice a whispering hiss. "I need your help."

"Ghost stories," Amandine said, but a chill crept over her skin. Faven had the look of a woman who'd seen a few ghosts.

For one dreadful moment, Amandine looked into eyes that saw the ways between the stars, and feared. Feared the navi knew Amandine's secret. That the rebellious navigator had dropped down from on high to grasp Amandine's arm and tell her that she knew. That Amandine's past had come home to roost and her world was about to unravel beneath her feet.

T0385165

Praise for
the Devoured Worlds

"I know it's a cliché to say, 'You won't be able to put it down,' but that's exactly the effect *The Blighted Stars* has on you! Riveting adventure at a rocketing pace, with engaging characters thrown in for good measure!"

Connie Willis, Hugo Award–winning author

"O'Keefe delivers a captivating exploration of identity in this smart, addictive space adventure full of intrigue, visceral danger, and deeply personal stakes. Come for the epic sci-fi action, stay for the charmingly broken characters just doing their best"

J. S. Dewes, author of *The Last Watch*

"Full of deftly plotted twists and turns, *The Blighted Stars* is a body-hopping, zombie-popping, rock-licking thrill ride"

Emily Skrutskie, author of *Bonds of Brass*

"*The Blighted Stars* is everything I want in a book: lots of action, lots of character, and lots of heart. Megan E. O'Keefe delights with every page, from her stunning action sequences set on alien planets to her exploration of the twisted pathways taken by the human heart. This is space opera for the ages, wrapped in complicated and delicious layers of family and loyalty and science and love and duty. I couldn't put it down!"

Karen Osborne, author of *Architects of Memory*

"Emotional arcs and action sequences, vivid worldbuilding, and interesting explorations of body printing and corporate servitude provide an immersive story...O'Keefe's latest has the intrigue, surprises, and high stakes of her previous novels"

Library Journal (starred review)

"*The Blighted Stars* yields enjoyable adventure full of romantic tension and alien mystery"

Wall Street Journal

"O'Keefe is a master world builder, and *The Blighted Stars* has one of the most fascinating sci-fi concepts of the year...If future entries in O'Keefe's Devoured Worlds saga are as exciting as this book, sci-fi fans will be thanking their lucky stars for years to come"

BookPage

"Thrilling, yearning, and paranoid. This book kept me up way too late!"

Max Gladstone, Hugo and Nebula Award–winning author

"Brimming with unconventional gender dynamics and shifting identities, *The Blighted Stars* is character-driven science fiction at its best—a taut novel with human questions at its heart"

E. J. Beaton, author of *The Councillor*

"Smart, incisive, and utterly gripping. Megan E. O'Keefe's masterful storytelling will draw you into a complex, brutal, yet hope-charged world, break your heart, and leave you begging for more"

Rowenna Miller, author of *The Fairy Bargains of Prospect Hill*

"A delightfully twisty space opera filled with unique worldbuilding and deft explorations of humanity, family, and power. Add in a dash of rebellion and a hint of romance, and I'm hooked—I can't wait for the next book!"

Jessie Mihalik, author of *Hunt the Stars*

By Megan E. O'Keefe

The Protectorate

Velocity Weapon

Chaos Vector

Catalyst Gate

The Devoured Worlds

The Blighted Stars

The Fractured Dark

The Bound Worlds

The First Omega (*novella*)

The Two Lies of Faven Sythe

THE TWO LIES OF FAVEN SYTHE

MEGAN E. O'KEEFE

orbit

orbit-books.co.uk

ORBIT

First published in Great Britain in 2025 by Orbit

1 3 5 7 9 10 8 6 4 2

Copyright © 2025 by Megan E. O'Keefe

Excerpt from *These Burning Stars* by Bethany Jacobs
Copyright © 2023 by Bethany Jacobs

The moral right of the author has been asserted.

*All characters and events in this publication, other than those
clearly in the public domain, are fictitious and any resemblance
to real persons, living or dead, is purely coincidental.*

All rights reserved.
No part of this publication may be reproduced, stored in a
retrieval system, or transmitted, in any form or by any means, without
the prior permission in writing of the publisher, nor be otherwise circulated
in any form of binding or cover other than that in which it is published
and without a similar condition including this condition being
imposed on the subsequent purchaser.

A CIP catalogue record for this book
is available from the British Library.

ISBN 978-0-356-52634-8

Printed and bound in Great Britain by Clays Ltd, Elcograf, S.p.A.

Papers used by Orbit are from well-managed forests
and other responsible sources.

Orbit
An imprint of
Little, Brown Book Group
Carmelite House
50 Victoria Embankment
London, EC4Y 0DZ

The authorised representative
in the EEA is
Hachette Ireland
8 Castlecourt Centre
Dublin 15, D15 XTP3, Ireland
(email: info@hbgi.ie)

An Hachette UK Company
www.hachette.co.uk

orbit-books.co.uk

For the intrepid fishers of the Eorzean Aquarium, and all other found families who come together to build safe havens

ONE

Faven

Faven Sythe was told two lies on the day her mother's organs finished crystallizing. The first was an updated work assignment. The banal notice only reached her because she'd flagged the name attached. It told her that Ulana Valset, Faven's mentor, had been reassigned to Amiens Station. A mere microdot of an orbital on the lacy edges of the galactic center. There, Ulana would train younger navigators—as she had once trained Faven—until the crystallization took her.

Alone in her rooms high in the Spire, Faven touched the petrified cheek of her mother's corpse. She had chosen a gentle position in which to spend eternity, kneeling upon the floor with her arms cradled across her stomach, as if rocking a babe.

Soon Faven would have to alert the architects that her mother had fully succumbed. That the last vestiges of her skin had transmuted to scales of aquamarine, and at long last, even the irises of her eyes had switched from dusky umber to the teal glow of the cryst. Faven kissed her mother's forehead, the mineral scales smooth and cold beneath her lips. A small patch of scale already marred the corner of Faven's own mouth, bracketing her smile and tugging at the skin when she laughed.

"I'll see you moved to the Rosette Pond," Faven said. "Where you can watch the gleamfish swim. I promise."

She did not tell the corpse of her mother that the order would be sent remotely, and that Faven would not be there to see the enshrinement done. The statue kneeling on Faven's floor was just that—a statue. A memory. Her mother's consciousness had long since transmuted to light. Her mother had become a star.

Faven wrapped a plain grey cloak around herself and flipped the hood up to hide the shining web of sapphires that veiled her hair and shoulders.

That her mentor had been sent to Amiens was a lie as pretty as the lustrous corpse kneeling on soft velvets in Faven's sitting room. Faven's world was constructed of such lies, the dull solder between shining panes of cryst-glass. Most of the time she did not see those lies, for she did not care to look.

But when Ulana had last left Votive City, there had been tension in her eyes. An anxious clutching in the long fingers of hands armored with the aquamarine blue scales of cryst that eventually took all those who walked the paths between the stars. After leaving, Ulana had stopped answering all attempts to contact her.

And so, Faven had snooped. A grave sin. A terrible violation. The paths a navigator wove were sacred, the creative expressions of their very souls.

Ulana Valset's soul led her into the dark.

Faven had been certain she was incorrect. That in spying upon the starpath Ulana wove into the lightdrive of her ship, Faven had somehow corrupted it. When you live steeped in lies, you grow used to telling them to yourself.

Ulana's route did not go to Amiens Station. It led into the Clutch. A dark fist of a dyson sphere seized around a whimpering star. It was the graveyard of their predecessors. An expanse of rubble held sacred only because it was the last known concretion of the technological artifacts of the cryst, the ancient species whose leftover research had given the navigators their art.

A place of reverence. A place for dying. And all that technology was as dead as its progenitors. Save the *Black Celeste*.

A rumor. A fairy tale. A derelict ship called the *Black Celeste* was very real, but the stories that clung to it breathed mystery into its dead walls. Young navigators titillated one another with stories of it waking up. Of its halls filled with the spectral shapes of the cryst. Sometimes, the young navigators would whisper, you could see a light inside, burning. Sometimes that light moved.

The stories had fascinated Faven when she was too young to have learned that the unknown was a lot less scary than the ugly truths of the world.

Ulana's starpath was a twisted, frayed thing. A jumbling of punch-through points and scrambled orbital grooves. But its intended terminus was clear, for the *Black Celeste* was the only known structure within the Clutch said to move outside of orbital drift, and the path accounted for such a possibility.

Ulana had gone into a ghost story, and Faven couldn't even ask her why. But the second lie, well. That might have something to tell her after all.

Faven skimmed the other message—the ugly, clumsy lie. It was simple enough. A contract offered, with saccharine platitudes, for Navigator Sythe's services in weaving a starpath into the lightdrive of a merchant vessel that wanted to transport quartz wine from Votive City to Orvieto Station.

Faven knew that she was coddled. That her thirty-six years of life had slipped by wrapped in fine silks studded with gemstones. But she was not uninformed on matters of commerce. Quartz wine was plentiful in Orvieto Station, and the fee involved in her weaving a custom path would far outweigh any profit. The merchant wished to meet to discuss the matter in a sector of the docks known for dark-dealing. A place infested with the pirates that plagued the skies presided over by the Choir of Stars.

Faven was being fished.

The hubris of such a thing, to bait your hook for the mouth of a god, amused her. But the Choir of Stars would not tell her about the *Black Celeste*. Would not tell her why her mentor had gone into the dark.

Ulana wasn't the only one to have disappeared in recent years, and the Choir refused to answer the questions of those who'd gone looking for their loved ones. No, Ulana was not the first. She was merely the first that Faven cared about.

She'd lost two mothers on the same day, and she was so very weary of being lied to. Pirates, while not known for their honesty, made a habit of scavenging the Clutch. That baited hook might very well possess the answers she sought.

Faven had not been born of her mother's womb. She'd been a shard of sacred cryst that had grown beneath her mother's skin and then been plucked free to be nurtured into a woman, or something like a woman.

When she closed her eyes, she and the other cryst-born could read the paths between the stars. Find the secret ways through the fabric of the universe and teach them to the lightdrives of ships. Sometimes, the navigators saw other things when they closed their human eyes.

She was no auger. No farseer nor futurespinner. If a confidant were ever to ask her if she believed in fate or magic, she would scoff like all the rest of her kin. Their craft was trade. Travel. Gods of commerce and expansion, and the rest was fairy-whispers.

But they all had their little quirks. Some cryst-born heard notes of music when they charted their paths. Discordant vibrations that warned them off dangerous routes and sweet notes for safer shores. So common was the phenomenon that they named their governing council for it—the Choir of Stars.

Faven saw light. Shades of color guiding her way, illuminating secret pitfalls to her as she worked paths between gravitational grooves. When she closed her eyes and meditated upon Ulana's lie, she saw an empty space in her future. A violet-soaked nightmare of a moment, red-shifted, rushing closer.

She conjured the fishing message to mind and was filled with the wavering glow of indigo. Safe, perhaps, though eager to shift into the dangerous realm of violet, if she was not careful. A static moment. A moment she could take, or leave, while the other came for her all the same.

In the end, it was no choice at all.

Faven summoned a travel censer and went to be kidnapped by pirates.

TWO

Amandine

Bitter Amandine was reasonably certain that Tagert Red was about to get himself killed or mortally embarrassed, and she wanted to be there to see it when it happened. Tagert thought himself so clever, scheming with his crew in a dingy side room of the Broken Mast. Their voices were tight with anticipation, and not nearly soft enough to evade being picked up by the listening devices Amandine had planted in every single room of that pirate-lousy bar.

The owner, a person with more sense than muscle but a deft hand on a shotgun trigger, chose to ignore Amandine's spying. It was a pirate bar. Any pirate daft enough to talk real business in a pirate bar deserved to have their score scooped on them.

Every so often, some soul with a lick of sense would scan the bar before talking plans with their crew, then make a damn racket about the devices. The owner would, with a shrug, toss them in the incinerator. Amandine was always back within the week with one fist full of bugs and the other fist full of cash.

And so the cycle repeated. And Amandine stayed one step ahead of every dodder-headed pirate working in Votive City.

Tagert's crew left the Broken Mast, making their way to the

nearby docks for their supposed "meeting." Amandine flipped up the camera feed Kester had patched her into. She leaned back in the captain's seat of the *Marquette*, cradling a hot mug of tea with a dash of rum tossed in to really warm her up, kicked her boots up on the dash, and watched in real time as Tagert's crew made a mess of getting into position.

It was almost painful to watch. She had half a mind to make Kester patch her into the dock's speakers so that she could bark out some real orders. Tagert had put his lookouts in positions where they only had 120 degrees of view, for light's sake.

"He gets worse every year," Becks said. The mechanic slotted themself into the second-in-command seat and wove their fingers together, stretching their arms forward until their knuckles cracked.

Amandine smiled into her tea. "He stays the same, but the world changes around him, and his already questionable techniques grow clumsier in their execution."

Becks wrinkled their nose and jabbed at the console, checking the cloaking tech wrapped around the *Marquette*. It'd been fritzing lately, and it'd be rather embarrassing if it fuzzed out now and revealed her position, hovering above Tagert's pitiful tableau. Amandine had checked it twice herself. Becks checked it three more times.

"Didn't sign up to stomp boots with no philosopher-cap'n," they grumbled.

"You didn't sign up at all, Becks. You tromped up my gangway and told me my thrusters were overheating and going to strip the enamel if someone didn't do something about it, and that someone was going to be you."

"If I hadn't, you woulda been stuck out in the black somewhere twiddling your thumbs with a hold full of stolen cargo waiting for a tug and hoping they didn't look too hard and start asking questions."

"And every day I pray my thanks at the altar of your illustrious being for that timely intervention."

"Best be praying for better pay, Cap'n," Becks said, but a curl to the corner of their lips meant their ego was assuaged, and now Amandine needed to bite her tongue and let them work, lest she annoy them into distraction.

Amandine had her own distractions. A travel censer swept down from the high peak of the Navigator's Spire. The hexagonal conveyance was constructed of the same multicolor glass as all Votive City. It hung perfectly straight, a teardrop in variegated shades of blue dripping toward the docks from on high.

She leaned closer to the screen and set her mug aside. A silhouette of a person waited within, their shape obscured by the soft fall of a cloak, a hood pulled up to hide their face.

Amandine couldn't believe it. She really couldn't. Faven Sythe hadn't exactly made a name for herself, but she'd spent all her life training and working in the Spire's hallowed halls. She should be too clever and too skilled by far to fall for Tagert Red's clumsy attempt to lure her out. Either the woman was daft, desperate, or had a trick up her sleeve.

The first two options were more likely. The last was more fun.

"Kester." Amandine jabbed her finger onto the button for the intercom between the pilot's deck and the armory. "Tell me your scans are picking up weapons, or guards, or something. Tell me this fool-headed goddess isn't going to meet with Tagert Red about a phony deal *alone*."

"I cannot tell you such a thing, Captain," she said.

Amandine rubbed her hands together. That delicate bird riding down from on high was up to something. It'd been a long, long time since Amandine hadn't known what, exactly, she'd be walking into.

"You sure about this, Cap'n?" Becks's hands stilled on the console as they cocked her a sideways glance. "Tangling with a navigator, I mean. Our cloaking is up. We could sail out of here without any-one ever knowing we'd been."

"Come on, Becks." She clapped them on the shoulder. "Live a little."

"I'd like to keep on living—that's the trouble!"

Amandine tapped a small photo she kept taped to her dash for luck—the cabin her grandfather had built, swaddled in the mists of Blackloach—and gave Becks a thump on the back as she swung out of her chair.

Whatever they shouted after her, she didn't hear it. She was already striding toward the armory to join Kester and Tully in pre-paring. The more scores they scooped up, the sooner Amandine could get back to living life in that peaceful cabin, spending her days baiting hooks for fish instead of ships.

The sooner she could retire her captainship of the *Marquette* and stop looking over her shoulder every damn time someone so much as sniffed in her ship's direction.

Tagert Red might be about to have a very bad day, but things were looking up for Bitter Amandine.

THREE

Faven

F aven twitched the hood of her cloak forward to better hide her profile from prying eyes. Though the cloak was plain grey, soft as water and thick with warmth, the Vigil stripped away all pretense of simplicity.

The largest of humanity's stations, the Vigil was a many-faceted jewel whose exterior walls were constructed entirely of cryst-glass plating salvaged from the derelict constructs of the Clutch. Cryst-glass was the most resilient material in the known universe, the gleaming panes letting through the brilliant wink of stars and passing lights of ships while still shielding the station within from radiation and the endless, hungry maw of the vacuum beyond.

In the dock district, the ceiling was patterned with the Sixteen Cardinal Weaves. Spiky compasses representing those starpaths painted myriad shades of gold and violet over the plain grey of her cloak. Auspicious and dangerous colors.

Those sixteen starpaths were free for any starship captain to make use of, no votive required, as they were the starpaths that kept their society operational. A gift. A necessity. Anything more refined than that, any clever path that shaved hours or days off the cardinal routes or brought you closer to your destination, cost dearly.

The man awaiting Faven could not even afford the deposit for a custom starpath.

He wore last year's fashion, a tunic cut tight to his waist in the seven colors of the visible spectrum. The cloth was ratty at the seams, his slim trousers deep black to offset the prismatic hues of his tunic. He held himself with the stiff posture of an amateur actor playing an aristocrat, and the bulge of a weapon hidden against his back rather ruined the sleek lines of his outfit.

She guessed him about forty, or in the early range thereof, though hard years spent living on ships with haphazard radiation shielding had drawn deeper creases across his face. Laugh lines framed his lips and furrows traced old frustrations across his brow.

This man had lured her to an abandoned corner of the docks to take advantage of her in some way, but those wrinkles told her he was quick to laugh and often befuddled—crunching his brow as he thought. A pang of sympathy rang within her. Was it right to take advantage of a man who would send her such a clumsy fishing attempt, and be foolish enough to believe it had worked?

No matter. She had questions about the Clutch that she needed answered. Whether or not this man realized he was in over his head, he was a pirate. He'd know a thing or two about that field of dormant treasures. She met his eyes and inclined her head at the sharp angle of a superior greeting their inferior.

"Mr. Clairmont?" Faven asked.

He swept her an elaborate bow. "Navigator Sythe. I'm so very pleased that you agreed to meet with me to discuss a votive."

Faven *tsked*. There was only so much pageantry she could take. "Dear man, you and I are both quite aware that the cost of a shipment of quartz wine from the Vigil to Orvieto would never provide enough profit to cover the expense of a custom starpath. What is it you truly desire?"

He blinked, a foot sliding back instinctually, a very unnoble motion. That was not a merchant's or trader's natural reaction to surprise, but the bracing foot of a brawler. Faven gave him a flat smile, cryst-scale tugging at the corner of her lips, and lifted her eyes deliberately from that foot to the man's eyes.

"Gotta admit." He dropped the crisp elocution. Faven arched a brow. His accent had been convincing enough that she hadn't thought twice about it. The man had some experience in the upper echelons, then. Perhaps this would make her dealings with him easier. "Didn't think you'd bite. Clumsy letter like that, only the dullest would take the bait."

"Ah." She fingered the cool metal of the armillary hidden within her flowing sleeve. "That explains the nature of your overture but not the desired outcome."

"Coin, Navigator." He rolled his shoulders in a halfway apologetic shrug and reached back, producing a snub-nosed shotgun. He didn't point it at her, not yet, but instead rested the barrel against his shoulder, finger on the trigger guard in silent promise. "What else is there? I don't mean you any harm, but you should know you're surrounded."

At the word, five unsavory figures emerged from various hiding places around the dock. These hadn't bothered with the false finery the man wore; the weapons in their hands were better cared for than their clothes. Faven's heart gave a delightful kick. Her vision felt sharper, her mind bright. It was the most vibrant she'd felt since her mother had stopped speaking, and she craved more.

"Ransom, then," she said. "I suspected as much. Who am I addressing?"

Beneath the cover of her sleeve, she clutched the armillary, assuring herself by waking the familiar thrum of its energies. If things went too poorly, she could weave herself a path to safety in seconds. And if she was truly motivated, she could weave the pirates a path into the heart of a star, and brush her hands of their ashes.

"That dunderhead is Tagert Red," a drawling voice said, rich with amusement.

Faven turned to meet this new curiosity. A tall, broad-shouldered woman strode into the center of the pirates. Her copper-red hair was tugged back under the wrap of a bandana, but Faven caught glimpses of gems woven into thin braids. The brown leathers she wore were scuffed but well mended, and the matching coat that flowed open around her frame did a much better job of hiding extra weapons than Tagert's tunic had.

Between the woman's swagger and the easy way she tapped the barrel of her own shotgun against her shoulder, Faven would have believed it if the woman were to tell her she'd wrestled the leather she wore off the animal that'd grown it.

"Amandine," Tagert said with a growl of frustration. "This ain't any of your concern."

"*Bitter* Amandine?" Faven asked, unable to help a small gasp of surprise. The infamous pirate shot her a viridian-eyed wink.

Bitter Amandine. Even in the high towers of the Spire that name had floated up to Faven's ears. The only surviving protégé of Captain Amber Jacq, a man whose name still made Choir captains look to the stars in silent prayer. The Choir claimed Amandine was little more than a nuisance, but the fact that they knew her name at all revealed she was more than that. Infamous for exclusively targeting corporate vessels, she was rumored to have ears to the ground in every corner of the galaxy to facilitate her daring heists.

If anyone had answers, and access, to the Clutch, it would be her.

"That's what they call me." She stopped a few feet away from Tagert, spreading her arms wide. "But my friends call me Amandine, and we're all friends here, aren't we, lovelies?"

Tagert responded by leveling his shotgun straight at her heart. Amandine didn't seem to mind. "Scurry off," he said.

"Nah," she said. "You're here to take advantage of a navi responding to a genuine request. For shame, Tagert, for shame. We got a code, don't we? Mess about with the navis too much and they might stop doing business with us." She leaned toward him and dropped her voice. "With those of us who can *actually afford them.*"

"You overstep." Tagert's finger slid off the guard to rest on the trigger.

"I step where I fucking like." Amandine snapped her fingers.

Faven flinched at a sudden brightness. Floodlights stung her eyes, made her throw up an arm to shield her vision. A ship hovered a dozen or so feet above their heads, its spotlights pointed straight at them.

It appeared to be a Rayonnant model, a favorite of merchants and mercenaries both, but its sleek body was longer and broader than any Rayonnant Faven had ever seen. Trefoil windows banded its hull with cryst-glass scenes. In the nearest, an abstract woman with carnelian hair stood victorious above three crashed ships that looked suspiciously like Choir freight haulers. Faven had no doubt that the red-haired woman depicted in the glass was meant to represent Amandine during her many exploits.

The light faded back to bearable levels. As Faven lowered her arm and blinked tears from her eyes, she could make out another figure circling the knot of pirates with predatory grace. There was an angularity to the person's frame that prickled Faven's senses, and the light seemed to bend away from them, so that it was difficult to see them clearly.

Amandine's shotgun was still propped against her shoulder. But she'd taken Tagert's, and had his own weapon pointed at his chest, one-handed.

"Scurry off," she said.

Tagert's cheeks went so red he nearly turned purple. "This ain't over, Bitter."

She merely waved the barrel of the shotgun at him in response.

Tagert's fists clenched, and a fake smile that Faven believed was supposed to be an intimidating sneer painted his lips. He spat at her feet, then waved a hand through the air and stomped off, vanishing between the crates with the rest of his crew. Amandine waited, unmoving, until her head tipped to the side and she nodded to herself. Then she slung her own shotgun back into its holster inside her coat, letting Tagert's rest against her shoulder in its place.

"Right, then." She turned to face Faven. "It's time you and I had a chat, Navi."

Faven gave the pirate a wide and genuine smile, inclining her head with far more respect than she had for Tagert. "At last," she said. "I was beginning to worry I had wasted my time."

FOUR

Amandine

Faven looked a fragile thing, by Amandine's reckoning. She had the kind of long, willowy limbs that Amandine could grab in either hand and snap over her knee, should the mood strike her, but not the height to go with the narrowness, which only added to the impression of being insubstantial. A twig that could wash away on a strong breeze.

But her chin was held high, and the white freckles that painted her night-dark cheeks gleamed like stars. Cryst-scale had broken out around one side of her mouth, adding a sucked-in look that gave the impression of a permanent smirk.

Long enough ago that Amandine filed the story under "legend" and not "history," the cryst had come to humanity and lifted them up. Gave them starfaring ships and stations and then they'd either left or died off, depending on the favored theology of the person telling the tale. Their reasons aside, the result was the same: Humanity had foundered until the intrepid souls who'd become the Choir of Stars discovered a way to fuse leftover cryst-tech with human biology.

They'd kept on doing it until they got a result that wasn't quite human anymore, nor was it purely cryst, but the cryst-born were capable of making starpaths and forging lightdrives, and that had been good enough to keep humanity alive in the structures the cryst had left behind.

Amandine didn't know what the cryst had looked like. No one did. The only depictions they'd left of themselves were abstract, floating points of light rendered in cryst-glass.

To hear the navis tell it, the cryst-born were more cryst than human. Amandine had heard rumors that the two species couldn't interbreed, but Faven looked human enough to her. Stuck-up, to be sure, but all the confidence in the world couldn't have tricked her into thinking that meeting Tagert alone was a good idea. The navi had something else in mind. Something she hadn't yet said.

She was an interesting woman, this Faven Sythe, but the most interesting part of all was the thrill that had sparked in her eyes when the guns had been drawn. And the obvious weapon hidden up her sleeve.

"I've shown you mine." Amandine hoisted Tagert's shotgun for emphasis. "You show me yours."

"I'm afraid you're going to be disappointed."

Faven drew her weapon and held it up to view. It appeared flat at first, the size of a dessert plate, but it unfolded, rising to hover above her palm. An elaborate silver-toned metal and gemstone-encrusted armillary. Holograms teased between the orbital rings, hinting at the paths the navi's power could draw between the stars.

Amandine had been told two things about armillaries: A skilled navi could preprogram starpaths into them to pull upon in a rush, and most importantly, they held micro lightdrives in their cores to facilitate short jumps. In a battle, those jumps included weaving a path between a poor soul and the fiery heart of a star. Amandine had seen plenty of that, when she'd fought in the Push.

"A mere tool of my trade," Faven said with a one-shouldered shrug. The spinning rings of the armillary painted shadows across her star-speckled face.

"Sure," Amandine drawled. "Which star had you planned on dropping Tagert into, if he wasn't amenable to your plans?"

Surprise widened the navi's eyes, and that permanent smirk deepened. "You are educated in our methods."

"I'm educated in a great many things that aren't any of your business." She gestured to the side. "Kester, take it down."

Faven's head whipped around when Kester emerged from the shadows. At first glance, Kester didn't look particularly intimidating. She wore a gold-trimmed tunic in crisp white above precisely tailored slacks, her high collar as stiff as her posture. Kester kept her ash-blond hair cut short, the amber-hued sunglasses perched on her nose hiding a pair of gelid eyes that could make even Amandine's guts turn to water, if she glared at her just right. She would have made a better fake merchant than Tagert in his ridiculous getup.

Most people who tangled with Kester thought she was too prim to get her hands bloody. Those people didn't live long enough to revise their opinion. Faven Sythe surprised them all by taking one look at Kester and shuffling back a step, her sapphire-laced veil slipping down to puddle about her shoulders. She held the armillary out to the side, as if it was a hammer she was preparing to bring down.

"If you don't wish to visit the star I'd planned for Mr. Red," Faven said, "then I suggest you don't attempt to take my armillary." Her tone was all cool indifference, but Amandine caught the tremor in her voice that said she didn't want to be put to the test. A Spire navi like her, she'd probably never had to make good on a threat in her life.

Kester paused. Amandine suppressed a smile as Kester flicked two fingers against her collar in mild agitation before she pressed a forearm to her abdomen and bowed over it.

"I do not mean to disparage the lady's hospitality," Kester said in that deep, silky voice of hers. "But I do not believe I would enjoy such a visit."

"Now, now," Amandine said. "No one's going to take your trinket. I told her to take it down. She's already done so."

Kester gestured, almost sheepishly, to her collar and pulled it aside so that Faven could see the fine wires concealed in the fabric. "Weave disrupter, Navigator."

"Educated and prepared," Faven said. "It appears you have me at a disadvantage after all. I should have expected no less, from Amber Jacq's disciple."

"Disciple ain't the word I'd use, but now you've got me wondering, Navi. Just how educated are you on me and mine? Because while it's a fact I crewed with Jacq, it's also a fact that those who know I did are too clever to say that name to my face."

"And why's that?"

"We disagreed." Amandine rolled her stiffening shoulder, easing the scar there. "Often. So if you've come looking for a pirate as bloody-minded as he was, sorry to say you've missed your mark. But you're lucky, too, because ol' Jacq would've had you bound and shoved in his cargo hold by now."

Faven didn't so much as twitch at what most would have considered a thinly veiled threat. She merely tipped her head to the side, thinking. "Why haven't you?"

"I don't much like violence," Amandine said. At Faven's light scoff, she added with a wink, "Not if I can help it, anyway. Truth be told, only the daft and the suicidal like tangling with you crystborn. So, I'm going to make this real easy for you. In payment for your timely rescue, I require two things: cash and information."

"What kind of information?"

Amandine let her smile turn coy. "I'm a curious sort. I gotta know, Sythe, what's a smart girl like you doing wandering into a clumsy trap set by the likes of Tagert Red? You wanted him for something. What was it?"

"Perhaps we should have this conversation somewhere more private?" She lifted her eyes, indicating the looming shadow of the *Marquette*.

A chorus of protests exploded across Amandine's comms, loud

enough to make her suppress a flinch. Becks was, unsurprisingly, the biggest dissenter, droning on and on about letting a navi anywhere near the ship's drive, where she could sabotage their navigational systems and none of them would have the skill to fix whatever problem she'd caused.

"I got a better idea," Amandine said. "Why don't you pull that hood of yours back up and let me buy you a proper dockside drink? Then we can chat."

"What I have to say cannot be overheard."

Amandine gave her a broad smile. "The only ears where we're going are mine."

FIVE

Amandine

Amandine led Faven through the labyrinthine roads of the docks, waving in greeting to those who recognized her as she passed. The Vigil wasn't her favorite station in the cluster, but it was the richest. The vast majority of goods she pushed through black and grey markets ended up here one way or another. While Votive City itself kept a tight watch on all trade, the sprawling suburbs and townships surrounding the capital city were more than willing to keep their questions to themselves about the origins of certain items.

Nothing illegal was ever technically done at the docks. Pirates weren't foolish enough to risk the wrath of Votive City's mechanical guards, the Blades. But hands were shaken, palms were greased, and meetings arranged for later in friendlier territory.

"Hey, Bitter!" a woman shouted, tone light and welcoming.

Amandine craned her neck around to spy a stocky woman with a shock of short, spiky, electric-orange hair. The woman hopped off the side of the ship she'd been fiddling with and waved. Amandine squinted—that ship was running refabbed tail stabilizers. Old, discontinued stock that wasn't manufactured anymore because the profit margins were too low, even though plenty of ships relied on them.

Two months ago, Amandine and the crew of the *Marquette* had broken into the manufacturer's warehouse to steal the last known pallet and, naturally, the mold and specs to make more. She cracked a grin and lifted a hand to the woman.

"Stabilizers holding up all right?" Amandine asked.

A smile overtook her weathered face. "Better than when those vultures at Vertue Corp were making them. You don't know me, Bitter, but I can't thank you enough. Couldn't afford a full refit of the housing, and I sure couldn't afford a whole new ship."

"Ain't a problem, friend," Amandine said, feeling Faven's eyes on her back. "Take good care of your bird for me, eh?"

"Will do, Cap'n." The woman bobbed her head before scurrying back to work.

"For a pirate," Faven said, "people appear to view you quite favorably."

Amandine barked a laugh. "Come down from that big ol' cage of yours sometime, Navi, and see how people live. We're all making do, and people, well, people always appreciate a hand up. Don't much matter who's holding that hand down."

Faven fell silent, twitching her hood to better hide her face. That was fine by Amandine. She'd much rather be buying the mechanic with the orange hair a drink—but the navigator had captured Amandine's curiosity for the time being. There'd be time enough to chat up the mechanic later if Faven's story turned out to be more boring than Amandine hoped.

The Broken Mast reared up on her left, a squat building hunkering down under the brilliance of the Sixteen Cardinal Weaves. Most of the buildings in this section of the docks were getting shabby around the edges, but Yalton kept the Broken Mast's exterior pristine. Its vibrant blue paint mingled with the stained-glass light to give the illusion of waves crashing against the walls.

Amandine and Kester closed ranks around Faven when they walked through the door, sheltering the navigator from prying eyes as shouts of welcome burst up from the bar's patrons.

The Broken Mast's owner was lingering behind the bar, as per usual, a rag over their shoulder and an eyebrow cocked in question. Amandine held up two fingers, signaling she wanted the second-largest meeting room. They gave her a nod before shuffling off to open the door with a clunk of the oversized key they wore around their neck.

The doors were actually locked with biometric encoders that read a chip beneath Yalton's skin, but the patrons liked the aesthetic of the heavy keys. So, they kept up the act and raked in bigger tips. Yalton swung the door open and squinted at Amandine.

"Four?" they asked.

"Four," Amandine confirmed.

She slung herself onto a thinly stuffed bench and kicked her ankle up on her knee, spreading her arms across the back of the bench. A slow, easy sigh left her lips.

"Four?" Faven asked.

"Tully'll be along once they finish making sure Tagert's cleared out."

Tangling with Tagert was never worrisome. They pinched at each other every so often, and that was that. The squabble wouldn't escalate beyond petty snipes, because neither one of them wanted to break from their usual thieving to deal with a full-scale rivalry. But Tagert couldn't be trusted not to attempt something childish, like dumping quick-sealant in their thrusters.

"Kester, scan it." Amandine waved a hand lazily through the air.

"Aye, Captain."

She pulled a slim device from her sleeve and ran it over the walls, floor, ceiling, and furniture. Faven stayed standing, shuffled off to the side in the shadowy room, trailing her gaze over the dust-coated nautical decor. Amandine was pretty sure Yalton had never stepped foot on a seafaring vessel in their life. It was all more theater for extra coin, but Amandine couldn't fault them for a good hustle.

"Chairs won't bite," Amandine said.

"What is she doing?" Faven pointed at Kester.

"She has a name, and you can ask her yourself."

"I'm scanning for listening devices." Kester shot Faven an annoyed look. "And have found nothing but the ones connected to the *Marquette*."

"Marvelous." Amandine sat straighter when Yalton returned with a tray full of rough clay cups and a bottle of spiced rum.

Amandine dragged the cork out with her teeth while the others got themselves settled and poured for her crew first, including an extra cup for Tully, then Faven and herself. The navi's nose wrinkled when she sniffed the cup, making Amandine smirk into her own drink. She took a swig, eyeing the navi.

"Now that we're cozy, I'll take the first half of my payment. Why'd you take Red's bait?"

Faven took a careful sip and actually smiled at the experience. "I require information that is not readily provided by the Choir of Stars and had hoped that a pirate's...habits...would provide what I'm looking for."

"Only habit Red's got is avoiding a bath. Why him?"

"You may be shocked to learn that I don't keep a diary of pirate contacts to hand. He reached out to me in a moment when I required information he could deliver. My kind are just as capable of being impulsive as yours."

She'd gone stiff from her spine all the way down to her manner of speaking. Sore spot. Interesting. "And what got you so wound up you jumped on the first hook tossed your way?"

Faven took a breath. Amandine waited, knowing the look in the woman's eyes, even if she didn't know the woman. She was steeling herself. "I'm seeking information regarding the Clutch."

Jacq. The Clutch. Two shadows of her past sewn together at the seams, and she didn't much like the shape this story was taking.

"The Clutch is a graveyard. Best thing a grave can do is stay buried," Amandine said, and started to stand.

"I'm willing to pay in a starpath of your choosing," Faven said quickly. "One I will weave into your lightdrive myself."

Amandine hesitated. A custom weaving could give them an incredible advantage, allowing them to skirt the sixteen thoroughfares and cut substantial time off their favored runs. It'd be exponentially more valuable than a single payout. Faster runs, more runs, more money over time. Her crew could end up rich. Stupidly rich.

She'd be hanging up her shotgun faster than she'd dreamed, slipping out of the black to retire on a foggy little planet called Blackloach. Back to the cabin of the grandfather who'd raised her, and the old oak tree she'd buried him beside. Amandine licked her lips. Nothing that good came without a price.

"Why?" Amandine said into the stretching silence.

"My reasons are personal," Faven said crisply.

Amandine chuckled, a low rumble in her chest. Kester swirled her cup, eyeing Faven like she was a venomous snake rearing up to bite, and maybe she was, but Amandine had never feared to tangle with snakes.

"I'm sure you could find anything you liked in the Choir's archives, Navi. Don't need no pirates who've never been within spitting distance of that graveyard to read off a 'pedia entry for you. Maybe you've forgotten, living in that birdcage of yours, but travel to the Clutch is illegal for scrubs like us."

"I'm not here to entrap you." Faven's eyes narrowed. "And I don't appreciate the implication that I would be so naive as to believe that you and your 'crew' have never been to the Clutch, Bitter Amandine. You and your ilk scurry about the place like rats."

Amandine bristled. It was one thing for Faven to take jabs at her, she'd suffered plenty worse insults by people whose opinions she actually valued, but no one spoke that way about her crew and got away with it.

She tossed back her drink and dropped the cup on the table with a thunk. "You've insulted my crew, Faven Sythe, and that's a slight I won't stand for. I suggest you learn to mind your manners, even at a pirate's table, otherwise this conversation is over."

The color drained from her face. "Forgive me, I allowed my frustration to be redirected at you all. It's only that—"

"Cap'n," Tully said through the comm gem piercing Amandine's ear. "Trouble. Got a Blade headed your way in a hurry."

"Copy that," Amandine said to Tully, then focused her attention on Faven. "What did you do, Navi? Got a Blade coming our way, and you're too old to have been caught out skipping school."

Amandine watched with mild fascination as Faven's already color-washed expression turned positively ill. "Shit," the navi said with as much enthusiasm as Amandine had ever said the word.

Amandine's lips parted in surprise. "Don't tell me you've broken Choir law?"

"I was supposed to be somewhere I am not. The Choir have noticed my absence and are coming to collect me. That is all."

"Really." Amandine dragged out the word, then exchanged a look with Kester and pushed to her feet. "It's been interesting, Sythe, but I'm not getting mixed up with the Blades when you're not being straight with me. Time to make our exit."

Faven lunged across the table, curling thin fingers around Amandine's forearm and knocking aside Tully's still-full cup in the process. Amandine froze, bewildered, staring down into eyes huge with genuine desperation. Kester's hand drifted to the fléchettes she kept hidden up her sleeves, but Amandine held up a forestalling hand.

"Please." Faven's voice was unsteady with the necessity of begging, something the navi didn't have much practice at. "Take me with you. Do as Red was going to do—kidnap me for ransom. They'll pay handsomely."

"We're not that stupid." Amandine started to peel the woman's hand off her arm. Faven tightened her grip, digging her nails in.

"Navigators are being sent to the *Black Celeste* and aren't heard from again," Faven said, rapid-fire, her voice a whispering hiss. "I need your help."

"Ghost stories," Amandine said, but a chill crept over her skin. Faven had the look of a woman who'd seen a few ghosts.

For one dreadful moment, Amandine looked into eyes that saw the ways between the stars, and feared. Feared the navi knew Amandine's secret. That the rebellious navigator had dropped down from on high to grasp Amandine's arm and tell her that she knew. That Amandine's past had come home to roost and her world was about to unravel beneath her feet.

No. The connection to the Clutch was incidental. Faven was here for her own reasons, and they had nothing to do with Amandine's buried past. Though they might give her some answers. Answers she'd never dared hope to uncover.

"Honesty now, or you get nothing: Where were you supposed to be?"

"My mother's interment."

Amandine drew her head back, sucking down a sharp breath. "Price of rescue just went up."

"Whatever you want," Faven said.

Foolish of the woman to commit to something so open-ended, but desperation was driving her now, and Amandine knew how to steer those waters better than most.

"Well, then." Amandine unslung her shotgun. "I never could say no to a pretty face."

SIX

Faven

It was one thing to make dramatic proclamations, but quite another to see them through. Faven struggled to keep her terror from showing as she followed the pirates around the side of the Broken Mast, skirting the edge of the docks until they could get somewhere Amandine deemed "clear" for the *Marquette* to drop down and pick them up.

A rough hand—the quiet woman, what was her name, K-something?—grabbed her arm to keep her moving. Faven flinched, but she was grateful for that grip. The pain cut through the fog of rising panic in her chest, the constriction of her breath that didn't have anything to do with how fast they were running.

She couldn't go back to the Spire. Not after this. Amandine might make a good show of pretending to kidnap her, but if Faven returned, then the Choir would scent the truth on her. Discover that she'd meant to investigate the Clutch, and the reason Ulana had been sent to it, without their permission.

Even if Ulana was safe after all, that didn't mean Faven would be. If they caught her consorting with pirates to circumvent their authority, banishment to the outer stations, where she'd be forced to weave tiny paths between inconsequential stars for payment that went straight to the Choir's accounts, would be a kind punishment.

THE TWO LIES OF FAVEN SYTHE   29

Despite all that, her feet kept moving. She couldn't renege on the one thing she'd ever decided for herself. Faven was going to either find out why Ulana had been sent to the Clutch, or die trying. The corners of her lips twitched, the scales pulling her skin. She was dying anyway.

The comm gem piercing her ear buzzed. Before she could think better of the motion, she brushed her fingertips against it.

"Navigator Sythe, please announce location and wait for further instruction," the cool, mechanized voice of one of the Blades said.

"I—I don't—" What in the light was she supposed to say?

Kester plucked the comm gem from her ear and dropped it to the ground, giving it a quick grind beneath her heel. "They can use the signal to track your whereabouts."

The earring was worth a small fortune, but Faven was grateful to have the choice of responding taken away from her. She was, after all, being kidnapped.

"We hold here." Amandine drew the rushing group to a halt at the end of a crowded dock. Along the sides, blue-painted crates formed a corridor, while a mountainous pile of green crates waited at the end. The still water of the harbor surrounded them. There was no way out that Faven could see.

"Why here?" Faven asked.

"Defensible. Open enough for a pickup. For the rest, you'll see."

Amandine winked one of those verdigris-green eyes at her and Faven caught herself smiling, even though fear coiled through her belly and brought cold sweat to her skin. Amandine's confidence was infectious.

Amandine's *everything* was infectious. Faven had spent weeks and months and endless nights gathering calm into herself. Hollowing out a place in her being where she wasn't afraid, listening to her mother's breaths slow. A safe place from which she could watch with clinical detachment as the scale crept across her mother's sclera.

And in not even an hour's time with the pirate, she'd found fear again. Fear that didn't feel brittle, her whole being liable to shatter at the slightest pressure, but vital. Thrilling. Alive.

Maybe it was grief making her reckless, or perhaps it was loneliness—which was just a different kind of grief—but for the first time in longer than she could remember, Faven trusted that someone else would come through for her. Believed that she wouldn't have to do this alone.

Believing in the pirate was unhinged. Faven knew well what a Blade was capable of, and should have run screaming into its arms to beg forgiveness for making it come look for her. She almost did precisely that, when the Blade stepped from between the blue crates.

Her breath caught. Kester grabbed her shoulder and shoved her backward, pressing her against the tower of shipping crates. Her thoughts scattered—she was *not* accustomed to being manhandled. Before Faven could make a sound, Kester's knife was to her throat. It didn't matter that they were acting, her whole body locked up in terror.

The blade was startlingly cold. Every time her heart beat—frantic as a hummingbird's wings—she feared her pulse would expand her throat and split her skin against the cutting edge.

Amandine moved in front of Faven, her own shotgun back in her hands, Tagert's hanging off her hip.

The Blade stopped its advance. A bipedal, eight-foot-tall construct, it was encased in dark panes of armor with a visor of indigo obscuring its ocular sensors. It held no weapon, but there were projectiles hidden within its arms. Mostly sedative darts and stun rounds. The Choir of Stars liked to take those who threatened their navigators alive, if they could help it. For questioning.

"Release and step away from Navigator Sythe," the Blade said.

"Now, now, my lovely," Amandine said, as if she were talking to an old friend. "We were just having a chat with the navi. Weren't we, Faven old girl?"

She licked her lips, started to say something, but Kester gave her a squeeze. Faven clamped her mouth shut.

"I am authorized to engage in lethal protection measures," the Blade said. It turned its attention back to Faven. "Prepare for retrieval."

Faven had about two seconds to contemplate that before the Blade's arm lifted. Coppery light crackled over its forearm.

"Lethal protection?" Amandine mused. "Bit of an oxymoron, isn't it?"

"I will not ask again," it said.

"Figured you wouldn't. So I had a surprise cooked up. Just for you."

A net of energy burst from the Blade's hand and slammed into an invisible wall an arm's length from Amandine, fizzling and crackling as it dissipated against the barrier. Faven's heart lodged itself in her throat and stayed there, but Amandine wore a relaxed smile. Kester released a sound that might have been a chuckle.

"There's a reason we use old-fashioned projectile weapons." Amandine lowered the shotgun, pumping it once as she took aim at the Blade's chest. "They're not susceptible to field disrupters."

"Energetic field disrupters are illegal," the Blade said in its deadpan voice. "Disengage your device."

"Oh, are they? How silly of me, I didn't mean to break the law!" Amandine mock-gasped, and Kester definitely chuckled this time, which jostled the blade against Faven's throat and made her hold her breath.

"Engaging kinetic weapons," the Blade announced.

Thin fans of cobalt unfurled from its arms like feathers ruffling, the lethal edges flexing as the robot brought its arms across its chest, preparing to launch itself into Amandine.

"Careful," the pirate said. "Field disrupters play havoc with constructs like you. Wouldn't want to trip and stab Navigator Sythe because a motor gave out, would you?"

The Blade hesitated. In that stretched moment of indecision, Faven thought she could hear a soft whir on the air, though she couldn't find the source. A crackling sound tickled her senses. Someone shouted, "Got 'em!" in the split second before one side of the wall of crates shuddered and then *slammed* into the other side, crushing the Blade between them. Faven's mouth dropped open.

Amandine rested her shotgun back against her shoulder. "If you'd waited any longer, the Blade would have given me a shave!" she hollered toward the wreckage.

"Maybe I was hoping it would," a bright voice shouted back. "Light knows you need one!"

Amandine laughed, and Kester lowered the knife from Faven's throat at last. "What was that...that *thing*?" Faven asked.

Amandine gestured absently to the wiry figure scrambling through the wreckage at the other end of the dock. "That's Tully."

"No, not them, I meant—whatever that thing was that crushed the Blade?"

"That was also Tully," Amandine said. "But the contraption they employed was a clever stunt with magnets."

"How does it work?"

Amandine shrugged. "Beats me. I don't think anyone knows."

Faven narrowed her eyes at Amandine's mischievous smile. "I suppose our agreement doesn't require you to reveal the secrets of your trade to me."

"It does not."

Amandine turned and cupped a hand around her mouth. "Hurry up, Tully. You set off every damn alarm in the place!"

"You weren't specific about the method of 'dealing with it'!" Tully called back good-naturedly, but there was strain in their voice.

"Captain," Kester said.

Amandine held her hand back expectantly, never taking her eyes from Tully as they scrambled over the wreckage. Kester placed a thin device onto Amandine's hand, which she fit over her eyes like amethyst-shaded sunglasses. A HUD glass. Faven's brows lifted. Comm gems were common, but HUD glasses were supposed to be the purview of the Choir's military alone. Whatever Amandine saw in those lenses made her jaw tighten.

"A dozen incoming," she said.

Kester touched her comm gem. "Becks is shaking a tail and will not be in position in time."

"Shit." Amandine lowered her shotgun and took one long stride toward Tully. Kester stopped her with a hand on her shoulder.

"You cannot fight twelve Blades, Captain."

Amandine ground her teeth and glared sideways at Faven. "What in the void did you do, Navi? A baker's dozen of Blades don't come out for a navi missing a funeral."

"I told you the truth," Faven said. "Navigators are going to the Clutch, their true destinations hidden, and aren't heard from again."

"Ghost stories," Amandine insisted.

"Thirteen Blades don't mobilize for a ghost story," Faven shot back.

Amandine's nostrils flared, her gaze tracking to the rubble. The high points of the Blades appeared behind the wreckage, drawing closer. They would cut off Tully's escape path before Tully made it out.

"Becks," Amandine said into her comm gem. "I need a swoop on me in three." Amandine slung her shotgun into its holster, then took Faven's arm in one calloused hand. "Can you swim?"

"Of course I can."

"Then I'm sorry about this, goddess, I really am, but my crew comes first. Always."

"What—?"

Her question dissolved into a startled shout as Amandine dropped her other hand to Faven's waist, spun around, and flung

Faven with all her strength into the still waters of the harbor. Faven let out an undignified squawk of surprise, too stunned to remember to close her mouth.

Cold water rushed over her, sodden robes dragging her down. Faven thrashed for one frantic moment, then oriented herself toward the surface and kicked. When she broke through, she sputtered and wiped a hand across her face to clear the hair from her eyes—her braids would take ages to redo properly, damn that pirate—and whipped around to tell said pirate off.

The dock Amandine had been standing on was empty. Faven blinked and turned to find the water foaming as a mass of Blades rushed to secure her safety. She rolled her eyes, letting out a resigned sigh.

The *Marquette* sailed by above. Amandine dangled from a ladder hanging from the open cargo-belly doors, Kester from another. The pirate's face was taut with concentration, wind whipping her hair straight back as she leaned down, straining as far as she could, and held out a hand.

Tully scrambled up the side of a pile of crates, freed from the attention of the Blades, and snatched her hand. Amandine yanked them up, then threw a glance over her shoulder. Her eyes met Faven's. Amandine pursed her lips in a blown kiss.

Faven made a vulgar gesture at the fleeing pirate, and caught the flash of her grin before a burst of glittering chaff rained down from the *Marquette* to obscure their path. The ship's cloaking device stuttered on, winking them out of existence.

Faven closed her eyes and let herself lean back, floating on the surface of the water while she awaited her ill-timed rescue. Strange, that she could still float when she felt so very heavy.

How silly she had been to think, even for a brief and wonderful second, that she could rely on anyone but herself.

SEVEN

Amandine

Amandine slung herself into the pilot's seat and unfolded a fan of cryst-glass from the control board. The vital signs of the *Marquette* thrummed beneath her fingertips, the beating heart of her ship. Her world. They were singing in harmony, the ship responding happily to her orders to burn faster, fly darker.

"Bad idea," Becks said, fussing with their own display next to her.

Amandine scowled and peeked at their interface. They'd pulled up the lightdrive's diagnostics and nothing else, all their focus bent to that singular section of the ship, where the shielding was starting to wear thin.

"We'll get another job lined up, but we can't loaf around Votive City after brushing muskets with the Blades."

"Wouldn't have tangled with the Blades if you hadn't let that navi get in your head."

"You didn't see her, Becks. Desperate as a dehydrated mollusk."

"Sure she didn't blink those pretty eyes at you?"

Amandine thought, wistfully and briefly, of the orange-haired mechanic on the dock, then shook her head to clear it. "Ain't got a thing for prissy attitudes, and skies surround us, she is a Spire navigator to the core. Wonder if they get neck pain, craning to keep their noses so high in the air all the time?"

Becks snickered. "They'd never admit it if they did, Cap'n."

"True enough. Now stop shoving your head up my lightdrive's skirt and get me extra eyes on the exit points around here. Those Blades are going to send up distress signals soon, and I don't want to have to shake a tail. We gotta blow this station, and we gotta do it now."

"We may have more time than expected." Kester leaned in the doorframe between the cockpit and the ship's main hall. "I tossed the Blades a present before we jumped the ladders. Local disrupter. Should fuddle them for a while."

"Don't they have protections against that kind of thing?" Amandine flicked through a wireframe model of the Vigil's station schematics, searching for a lesser-used soft spot in the glass.

The greater shape of the Vigil resembled the tower structure of the Spire itself, crossed near the top with another level, the transept, where those wealthy enough to dwell in Votive City proper made their homes. The lower levels were a sprawl of townships and loosely correlated districts.

Each pane of glass in the overall construction was flagged with a permeability rating. Lightdrives would handshake with the crystglass, letting the ship slip through between station and open space without all the fuss of pressure.

Ships with cheaper, or older, drives had to make use of panes with higher permeability ratings. While those panes were large as skyscrapers, they were well-monitored by Choir security. Amandine had a reputation for being slippery, but most assumed the *Marquette* was any other Rayonnant-model ship—a favorite of pirates because they were quick, easily armed, easily maintained, and cheap enough to scrounge up. Amandine had gotten her start in one of those ships, crewing with Captain Amber Jacq.

Void, but she hadn't willingly thought Jacq's name in well over twenty years, now. Not since the day he'd died. When she'd first signed to his crew, he'd seemed larger than life, a pirate as brutal to his marks as he was generous with his crew.

In death, his shadow loomed larger than his life ever had, haunting her nightmares. For a second there, when Faven had gripped her arm tight, she'd thought she'd seen him. The glint of his teeth, gums bloody with the lightsickness that'd killed him, shining out of the shadows of her past.

Amandine should have died with him and the rest of his crew, but she'd made it out. Stumbled onto the *Marquette* and stolen away with it.

Becks knew the *Marquette* had more going on under its proverbial hood than the average Rayonnant, though they'd never actually talked about it. The mechanic may have pushed their way onto her ship to fine-tune the engine burn, but they'd stayed because this ship was a riddle worth solving.

She sensed its mood, a mirror to her own, anxious to get going. To be back in the endless empty between the stars, but there was trepidation in it, too.

Amandine ran a soothing hand over the ship's control panel and made herself focus on the task at hand. The permeability ratings were always changing, though the weaker sections remained constant. She found a panel rating higher than any sane captain would want to tackle, in the down-side of the Vigil, right at the edge of where the glass started to curve back up to make a wall instead of a floor. They'd cut it close to the buildings in the area, but they'd threaded finer needles under tighter circumstances.

"There," she said. "That's our exit."

"Bit thick," Becks said.

"Never been a problem before."

"Wasn't talking about the glass, Cap'n."

Amandine snorted and patted them on the back before abandoning the pilot's seat to leave them to it. She should probably hang

Becks up by their bootlaces to drain the insubordination out of them, but they worked best when allowed to indulge their bitter streak, and anyway, she found their constant grumbling entertaining.

Amandine let herself into the cargo hold—looking far too empty, these days—and paced back and forth, hands hooked in her belt, a thundercloud of disquiet dogging every step she took. The *Black Celeste*. A ludicrous story. Proof enough that the navi had knocked a few screws loose and needed the care of her people to get her thinking straight again.

Losing a mother could do that to you.

But she'd been so earnest. So scared. And Amandine had heard her own rumors, hadn't she? About ships going out to the Clutch and not coming back. About a light that moved through that graveyard, never in the same place twice.

Thirteen Blades don't mobilize for a ghost story.

She shook her head. Scowled at herself and the wall and every step that'd brought her to this place, this point in time, where for once in her life she didn't think she'd made the right call. That her gut had been wrong. That she should have found a way to take Faven with them.

The metallic click of a door closing echoed to her right. There was nothing there but empty shelves—shelves, and the square-mouthed opening of a ventilation shaft.

Amandine crept closer and heard the hiss of a chair being scraped across the floor, made tinny by the vent. The galley was on the other side of that wall. She strained to listen.

"Well?" Becks's voice, gruff with their usual impatience. "What'd the navi want?"

"Information on the Clutch," Kester said.

"Shouldn't she have her own people for that?" Tully, this time.

"She believes her own people are being banished there, for unknown reasons."

"Void," Becks swore. "And you didn't try to stop the cap'n from bringing her aboard?"

"The captain is the captain," Kester said simply.

Amandine bit her tongue.

"Anyway." Tully sniffed. "I handled it, didn't I?"

"And almost got yourself skewered by Blades in the process," Becks said.

Even through the vent, she could hear Tully inhale to launch into a justification.

"It is our duty to protect," Kester cut in. "You should not have intervened."

"Sorry," Tully muttered. "It's just—I don't want to go yet."

"We're not leaving," Becks said firmly.

Solemn murmurs of agreement all around.

Leave? Amandine's stomach fell and she strained closer to the vent to better hear them, but their voices had dropped too low—and then she heard the soft snick of the galley door.

Amandine scrambled away from the shelves and resumed pacing, as that's what Becks would expect of her. A few seconds later, Becks knocked on the door before letting themself in.

"Gonna wear a hole in my floor," they said.

Amandine turned a half-hearted scowl on them. The mechanic stalked into the room, a permanent lift to their brow that never failed to make Amandine feel like she'd stepped in something and hadn't yet noticed the stink.

"It's my own damn floor."

That brow got higher. "Touchy. We're through the wall, Cap'n, which means we need a new job, and quick. I pulled the manifest on that cargo hauler you had your eye on for the new wiring harnesses."

"And?" she pressed. Becks had a way of drawing out news—good or bad. Normally she found their dance charming, but she was running short on patience.

"Oh, they got 'em. Netted in containers near the bottom of the hauler, too. Easy pickings. But it's the harnesses I'm sour on. Checked the specs, you know. The manufacturer claims they push out ten percent more power at a third of the weight, yeah? Real streamlined."

Amandine crossed her arms and let her glare do the talking.

Becks held up their hands in defense. "I know, I know, get to the point. I checked the weight against the quantity on the manifest. Ain't no different than the usual arrangement. Maybe they've tightened up the styling, but those harnesses weigh the same as they always do. They're not going to cut down on a ship's dry weight, they just look fancier."

Amandine sighed heavily and dragged a hand down the side of her face. "Our buyer's not interested in looks, they want performance. Even if they buy the stuff, they'll negotiate us down so hard we'll be walking away with enough to cover the cost, if that, and we'll have bought ourselves some ill will for our trouble."

"I agree with you, Cap'n."

Amandine wrinkled her nose. "Call the buyer. Tell 'em the product's no good so the deal's off."

"Consider 'em called." Becks lingered, body language begging Amandine to ask what else they wanted, but she was tired and frustrated and if they pushed her buttons again, she might lose her head and demand to know what that conversation in the galley was really about. Becks got the hint and shifted their weight. "One more thing." They tapped the toolbox tucked under their arm. "The shielding on our lightdrive housing is running thinner in some spots than expected. Gonna have to recoat, and soon."

"How soon?"

"Couple weeks?" Becks rolled their shoulders. "Hard to say for sure, depends on how much we use the thing, but sooner rather than later."

Her stomach sank. The *Marquette* was their home. While

Amandine maintained ownership of her grandfather's fishing cabin, the rest of the crew didn't keep apartments at stations or planets. Every red cent they squeezed out from between the stars went into their private savings. If the shielding started to wear thin enough that radiation from the lightdrive bled through to the rest of the ship, they'd have to move out until it was fixed.

Part of Amandine would always want to relinquish her captain's seat. Return to the cabin and the mists and the quiet life her grandfather had left for her to inherit. But when she'd been young and hot-headed, she'd scarpered off and crewed with pirates. Found herself the *Marquette*, and built a crew of her own that relied on her leadership. On her to bring in the money they needed to survive.

If she couldn't keep them in the most basic comforts, then why stay? Amandine tried to imagine the halls of the *Marquette* empty once more, in the way they had been after she'd first stolen the ship for herself, only her own thoughts and the creaking of the vessel for company, and shivered.

"Why's the damn ship always break when we're close to getting comfortable?"

"Maybe she don't want you to go, Cap'n," Becks said.

Amandine scoffed, but Becks's face was wary, their eyes tracking to the walls.

"I'm not going anywhere," Amandine said. "Blackloach's an anchor, and I ain't ever cared for those."

"So you say."

Maybe they were only talking about leaving because they feared she'd leave them first. Amandine closed her eyes. Rubbed her forehead to chase the shadow of that misty landscape from her mind. It wasn't her home, not really. Hadn't been for a long, long time. It was just a dream. Something to orient herself toward when her life lost all bearing.

"I'll figure something out," she said.

"I'm sure you will." Becks turned to leave but paused, pressing their hand to the wall by the door as if they could sense the ship's moods the way Amandine did—but they never could. "It's a slow leak. We got time."

If it was a slow leak, lightsickness wouldn't come right away. She'd seen rigs where people had been running for months or weeks on a ship with a leaking core. They started to look sun-baked. Tired. Deep lines in their faces and leathery, chapped skin. Talking nonsense. Soon enough they started bruising too easily. Once that happened, there was no undoing the damage.

The containment coating was cryst-tech, made by the naviga-tors, and cost—well, cost about as much as ransoming Faven Sythe would have paid. Amandine frowned at the thought. Tagert had been looking rough in the skin department, though he'd been so red about the ears it was hard to say. If he was running his ship, the *Stamping Bull*, with a bleeding lightdrive, that explained his will-ingness to attempt the ransom of a navigator.

If Amandine couldn't rustle up a large score, she'd be staring down that same choice soon enough.

EIGHT

Faven

Faven wasn't in handcuffs, but the omission was illusory. The Blades marched by her side all the way back into the heart of the Spire, their presence a silent threat, the weight of what she had done—what she had been about to do—the binding chains between them.

By every tenet of her people, she should be ashamed. She reached for that feeling. Rooted around in the hollows of her soul for the place where that hot coal should smolder, and found nothing.

She followed the Blades through the straight halls of the Spire, leaving damp footprints in her wake. All around her the glories of other navigators were depicted in shining stained glass. Not the people, never that. By the time a navigator was talented enough to weave a triumph of a starpath, their bodies were too far gone to scale. A few reveled in it, viewed the petrification of their mortal vessels as beautiful, ascendant, but most took to wearing thicker veils and looser clothing to hide joints that no longer bent.

All cryst-born were keen to embrace their fate so long as they lived in this jewel box of a world. As long as they were admired and protected and rich beyond most imaginings. Faven's own mother had whispered of being safe in the Spire, before the scales had stopped her voice.

Diamond-speckled gauze curtains parted at her approach. The Blades left her side, turning their backs to the wall alongside the door where they became motionless sentinels.

Choir Gailliard's office was an ocean of calm. Pale tones of smoke and mist, greys tinted with the softest breaths of blue and green, made up his decor. Gailliard himself wore simple, if finely crafted, clothes in those same shades, his golden thatch of hair and the scale patterning his skin the only saturated colors in the room.

Faven paused before his desk as he looked up from his work. She nodded to him, careful not to let her gaze linger overlong on the scales that washed across his cheek, neck, and collar to disappear beneath his sleeve and lock one arm, slightly bent, forever in place.

Young to have joined the Choir, Gailliard had managed to weave two great starpaths before the scales had frozen that arm. While he could still easily weave less complicated paths, rumor said he'd been eager to take the promotion to become a Choir administrator.

When last Faven had seen him, three months past at some banquet or another, he hadn't worn a glove on the hand of his frozen arm. He wore one now. The glove didn't surprise her—some people were consumed faster than others—but the warmth in his voice did.

"Faven!" A genuine smile lit up his face. "I'm told you were caught consorting with pirates. Is it true?"

"'Caught' implies I was trying to hide the matter, Choir. I was merely pressing the pirate for information about a certain starpath."

"Please." He waved a hand sideways over the top of his desk. "I'm not angry with you. Truth be told, hearing about your adventure dockside is the most amusement I've had in months. Was it truly Bitter Amandine who swept to your rescue against Tagert Red?"

Faven's eyebrows climbed high despite her best efforts to school her expression. Usually Gailliard quailed at the mention of pirates, but Amandine's name had been delivered with a curious dash of gusto. "You are very well informed."

"When Choir Hatriel came to me spitting mad about you endangering yourself by answering an obvious fishing attempt, I had to review the footage myself."

A whisper of heat rose up her neck. "I'm sorry to have worried Choir Hatriel."

"I had to talk her out of going to the docks to recover you herself. Could you imagine, a Blademother descending upon the dockside rabble?" Gailliard laughed. "The people would think another war had started!"

The heat on her neck turned scalding. Faven's mother had always referred to Hatriel in the warmest of tones. Had insisted upon Faven calling the rigid old warrior her aunt, even though Hatriel barely seemed to notice Faven's existence.

Faven imagined Hatriel—the towering, vicious angles of her body, the way her legs had gone to scale and she walked around barefoot as a result, the clawlike clack of her feet sending shivers down Faven's spine—appearing on the docks with her whip-thin, armillary-hilted blade in her hand, and wanted to crawl into a hole to escape the possibility.

Thirteen Blades didn't mobilize for a ghost story.

But they would, if a Blademother bade them fight.

"I didn't mean to cause such a commotion," she managed through a knot in her throat.

Gailliard gave her a smile that once, when they'd been children together at school, would have spelled trouble, but now made her feel old, and a little sad. "The rigidity of one's body does not correlate to the rigidity of one's mind, Faven. Did you learn anything of use? And what in stars' light were you hoping to discover, precisely?"

His smile stayed in place, but it'd lost some of its charm. A sheath of golden hair fell across the scaled side of his face, where he wouldn't feel the contact. It gave him a boyish appearance. For an aching moment, she was reminded of the countless times after classes when they'd sneak off to test some harebrained theory or another without the watchful eye of their tutors over them.

Of course, their tutors were always watching. And so was the Choir, never mind that this one had been her friend, once. His question was delivered in a light manner, but she had no doubt she was being interrogated.

"I wanted to know the nature of the routes Bitter Amandine and those like her use to pillage the Clutch," Faven said.

Gailliard lifted his sole mobile eyebrow at her. The other had been frozen in place in a subtle arch that hinted at the surprise he'd felt when he'd first noticed the spread there.

"They use stolen lightdrives with starpaths legitimate buyers already worked into them. Or their own dangerous paths charted by would-be navigators with a larger need for coin than sense. These methods are known to us."

It wasn't a question, but he let the implication stretch between them, imploring her to fill the silence with something that might reveal her true purpose.

Faven slipped her hands into her sleeves and considered him, letting her own silence grow, letting him understand that she would not be manipulated by such petty methods. She was a navigator of the Spire, and despite her uncouth behavior and the fact she was dripping harbor water across his pristine floor, she would not be played so easily.

Eventually, his smile relaxed, becoming something real, and she took the opening in hand.

"My mother's crystallization completed this morning. I suppose I sought merely to feel something... different."

His smile fell, the vibrancy draining from his eyes, and again she looked for the shame, for the guilt she should surely feel at using her mother's death against him in such a way, but found nothing. Perhaps she wasn't built for such feelings.

Faven reached her thoughts back while Gailliard leaned across the desk, sympathy writ clear on what little remained of his face that he could use to emote, and found she could not recall a single moment in time when she truly, deeply, felt guilt. Curious. Could one's goals ever be noble, if they didn't know what it felt like to be ashamed? How could you ever tell what was right?

Faven caught herself wondering if Amandine ever felt guilt about what she did and pushed the thought aside.

"I'm sorry," he said. "I didn't know."

"It had been coming for months." She paced a slow circle around the room, examining the various awards and trinkets he left propped upon his shelves. Tiny splashes of color against the subdued tones he preferred.

Faven's mother had always been a distant figure in her life, a dim star in a faraway sky. She had been warm, and she had been kind, but by the time Faven had been born, some vital spark had faded beneath the spread of scale.

There was nothing unusual about that. All her kin tended to be remote, islands unto themselves. The older they grew, the further away they retreated from society. From one another.

Ulana had brought a vibrancy into Faven's life that she hadn't even known she'd craved. She'd been firm with Faven when required, and kind in her own way. Praise was always earned from Ulana, while it was meted out with a sort of droll disinterest from her mother. Faven had loved her mother, of that she had no doubt, but it had always been Ulana's approval she'd chased after. Ulana she feared to disappoint.

Her mother's loss was banal, perfunctory. The expected sacrifice of their society. There was nothing surprising in it, aside from her own personal ache yawning wide and barren despite the fact she knew better. Knew better than to hurt. What was the point of hurting over something that was inevitable?

But Ulana's loss wasn't *fair*.

"I'd heard she had stilled," he said when she'd been quiet too long, and flicked an uncontrolled glance to his own arm. "But I hadn't realized she was that far along."

"It takes everyone differently."

Faven let him see her look at his arm and then away. It started with the skin. Cryst-scale liked to announce itself. It made its appearance known on the surface while it did its work below. Once your skin started to scale, your muscles weren't far behind. Your nails.

As it spread across the scalp, your hair would fall out. Soon, the muscle would grow so stiff that you could scarcely move it, and then you'd have to choose what pose you wanted to remain in for eternity. Faven still hadn't decided how she wanted to be posed, when it was her turn to still.

When all your skin was consumed in scale and your muscles locked tight, your very bones turning to cryst, it invaded the organs. Firmed lungs. Stopped hearts. It was hard to say, in the end, what really killed you. By the time a person finished crystal-lizing, they'd lost the ability to scream, to gasp. If they suffocated, they did so in silence.

The iris of the eyes went last, always, but Faven hoped that they stopped seeing long before that final step. Hoped, for her own sake and her mother's, that by the time the eyes turned, you'd been dead awhile, and it was just the cryst catching up. One last sign to let your loved ones know you'd gone at last.

"Did she request a place of interment?" he asked.

His tone was controlled, the appropriate mix of gentle concern and sympathy, but Gailliard hung on to that control by a nanofila-ment. When he had been a child, his own mother had tried to sell him into the service of pirates—not people like Amandine, Faven thought. Or maybe she merely hoped that Bitter Amandine would draw the line at buying a child.

Regardless, he'd been taken all the way to the outer layers of the Clutch before the Choir realized what had happened and sent a squad of Blades to collect him. He'd been injured in the fighting, a knife carving a scar along his back. His scale had formed there first, then spread to overtake his arm. After that, Faven's mother had looked after him more often than not. But when the scale stopped her mother's walking, Gailliard came to see them both less and less.

Her mother had understood his distance. It was difficult to look your own death in the eyes. Faven was less forgiving. And so she took small pleasure in watching his careful facade crack as she drove a knife of words into his heart and twisted.

"Her voice went early," Faven said. "She wasn't able to express a desired place of rest."

He pressed his good hand into the desktop to steady himself. "What will you do?"

"She always loved the gleamfish. I arranged a location where she can watch them swim in peace."

He nodded, satisfied, and she wanted to take his shoulders in hand and shake him, shout at him. Make him realize that for all their beautiful trappings there was nothing lovely in her mother's death, only suffering. Not crystal and pond and manicured fish. Just a cold void where a warm soul once burned. But he was Choir, and she was not, and while she'd found a chink in his armor, there was no denying that she was here to be punished for her misadventure on the dock.

"I understand you were distraught. The Choir can be lenient on the basis of that, but really, Faven. Pirates? The risk was too great. They could have taken you, and then you'd have your answer for how they make their way into the Clutch, because you'd be forced to provide them the means."

Faven pressed her lips together, considering her estranged friend, but said nothing. He sighed.

"I can't help you if you aren't honest with me. Why this sudden obsession? What has you so curious that you would risk dealing with pirates to find out their secrets?"

Faven was tired and frustrated and feeling reckless for once in her life. She'd thought she'd been skirting danger. Thought she'd finally broken free of the mold she'd been cast in. But physical danger was as far away from her as the Clutch.

She was valuable, and only valuable alive and whole. Her body had never been in danger, no matter what her pounding heart had told her. But there, standing before a Choir—never mind that he had been her friend—she saw danger looming for the first time. The world of a navigator was stable. Safe.

But secrets were worth more than flesh and blood and talent.

"Ulana Valset went to the *Black Celeste*, not to Amiens, and I mean to find out why," she said, and felt the thrill of sticking her neck out at last.

"Faven, my friend." Gailliard's voice was devastatingly kind. "Ulana Valset is dead."

NINE

Faven

Denial bubbled up within her, swift and certain, the way one puts out a hand to protect their face when they've tripped and the ground is rushing up to meet them. But Gailliard, damn him, was too much an open book, and the terrible sympathy writ across his features ripped that false comfort away.

"When?" May not have been the best question to ask, but it was the first that came to her. A fact she required to find her footing once more.

"During the transit to Amiens," he said. "The shielding on her lightdrive failed, and the ship . . . Well, there was an explosion."

"An explosion."

Explosions were things that happened to other people. Events described in news reels as *tragic accidents* that, almost inevitably, *could have been avoided*. The ships of the cryst-born didn't have loose screws, or old wiring, or any other number of mundane bits of machinery that hadn't been maintained.

No, no. Ulana wasn't dead. She couldn't be.

"Faven?"

"If a ship was lost in transit to Amiens, it wasn't hers. Ulana's last starpath was destined for the Clutch."

Gailliard went stock-still. Faven reveled in the slow shock he struggled to conceal. A tingle spread across her skin, reminiscent of having a warm blanket draped around her shoulders after a long, cold night's work, and it was all she could do to suppress a shiver.

"You're certain?" he asked.

"I checked her path myself."

"A violation."

"The path she wove was too erratic at the end for me to follow, but the destination was clear enough. You cannot look me in the eye and tell me that job reassignment posted by the Choir was meant as anything but a distraction from whatever her true task is. And once more." Faven took a breath. Braced herself. "She's not the only navigator to have gone to the Clutch in recent time, is she? Our numbers dwindle. We notice. We whisper among ourselves. We always have. You used to join in those whispers, Gailliard."

"So I did." His gaze skimmed around the room, came back to her, and when it did, there was a resolve in him she didn't recognize. "Walk with me?"

He was moving before she could answer. She fell into step beside him. The vast majority of the Spire was empty, these days. Coffered ceilings inset with skylight panels of stained glass bathed the floor in myriad lights and cast the lonely echo of their footsteps back to them, but muted. A permanent hush in the once bustling halls of the navigators' home.

Faven had been born long after their population began to wane, and though the quiet was normal enough, it had always prickled her senses. Sometimes, when she walked alone through halls meant to accommodate hundreds at a time, she thought she heard the whispers of those gone past. Felt them like fine needles brushing against her skin. A weight pressing her down. Stifling.

None but the Blades were there to mark their passing. Gailliard led her away from the offices of the Choir, through long, straight hallways dripping with ornamentation. Stained-glass mosaics of navigators long passed dotted the silk-swathed walls, eyes in shades of cerulean to indicate that the portraits had been made after the subjects' deaths.

Only one place within the Spire featured portraits. One day, her mother's countenance would adorn these walls.

"We go to the birthing hall?" she asked.

A subtle grimace graced his lips. "It's where we're most likely to find privacy."

Faven thought it unlikely that they'd have been overheard in Gailliard's office, or anywhere else they'd passed by, but bit her lips shut. Gailliard had experience with the other members of the Choir, and Faven did not.

She thought of Amandine's boast that the only ears listening in the pirate bar were hers and had to stifle an inappropriate smile as they crossed the threshold into the birthing hall. She couldn't imagine Gailliard scanning the walls for listening devices.

In the womb-warm dark, all pretense of opulence washed away. Beguiled as her people were by a shining gem or artfully crafted artifice, there was nothing in the worlds presided over by the Choir of Stars more beautiful than the origin of themselves.

Faven and Gailliard paused on the threshold, folding their arms across their stomachs as they lifted their eyes to the ceiling, and in turn the endless stars beyond, in prayer.

Faven's prayers had always been more reflex than reflection. Thanks given to her ancestors, as was expected. As brief and rote and empty as the hollow where her sense of shame should be.

This time, she found herself praying that her mother rested well. That she hadn't suffered, or been aware, as her scale progressed to its end. And a sentiment that was more wish than prayer—or maybe prayers had always been wishes, and Faven hadn't bothered to notice until she needed them—that she would discover the truth of what had happened to Ulana.

Gailliard released his prostration. They walked on.

A cavernous space tucked into the heart of the Spire, the birthing hall's lights were kept so low that the ceiling above was lost in darkness. Slender pillars speared down from those shadows, the cryst-rich amniotic fluid within imbuing the space in a soothing teal luminescence.

It was no wonder that Gailliard had assured her they wouldn't be overheard in the birthing hall. All around her stood empty pillars, not a single one sheltering a cryst-born child in any stage of its development.

Faven breathed deep of the mineral-laden scent, the knots in her shoulders relaxing with each breath.

"Ulana used to bring me here," she said. "When I misbehaved. To remind me that our people had once changed our very species to preserve humanity against extinction, and in the shadow of that effort, I could manage to whine less about my lessons."

Gailliard laughed. "Ulana was always an overzealous teacher."

"She was. I needed that, at the time. Mother...I think she lost something, when the spark of a new life called to her."

"Have you ever felt the spark?"

She shook her head. "I haven't. Truth be told, I don't think I would be suited."

"I haven't felt it, either." He paused to rest his palm reverently against a pillar. "So few of us do."

"We will again," Faven said, but the platitude was strained even to her own ears.

Many of her people spent lifetimes waiting for the spark of another life to call out to them during their meditations. Praying for it, trying to find ways to induce the growth of a cryst-shard beneath their skin so that it could then be excised and placed into a birthing pillar to be grown into the shape of a human baby.

Wasted effort, in Faven's opinion. No contrivances lured the spark. Life called to you, or it did not, and looking upon that forest of lifeless glass, a chill caused her to hug her arms closer. She'd known their numbers dwindled. She hadn't realized that there were none being born to replace them.

"How long has it been like this?" she asked.

"Years," Gailliard admitted. "We've one or two who feel the spark in a year, but no more than a handful. The Choir is not as concerned as I would like."

She cut him a glance at that, trying to read his intention, and thought she sensed desperation lurking below the surface of his cool facade. "Is anything being done?"

"Research."

Faven glanced pointedly at the lack of activity in the birthing hall. "But not here?"

"No, not here." He turned the cryst side of his face, immobile and lacking emotion, to her. "An expedition was mounted to the inner layers of the Clutch to, I am told, study what remains of cryst technology and seek ways to revitalize our birthing practices."

Faven's heart startled her by thumping heavily. She pressed a hand against her breastbone, unsettled by the strength of the emotion. "Have they found anything?"

"I don't know. It's not considered my business within the Choir, no matter how many times I ask. But I have suspected for some time..." He paused and turned to face her fully. "After the initial team went, many who had not yet felt the spark themselves followed. Sometimes officially. Sometimes, they simply disappeared or were lost in transit. I asked to be sent myself, as I desire the spark with all my heart, but was declined."

"Why?" Faven asked. Gailliard was well respected, and drawing near the end of his life. The Choir should have seen him as a prime candidate to receive the spark.

"They told me that those who were sent were required to assist with maintenance, not in potential birthings. I found this difficult to believe and did some digging. Those who are sent are all of a particular bent."

"Which is?"

He eyed her. "Seditious."

She scoffed. Couldn't help herself. "Ulana Valset is many things, Gailliard, but seditious does not rank among them."

"Don't be so certain," he said with a slow shake of the head. "I didn't know her as well as you, but the Choir kept extensive notes on her teachings. They believed she was encouraging navigators to give up their service, if they so wished. That their work was not compulsory."

"All navigators serve," Faven said by reflex, confusion puckering her brow.

Gailliard's smile turned sad, his eyes downcast. Though he said nothing, her cheeks flushed claret all the same. She knew better. There were navigators who would give up their talent, given the chance. Turn away from wealth and comfort for the opportunity to die however they liked, not slowly consumed by the very power they wielded until there was nothing left but a beautiful edifice.

Faven had considered it herself. She was certain all of them had entertained the thought at least once. How could you not? There must even be those in the universe who had fled and hid themselves so well the Choir never sensed the pull of their strength. Never came to collect. But those were fairy stories.

Like ghost ships that moved in the Clutch.

"Then it's a punishment for dissent," she said.

Putting the words to the truth rubbed the shine off the conspiracy. People who said bad things were punished. There was no mystery in that.

"You sound disappointed." Gailliard let escape a small, bitten-off chuckle. "I should have expected as much from a woman who sought pirates for information. But set aside your boredom, my friend, and think. Why the sparkless? Why the secrecy? And once more—what form of maintenance could require so *many*?"

"A makeshift prison, perhaps? Get the troublemakers away from prying eyes and put them to work while reeducating their undesirable proclivities? Perhaps Ulana has been recruited to perform that instruction. Once reeducated, they could assist the researchers in their work."

"Possible," Gailliard said. "But I cannot say for certain, and I fear that if I continue pressing, I may find out firsthand. I wouldn't be the first member of the Choir to be sent into the dark. To be perfectly honest with you, I'm not certain I could stomach being sent there to make that discovery."

"But you wanted to go?"

"Of my own volition. To be sent there as a prisoner of any kind..." He shuddered, and she rested a hand against his flesh-and-blood shoulder in comfort. It had been in the Clutch that the Choir had found him, and the bloody rescue commenced.

"I don't blame you for that," she said.

"Then I hope you'll also not blame me for the suggestion I'm about to make. If someone seditious, not on the Choir, were to be sent there with a Choir ally in place, then it would be easier, I believe, to retrieve that person from the Clutch and determine what has really happened out there."

"And I have been acting in a seditious manner, consorting with pirates."

He threw up his good hand to stop her speaking. "This is dangerous. More dangerous than either of us know. You'd have no information beyond mere speculation, and only my admittedly precarious hand on the string that can yank you back to safety. I can give you a beacon to secret on your person, to alert me if you find yourself in grave peril, but we are old friends, you and I. If the rest of the Choir suspects that you mean to report to me all you see out there, then we could both end up at whatever horrible institution they've built."

"I'll do it," she said without hesitation.

"We'll have to be careful," he warned. "Lay the groundwork so that they believe we aren't putting our heads together. In a week or so, if—"

"A week?" She let out a rough laugh. "Gailliard, the time is now. I've just been caught with pirates. My mother and mentor are dead. Right now, right this second, you and I must have a blow-out fight that draws attention from every corner of the Spire."

His eyes widened and he took a half step back. "A fight? I'm not known for my temper."

Faven pushed up her sleeves. "I am."

TEN

Amandine

Amandine treated her crew to the one thing that never failed to buoy their spirits: good food, good booze, and a movie just terrible enough that they all had something they could vociferously complain about.

The movie was an hour and a half long. They'd been watching it for two hours, now. Tully paused on a scene about 25 percent of the way through and threw up their hands.

"See?" they demanded. "This is what I'm talking about. If Mr. Handsome here was so determined to get into that bank, he could have dropped a short-wave trigger explosive in the safe-deposit box when he was busy flirting with the bank manager, and *then* come back later that night and popped a hole in the wall to thread a larger device through. That would—"

"Make so much racket he called every authority in the station down on his head?" Kester cut in smoothly. "No, I think not. A localized field disrupter, however, would have—"

Tully groaned dramatically. "Field disrupters are your answer to *everything*."

"Have they steered us wrong yet?"

"No," Tully grumbled.

Amandine smiled into her drink.

"What their problem is," Becks said, "is that none of those fools ever listen to one another."

"If we listened to you every time you got an ill feeling," Tully said, "we'd never leave the dock."

They fell into a well-worn pattern of bickering. Amandine leaned her head back on the couch, cradling her drink against her stomach, and let her eyes slide half-shut as the argument swirled around her. Eventually they decided to "wait and see," each one of them convinced the movie would prove their theory right, and pressed play again.

Pause. Bicker. Pause. Bicker. The night slipped away and Amandine didn't interject overmuch. Despite the rich food in her belly and the better drink in her hand, her mind kept drifting back to the shielding on the lightdrive. To their stuttering cloaking.

The credits rolled. The argument wound down. Kester turned to her, eyes settling on her like spotlights, and asked, "Well? How bad is it, Captain?"

"Bad," Amandine admitted. "We need shielding yesterday, and no one's biting my usual lines."

Kester frowned, tugging self-consciously at her sleeves. She knew what that meant. Brute-force runs, and the potential for spilled blood. Amandine didn't ask many questions when it came to her crew's pasts, but when Kester had sworn into Amandine's service she'd also sworn off dropping bodies. A lifetime as a corporate assassin, and Kester had decided pirating suited her moral compass better. Amandine had promised her no bloodshed that wasn't in self-defense and had meant it.

"If nothing turns up," Amandine said, "I'll call Ma Sere."

Grimaces all around. Nothing Sere Steel gave came free of strings, and Amandine's relationship with the pirate queen of Turtar Glas was rocky at best. Sere had a habit of swinging between generosity and parsimoniousness, and there was no telling where that pendulum would come to rest.

"Could just keep an eye on Tagert," Becks said. "He's liable to do something else foolhardy again soon, if he's desperate enough."

Amandine wrinkled her nose. "Nah. We tangle with him too much and we'll have a real rivalry to deal with. Ma Sere won't like it, and if we do ever need a hand up, she won't be likely to hold hers out."

Amandine's comm gem alerted her with a soft chime. The *Marquette*, telling her that one of her many networks had pinged with a possible lead.

"Hang on." She dug around in her pocket for her cryst-fan. "Might have a line on something after all."

"Fortuitous timing," Kester said.

"Isn't it just?" Amandine mused. "Nice of the *Marquette* to wait until after the movie's over."

Becks shot Kester a curiously pointed look, but spoke to Amandine, "Ship doesn't know to do that unless you programmed it to, Cap'n."

"Yeah, yeah. Here, look."

Amandine flicked her cryst-fan open and turned the projection around to show them. A flight map filled the view, multicolored dots that represented the various ships traveling in and out of the Vigil swarming around preordained traffic patterns. One ship, tagged with a dark violet flag, was the focus of the projection. In the side column where all the ship's data would go—make, model, destination—the fields had been left blank. A Bladeship, then.

A possible heading had been estimated based off the ship's current trajectory. A Bladeship, flying dark, straight for the Clutch. That matched with what Faven had to say. Amandine squinted. A tiny beacon winked up at her from the display.

"Is that—what in the void-crossed black is one of my cargo trackers doing on a Bladeship?"

"Ah, that." Becks rubbed the back of their neck. "Want to take that one, Kester?"

"I planted a tracker on Navigator Sythe's armillary when she was distracted by my knife to her throat," Kester said, then re-straightened her collar with an anxious twitch of the fingers when she noted Amandine's widened eyes. "Old habits, I'm afraid."

"Fuck's sake, Kester, you know if they find that thing they can route it back to us? Our security's good, but it's not hiding-from-the-direct-scrutiny-of-the-Choir good."

"Maybe they won't notice it?" Tully said.

"They will." Amandine bent over that dot, rubbing her forehead. "I'm only shocked they haven't already. *Marquette*, when did this ship take off?"

A time flashed in the display—about two hours after they'd left the navi to her bath at the docks. Black skies, that was fast. It took at least fifteen minutes just to get all the way up to the Spire from the docks. Either Faven had gotten her ticket to the Clutch by asking, or she'd gotten it by force, and Amandine didn't have to think twice about which outcome she'd bet on.

"We've got to get it back," Amandine said.

"No way." Tully sliced a hand through the air, shaking their head. "Cap'n, c'mon, that navi almost got us shredded by Blades and you want to go back for more?"

I handled it, didn't I?

Amandine kept her eyes on the display. The last thing she wanted was for any of them to realize she'd eavesdropped on that conversation, but she had to know.

"You got a personal objection to tangling with the navi, Tully?"

"What?" Their voice was a surprised squeak. "No! But that doesn't mean I want anything to do with the Clutch."

"We ain't touching that cursed place," Becks said firmly.

The lights seemed to dim on the tail end of that statement. Amandine glanced upward at her ship, wondering. Had that been a trick of her imagination? No one else seemed to have noticed.

"Wouldn't have to get near it," Amandine said. "We'd snag the navi long before she got close."

"I don't see why we have to get it back at all," Tully said.

"Because," Amandine said, "we go and get it ourselves, we've got the high ground. We wait for them to find it and come to us, we'll be dead before they finish knocking."

"Oh." Tully slumped.

How many years since she'd even thought about the Clutch? And in one cursed day that place had gone from being a buried memory to a resurrected nuisance. Coincidence. Probably. Maybe. She felt like she'd been snagged by a riptide and was just now noticing she was miles out from shore.

Amandine shook herself and flipped the cryst-fan closed, tapping it against her open palm. "Don't look so glum, Tully. We'll be in and out, no mess. Grab the tracker, ransom the navi for a nice chunk of change, and strip out any spare shielding they might have lying about." She pointed at them with the fan, summoning up a cocky smile. "Or are you afraid of a little tussle?"

That got a grin out of them. "Haven't met a Blade whose head I couldn't crack."

"You haven't actually met any Blades," Kester said. Tully stuck their tongue out at her.

"We're really doing this?" Becks asked.

Amandine wasn't yet sure if Faven was bonked in the head about the *Black Celeste*, but it didn't matter. A conspiracy nut ransomed as easily as any other navigator. And besides, Amandine felt that insistent, niggling curiosity she had when she'd first met the woman. The same feeling that told her she'd been wrong to leave Faven Sythe behind.

The Choir of Stars was up to something in the Clutch, and that answer might be worth more than ransom or salvage combined.

Her crew was looking up at her with eager, hopeful eyes. Snagging the navi could get them out of hot water without having to call Sere, that was true enough. But the real truth was—it'd been too long since they'd had a proper challenge.

"Let's go kidnap a goddess," Amandine said.

ELEVEN

Amandine

Amandine pressed her hands into the control panel of the *Marquette* and hummed to herself as the ship thrummed awake at her touch. They'd been nipping at the tail of the Bladeship for the past hour, darting in close and out again to test their ability to stay cloaked in the Bladeship's presence. So far, they'd been successful.

Becks muttered as they worked alongside her, a constant litany in their own language that Amandine never bothered to have her translator explain to her. As far as she was concerned, that litany was private. Right now, though, she couldn't help but wish they'd knock it off. Foreboding caressed the back of her thoughts. Not enough for her to call the whole thing off, but enough to make her wary.

Maybe it was the Bladeship itself, that brutal piece of machinery slicing through the vacuum dangerously close to them. Amandine's run-ins with the Blades thus far had been brief, and with a strong emphasis on the "running" part of the equation.

"Can't keep playing cat 'n' mouse forever, Cap'n," Becks said. "We're in a good position. Got a good plan. They haven't seen us, and the longer we keep chasing their tail, the more we risk them entering a unique starpath and leaving us in the dust."

Or the *Marquette*'s cloaking stuttering out again. Amandine caressed the controls, checking for irregularities. They were golden. The ship, anticipating her mood, was practically champing at the bit to launch the capture nets that'd keep the Bladeship from slipping away.

Amandine's gut was law on the *Marquette*. If she said something didn't feel right and they needed to bail, then that's precisely what they'd do, and no one would gripe about it. Not even Becks. Her gut was telling her to abort, even though every check was coming back A-okay. She swallowed against the word, ground it between her teeth. It was just fear, crawling back up from the secret, swampy places she kept it smothered.

The Bladeship, a dart of a vessel with fins expanding from its sides like arrow fletching, burned ahead of her on the cameras, oblivious to the shark following its trail. It wasn't the same ship that had come for her old crew the first time she'd raided the Clutch. Similar, yes, but not the same. And she was older and wiser now, with a few new tricks up her sleeve.

"Prep the net," she said to Becks, then reached over and hit the button for the *Marquette*'s intercom. "Kester, Tully, you suited and ready to drop?"

"Aye," came their duet reply.

Despite her earlier trepidation, a grin printed itself onto Amandine's face. This wasn't a real battle—nothing near like what she'd faced during the Push, when she'd picked the wrong side and gotten her ass handed to her along with all her allies, because they'd never stood a chance against the Choir in the first place. But it was close enough, and her body remembered the thrill of battle, even if the reasons had changed.

"Capture in ten," she said.

Amandine ran a hand across the harness holding her to her seat, checking the seals on her hard suit. The suits were the most expensive things any of them owned, outside of the *Marquette* itself. In theory, every citizen under the Choir was entitled to a free hard suit. They had only to request it directly from their local administrative branch of the Choir. Or, if their suit was damaged, submit whatever was left of the original and file a report on how the damage had come to be.

Pirates, naturally, weren't given the same luxury. Bureaucracy wasn't likely to hand over a suit with a smile if you filed a report saying the leg had gotten torn wide open by a rifle ball while raiding cargo off a Choir-ordained merchant transport. Their suits were pilfered from the ships they raided, with backups tucked away in shielded lockboxes.

Black as the bonding agent used to adhere panes of cryst-glass together, the suits were woven through with a fine mesh of cryst-glass, the pieces small enough to be indistinguishable to the naked eye. It was scale in miniature. Amandine brushed her hand along her torso, thinking of that small patch of scale by Faven's lips. Would the navigator be thankful, or furious, for this intervention?

Amandine shook her head to clear that puckered, curious smile from her mind's eye. It didn't matter what Faven wanted. What mattered was what she was worth.

Amandine tapped the picture of her cabin on Blackloach for luck and nodded to herself. "Golden," she said, and fired the nets.

A trio of nets burst out of the *Marquette* and arced, single-minded as predators, for the sleek and biting body of the Bladeship. The Bladeship's antipiracy measures kicked in, but fractions of a second too late—Amandine didn't skimp on the tools of her trade, and the nets remained stealthed until they were well within the other ship's envelope for evasion. Still, the Bladeship's automated systems struggled to do their job, dropping the ship down, out of the plane of assault, even as it bristled with sharp fletching and rolled.

A TARGETED alert flashed across the forward screen of the *Marquette*. Amandine held her breath, preparing to fight or evade, but the nets clung tight and pulsed on contact, wrapping the Bladeship in a bubble of a field from which it couldn't wrest free.

The TARGETED warning blinked off. At this range, without the ability to evade, any weaponry launched at the *Marquette* ran too high a risk of damaging both ships. Self-preservation, Amandine had found, was more common than thrashing rage.

Right on cue, a comms request flashed across her controls. She leaned back in her chair and put on a nice-to-meet-you smile as she accepted the video request.

The captain of the Bladeship was a red-cheeked man with a shaved head. The gold-and-aquamarine choker that denoted his status as a pilot for the Choir of Stars gleamed at his throat. A bit pale, a bit nervous. One side of his lips was redder than the other, indicating he'd been chewing on it, and though his privacy filters were in place, Amandine could make out the angled body of a Blade looming behind his chair. Young, she thought. Maybe mid-twenties. Poor kid had probably never had to make a decision more difficult than which dock to put in at. Lucky for him, she was an old hand at this and would make it easy for him.

"What's your name, Captain?" she asked, friendly as could be.

He blinked. Sat a little straighter. "This is Captain Emmanuel of the Bladeship *Vermeil*, under ordination of the Choir of Stars. You are interfering with Choir business. I order you to release this ship immediately or face the consequences."

"Oh dear," she drawled, pressing a hand to her heart in mock surprise. "A Bladeship under the ordination of the Choir? How very serious. Would you believe me if I said my finger slipped and I accidentally fired those nets?"

The thinnest wash of relief tinged Captain Emmanuel's face. Poor sod was as guileless as a compass. "I believe we can come to an understanding."

Out of view of the video feed, Becks gave her a thumbs-up. She'd talked long enough for their virus to worm its way across the connection, keeping the Bladeship from sending out any pesky distress signals.

"You know," she said, "I really *do* think we can come to an understanding. I'll make this nice and simple for you, Captain. I am Captain Bitter Amandine of the *Marquette*, and I can see by the shock in your eyes that my reputation precedes me. I don't want violence, but I won't hesitate to fry your ship's systems if you give me the tiniest touch of trouble, understand?"

He licked his lips and pressed shaking hands into the armrests of his big, cushy chair. "This is a Bladeship, Captain. The Blades will defend themselves if you attempt a boarding."

"I am, in fact, not an idiot. The Blades respond to the orders of their handlers back in the Choir or perceived threats of violence. So, you and I and everyone on that ship, we're going to have a real calm time of it, aren't we? You tell your bot friends it's all right, everything's right as starshine, and I won't send a pulse through the nets holding your craft to permanently short your life-support systems. Am I clear?"

The glittering collar around his throat bobbed as he swallowed. "I don't have the highest level of authority over the Blades on this craft. I cannot make you any such promises."

Amandine leaned forward to stare hard into the camera. "But your navigator does. Arms down, weapons on the floor by your starboard airlock. I see a single fucking Blade when I step foot on that ship, Captain, and we're going to have trouble. Now, I don't *want* trouble, so I expect you and your passenger to rub your two brain cells together and get this done nice and neat."

"What—what do you want?"

"Bring me Faven Sythe." She cut the feed.

Amandine slung the velocity harness off her chest and stood, stretching, as the vacuum hood slipped up over her head and the clear globe pulsed with light once to let her know the seal held. A HUD popped up in the corner of the helmet, relegated to simple status checks for the moment, and she opened a team channel.

"Ready?" she asked.

"Aye," came the chorus. If they all sounded a little trigger-happy, Amandine didn't mind. Her own shotgun felt too comfortable in her gloved hands.

TWELVE

Faven

Faven was pulled from her meditations by the harsh rap of a fist against the door to the astarium. Wincing, she cracked her eyes open. Twisting orbital paths of celestial bodies danced behind her eyelids, whispering to her of starpaths she'd almost gotten her fingers around before that knock shattered her concentration.

There were protocols on all Choir-ordained ships. If a navigator's attention was urgently required, the staff should have gently pulsed the lights and allowed her to ease herself out of the meditation instead of pounding on the door.

Frustration bubbled hot in her throat and she pushed to her feet, smoothing the jewel-toned robes that swathed her body into some semblance of order. She slashed a hand through the air, dashing away her armillary's projection of the local star system that had painted the otherwise smooth, blank walls that surrounded her.

"What is it?" she demanded as she waved the door open.

A wide-eyed Captain Emmanuel bowed his head in apology. Faven frowned, her hyperaware state allowing her to sense the twitchy fear that radiated from him. She shook her head again, violently, and felt more herself.

"I apologize, Navigator Sythe, but we've been temporarily delayed."

Faven skimmed her gaze up and down the halls, seeking the presence of the Blades that usually watched whatever door she was tucked behind, and found her silent sentinels missing. Thin sweat misted her palms.

"What happened?"

"Please don't be frightened, but there's no easy way to say this. We have been waylaid by pirates. Bitter Amandine and the crew of the *Marquette*, or so their captain claims. If her identity is true, then she has a reputation for allowing her marks to go free without harm as long as they cooperate. She'd like a word with you, Navigator. Requested by name."

Faven's lips parted with surprise. Mingled fear and fascination provided a giddy sensation that made her nearly as lightheaded as being yanked out of her meditation. She had no doubt their pirate attackers were Amandine and her crew; nothing else made sense. Her thoughts tangled with questions as she followed Captain Emmanuel down the hall.

She could think of nothing the pirate would want from her. Faven had asked to be taken but had been left behind. Though the moment had stung, it had, eventually, led her to this ship—the Clutch nearly in her grasp. She should be furious by the interruption, but with every step she took, all she could feel was excitement.

By the time Faven reached the rendezvous, Amandine was already there, her sturdy frame hidden behind the rigid panels of a vacuum suit, her red hair tucked under the tight control of a bandana, scarcely visible within the globe of her helmet. She carried her shotgun easily in one arm, cradled against her side like a toddler.

The wiry person to Amandine's right—Tully, Faven presumed—had a stun gun clutched tight in one fist and brought it up to level at Faven and Emmanuel as they approached. Kester, standing on the other side of Amandine, was perfectly still with no obvious weapon in hand, awaiting her captain's orders.

"Hello, lovelies," Amandine said, then addressed Emmanuel directly. "You see? This isn't so bad. I'll be out of your hair before you know it."

"Retaliation will be swift and devastating." Emmanuel slipped a finger beneath his pilot's collar and tugged on it. "You've overstepped, Bitter Amandine."

Her gaze slid off the captain, settled on Faven, and she gave her a curl of a smile. "I get that a lot. Come along now, Sythe. I assume you have a hard suit nearby?"

Faven's brows lifted and she stopped her advance, folding her hands neatly in front of her body. "I don't believe I've agreed to go anywhere with you, Amandine."

"Not really looking for agreement, but I do require compliance. Suit up."

"Navigator." Emmanuel placed himself bodily between them. "You don't have to go with this woman."

Faven tapped a finger against the back of her folded hands, considering. There was a sly nature to Amandine's smile, but tension tugged the corners of that smile too tight, made her back too rigid. She wanted to ask what game Amandine thought she was playing, but she'd already gotten herself in a fair amount of trouble. She didn't need Captain Emmanuel reporting that she was overly familiar with a pirate who'd been bold enough to waylay a Bladeship.

"This is a Bladeship." Faven watched the other woman's face, curious to see any flicker of fear or dawning realization that she truly had overstepped, this time. Amandine's expression didn't so much as twitch. "Surely you understand that you are outgunned, madam. I have but to snap my fingers and the Blades of this vessel will come swarming to my rescue."

"Snap all you like," Amandine said. "If I give a shout, or my vitals cut off, my crew back on the *Marquette* will send a pulse through the nets that hold this ship. A pulse that'll destroy your life support." She tapped a finger against her chest, the cryst woven into the material clinking. "That's why we're in the suits."

Faven tilted her head to the side. "Is that true, Captain Emmanuel?"

"I'm afraid so," Emmanuel said through gritted teeth.

"Then I had better get my hard suit on."

"Navigator, no, you don't have to—" Captain Emmanuel spun around and gripped her upper arm to stop her.

Faven froze, staring at the hand clamped around her arm. She was so rarely touched by subordinates that the shock of the contact momentarily knocked her senseless.

Being manhandled by pirates had been strange enough. But staff did not *grab* navigators. Not only was it profoundly rude, one could never be sure if a navigator's skin had begun to turn to scale, and sudden compression or friction could be terribly painful. Luckily, her arm was unmarred.

Captain Emmanuel realized what he'd done and jumped back, releasing her. "Forgive me, I meant only to keep you from—"

"I know what you meant," she snapped, and straightened her sleeve. Amandine let out a rumbling chuckle very much akin to a purr, but Faven ignored the sound to focus on the wide-eyed captain. "You're concerned that you'll be reprimanded for allowing a pirate to abscond with your navigator charge. Well, that's precisely what's already going to happen. But if you make things worse, if you try to hold me here bodily or otherwise engage in battle with this woman and damage the ship or myself in the process, your punishment will be severe."

He found his spine and thrust a finger at Amandine. "There's no telling what these people will do to you, Navigator. Please, you mustn't go with them."

"She comes with me now," Amandine said in her usual amiable manner, but this time the words tightened down with each syllable. "And we'll all get along just fine. No one gets hurt. If she tries to hunker down here or fight back, then we're going to have a problem you won't live to explain to your superiors, Captain." She stroked the side of her shotgun absently with her free hand. "You do want to live, don't you?"

"I..." He stammered, folded his hands together, and looked down at his feet. "Forgive me, Navigator Sythe."

Faven rolled her eyes to the heavens, and Amandine gave a soft snort. This time, Faven hesitated, the implications of what was about to happen finally sinking in. Amandine had given her no choice. Even if Faven had been shaking in her slippers with terror, she'd go with the pirate—because that was the protocol. Go along, stay alive, and wait for rescue. Navigators were always worth more alive and unharmed.

But now...She bit the inside of her cheek, considering Amandine with an appraising gaze. Faven had already gotten what she'd wanted: a ticket to the Clutch. If she had to be rescued from pirates yet again, the Choir wouldn't let her out of its sight, even if she were being troublesome in other matters.

A needling curiosity wanted to find out why the pirate had experienced a change of heart and come back for her. If that was indeed what had happened—Faven couldn't even begin to guess at her true motives.

Maybe Amandine could be relied upon, after all. But Faven had experienced too many times the chill of holding out her hand for help, and feeling nothing but the draft of the person she'd trusted walking away.

The shadow of the Clutch weighed heavily on her shoulders. She wouldn't lose her chance to find answers about Ulana and the others just because a pretty-eyed woman had turned her head.

Faven tipped her chin down slightly, the only indication she'd give in apology, and snapped her fingers twice. Bloody red light filled the room. Sirens blared out a shrill alarm.

Amandine arched one brow and puffed up her cheeks before blowing out a long, slow sigh.

"Shouldn't have done that," Amandine mused aloud. Faven felt certain she'd been shot in the chest before she realized blue energy crackled across her skin, wrapping her tight. Not a stun gun. A net gun. Her eyes widened, and she made to cry out, but the net had already crawled across her face and held her jaw shut.

THIRTEEN

Amandine

Captain Emmanuel did about the stupidest thing a captain can do when fighting breaks out on their ship; he tried to intervene. Amandine clocked him in the jaw with a lazy sweep of her shotgun's stock, the crack of oiled hardwood against bone loud even above the screech of the alarms. She shook her head, disappointed, as he crumpled like discarded tissue to the floor.

"Fool man musta been new to the job. Alarms start blaring, captains bolt for the cockpit. The only things they can do to fix a bad situation happen there."

"You never go for the cockpit," Tully said.

"I'm more versatile than a damn Choir captain."

She nudged the unconscious man with her boot. What'd he think he was going to do, wrestle her for her gun? Didn't look like he'd seen a fight in his life, and he'd been flinging himself toe-to-toe with a pirate he knew the name of. Brave. But brave often equated to dead, and now he'd given up any advantage he had.

"Should I pulse the capture nets, Cap'n?" Becks asked through comms.

The unconscious captain wasn't going to be a problem. When he came to, he might try to pursue, but by then they'd be long gone.

The only recourse he'd have left would be filing a very embarrassing report to his superiors.

Cutting the life support would give them a lead, but it'd also kill the captain. The man hadn't even been at the job long enough to earn a second aquamarine on his collar.

"What in the cursed black were they thinking, giving a rookie a transport job like this?" she muttered to herself. "Naw, Becks, don't fret none. We ain't killers unless we have to be."

That last was said to Faven, more than anything, but the woman's glass-cutting glare didn't soften. Amandine checked her HUD, saw red dots racing toward her through the halls, and sighed. Not much time.

She dropped to a crouch in front of Faven and met that hateful stare. "You chose to do this the hard way, and I ain't one to complain when my bluffs are called, but woman, you're on a transport with a green-gilled captain for a pilot. I know you don't get out much, but it'd serve you well to practice some survival instincts, eh?"

She glared hard enough that her eyes scrunched.

"You won't be harmed under my care," Amandine said. "But I suspect you already knew that."

Amandine hefted Faven over her shoulder. She was surprised to find the navi was muscular beneath her delicate robes, and wondered when she would have found the time for physical activity. As far as Amandine knew, the navigators of the Spire were trotted out only when required to weave starpaths into lightdrives. Otherwise, they led a life of indolence.

Silly of her, to think they all spent their time lying about drinking fancy teas or what have you. People had hobbies, passions. The navigators, of all people, would have the time to indulge in them. Maybe Faven liked a bit of sport or dance. Judging by the way Faven squirmed ineffectually against her grip, it certainly wasn't martial training that granted the navigator her compact musculature.

"Blades incoming," Tully said.

"Handle it," Amandine said.

Tully and Kester grunted understanding. The hall was filled with the low whine of two stun prods being charged. Funny, Amandine thought as she worked the security interface on the airlock to override the emergency lockdown, that a navigator like Faven was on a ship with a rookie captain and a minuscule guard of Blades.

Slow to respond, too. Almost like something was holding them back. Amandine glanced at Faven, but she'd gone limp as a sullen cat and her head dangled against the chest plate of Amandine's hard suit, refusing to look at her.

Amandine got the feeling that she wasn't the navigator's biggest problem right now. She half turned, watching Tully and Kester mow down the advancing Blades with deliberate shots, short-circuiting the horde with ease, and frowned.

"This is too easy, isn't it?" Amandine said over comms.

"You think?" Tully said, all acidic sarcasm.

Amandine checked her HUD on a whim, searching for more indicators of the Blades, and found three red dots converging on the lightdrive containment. Her blood ran cold. The world felt sharper, brighter, as her oh-shit instincts kicked into gear. She jabbed at the pad she'd been trying to hack. The digital display jittered under her touch, making the symbols unreadable. This wasn't a normal emergency lockdown.

The pulsing red light of a security alert switched to the eye-searing canary yellow of a containment breach.

"Lightdrive containment breached," the Bladeship's automated voice intoned, "please acquire hard suits and prepare for evacuation. Lightdrive containment..."

"Shit." Amandine slammed the side of her fist against the fizzing airlock control. No luck. "Someone didn't want you making it to your destination, goddess," she said to Faven.

"What do we do?" Tully asked.

Amandine glared at the malfunctioning airlock. She could force it, but if she was right, then this ship had been sabotaged. Designed to fail in ways that would keep Faven from escaping the lightdrive leak.

More than likely, whoever had thrown the wrench into things had thought to make forcing the mechanical override for the lock a damaging process. Amandine and her crew were suited, but Faven and Captain Emmanuel...She sighed.

"Fuck it all." She dropped Faven back to her feet and spun her around, pressing her against the airlock with her forearm to keep her in place as she lifted a hand to the net locking the woman's jaw shut. "You've been sent out to die, and I'm not inclined to let that happen. Not when that death's going to be pinned on my hands. But you gotta do exactly what I say if you want to make it out of here. Understand?"

Faven nodded. Amandine snipped the thin cords holding her mouth shut, but didn't unleash the rest of her. Not until she could be sure.

"Those void-hearted bastards," Faven spat out, working her jaw over to ease the ache. "I'll have them for this, I swear—"

"Anger's good," Amandine said. "But right now, you gotta focus on the next step. Where are the hard suits? We're not getting out that airlock without damaging both ships and wasting a ton of time, so we're going to have to do this a bit old-fashioned."

"I see." Some of the righteous fury bled out of Faven, replaced by an iron streak of focus. "Nearest hard suits are in the astarium. You'd better keep your word and get me out of here, Bitter Amandine. It seems I have a score to settle."

Amandine grinned. "I knew you had some teeth, goddess."

FOURTEEN

Faven

Faven wanted to tell Amandine to stop calling her a goddess, but the pirate cut the nets that bound her arms and legs, and the relief that flooded through Faven was so intense she found she didn't care what the pirate called her, so long as they got out of this alive.

She chafed her arms to get some life back into them, stepped over the unconscious body of Captain Emmanuel—an earnest but useless man—and did not have to ask to be followed as she rushed to the astarium. Amandine never left her side.

Without her armillary's projection covering the walls in the myriad hues of the celestial landscape, the room was a drab domed affair with blank white walls and a single pillow in the center. The divots from her knees were still visible in the cushion.

Though the feeling had long since come back to her arms, she kept rubbing them, tempted to curl her nails in and scratch the itch that lurked beneath her skin. Once you started scratching that itch, it was very hard to stop.

Usually she'd have time to come down off a meditation in peace, but she'd been yanked out by Amandine's arrival, and now her body was screaming with the anxiety of the broken containment on top of everything else. She hoped that if her movements were stiff and jerky, Amandine would ascribe the change in her demeanor to the general terror of the situation, not the simple fact that stars still spun behind her eyes, calling her name.

"This is an astarium?" Amandine brushed her fingertips against the wall. "Thought it'd be fancier."

She almost laughed her off. Everyone knew that an astarium was a calm, blank slate meant to take the projections of a navigator's mind without interference. Faven shook her head, frustrated with herself. She might have sworn she'd never become a docile, close-minded navi of the Spire, but when she hadn't been looking—when the years had been long and comfortable and without a single thing to spark her curiosity—she'd lost track of the world. Of how normal people lived in it.

"Ornamentation is a distraction from meditation," she said.

Where were those hard suits supposed to be? They must be close, safety was never far from navigators in case of emergency, but where *precisely*? Light, it'd been too long since she'd done any sort of travel training. Too long since she'd been on a ship at all. Faven spun in the center of the room, rubbing her arms, glaring at the walls.

Amandine cleared her throat. Faven whirled to face her.

"Having trouble remembering where the closets are?" Amandine asked.

"No," she snapped, though she couldn't say why she felt the need to be so defensive. Kindness, and maybe a tinge of sorrow, softened Amandine's laugh lines. Faven scowled, irritated that a pirate would feel anything near to pity for her. She could find the cursed hard suits.

"Cap'n," Tully said from the hall, voice a warning.

Amandine nodded. "Light's getting to her. I see it."

Faven shied away from Amandine as the pirate moved closer, arms out and to the side like she was placating a panicky animal.

"I'm perfectly all right," Faven said.

"I bet," Amandine said. "I bet you feel real fast, right? Quick-witted? But your thoughts are running together so much they're chewing each other up before you can get ahold of them. The world's a little too bright, a little too sharp, and you believe that if you could just *think*, you could get a handle on it all."

"It's just—"

"Lightsickness," Amandine said. "First sign of a containment breach. I bet you're itchy, too, huh? Stings like hell, once you start scratching, so don't do it or the next thing you know you'll be peeling your skin off. Stay here. Don't move if you can help it. We'll find the suits."

Faven's thoughts were too clotted up for her to try to explain that it wasn't the lightdrive making her feel this way, it was her interrupted meditation. She stilled, hugging herself to keep from scratching as Tully and Amandine expertly checked the wall panels until one popped open and five suits were pulled out on a rack.

Amandine handed Faven one and gave Tully another, sending them back to suit up Captain Emmanuel. Faven almost blurted out that the captain didn't deserve to be saved, he must have been in on the sabotage, but got her tongue under control. He was young, inexperienced. The perfect fall person to blame a ship's malfunction on.

A terrible accident, just like Ulana's ship.

"Do you need help putting it on?" Amandine asked.

Faven wrinkled her nose and readied a scathing reply, but that, too, died on her lips. She'd been standing there for nearly a full minute since Amandine had handed her the suit, clenching her jaw and fists in rhythm, too mired in her thoughts to act. She nodded jerkily. Amandine flowed into motion, clipping the shotgun into a holster at her back.

"I'm going to have to rearrange your clothes," Amandine said.

Faven nodded again, jaw clenched, not trusting her voice to be anything more than a staccato burst if she tried to speak. Amandine's gloved hands were firm and cold against her. She tucked the many wrapped layers of silk and velvet into Faven's sash of a belt, then tightened them across her chest. Her legs, bare to the air, made her whole body feel exposed, every nerve raw. A tear slipped down her cheek and she didn't know why. Amandine brushed it aside without comment.

Faster than she'd adjusted the clothing, Amandine clamped the hard suit around her, making her step into the boots before she closed the jaws of the leg panels over her calves, worked her way up, over her thighs and hips and stomach until she had to gently, but firmly, unwind Faven's self-hug, and hold her arms out so that she could get the chest and arm plates into place. When it was finished, Amandine held both sides of Faven's face between her hands so that there was nowhere else to look but into her eyes.

"I'm going to put your helmet up," she said, which seemed an innocuous enough thing to do, but the warning in her voice made Faven's chest tighten. "Getting cut off from the light-leak so suddenly might make you feel disoriented. I'll get you out of here, but I need you to trust me. Clear?"

Faven nodded again, chewing the inside of her cheek. Amandine hesitated a breath, then triggered the helmet.

She gasped as if she'd been tossed in a glacial lake. Her body went rigid, and though the steady thrum of lightsickness remained, she realized how foolish she'd been to attribute everything she'd felt to her interrupted meditation. The sensations were similar, but lightsickness was dialed up to another level entirely.

"That was—" She pressed a hand to her chest, heaving for the recirculated air of her suit. "I had no idea it could be that bad."

A shadow passed over her eyes. Amandine looked away. Cleared her throat. "It's common enough knowledge to those who live on ships. Navigators are more sensitive to the effects."

"Why do they not warn us?"

"Why should they?" There was a caustic edge to Amandine's voice that startled Faven. "Your ships are state-of-the-art, well maintained. And when they want to get rid of one of you... Well, that's an easy lever to pull."

Faven's mind was too jittery, the reverberations of lightsickness making her muscles ache, her limbs heavy. She wanted to ask Amandine something, and thought the pirate might be in the mood to answer her honestly, but she couldn't remember what the question had been. Amandine straightened, and when she looked to Faven again, the humor was back in her eyes, her smile easy as she grabbed Faven's wrist, not unkindly.

"Come on, goddess, let's get you off this sinking ship."

FIFTEEN

Amandine

Being the captain was a pretty cushy deal most of the time, but when things started swirling down the drain, Amandine wished she'd picked a less stressful profession. Like black hole racing. As things stood, all the warnings in her helmet were things she'd rather not be looking at. Unfortunately for Amandine, she was the only one who could shuffle those facts around until they squeaked out of danger into a comfortable, if close-shaved, retreat.

She hoped.

Becks pushed through a docket of data that could be summed up as: The Bladeship wasn't going to let the *Marquette*'s airlock go anytime soon. While Becks was working their tail off to get that straightened out, Amandine didn't like their odds, because she'd seen something like this once before.

"I want us decoupled in ten," she said to Becks through team comms.

They grunted in response. "Might have to break something to get loose on that timeframe, Cap'n. The usual software work-arounds aren't working around. It's like the Bladeship's turned itself off, but I don't see how that's possible."

"This thing was sabotaged to take Navigator Sythe down. I'm

guessing that when we tried to exit the airlock, we triggered the leak early. They wouldn't want to risk her being rescued."

"Why not blow her up? Easy enough to rig an explosion."

"A lightdrive leak is a tragic accident. An explosion is dramatic and suspicious."

"Then whoever did this is powerful and cares about optics," Kester said.

"Which is why we need to get off this thing." Amandine didn't bother to elaborate. The others were capable of arriving at the same conclusion she had.

Whoever had rigged the ship to poison Faven wouldn't have taken any chances. All ships came with biological life detectors. Amandine had no doubt that this one's would be monitoring for any and all signs of life after the lightdrive was breached. She'd seen similar traps on scuttled corporate ships, bio-trackers set up to trigger a catastrophic failure if they registered a presence of life that wasn't on the official roster. Amandine would bet her teeth that the trackers on this ship would, after a countdown, recognize any life left standing as unofficial.

An explosion would be an annoying catastrophe to explain, true enough, but a furious navigator surviving an obvious assassination attempt would be even more inconvenient.

Amandine kicked the release lever on a hatch to a maintenance shaft and passed Faven off to Tully. A narrow passage led down into the cargo bay. Amandine switched on her suit's external lights and swung over the ladder, sliding down with one hand on the side rail as she pulled her shotgun free.

She hit the ground in a puddle of her own light, caught a glimpse of a red operation beacon moving toward her, brought up the gun, and fired. The Blade shuddered from the impact but didn't stop moving. Amandine swore, scuttled back a step, and pumped the shotgun, taking aim again. She'd left the stunners with Tully and Kester, thinking any opposition she'd face down here was bound to be human—they'd flagged all the remaining Blades on board and those should have been clustered in the engine bay.

Not a lot of time to consider what had gone wrong with your plan when you were busy being swarmed by murderous robots. Amandine backed up again, took aim, and fired. The shot pebbled the cryst-glass encasing the construct, leaving thumbnail-sized divots all over its exterior plating. One of the many reasons Amandine liked to use shotguns on ships and stations was because they weren't likely to cause a breach in cryst-made hulls. The very material the Blades were made of.

"Blades!" she called over crew comms, backing up another step.

The lights flared on. Amandine almost wished they'd turn the lights back off. The cargo bay was short of supplies—this run had been meant to be short, and end bloody—but that didn't mean it was empty. A half dozen Blades fanned out around the space, the red status lights in their eyes blinking as they turned their sensors toward this new disruption.

No one was getting off this ship alive, or so the saboteur hoped. Those bots were a last line of defense, prepared to shred whoever came down the ladder, then blow the cargo bay doors once there weren't any signs of life left, dumping the evidence.

"Next time," she called across open comms, "could you inspire less clever people to try to kill you?"

Whatever Faven said, Amandine missed it, focusing instead on cracking off shots at the bots before they could fully assess the situation. Didn't last long. Bots didn't need a lot of time to process when they'd been given a singular order—kill. A lot like some people in that regard.

Kester dropped down the ladder, landing in a featherlight crouch. She whipped an arm out, fine cables extended from the fingertips of her gloves. The crackling filaments arced and popped when they connected with the nearest Blade. The construct's body seized into a tightly clenched spire of metal and glass and killing intent before its power cut out and it slumped to the ground, bone-less as a sleeping cat.

A Blade darted for Amandine. Articulated, scalpel-like knives extended from its own would-be fingertips to slash at her throat. She jumped back, cracked off another shot and another in rapid succession. The shots scattered off the bot's plating, and before she could take aim again, another Blade had swooped in on her flank and slashed clawed hands at her arms.

Amandine swore and danced out of the way, hoping against hope that Kester was having an easier time than she was, because if she wasn't, then they were all dead. Blue light arced, snapping in the air, and a Blade that'd been clawing for her guts went down.

Faven blinked at Amandine over the crumpled body of the con-struct, a stunner in one hand and a look in her eyes like she had no idea who she was or what she'd done. Amandine didn't have time for reassurances. She snatched the stunner out of Faven's hand and holstered her shotgun, then swung around and slammed the end of the prod-shaped stunner into a Blade that'd been going for her ribs. The Blade sizzled, jerked, and fell.

"Come on." Amandine grabbed Faven's arm in her off hand.

The navigator stumbled over the body of a Blade, and Aman-dine turned her yank into a protective curl, tucking the navigator against her chest. Faven trembled, the vibrations of her body force-ful enough that Amandine could feel them through both hard suits. Amandine slammed the end of the stunner into the face of another Blade and walked backward, sweeping the area in front of her with the stunner, until she was almost back-to-back with Kester.

"Ideas?" she asked.

The remaining Blades regrouped, approaching them warily, assess-ing their numbers versus the number of stunners in the room. Aman-dine didn't think it'd take them long to work out the math. They were constructs, after all. Pretty soon they'd realize rushing them as a group was all it'd take, and then they were well and truly fucked.

"I believe Tully was working on something," Kester said, voice smooth as silk, unflappable as always.

Amandine flicked a glance at the open hatch and frowned, wondering where in the void Tully had gone, and why they thought it had been a good idea to drop Faven down here with the stunner. The navigator clearly didn't know a thing about a fight.

"Sooner is better," Amandine said through crew comms in a singsong voice that belied her terror. She always got sing-y when things were dire.

"Got it!" Tully shouted.

Amandine was about to ask them what *it* was, precisely, when Tully jumped down the hatch and landed with a thud. In one hand, they carried the unconscious Captain Emmanuel tossed over their shoulder. In the other, a slim, light grey rectangle about the size of a deck of cards.

"Oh shit," Amandine said.

Tully cracked a world-eating grin and hucked the device at the cargo bay doors.

Amandine spun, putting her back to the doors, and tightened her arm around Faven. The navigator looked up at her through the clear globe of her helmet, eyes huge, lips parted as she started to ask a question—then the blast ripped the words away. The hard suit muffled the heat and sound of the precision buster, but Amandine felt the backflow of pressure slam into her in the fraction of a second before the doors destabilized and the bay decompressed.

Amandine kept her eyes open, previous experience overriding her fear instinct to squeeze them shut as she—and everything else in the cargo bay—was ripped out into hard vacuum.

She'd locked the joint of her suit's elbow before the blast, so she kept Faven tucked against her body, but the stunner was long gone. Amandine wrapped that now-empty arm around the navigator, too, and held on tight as she could while they corkscrewed through vacuum, the Blades distant glimmers, and waited for her suit's stabilizers to get a handle on things.

In her helmet, Tully was letting out a whoop of triumph while Kester muttered about their uncouth methods. Amandine cut them both out of her channel, focusing on what she could do while her body spun out of control, drifting farther and farther away from the Bladeship. She pulled up a private line to Becks.

"Tell me you've decoupled that airlock and are coming to pick us up."

"Uh," they said.

She bit down hard enough on her tongue to taste iron. "Becks. We're drifting. I don't fancy becoming a human popsicle because you can't get your ass turned around and come pick us up in my own damn ship."

"Well—" Becks started to say, but was cut off by Tully asking across the crew channel.

"What's the holdup, Becks? We do this all the time, come on now!"

Grudgingly, Amandine switched back over to the crew channel. "The airlock is stuck."

"What? Still?" Tully asked, genuine bewilderment in their voice. If Amandine had been anywhere near them, she would have punched them square in the gut.

"Yes. *Still*. You didn't wait for the all clear before pulling your stunt, Tully, so now we're going to float awhile and think about how much we don't love it when you improvise."

"Hey," they said, "we pull that trick every other hit; how was I supposed to know Becks picked today to forget how to override an airlock?"

"It's not an override we're dealing with," Kester said, almost quietly. Amandine had been having the same thought, but finding the Blades in the cargo hold had distracted her enough that she hadn't had a chance to mention her suspicion. Also, she hadn't wanted to freak anyone out prematurely. Which, in retrospect, seemed like a silly worry, because they were definitely going to freak out now.

"Then what is it?" Tully asked.

"I don't know," Becks said, "if you could give me a second in silence to think—"

"It's a gator trap," Amandine said. "Like an alligator's jaws. Clamps on tight and when you try to disengage, it brings you down with it, rolling into dark waters. It won't let go until both ships show no signs of life."

Silence expanded in the wake of that statement.

"Why in the star-crossed black would they have something like that?" Tully demanded.

Amandine flicked a glance at the woman gathered in her arms. Faven's face had gone grey around the edges, her freckles stark against dark skin washed out by fear. Amandine sighed.

"To make sure there wasn't a rescue."

Tully whistled. "Wow. They really want that one dead."

"Break it," Amandine said, a sense of dread clutching her chest so tight she could scarcely breathe. "Break the airlock off if you have to, but get away from that Bladeship *now*."

"I—shit. Okay, okay," Becks muttered to themself as they worked.

Amandine craned her neck to look back at the mated ships. Blades sparkled in the dark between them and the open cargo bay, their cryst bodies shining in the exterior lights of both ships.

The light in the open cargo bay took on the pulsing dark red of an alarm. She squeezed Faven tight, and the navigator clung on to her.

"What's happening?" she asked, voice soft and jittery from the aftereffects of lightsickness. "I sense...something. Something scratching inside me, under my skin."

"Lightdrive overload. That thing's a bomb," Amandine said. "Becks, shield us. Everything you got."

Becks let loose a litany of curses that almost sounded like a song. The *Marquette* broke away from the airlock at last, bits of metal and glass flying away from the shattered mating. Amandine held her breath as her ship rolled, Becks using all their considerable skill as a pilot to wrench the vessel around.

A second heartbeat took up residence beneath her breastbone. Amandine couldn't say if it was the *Marquette*'s lightdrive, or the Bladeship's, or maybe it was just Faven's heart beating so hard Amandine could feel it through two hard suits, but whatever it was, it left her mind numb, her body locked in place, as the pulse grew heavier. Faster.

The *Marquette* yawed and a bubble burst into life around its arrow-head body, foaming white for a flash before the shielding settled into place. Amandine thought she could sense the urgency in her ship, could taste its desire to get into position in time. But that was wishful thinking, a captain anthropomorphizing her ship, because some nights that ship was the only thing in her life worth knowing.

A yellow-tinged fractal of destruction unfurled from within the Bladeship, cracking its hull. All that cryst-glass and high-end metal and Choir-led engineering was little more than dried grass beneath the strength of a lightdrive unchained.

Amandine couldn't look away. Though it happened in an instant, she felt as if the universe had slowed. Stretched the moment so that she could see every single detail. Faven was weeping without sound, the trembling of her body a struck chord.

"Wake," Faven whispered.

The lightdrive itself couldn't harm them, not after it had spent its initial energy in rending the ship, but the debris didn't play by the same rules. Scrap peppered the shield of the *Marquette*, the clear bubble becoming a mass of frothy milk, churned by countless minuscule impact sites, battered by larger ones.

Amandine winced, feeling the pain of her ship as if it were her own body undergoing the onslaught. An old ache took up residence in her shoulder, across her back, throbbing in time with the second heartbeat.

The protocols for a breach spun through her mind, but there

was nothing she could do, drifting in the black clutching a left-for-dead navigator to her chest. Her fingers itched for patch kits and switches and all the things she'd be doing to put her ship, her home, back to rights.

"Becks," she said over the channel, annoyed by the anxiety in her voice. A captain needed to be clear. Focused. Not sound like the grains of their life were slipping through their fingers. "Report."

"Shredded the rear bul—"

DISCONNECT flashed in her HUD.

SIXTEEN

Amandine

There wasn't a lot you could do when you were drifting through space, untethered, outside of your ship that may or may not be scrap. Amandine considered, briefly, giving in to the absurdity of the moment and laughing until her air ran out. But she'd gone and made a play for a navigator, and while Faven was collateral, Amandine had never intended for the woman to die. So she swallowed her rising panic and came up with something that looked like a plan, if you squinted at it just right.

"Sythe," she said, "any chance you could weave us a short teleport into the *Marquette*?"

"Not without my armillary to power the jump, and you tucked that inside my suit."

"Right," Amandine said. "Then I'm going to use your stabilizers to thrust us toward the *Marquette*. The disengagement broke the airlock, and if we get close enough there's a big hole we can crawl inside of."

"Aren't the stabilizers tied to the suit's air supply?"

"Yes," Amandine said, "but I burned through twenty-three percent of my supply stopping our spin, so it's time to spread the burden around, eh?"

"Can't the ship come to us?"

"It's this or we risk opening your suit for a few seconds to get the armillary out. Your call."

Faven winced but gestured for her to go ahead. Amandine was struck by how fragile such an otherwise powerful person could seem when all their trappings of grandeur had been stripped away.

She clipped a tether onto Faven's belt and then used the same hacking software they'd used on the Bladeship to access Faven's suit controls via her own HUD. The onboard controls did most of the math, but Amandine double-checked the trajectories herself before allowing the first burst of air to vent free.

Faven gave a squeak of surprise when her suit jerked, pushing them closer to the *Marquette*. It would take more air to move both of their masses, but Amandine and Faven were closer to the *Marquette* than the others. And Amandine would never forgive herself if Kester or Tully accidentally missed the mark and went hurtling past the ship.

Faven twisted, craning her neck to see the ship rushing toward them.

"Easy," Amandine said. "Don't move."

Faven went still as stone. Amandine marked another path, released a little more air. The *Marquette* drifted, twisting along its center mass, a pirouette predetermined by whatever the last thing was that had hit it, because there was no way Becks would make the ship spin like that on purpose.

It looked deathly quiet. Her mind screamed at her that something terrible had happened—something worse than what she could see—but she took a breath and pushed through the fear. Ships weren't homes, with windows to shine light through, reminding those outside that life thrived within. There was nothing strange about her ship looking dark.

"Easy," she said again, but this time as a soft murmur to herself as she thumbed the controls.

They were close enough to make out the extent of the airlock damage. One of the jawlike doors had been ripped free, tearing a chunk out of the hull in the process. The frame bent back and up, a scraggly-looking hangnail of metal. Beneath the torn cryst exterior, Amandine could make out the thin, obsidian-black plating that made up the original hull. Her heart kicked, hoping Faven was too distracted by their predicament to recognize anything unusual.

She gave the thrusters one last push. They hurtled toward the half-moon opening, Amandine clenching her jaw hard enough that she was certain her teeth were going to crack. The ship kept spinning, pulling the opening farther and farther out of her path. If she could just get a handle on the ship, then she could drag them to that opening.

Amandine reached out, and swore as the gap in the hull turned past faster than she'd anticipated. A piece of metal frame whipped around and slammed into them, snagging on her hard suit. Faven shouted as she was knocked away. Amandine had a half second to think *shit* before the tether between them tightened.

She grabbed a twisted piece of metal and clung on for all she was worth. Her shoulder ached, but she held on, waiting until the pain faded before starting a careful, hand-over-hand crawl along the edge.

"Everything all right, Cap'n?" Tully asked. While Amandine had a mind to tell them off for asking stupid questions, the worry in their voice made it clear they weren't really asking if she was all right. They were asking if something else catastrophic had happened. Something deadly.

"I've got hands on the airlock. Crawling inside now."

"Copy that," Tully said.

Her stomach flip-flopped as she dragged herself over the ragged threshold of the airlock, the ship's artificial gravity taking shaky hold. At least that was still working. Relieved to be inside, she flipped herself around to let her feet be dragged to the ground and pulled on the tether, reeling Faven in until the gravity caught her as well. She staggered but stayed upright.

"I'm leaving you tethered for now," Amandine said. "Stay close."

Faven nodded. She still had that bright-eyed, twitchy look that came from lightsickness, but she was responding to verbal commands and moving more or less in a straight line. Really, that was all Amandine could ask for under the circumstances.

Amandine crossed the small room to the door that led into the central hall of the *Marquette* and pressed the mechanical intercom button, a backup they'd installed in case of digital sabotage. It crackled to life.

"Tell me you're alive somewhere on this bucket, Becks," Amandine said.

"Alive but angry," Becks said. "Everyone in one piece?"

"More or less." They'd been answering her hails. If anyone was injured, it was mild enough that they could hide it. "You?"

"Bruised and angry, but kicking."

"You already said the angry part."

"It's the important part."

Amandine let her eyes slip closed in relief, because Becks being grumbly was the best sign of health in them. "Why'd we lose comms?"

A big sigh. "Not sure. Our lightdrive started pulsing in sync with the Bladeship's before it went up. The containment held, but something fritzed. I'll get a proper look at it once we pick up the others."

"Which we haven't done yet because . . . ?"

"Because I've spent the past however-the-fuck long running checks on our systems and trying to get the comms back online."

"How bad?" She pressed a hand against the door. A tingle ran through her, an unknown sensation rousing in her chest.

"Not very, truth be told," Becks said. "Mostly that airlock is mangled, some pebbling on the hull plating. Nothing that looks like a proper crater or real damage, yet. I think we lost comms due to lightdrive flux, that's all. Should settle down soon-ish. Though I don't like the idea of our drive pulsing with the state of the shielding around it."

"Nothing to be done for that. Is this room the only breach?"

"It is."

"Good. We'll wait in here and bring out the tethers when you swing us around to pick up the others."

"Right-o. What's the plan after that, Cap'n?"

Amandine puffed out her cheeks. "People first. Plans later."

"Aye," Becks said. The subtle vibration of the sublight engine kicking on tickled her palm through the door.

Amandine switched to helmet comms. "Hang tight, team, we're coming for you."

SEVENTEEN

Faven

Faven clenched her fists in the snug fit of her gloves, glad that the hard suit hid her knuckles from view, lest Amandine see them lighten. A small, caged part of her didn't want the pirate to see that she was anything but collected. Calm.

She'd built that cage the day her mother's voice stopped. Gathered up all she was feeling and locked it tight, because that was what had been necessary, to make it through. To walk the halls of the Spire with her head held high even after her mother's friends stopped coming to visit—saying she needed *rest*—when what they meant was that they were too afraid to look into their own future.

Faven had gathered and gathered, scything out the small hurting parts of herself, until she had compressed it all into a nodule so small she could almost believe she'd scraped herself out. That she was truly as empty inside as the corpses of her kin.

Nothing could hurt, anymore, when the tender parts were shoved out of reach of the surface. She hadn't thought about her self-imposed cage in a long, long time. Only the hollow that its making had left behind.

Amandine's slantwise glance rattled the bars of that cage.

It was the aftereffects of lightsickness. Making her feel raw, exposed. If she'd been without the hard suit, she'd be digging her nails into her palms to hold back the jittery urges bouncing through her. It was all she could do to keep from throwing open the door and sprinting down the hall to the *Marquette*'s lightdrive.

She knew exactly where it was, nestled in the heart of the ship. Could feel it pulse and stutter, flickers of the drive's frustration licking against her senses, the sharp-burning sensation akin to running her tongue along the edge of a razor blade, and letting that blade cut.

What had come over her? The moment Amandine had sealed her up, she'd stopped feeling the bleed-over from the lightdrive on the Bladeship. But here, on the *Marquette*, the lightdrive was practically singing her name. She couldn't work out if it was real, or stress giving her an overactive imagination.

Lightsickness was one thing. This was something else. Something with hooks and teeth and claws that burrowed beneath her skin even as it hugged her close. She wanted to scream and simultaneously throw herself on the lightdrive or out of the broken airlock, and neither impulse made sense.

Amandine was talking. Probably had been, for a while. She had a device in her hand like a small backpack, a tether extending from the bag to a long object that looked very much like the stun prod Tully had given her on the Bladeship.

". . . because they lock in on any hard suit, they don't take much aiming," she said.

Faven nodded, as if she'd been paying attention.

Amandine lowered the device, narrowing her eyes. "You're not going to do anything foolish, are you?"

Faven let out a rough laugh that sounded shrill in the hollow of her helmet. She crossed her arms and planted her feet, looking the pirate dead in the eye, and wondered how tiny her pupils must be right now. "I would prefer not to."

"But you can't make any promises," Amandine said.

In the room exposed to vacuum, the gravity field was an unsteady thing, every twitch of the ship a flutter in Faven's belly, a stutter in her heart as her blood pressure rose and fell. Maybe that's what she was feeling. Some sort of paranoia born of being in an unsteady gravity field. Yes. That made sense. Once she was inside the *Marquette* properly, her nerves would settle down.

"I'll manage," she said briskly.

Amandine gave her a look that said she wasn't so sure, but the pirate shrugged and went back to checking over her device, the subtle gleam of her HUD tracing strange constellations across her face. Even encased in a hard suit with a spaceship as her backdrop, there was an earthy solidness to Amandine that captured Faven's attention.

The vibrant splash of her hair was peppered with fine strands of grey, the corners of her eyes creased with thin wrinkles that whispered at grins and laughs and smiles so wide they pushed out all the details of her face. Amandine's world was not one of fine silks and jewels and safety—certainly never safety—but Faven found in her a stability she didn't understand.

It grounded her, even if she couldn't make sense of it. The firm, sure movements of Amandine's fingers a dance of competence that lured her in and shook off the screeching anxiety that was boiling in her heart.

"Strap yourself to the wall there." Amandine gestured to a cable hook. "In case things get dicey."

She meant—in case you lose your marbles and do something suicidal—but Faven nodded anyway and shuffled over to press her back into the wall, willing her hands to stop shaking as she hooked herself in.

A flush raced up her neck and heated her cheeks. She was a navigator of the Spire. Faven should be the one giving orders, taking control. She'd been kidnapped by this ridiculous woman with her laugh-worn face and nearly killed in the process. Why, by the light, was she fumbling along and rushing to meet her every command?

Faven blinked some clarity into herself and took a series of slow, steady breaths akin to those she'd take before slipping into a weaving meditation.

The *Marquette* maneuvered slowly through the rubble of the Bladeship, angling to get them a better shot at firing whatever that thing was that Amandine was holding at the drifting crew members and Captain Emmanuel.

Amandine approached the breach, a thin cable connecting her hard suit to the wall, and peered out into the inky black beyond. "Got 'em," she said to no one in particular, bringing up the device. She fired. A blunted bolt lurched from the gun, expanding into a fine-webbed net as it barreled through space, a sturdy cable whipping out behind it.

After a few moments of grunting over winding the cable, Amandine reeled Tully through the broken door and helped them steady themself. Captain Emmanuel's suit had been clipped into Tully's, his head lolling inside the containment of his helmet. Tully took less care with him than Amandine had with Faven, and let him thump to the ground.

"Is the captain all right?" Faven asked.

"Had a little shock," Tully said with a mean-edged chuckle. "He'll be fine, excepting a nasty headache."

"Help me with Kester," Amandine said.

Tully nudged Captain Emmanuel aside with their boot, taking up position alongside Amandine at the broken airlock. Emmanuel rolled away, coming to rest against the wall. Faven glanced from Emmanuel to her captors. Their attention was focused outside the ship.

Faven unhooked herself from the wall and crept as softly as she could to the captain's side. The pirates talked between themselves as Tully pointed and Amandine shook her head in negation. Faven knelt beside Emmanuel and, gently as she could, gave his shoulder a shake.

Emmanuel's limbs twitched as if he were dreaming. A thin line of drool trickled down his chin. Faven bit back a curse and gave him a firmer shake.

His eyes flew open and he jerked away, jackknifing into a sitting position. Faven planted both hands on his shoulders, holding him still to keep him from thrashing. He blinked a few times, sleepily, before understanding settled over him, the panic fading. Faven pressed a finger against her helmet over her lips.

A private comms request flashed in her helmet. She accepted.

"Navigator Sythe, are you all right? What happened?" Captain Emmanuel asked.

"I'm unharmed," she said, and wondered what else she could tell him. That the ship had been sabotaged, she had no doubt. Who had done it was another story. "The Bladeship is no more. The Blades attacked the containment, and the lightdrive went critical. We're on the pirate vessel now, the *Marquette*."

He took it well enough, sucking in a sharp breath as he swiveled his head to get a better look at his surroundings. Amandine and Tully were busy reeling the other one in, the cable winding back through both their hands.

"The Blades broke the drive containment?" he asked, frowning. "Are you sure?"

"As sure as I can be. When we attempted to escape via the cargo bay, they attacked us there as well."

"Why not use the airlock?"

"It was stuck in something Bitter Amandine called a gator trap."

"Oh fuck," he whispered, then turned about thirty shades of crimson. "Forgive me, Navigator, it's just that—I didn't think pirates had access to that kind of technology."

Faven let out a small, soft sigh. "I don't believe they do."

There were two conclusions to be drawn from that statement. The first, and most obvious to Faven, was that someone else had orchestrated the sabotage. If the pirates could not have access to such technology, then someone else had done so. It was simple, neat, and didn't raise mind-aching questions about how the pirates had managed to set it all up.

Captain Emmanuel, loyal to a fault, young and starry-eyed, arrived at an entirely different conclusion.

"We have to take over this ship and get word back to the Spire," he said. "The Choir must be warned that pirates have this technology."

"Gotcha," Amandine said, drawing Faven's attention. Kester was peeling the remains of the capture net off her hard suit. Amandine turned back to her two captives, and seeing them together, a deep furrow worked its way between her brows. "Tully, see our guests to separate rooms. Kester, cut their comms."

Captain Emmanuel gave Faven a grim smile. "Don't fear, Navigator, I have a plan."

Tully's hands closed heavily around her upper arms, yanking her to her feet, and the comm channel fizzled away into static.

Faven craned her neck as she was ushered toward the door to the interior, ignoring all the chatter about making sure the hallway beyond was sealed off to the rest of the ship before they opened that door. Her gaze latched on to Amandine. Absorbing the way she hesitated beside the breach in the hull.

And the way, when Amandine rested her right palm against that gaping wound, the anxious pulsing of the lightdrive stopped at last.

EIGHTEEN

Amandine

Amandine gathered her crew in the cockpit after the captives were safely tucked away, put her hands on her hips, and met each and every set of eyes watching her before declaring, "I do not believe we have ever been this fucked before."

"I dunno." Tully crossed their arms and slouched against the wall, chewing on the side of their thumbnail between words. "Remember when we got that corp hauler's cargo that was loaded with trackers, and every bounty hunter in the verse was up our cones?"

"I remember." Amandine cut Kester a look, because she'd been in charge of checking for trackers and had failed to a degree Amandine hadn't thought possible.

"Would you like me to recover my tracker now, Captain?" Kester asked, almost sheepishly.

"Not yet. That armillary's locked up tight, but as long as the navi's on my ship, I want to know exactly where her weapon is at all times."

"What happened out there, anyway?" Becks asked. They sat backward on the copilot's chair, arms draped over the back while Amandine leaned against the back of the pilot's chair beside them.

"I've never seen a gator trap on a Bladeship. Never seen one on something that wasn't bait we were too clever to take, as it happens."

"I don't think that was for us." Amandine adjusted the bandana keeping the hair out of her eyes. "Everything on that ship was designed to make sure its passengers didn't live to tell the tale. Bit overkill, even."

"So." Kester plucked at the cuffs of her jacket as she spoke. "That leaves the question—was the navigator, the ship itself, or Captain Emmanuel the target? It couldn't have been us. Navigator Sythe was genuinely taken by surprise, and I don't believe that, even though she found our encounter disappointing, she would have bothered to rig such an elaborate trap on the off chance we'd come for her. A trap that put herself in danger, no less."

"No way was that trap meant for us," Amandine said, "and the captain's too green to have enemies with those resources. Whoever rigged the ship wanted Faven Sythe dead."

"Ugh." Tully bumped the back of their head against the wall in frustration. "We'd intended to ransom her, and it turns out her own people don't want her back. She's deadweight. Worse, dead-weight with a target locked on her back."

Amandine frowned but inclined her head. "Until we can be certain who was after her, we can't be sure who'd be willing to pay for her recovery. Ransom's off the table."

Kester cleared her throat. "In my previous line of work, it was not unheard of to pay for the recovery of an individual who survived an attempt against their life. It's possible that the saboteur would be more than happy to pay for her to be returned. And pay more again for our silence."

Amandine watched them do the math, even as she did it herself, and wondered how her crew was tallying that information. The *Marquette* was more damaged than when they'd started this venture. Potentially more damaged than the ransom of a navigator could cover. If the saboteur was willing to pay a bonus for their silence, then they could be flying true again in a matter of days, paying peak pricing to get the ship fitted with the best materials available.

"The *Marquette* needs a lot of work," Becks said, each syllable hesitant.

Kester's fingers twitched as she smoothed sleeves that hid a variety of weapons—Amandine could never be sure what the woman was packing at any given time. She'd met Kester in Votive City some five years ago now, when Kester had unexpectedly, to herself and her employers at the Spire, found her breaking point.

She'd been asked to carry out the assassination of a child. Amandine had never had the guts to ask Kester if it'd been the first child she'd been assigned, but the haunted look in the assassin's eyes had told her that it was, at least, the second. Kester had been slinking around the docks, waiting for a ship to come in that she could stow away on.

Amandine had spotted her a mile off and left one of the cargo bay doors unlatched, just in case. She hadn't been even a little surprised when halfway through her flight back out to Turtar Glas, Kester had emerged from the walls and asked for a hot meal, because she was tired of subsisting on rations. As far as Amandine knew, Kester hadn't killed another soul that wasn't trying to kill her back since that night.

"You'd be all right with that?" Amandine asked.

Kester frowned deeply, her fingers stilling against her sleeve. "If it's what's required to be certain this crew is safe, then I would be all right with that."

No, that was just the long way around to say she wasn't okay, but she'd suck it up and deal because she didn't want to put the words out there. Didn't want to admit she was tired of innocent blood on her hands. If Faven was indeed innocent. She'd come sniffing around the docks to parlay with pirates, after all, looking for information on the Clutch.

"I'll speak with her. See what she has to say for herself,"

Amandine said. "Once we have more information, a path might make itself clear."

"She's a navi, Cap'n, and already lied to us once," Tully said. "Think she's really going to be forthcoming? It's not every day a Bladeship is rigged to take out the person it's supposed to be protecting. She's in something up to her neck, drowning, and likely to drag us down with her."

"I said I was going to talk to her, not that I was going to eat up everything she has to say like it's sugar and starshine. Give me a little credit."

Tully threw their hands in the air and laughed. "Had to put it out there. Make sure you're not getting us in hot water over a pretty lady *again*."

Amandine scowled. "I didn't know she was a damn bounty hunter when I brought her back to my cabin, all right? Light in the dark, I'm never going to live that down, am I?"

"No, Captain." Kester's worried expression softened with the slight curl of a half smile. "Just as we shall never forget you running out of your cabin in your underwear, wielding a shotgun like a baseball bat."

The tension bled out of the cramped room as her crew laughed. Didn't matter if they were laughing at her, so long as they weren't all so wound up they'd be likely to do something they'd regret.

"Yeah, yeah. You treasure that memory of my freckled behind. I got a captive to interview. Maybe pretend to do some work and clean this place up while I'm busy saving our skins, eh?"

Tully clapped a hand on her shoulder and gave her a rough but companionable shake as she squeezed past them. Without her hard suit on, Amandine could taste a tinge of burnt metal in the air left over from temporarily depressurizing the hallway. The *Marquette* had refilled the air and pumped up the pressure quickly enough, but something about that exposure made Amandine feel more naked than charging down the same hall in her undies had.

She trailed a hand against the wall as she walked, stroking the ship as if comforting a pet. Or a friend. The *Marquette* felt prickly. Snappish. She wished she could soothe the mood of the ship as easily as she did her crew, reminding them of past antics.

Amandine tapped on the door with her knuckles, waited for Faven to say, "Come in," then flashed her credentials over the lock. She strolled into the room, letting her gaze drift around the stripped-down state of one of their spare bunks. Amandine had never liked a large crew—those she picked up she'd picked up almost by accident, save Tully, who she'd gotten into a brawl with in a bar and offered a job on the spot.

The *Marquette* could accommodate more, but Amandine didn't want more.

Faven had settled on the edge of a cot folded down from the wall, her hard suit still on, save the helmet. The extra fabric of her robes and her sapphire-studded veil bunched up around her neck. At a glance, the lightsickness seemed to have faded, or else she'd gotten better at hiding the mania that'd gripped her.

"Is Captain Emmanuel safe?" she asked.

Amandine leaned against the wall opposite her and crossed her arms and ankles, watching the navigator carefully. "You know he is. My crew don't deal in body counts."

"Is that so? Because you chased my ship, netted it, set all manner of traps and deadly devices loose—to your own detriment—and here I am, at your mercy. I thought you were quite done with me when you dumped me in the harbor, Bitter Amandine."

"We didn't have a single thing to do with the sabotage on your ship, Sythe. I suggest you start thinking long and hard about who wanted you dead, because someone went to a lot of trouble to make that happen."

Her lips creased as she pressed them together. She sat up straighter, folded her hands into her lap, and despite Amandine's effort to keep her gaze shielded with the droop of her lashes, Faven found her eyes and stared into them anyway. "If you had nothing to do with those traps, then why did they occur only after your arrival? Things had moved quite smoothly until you knocked on my door, pirate."

Amandine let her gaze slide off of Faven's, drifting down to the freckles that painted her cheeks with tiny white stars, to the cryst-scale lining the corner of her mouth. "You trying to accuse me, or convince yourself? It's funny, I can't tell with you."

Faven bristled, started to say something, but Amandine held up a hand and clenched it into a fist, cutting her off. "Don't matter to me, either way. But I'll give you the truth, even if you don't like hearing it. If I'd wanted you dead—which would be foolish of me, because you're far more valuable alive—you'd be dead. I'd have left you behind, or merely blown your head off right there in the hall-way. Wouldn't have needed all that pageantry to crack your head open, now would I?"

"Unless you wanted me grateful for your rescue. There's still the matter of your curiously timed arrival."

"That's easy enough. Whoever wanted you dead didn't want a rescue swooping in. When we tried to remove the airlock mating, that's when the gator trap kicked in—and I suspect the lightdrive overload was tied to that. Make sure no one walks away to say what happened."

Her cheek sucked in as she bit the inside of it. "You would have me believe my own people tried to ensure my death."

"I'd have you look at the evidence, and see that it's true."

Faven frowned deeply, her fingers lacing tightly together. Amandine gave her time, let her work through what she'd experienced, what the only logical outcome was, and was unsurprised when she let out a low, hissing breath. "I'd hoped... Well, it doesn't matter. You'll find you'll have a harder time convincing Captain Emmanuel that you and your crew had nothing to do with the Bladeship's destruction."

"We're watching him," she said, and let Faven intuit that meant they were watching her, too. "Now that you've shown some sense, we're going to have a very frank discussion about what happens next. See, we already needed the money for your ransom. Now we've got more damage to fix than we'd counted on, and we need it even more. I'm hoping you've got a good reason why someone with the money and power to sabotage a Bladeship wants you dead, and why maybe you don't deserve that fate after all."

"You're considering returning me to my attackers for a higher payment."

"It's an option that's on the table. You've got a chance to talk me out of it."

"I could lie to you," Faven said. "Tell you how persecuted I am, how put upon. That I don't deserve what was done to me. You have no way of knowing."

"I have a few ways," Amandine said with a roll of the shoulder, feeling the *Marquette* thrum against her back. The ship had always been a better judge of character than Amandine. It hadn't liked that bounty hunter for a second. "But I don't think you're going to lie to me, Faven Sythe."

"Why is that?"

"Because when we first met, you were sticking your neck out to find out a truth. This is about the Clutch. This is about what you think is happening there. And the only way you're going to get your answers now that you know someone back home wants you dead is by being honest with pirates."

She gave a little laugh, strained around the edges, and rested the back of her head against the wall, stretching her neck so that Amandine could see her pulse thump beneath soft skin. The motion struck her as startlingly vulnerable.

"I don't know," Faven said to the ceiling. "I don't know who wanted me dead, or why. You may think the Choir of Stars is a monolith, rigid in their ways, but there are factions. Disagreements.

I wasn't the only one curious about why navigators have been sent to the Clutch lately, and not heard from again. It could be any one of them. It could be for no reason I'm aware of at all."

"Then we keep it simple: Who ordered you onto that ship?"

Faven looked at her again, frowning in thought. "Choir Lisette. After my confrontation with Choir Gailliard, she thought it would be best if I went away from the Spire to cool my heels. It was not commanded of me, but..."

"But you wanted to come to the Clutch regardless, and I'm guessing after your run-in with the Blades on the docks, the rest of the Choir members more or less knew that."

"True," Faven said hesitantly. "I had, in fact, begun my altercation with Choir Gailliard with the intention of soliciting precisely the punishment I received."

Amandine chuckled. "Risky. But I suppose you're accustomed to getting your way."

Her cheeks darkened. "I've had my fair share of disappointments in life."

"Sure." Amandine brushed a hand through the air to dismiss the topic. She didn't feel like playing at who-suffered-more with a Spire-raised navigator. She liked Faven well enough, so far. Didn't want to be given a reason to feel like strangling that delicate neck. "Why'd you pick this Gailliard to tangle with?"

"Ah, well..." She diverted her gaze. "He invited it. It was his idea to begin with."

"Was it now," Amandine said dryly. "And what reason would Choir Gailliard have to send you away to the Clutch?"

"It's not what you're thinking," she said with sudden vehemence. "He doesn't know what's going on in the Clutch any more than I do. He said the others were keeping it from him, claiming they didn't want to unsettle him with talk of the Clutch because he—" She cut herself off. Bit her lip.

"Why?"

Faven wouldn't speak. Amandine watched the tumult churn across her expression with mild fascination. She wasn't used to people who felt so openly. Whose pain was obvious without so much as a scowl or a sarcastic barb to cover it up. Her crew had no problem telling her how they felt—and often with colorful clarity—but this was a woman on the verge of tears. A powerful, haughty, annoying-as-hell woman, but a person in need of comfort all the same.

Amandine pushed away from the wall and sat awkwardly beside her. Gave her back a rough pat.

Faven cough-laughed, shook her head, and scrubbed her hands across her eyes, though those tears had never fallen. "I meant to say, Choir Gailliard experienced some trauma at the Clutch, and the other Choir members make a habit of keeping him out of all Clutch matters. He suspects, however, that in this case they are using his known aversion as a convenient excuse."

Amandine watched her for a while in silence, trying to read a crack in her demeanor, trying to find some hint that she knew what had gone wrong and had an idea of who was out to kill her. But all she could find was exhaustion and confusion, a bone-weary heaviness that was hard to fake. Either Faven Sythe was the finest liar Amandine had ever crossed paths with—not impossible, navigators were political creatures by nature—or she meant the words she'd said. Unfortunately, her sincerity didn't help either of them.

"Thank you for your candor," she said, and stood. "Make yourself comfortable, and hit the intercom if you need anything. I'll send someone round later with a plate for you."

"Wait." Faven started to rise, then thought better of it and aborted the motion. "Why did you come back for me?"

"Money, Navi," she said, hand on the door, then hesitated, and cast a look back over her shoulder. Despite her earlier openness, Faven had stiffened in the way of someone shutting down to hide all they were feeling. Amandine puffed up her cheeks. Blew out a sharp breath. "And maybe because I didn't feel right, leaving you to float after I'd promised my help."

"Maybe?"

"Maybe."

Faven gave her a strained smile before Amandine slipped away.

NINETEEN

Amandine

Amandine took a pair of scoring clips from Becks's outstretched hand and glared at the mutilated plating of the *Marquette*'s exterior hull. They'd spent the past hour transforming the breach from a ragged wound into a surgical incision, filing away the rough edges and tucking and capping off wires that had been severed, rerouting what they could.

An hour of this—of muttering under her breath as she ran the scoring tool across the glass, then brought the clipper edge around and nipped off the edges, capturing the discarded pieces to store and sell to someone who had the equipment to repurpose them. An hour, and she was no closer to a decision.

"Between selling the scrap and our operating budget," Becks said, "we can get this hole patched up. Maybe even restock our food supplies with an extra bottle or two, if you're feeling generous."

"I'm feeling murderous." Amandine sanded smooth a piece of broken plating that had already been tidied up.

"Cap'n," Becks said, "you have to call her."

Amandine closed her eyes and thumped her helmet lightly against the hull of her ship. "I know. I know."

"Don't see why you're so fussed about it. She likes you." Becks tucked their tools away. They started the process of climbing back into the hull breach and reentering the ship.

"Oh, she likes me. Likes me begging at her feet."

"Thought you fancied that kinda thing."

Amandine landed an elbow in Becks's ribs and laughed when they gave her a sour look. "Mind your business," she said.

"Mind your ship, Cap'n," Becks shot back.

She winced, placing both hands over her heart as if they'd struck a heavy blow. "Yeah, yeah. I hear you. I'll make the call from the cockpit."

"I'll steer everyone clear." Becks squeezed her arm and left her to it.

Amandine shucked off her hard suit and let herself into the flight deck, locking the door behind. Becks was right. They had enough cryst scrap and funds to repair the hull breach, but that'd leave them even shorter on what they needed for the lightdrive shielding.

They needed a hand up, and there was only one place in the black a pirate could reliably hold out their hand without getting it cut off.

She brushed her palms across the dash, trying to sense the mood of the *Marquette*, but it was subdued. Pensive. Amandine thought it might be sulking. Absently, she tapped the photo of her cabin on Blackloach that she kept taped to the dash, wondering if that dusty pile of sticks was still standing. She hadn't seen it in years.

Amandine was stalling. She still didn't know what to do about the navigator, but one thing was certain—if she wanted to do anything at all, then she needed her hull intact, and that repair started on Turtar Glas.

Turtar Glas wasn't a place you wanted to end up in when you were vulnerable. Pirates could smell blood in the water a light-year off. She'd have small fish prodding at her defenses shortly after landing—there was no hiding the breach in her hull—but she was coming in fresh off a successful operation with those stabilizers.

They'd benefited half the souls that made Turtar Glas their regular haunt. She had social credit to spare.

More social credit than hard credit, at any rate.

Amandine spun up the heading indicator on her console and entered a seed into the scan that would search for a certain set of transponders in an area that, otherwise, looked like nothing but empty space.

Turtar Glas wasn't a singular station, nor a planet. It was a fleet of ships encased in an outer shell of deep green cryst-glass, the ships interlinked through a clever weaving of flexible docks and temporarily mated airlocks. Stolen leisure ships, massive yachts of the stars, made up the anchor points of the armada, but the spaces between were freckled with cargo haulers, chunks broken off stations mid-decommission, vicious-looking gunships, and even a handful of Bladeships, all stolen and grafted to the Turtar Glas armada like growths.

There was no official ruler of Turtar Glas, no governmental head or army. Alliances, yes. Factions and feuds and all the rest, and at the top of it all, Sere Steel. The pirate who'd originally absconded with a fleet of leisure yachts and determined they should all be linked together and draped in green. She alone held the keys to the armada's transponders.

One did not call Sere Steel. You knocked on her door and hoped she answered.

The search pinged with results, flashing a selection of headings onto the screen. Amandine scanned the list until she found one with the last three digits reading A33, and let out a soft sigh of relief. Every pirate had the codes to scan for Turtar Glas. Not every pirate was welcome to dock, and your favor could rise and fall in the blink of an eye.

If a transponder lit up with your unique identifier, then you would be welcomed with open arms. If you tried to dock without that invitation, you'd discover very quickly why Sere had named herself after steel.

The A33 designation was Sere's little joke, and it made Amandine smile as she keyed the order into the *Marquette*. Amandine hadn't picked her name, not exactly. It'd been given to her in jest by Amber Jacq in the days before he'd died—a wink to what he'd called her "poisonous attitude." Bitter almonds, for which he'd named her, were a common association with arsenic—atomic number 33.

She'd thought it was silly at the time. But then he'd gone and bled out at her feet, and she'd kept the name, if only because her own had died that day along with the rest of Amber Jacq's crew.

Her smile faded. A call request flashed upon the dash. Amandine accepted, eager to put old ghosts to rest. Sere's radiation-wrinkled face puckered in a grin and she poked her tongue through the gap between the two teeth she'd never bothered to have replaced, because she liked the way it looked.

"Amandine, my honeyed girl, the halls are singing your praises. Those stabilizers kept a lot of the regular scruff in fighting form. Had a few decent hauls roll in after some of the less experienced pups got their ships fitted out with your supply."

"Glad to hear it, Ma Sere," Amandine said, "but I suspect there's one who's not too fond of me at the moment."

Sere rolled her tongue over her teeth, making her lips bulge, and winked. "Ah, Tagert Red. Always was too big for his harness. You smarted him real good, taking that mark out from under him."

Amandine chuckled. "Was only a mark in his own fool head. That navi was playing him for information."

"Information on...?"

Amandine merely smiled.

Sere huffed overdramatically and waved a hand through the air, her fingers so thick with gold and gemstone-laden rings that she appeared part metal herself. "Fine, fine, keep your counsel. I don't ask much, do I?"

"Just ten percent of every trade that gets done on Turtar Glas."

"Twenty," she corrected.

"But ten for me," Amandine said with a coy smile that made Sere squint at her.

"Don't tell me you've been afflicted with the same braggadocio disease as Tagert."

"Not at all." Amandine made a brief show of examining the tops of her fingernails. "Unlike Tagert, I can back up my claims. I want ten percent, and I want it for life, and for that I'm willing to pay with a permanent addition to the armada of great value."

Sere leaned toward the camera, eyes hungry. "You have the navi Tagert Red lost."

Amandine looked up from her nails. Gave her a slash of a smile. "I do. My hull is breached and our bellies are empty, Ma Sere. But I've also got the most valuable cargo in all the black. I can deal with her—without violence—but I need your word on safe passage, and the percentage drop. The *Marquette* needs repairs, and I've been too busy cleaning up Tagert's mess to run any other jobs for the coin."

Sere leaned back and eyed Amandine critically from beneath hooded eyes. Amandine suppressed a smile. She'd stolen that same languid, evaluating stare from Sere to use herself, and it worked a trick on those who didn't know it was just that—a trick.

"You're vulnerable and carrying precious cargo. I think I'm in the better negotiating position, as a matter of fact. A nice enough position that I'm not sure about that percent reduction, but if you have her weave me three permanent paths—"

"One," Amandine said.

Her brows arched. "One measly path? I'm likely to rescind your dock access."

Amandine leaned forward, pressed her palms into the dash, and refused to be cowed. "One is all that's on the table. You know as well as I do that every time she uses that talent of hers, more cryst-scale sets in, and she gets a hair closer to death. Now, she's willing to trade for her own reasons, but I won't push her beyond what's necessary. Shortening lives that don't come for mine ain't my business. I don't think it's yours, either."

"I was dropping bodies before you were born, honeyed girl. Don't tell me my business."

Amandine's throat tightened. "The rebellion was a long time ago, and we're all just getting by now, aren't we? This navi's under my protection, and I ain't any nicer than you when it comes to a fight, so don't push me on this unless you want to get pushed back."

Something that might have been pride shone in Sere's eyes. "I find this moral streak of yours irritating."

"Anyone who doesn't irritate you every so often ends up boring you to death."

"Usually theirs," she drawled, and waited for a reaction, but when Amandine kept the hard smile on, she let out a puff of a sigh. "Fine. One starpath, fifteen percent, and I help you fix that ship of yours."

"Define help," Amandine said quickly. She liked Sere well enough, but she liked her because she was a shrewd business-woman who'd laugh just as joyfully at a bawdy joke as she would a loophole in a contract.

"Such little trust in these younger generations!" Sere threw her hand up, rings glittering, but Amandine could see the smile beneath her faux-outrage. "Is the word of a pirate not sacred?"

"It is not," Amandine deadpanned.

Sere roared with laughter and slapped a palm against an elegantly carved wooden armrest padded in raspberry velvet. "All right, all right. Say I give you, oh, let's see here." She turned her head to the side, fingertips tapping over a display that was out of view of the camera. "Insulation and enough plating to patch that hole in your hull at seventy-five percent under markup?"

"I don't need the insulation," she said, wary of the flash of concern in Sere. "Picked up extra when we grabbed the navi. But I'll take the cryst at cost, in trade for what we recovered in scrap—around three hundred granets' worth."

"Deal," Sere said. "Get yourself docked, grab the navi, then come pay me a long-overdue visit and we'll hash out the details."

Amandine tipped her head. "Looking forward to it."

TWENTY

Faven

Faven had been left to stew. No information, no check-ins. Just her alone in a tiny room for the past few hours while she felt the engines of the *Marquette* thrum, the lightdrive dormant as it traveled to what must be a nearby location. Her skin prickled at the thought. The Bladeship hadn't taken her far from Votive City. *Nearby* could easily be back to the Spire. Back into the hands of whoever had tried to have her killed.

But she knew who that was, didn't she? Even if she didn't want to fully admit it to herself. It's easy to lie, when you believe what you're saying to be the truth. Everything Faven had told Amandine had been true, in one fashion or another. True, but incomplete. Amandine's questions—logical, forthright, not bothering to hedge or account for feeling or tradition or friendship—had planted a seed of doubt.

Doubt that Gailliard's hands were clean. Doubt that anything he'd said to her was true at all.

Ulana Valset is dead.

Had Ulana discovered something about the Clutch, and Gailliard had tried to have her killed before she could investigate? Any member of the Choir could have sent out that work reassignment.

If Ulana had discovered that her ship to Amiens was sabotaged, then that would explain the jittery nature of the path she'd woven into the Clutch—done quickly, in desperation to escape an assassination attempt.

An accident. The shielding on her lightdrive failed.

Oh, the ease with which her old friend lied.

Though the room was small, it had a refresher in it, a chemical-based scouring cubicle that stripped the dirt and built-up oils from her skin and left her feeling clean, if a touch raw. Feeling more like herself, she sat cross-legged on the cot and meditated.

The *Marquette* listened. Impossible, she knew. Ships were not beings, not thoughts and moods. But as she summoned up the inner world that only navigators could access, she felt eyes on her for the first time in hours. Eyes all around, enfolding her.

Her heart thundered, the weighty presence of that other-mind threatening to press her down, to shove her out of her meditation and trap her within her flesh for all eternity, unable to enter the vaulted halls of her mind space where she saw the ways between stars. That threat loomed, imminent, but it did not act.

Faven thought of the gator trap. Thought that the *Marquette* might be waiting for her to do something before it struck. A security mechanism pirates must use to keep navigators from altering their lightdrives without permission.

Faven had no intention of altering the *Marquette*'s lightdrive, and she hoped that the ship understood that as she relaxed into the visualization. Her mind drifted through nameless stars until she settled, her breathing slow, her heartbeat even, and carefully allowed herself to recall the details of the starpath Ulana had woven the day of her disappearance.

The *Marquette* continued to observe, but its presence receded. Faven's full attention was subsumed in the fine details of Ulana's last weaving.

Chaotic, she would have called it, if a student weaver had

brought that path to her. Disjointed and meandering. Inefficient, sloppy. Now she thought those errors might be the result of fear.

It was the very ending of that path that most stymied her. It was fickle. Changeable. The ends appeared snipped off one second, then restored the next, the pathways too slim to ever allow something so large as a ship to pass through. There were intricacies to the path, but she lacked the skill and knowledge to tease them out.

Frustration skittered her heart rate up. She breathed out, focusing on relaxation. Intent. More than any of her old school teachers, Ulana had always pressed Faven to act with intent before weaving. Had taught her that clarity of purpose ensured clarity of action.

There was a secret in that starpath, Faven was sure of it. She turned it over in her mind, the framework spiraling, orbital lines branching off at seemingly random intervals, punch-through and turning points tossed in almost haphazardly, as if Ulana hadn't been sure where they would actually be, and so had hedged by including far more than reality suggested.

The model stopped spinning in her mind, and not of her own will. The *Marquette*. She'd lost track of its presence while she'd been mired in thought, but she could sense it once again, all around her, the starpath stripped from her control and into the ship's, frozen in place. A bug trapped in amber glass.

Fury overrode fear in a flash. How dare anything—even this strange ship with its moody, watchful lightdrive—manipulate her weavings without her permission. If the ship had broken her mental model of Ulana's last starpath, then she would—she would break it back.

She sensed gentle concern from the ship, a nudging curiosity. Her thoughts had fled, scattered by the whirl of anger, and she gathered them back, patched up the visual cues in her mental simulation. Looked again at the path, checking it for deviation from what she remembered.

It remained the same, as incoherent as ever, locked in the phase where she could see all those nonsensical turning points, splatters like paint, making no sense. She sighed to herself, and murmured under her breath.

"If you're trying to show me something, ship, I don't see it."

Tension pulled her spine taut. The emotion wasn't hers, but bleed-over from the *Marquette*. Faven frowned. The ship seemed to want to help her—why shouldn't it? The simple intelligences guiding the lightdrives were made to interface with navigators. She tried again to understand. And again.

Someone pounded on her door. Faven jumped, falling out of the trance, phantom trails of stars staining her vision as if those paths had been burned into her retinas. A groan escaped her, the twinges of a pounding headache tickling the back of her skull. She should have known better than to attempt a meditation on the *Marquette*. This was a pirate ship. They wouldn't have the same protocols for a navigator's rituals.

"Come in," she started to say, dragging a hand across her eyes, but the door was already being shoved open.

Amandine stormed into the room. She placed a hand flat against the wall, frowned briefly to herself, then let her face relax. Faven blinked up at her and rubbed her eyes again, but still Ulana's star-path clouded her vision, the chaotic spiral painting thin lines of shadow across Amandine's features.

The pirate hesitated, uncertain for the first time since Faven had met her. She pressed her hand harder against the wall and tilted her head to the side, considering. "Were you attempting to alter our lightdrive?"

Faven shook her head, which kicked off a pounding headache. She winced one eye closed. "No. I highly doubt that security system you installed would let me approach the lightdrive without your express permission. I simply entered a personal meditation and your ship watched me like a hawk. I've never sensed anything like the *Marquette* before."

Amandine stiffened. If Faven hadn't been so hyperaware, she might have missed it, but she caught a flash of fear—an emotion it seemed impossible for Amandine to possess—pass through the pirate captain and be soothed, immediately, by the gentle touch of the *Marquette*'s reassurance.

She'd seen the way Amandine rested her right hand against the ship, the flat of her palm giving the walls long, firm strokes, as if she were communing with something more than metal and cryst-glass.

The others didn't do that. It could be an affectation of hers—a captain's quirk—but Faven recalled a keen howling in her mind when the lightdrive of the Bladeship had gone critical. Confusion and sadness that weren't her own had raced through her, and she didn't think Amandine's bond with her ship was superstition, or showmanship.

Faven spoke before she could think better of the words. "It's not a security system, is it?"

"The *Marquette*'s systems aren't any of your business, Navi," she said gruffly. Amandine reached into the duffel she carried and pulled out a long, plain brown coat with a soft, woven hood, and tossed it to Faven. "Put this on. We're going for a stroll, the two of us, and trust me, you don't want to draw attention to yourself here any more than I want you to."

Faven caught the coat and tugged the wrapping of her top more snugly closed to hide the scale spreading along her collarbone. Amandine's gaze lingered on that spot, her expression unreadable. Faven ran the coat through her fingers, surprised by how supple the material felt, despite the rough look. A soft, spicy scent wafted from the hood as she stood and tugged it on, buckling the belt over her waist. "Is this yours?"

"I didn't have time to go on a special shopping trip just for you, goddess."

"Where are we going?"

"Turtar Glas," Amandine said, and smiled at the widening of

Faven's eyes. "I've made a deal with Sere Steel. She'll fix the ship if you weave a path of her choosing into the armada's primary lightdrives."

"You didn't think to consult me on this?"

Amandine crossed her arms and tilted her head to the side. "You are, in actual fact, a prisoner. But no, I didn't think to consult you, as I thought you'd be delighted."

Faven frowned at the amused lilt to Amandine's voice. "Why?"

"There's no pirate in the verse that's been to the Clutch more often than Sere Steel, and she's a talker."

"Oh," Faven said, and blinked. "I . . . Thank you."

Amandine grunted. "Don't mention it. I need information, too. And at least try to look a little frightened, will you?"

She bowed her head. "I will endeavor to show proper terror of your fearsome reputation, oh piratess."

Amandine scowled, but Faven thought it might be to cover a smile, then turned on her heel and strolled out the door, waving for Faven to follow.

TWENTY-ONE

Amandine

Amandine had lost track of the number of times she'd dropped anchor on Turtar Glas, but every time she did, something was different. This time around, Sere had given them access to a private berth bolted onto the side of one of Sere's personal yachts.

While the entire armada was encased in a bubble of cryst to shield it from the void, the interior lacked the stained-glass aesthetic of stations run by the Choir of Stars. Here, the walls were plain metal and construction foams. Blank sheets of unadorned steel, aluminum, and smart materials threw a hodgepodge veneer over everything—a middle finger to the Choir and their taste for all that glittered.

Citizens of the Choir, who spent their lives in gleaming cryst stations, might very well have found the inside of the armada ugly, but its brutish nature had always appealed to Amandine. There was something satisfying in the light all being, more or less, one color. There was a clarity to it that eased Amandine's shoulders. Made her feel like she could see people's faces better—see who they were better than ever before. The beauty of the cryst stations muddled people, stripped the details of their personalities down and washed them in Choir jewel tones.

Everything in the armada was plain, save for the exterior

shielding. There was no getting around the use of cryst-glass in the shielding, it'd be foolish to eschew such a useful material, but the pirates of Turtar Glas had made it their own.

While the exterior was cryst in shades of green, they'd double-walled the great shell of the armada and used clear cryst on the interior. Then they'd filled the space between with water, and water plants, and after a while Sere had declared that their great shell required wardens. Sere had taken her inner circle out to catch fish to fill those waters, and soon it became a tradition—catch a fish for the shell to pay your respect to the armada.

Amandine threw a sideways glance at Faven, curious what the Spire navigator would make of all this. She'd expected to see disgust, maybe even boredom, but Faven was looking around her with wide, appreciative eyes, one hand held to the top of her coat to make sure the collar didn't drape open and reveal her scale.

With Faven stripped of all the trappings of her station, Amandine had expected the navi's beauty to dull. Faven should have been just a small, round-faced woman with a pretty speckling of freckles, and nothing more. But Amandine couldn't make herself see her as anything less than beautiful. Even in the murky light of Turtar Glas, she seemed to shine from within with a subtle labradorescence. A warden swam above, and Faven's eyes went wider still.

"Are those fish?" she asked.

Amandine craned her neck to follow the path of the passing behemoth. One of the older wardens, the great fish was nearly as long as Faven was tall, its muscled body striped in scales that comprised all the colors of the spectrum and glittered with each firm swish of its tail.

"They are. Ma Sere takes parties out, sometimes, to catch them. They clean the interior wall of algae buildup, and that algae contains fine particles of cryst. It's what makes them so vibrant. Each one is unique, and every captain knows which warden they caught to look over the armada."

"Do they have names?"

"Sure." Amandine pointed to the warden who had first drawn Faven's attention. "That one is named Fruity."

"You're teasing me."

"I'd never." At Faven's pursing of lips, Amandine laughed. "All right, fine. That one over there is Zin."

"That sounds like a proper name," Faven allowed.

"And that other one is Beans."

"Now I know you're teasing me."

"It's true, I swear. Pirates take many things seriously, but rarely names. Mine's an arsenic joke, for light's sake."

"They're beautiful, though."

"They are." Amandine glanced to the scale bracketing Faven's lips. She brought a hand to her mouth, hiding it. Amandine grasped that hand before she could think. Faven's pulse jumped, their skin too warm together, and Amandine cleared her throat before releasing the navi's hand and taking a deliberate step back.

"Here." Amandine untied the bandana that covered her hair. "Cover your mouth. Pretend you have a cough, if anyone asks."

"Thank you," Faven said too quickly, and tied the bandana in place.

"Now." Amandine rubbed her hands together. "What pirates do take seriously is time tables. Come along. Sere Steel awaits."

Amandine led them out of the private dock and into the chaos of the heart of Turtar Glas. Suspended between the yachts that made up the cornerstones, the armada was a tangle of docks and bridges, small places for pirates coming in with hot scores to park their ships and set out their shingle for selling. Some of those shops had become something almost permanent; craftspeople and artisans settling in to service the endless churn of pirate vessels. The stained-glass art on the *Marquette*'s hull had been done by an artisan down in the lower levels. A gift from Sere, when she'd been feeling generous.

Faven shied closer to Amandine's side when she realized the walkways were open to the bottom of Turtar Glas's outer shell.

There were, supposedly, safety nets below the walkways, but Amandine had never seen them. The chaos of good-natured shouting washed over her, making her steps lighter, and she returned the waves of those who noticed her, but kept up her steady pace.

"How does it work?" Faven asked. "The armada, I mean. Is there a central control, or is each ship an independent part?"

"Depends on who you ask," she said with a shrug. "Ma Sere runs most things around here. She has her hand on the transponder keys and controls the primary lightdrives. Sere alone could drop the cloaking on the armada, and if she took her ships and left, it would dissolve, no one doubts that.

"But it's the smaller ships between that make up the life of the place." Amandine gestured to the dozens of pirate vessels crowding the market. "This is where most deals are done, where experiments are made and alliances shifted. Some of those alliances are larger than others—the Crocket Girls run about half of the Flamboyant sector of the armada, for example, and if they decided to take off on their own, it'd hurt the place. But ultimately, we're all individualists. Anyone gets any ideas of grandeur—of kicking Ma Sere off her yachts or otherwise taking brute control, we cut 'em down to size."

"Why does Sere get to maintain control? Why is she protected?"

"Sere Steel is our collective matriarch, understand? She fought in the rebellion, a long time ago. When she lost that fight, she started running raids on corps that were increasing the prices of necessary medicines until they begged for mercy.

"Then Ma Sere declared that a Bladeship she'd stolen was a hunk of junk and rammed it into the yacht we're going to now, the *Claribel*, because she'd heard the working-class people on board weren't getting paid what they were owed. So, she took the yacht. Made the workers her extended crew. Gave them a share of her profits and kept hitting yachts and taking them over, until the corps once again threw up their hands and promised to actually pay their damn workers, if only Ma Sere would stop."

Amandine smiled to herself at the thought. She hadn't crewed with Captain Jacq at that point in time, hadn't even left Black-loach yet, but she'd heard the stories often enough, and they always warmed her. Gave her something worth aspiring toward.

"I had no idea," Faven said. "I knew her only as the pirate who stole the yachts."

"That's the official story," Amandine said. "The official story's always sanitized, so no one else gets any ideas. That's what your Choir does, Sythe. You see that, don't you?

"They tried to kill you. And you know as well as I do that once this is over, once you go back to your fine wines and your silken sheets, they're going to tell the tale of Bitter Amandine destroying a Bladeship to kidnap and ransom a navigator, and what a terror I am, a menace to be stopped. And you know what? I like that story just fine. I don't need them to acknowledge my truth."

"But it is true, isn't it?" Faven said. "You destroyed a Bladeship in the process of kidnapping me."

Amandine snorted. "Thought you wanted to be kidnapped, goddess."

"It's not my usual fantasy," she said. "But I find myself enjoying the experience."

"What?"

Amandine stopped cold and turned to face the navi. Faven's small face was upturned, and though the bandana hid most of her expression, Amandine thought she detected a slight arch to her brow—challenge, or invitation? Amandine licked her lips, hesitant, but was rescued by a boisterous shout.

"Amandine! Come resupply with me!"

She turned, squinting down the docks, and found Short Gehry and her crew lounging in canvas chairs outside the open cargo bay doors of Gehry's ship. Amandine smiled wide and waved a hand in answer as she approached.

Short Gehry was, naturally, the tallest woman Amandine had

ever met. When she rolled herself out of her chair to stand, Amandine had to crane her neck up, and up, to meet those dark pools of eyes set in an even darker face. Her long locs swayed over her shoulders, studded with golden trinkets, and by her unsteady sway Amandine presumed that the sweet-booze smell on the air was coming from Gehry and her crew.

"Gehry, Gehry, Gehry." Amandine *tsked* but shot her a wink. "Doing business while three sheets to the wind? However do you turn a profit?"

She tossed her head and let out a booming laugh. "By procuring goods no one can resist." Gehry palmed something in her pocket and held up her hand, unfolding her fingers with a flourish to reveal a perfectly golden peach.

"Beautiful," Amandine said. "I grant you that, but how many of those beauties have been squashed to ferment for your current revelries?"

"Why don't you join us and find out?"

"Tempting, truly, but Ma Sere's expecting me, and we can't leave ol' Steel waiting too long. She'll rust. I'll send Becks round later to negotiate for what you've got."

Gehry pouted at her. "Becks is no fun to negotiate with. Stay and do it yourself."

"You only say that because Becks can't be bribed with a kiss."

"Now those are deals I've never come up short on." While her crew groaned and jeered at her good-naturedly, Gehry leaned down, placing a hand on the crate between them, and hefted the peach pointedly. "What say you, Captain Bitter Amandine of the *Marquette*, oh fearsome thief of skies and hearts?" Amandine couldn't help but laugh at Gehry's theatrical tone. "A small trade now, to tide me over? It'd break my heart if you got scurvy waiting for Becks to finish bloviating at me."

"I couldn't bear to break your heart."

Amandine brushed her lips against Gehry's in a quick kiss that

Gehry, predictably, deepened. She tasted of star-warmed peaches, sweet liquor, and far too many memories that Amandine would very much like to revisit. Reluctantly, she broke away and snatched the peach from Gehry's hand, taking a large bite.

"Thanks for the trade, lovely, but Ma Sere awaits."

Gehry sighed with overdramatic dejection. "Best hurry on, then. Give Ma Sere my love, and don't be a stranger yourself, eh, Amandine?" She tapped her comm gem with one finger in a call-me gesture.

"You know I won't."

Amandine waved farewell to Gehry and her crew and strode on, finishing up the peach as she walked. Faven had gone quiet, and Amandine felt her presence at her side like an anchor dragging her mood back down.

When Amandine finished the peach, she wiped her fingers clean and tossed the pit in an incinerator, then let them both into the elevator that would take them up to Sere's domain. She typed the armada's general access code into the panel. Amandine wanted to ignore Faven's sullen silence. She really did. But, eventually, she let out an explosive breath and hit the elevator stop button.

"What's your trouble?" Amandine asked.

"Was that pirate woman your lover?"

Amandine blinked. "Sometimes. Depends on our moods and the timing."

"Exclusively?"

Amandine let loose a startled laugh. "Light, no. It's crew first, always, for all the captains of Turtar Glas. Anything extra is just friendly. Why?"

"I was merely curious."

"Odd thing for you to be curious about, Navi."

"Is it?"

Faven took a step closer. In the small confines of the elevator, the soft scent of Amandine's clothes mingled with the cool musk of Faven's skin. Amandine's thumb joint ached as she held the stop button down hard enough to make the plastic creak.

Faven reached out, hesitantly at first, and Amandine's thoughts tangled and fell apart all at once as the navi brushed those chilly fingertips along Amandine's cheek. Started to trail them down her neck. Amandine grabbed her wrist.

"You're my prisoner. I don't mess about with hostages. If you're still interested when this is over, then we'll talk."

Faven tilted her head to the side and didn't attempt to wrest her hand free. "I won't be seen consorting with pirates once this is over."

Amandine snorted, the heat that'd been coiling in her belly cooling in a flash. The *Marquette* was a small ship. No doubt Faven had overheard the crew giving her a hard time about having her head muddled by a pretty face and had decided to put that information to use. She dropped the navigator's wrist and gave her a small shove, not harsh, just enough to put some space between them.

"Cute, goddess. But unlike Tagert Red, I can't be manipulated so easily."

Faven's cheeks turned the color of dark, lush roses, and she tugged forcefully at her hood with both hands. "Your loss."

"I've no doubt of that. Let's get this over with."

Amandine peeled her thumb off the stop button. The elevator rattled to life, whisking them up from the makeshift docks into the finer trappings of the yacht Sere claimed for herself. When the elevator stopped, Amandine recalled with a jolt what awaited on the other side, and held the stop button down again.

"Listen, Navi." Faven slouched like a sullen cat and wouldn't even look at her. "Brace yourself."

"Why?"

Amandine let the doors swish open. In the darkened room beyond, the fully scaled bodies of dozens of cryst-born were artfully arranged beneath brilliant shafts of light.

In death, every single one of them knelt.

TWENTY-TWO

Faven

It was the scent that nearly broke her. Mineral rich with the barest hint of sulfur, damp and burgeoning with the promise of growth in a place where only death presided. The scent of the cryst-born birthing chamber. Of the fluid that let them grow from shards into human-shaped children.

To find it here, where her people's corpses knelt in supplication to pirates, ripped free any defenses she had built. Left her reeling, feeling small and helpless as a child, and like a child not knowing what else to do with what she was feeling, she lashed out. Struck Amandine with a sturdy backhand that jarred the bones of her wrist, grounded her mind back into her body with pain.

"How dare you." Faven's voice shook, unsteady with outrage.

"Well." Amandine prodded at her cheek, working her jaw around. The joint popped. "Hadn't expected that."

Faven's face heated and she crossed her arms, slipping the offending hand into her sleeve as she struggled for the aloofness her kin were known for. Struggled to shove her feelings back down into the cage in which they belonged. "It's the least of what you deserve."

"You got it wrong, Navi. They came to us. Or Ma Sere, at any rate. Deserters of the Choir during the rebellion, every last soul. This is a place of honor."

"Honor?" Her voice rose, and she thrust a finger toward the nearest figure. Her wrist twinged, arm shaking. "Honor? They're kneeling, for light's sake!"

"Keep your voice down. Yes, they are, because that's what they chose. Now give me that hand, you've gone and hurt yourself."

"What do you mean, chose?"

Amandine ignored her. Snatched her hand and prodded at the bony ridges of her wrist, twisting it this way and that until Faven hissed in pain and tried to yank it back, but Amandine held on tight. She *tsked* softly under her breath.

"Fool woman. You've sprained it."

"You seem fine."

"I've been struck by people bigger and meaner than you, Sythe. Do me a favor; never try to throw a punch. You're likely to break all your fingers."

"I'm perfectly capable of looking after myself."

"You sure about that?" Amandine tugged a spare bandana from her coat pocket and began to wrap Faven's wrist, all her focus on the process. "Because the way I see it, you've barely started charting your own path. You don't know what it means to look after yourself. To make a real choice." She tied the bandana tight and let it go.

"These people." Amandine gestured to the kneeling cryst-born. "They knew the weight of a choice. What it meant to look after themselves for real. They were good people. And I won't have you throwing a hissy fit here, insulting their memory."

"We are not *people*."

"Maybe you aren't. But they were."

"Do not insult their sacrifice. The cryst-born gave up our humanity centuries ago to save you all from dissolution after the cryst left. We are not human. We are *more*. And we do not kneel to humanity."

Amandine let loose a snort so derisive that Faven came very

close to striking her again. "More what? Strength? Money? Fancy clothes?" She flicked a fold of Faven's robes that peeked out from beneath the coat. "All you made was a hollow inside yourself you fill with power. Look around, Sythe. Look into the faces of the navis of Turtar Glas and tell me if these edifices of the dead are as empty as the cryst-born living in the Spire."

"They're gone!" Her voice cracked. She didn't care. "There's nothing in there to see!"

"Faven." Amandine's voice was an ocean of calm, but Faven had never felt more adrift. "Look."

Light help her, she did. And at the very first face she glimpsed, serene and content, the ghost of a smile poised forever at the corner of the dead woman's lips, the cracks spiderwebbing her world shattered.

The life of a cryst-born was measured in the strength of their inner light. When their ancestors had first sought to rekindle the meditations that the cryst had used to weave starpaths, they had called to themselves sparks of the cryst's divinity.

That spark had taken root in human bodies. Burrowed beneath the skin where it formed a shard that could be excised and grown in the mineral baths of the birthing chamber until it became cryst-born, resembling a human but in truth a fragment of the cryst themselves.

Every time they used their talents, their light faded. Their minds growing distant, retreating into themselves. To call a spark to oneself to birth another cryst-born reduced your light further so that, like Faven's mother, most parents were cold and removed by the time their children were grown.

When the cryst-scale took a body entirely, there was so very little light left. Nothing, really, of the person they had been before. Merely a shell; faces blank and eyes vague.

And yet these cryst-born had died smiling.

"I don't understand," Faven all but whispered.

"They found purpose, in the end. One they wanted for them-selves. I don't claim to understand it. I don't really know how your kind work. I'm not even sure if you all do. But knowing what you want in life, making a choice for yourself. That's a powerful thing."

"But you kidnapped them."

"Void, no," Amandine said. "They ran away."

"I haven't heard of any of this."

"Why would you?" Amandine hooked her hands around her hips and stood before the cryst body Faven had approached. "No point in telling the young'uns that a cadre of their elders ran off before they were born to join the rebellion, is there? You might get ideas."

"Cryst-born fought *against* the Choir in the rebellion?"

"By the black." Amandine shook her head. "You really don't know anything, do you?"

"I—" A protest poised on her lips, but she bit the words back. No. No, it seemed she didn't know anything, after all. "I suppose not. Amandine, I'm sorry I struck you."

"Did you? Funny, I only felt a little tickle."

Faven scowled, but Amandine's wry smile had slipped back into place, bringing out the red on her cheek. The jab was a kindness, a bridge offered between them. Faven's scowl faded.

With the fog of outrage clearing, she let herself approach the nearest navigator. Their scale was old, widening to the width of Faven's palm in some places, where her own scales were only the size of her little fingernail.

Not a speck of dust had been allowed to settle in the cracks, and the shallow pool that surrounded their plinths was sprinkled with gemstones, sparkling under the shafts of light.

A place of honor.

Faven crossed her arms over her stomach and tipped her head back to face her eyes toward the stars above, and prayed. Prayed that they had been as content as they seemed, when their end came.

Prayed that their rest was gentle. Prayed that she might be as sure in her convictions as they were, one day.

When she released the prostration, Amandine was watching her with a quiet, contemplative look Faven couldn't name.

As if reading her thoughts, Amandine said, "It's the hardest thing in the world. Knowing what you want."

"How did you figure it out?"

"Who says I did?" Her gaze tracked away from the statues to a set of double doors, twin bronze panels towering above them chased with scenes from what must be Sere Steel's life. "Ma Sere's likely to tan my hide for a new coat if I keep her waiting much longer."

Faven hurried to match Amandine's long strides. "She'd do something like that?"

Amandine paused with a hand on the door. "Ma Sere does what's necessary. Remember that."

She threw the doors wide. Sere's guards had been cut down where they'd stood, throats slit in such a consistent and precise manner that it appeared to have all happened at once, each throat opened before a guard could move, or cry out.

Tagert Red stood beside Sere Steel, a hand on the woman's shoulder, a bloodied blade to her throat, sweat dripping from his brow, and gave Amandine a vicious smile.

"You're late," he said.

TWENTY-THREE

Faven

Faven had been a step behind Amandine, her shorter stature shielded by the pirate when she'd walked into the room. As soon as she'd realized what had happened, she'd felt nothing but cold calm suffuse her. A steady, enduring desire to survive.

While Amandine took a sure, firm step onto the blood-soaked carpet, Faven ducked to the side, pressing her back against the wall that framed the door. Her heart threatened to choke her, it was beating so fast, but she parted her lips, made herself breathe through her mouth to calm her nerves, and listened. There was no shout of alarm. No cry of *after her* or *catch that woman*. She hadn't been seen.

"Tagert," Amandine drawled, voice as calm and amused as it had been when she'd strolled onto the dock in Votive City, completely in control. A surge of admiration rose within Faven, wondering how Amandine could sound so confident. The resolve that had urged Faven to hide was already dissolving under the assault of fear. If she tried to speak, the words would come out squeaky and high with terror. "I don't mean to critique your methods," Amandine said, "but tangling with Sere Steel? You won't walk away from this."

Tagert let out a grating laugh that made Faven's chest clench. "Bitter, you've no idea what you're tangling with. Where is she?"

Faven held her breath, waiting for Amandine to realize Faven had fled. Waiting for the pirate to give her up, to say *she was right here, better go catch her*, in an attempt to get that blade away from Sere Steel's throat.

"Don't know who you mean," Amandine said instead.

"Bullshit." Tagert launched into a tirade denigrating Amandine's character in many elaborate ways.

Faven half listened, stunned to the core by Amandine's refusal to give her over to save her matriarch. This was an opportunity. Faven's one shot to get away, to set herself free of both pirates. She had skills to trade. She could get herself off the armada and back to Votive City. Bury herself in fine fabrics and foods and continue to be coddled until her bones turned to cryst, if whoever had tried to kill her let her live that long.

If she did that, Amandine would die here, today. Faven was quite good at lying to herself, at accepting the banal falsehoods others extended to her to keep her world safe and calm, but not even she could lie to herself about that. Amandine, despite her considerable prowess, would not make it out of this alone.

Faven's gaze snagged on the body of one of her predecessors, and she smiled. Amandine would make it out, because she wasn't alone. Faven wouldn't leave her to save her own skin.

But what was she to do? Amandine had taken her armillary—not that Faven believed it'd do any good at this point. She hadn't memorized a path between the armada and the nearest star, and attempting to dump Tagert unceremoniously anywhere else was more likely to damage the armada or harm someone else by weaving him into a position already occupied by a person, or ship.

What Faven needed was people versed in violence. People who knew how to think quickly when everything was on the line, and improvise in inventive ways.

She thought a silent apology to Amandine for leaving her alone, and crept along the wall until her path back to the elevator would be covered from the open door by a row of cryst-born. Faven took a breath, asked the Sixteen Cardinal Weaves to guide her steps, and sprinted as light-footed as she could.

Every navigator with an ounce of curiosity learned how to run without making noise—sneaking out at night to go exploring and racing back to bed before you could be found missing was practically a sport—and those old skills came rushing back, muscle memory forcing her to the balls of her feet.

She skidded to a stop by the elevator, cursing in a soft, hissing whisper as she struggled to recall what, exactly, Amandine had typed into the pad. Six digits. There had been six, she was sure of it.

Not certain if setting off an alarm would be a good or bad thing at this point, Faven shrugged and typed 161616 for the Sixteen Cardinal Weaves into the pad. It chirped acceptance, and the doors whispered open.

Faven had an instinct for direction that bordered on the pathological. All navigators did. There was no hide-the-ball game she couldn't win, no map she couldn't follow. She recalled every single step she'd ever taken, and she retraced the path back to the *Marquette* as quickly as she dared, smothering an urge to run, lest she draw attention to herself.

She was already drawing attention. The other pirate crews who'd been milling around the market, seeing to their own ships and socializing, looked up when the elevator swished open. Those eyes followed her with a mixture of curiosity, contempt, and hunger.

Pirates knew one another, and Faven had shown up alongside one of the most notorious of them all—clearly not a part of Bitter Amandine's core crew—and was now returning alone, too quickly, after a visit with Sere Steel, without Amandine herself, practically running.

Faven pulled her hood tighter around her cheeks, hoping they'd lose interest. She told herself she was unimportant. A new recruit to the crew on an errand for her captain and nervous about getting it right, and tried to radiate that energy. But when had she ever seen Kester, Becks, or Tully rush anywhere? Should she swagger? She'd look ridiculous if she tried.

"Oi," Short Gehry called, "you there!"

Faven turned to the sound before she could stop herself. The woman wore a singlet stained with various machinery lubricants, her baggy pants hanging loose about her hips, and despite Amandine's assertions that she'd been drunk, she seemed remarkably astute to Faven. Short Gehry stubbed out a cigar against a nearby crate.

"What in the black do you think you're doing?"

Faven had no idea how to properly explain herself, and so she whirled about and ran faster than she ever had in her life, throwing herself full-tilt toward the battered body of the *Marquette*.

Please be there, she thought, willing the crew to have stayed behind, to not have already gone out into the rest of Turtar Glas in search of the supplies the ship desperately needed.

The angular top of the *Marquette* came into view as she swung around a corner, boots pounding the ground behind her. Plasma-bright light stung her eyes and she threw up a hand to shade them, but kept on running. Becks, light bless them, sat on a crate outside the breach in the *Marquette*'s hull, a cryst-made shield pulled down over their face as they worked on the hull with a torch.

A hand grabbed her shoulder, heavy and muscular, and yanked her to a stumbling stop. Faven shouted, twisted, tried to kick back at her captor, but Gehry was too strong. Gehry grabbed her wrists and trapped them in one hand, holding on so tight Faven's bones ground against each other. The pressure on her sprain made her gasp in pain, false stars spinning across her eyes.

"I said," Short Gehry repeated, "what in the black do you think you're doing? Where's Amandine?"

"Becks!" Faven shouted.

Gehry gave her a shake, blurring her vision, but she thought she saw Becks start to stand. The plasma-bright light went away. Faven blinked a few times, feeling as if she'd been plunged into darkness, even though the light was perfectly set to daylight.

"Didn't you two morons see I had the cryst weld out?" Becks said. "Do you want to go blind?"

"Sorry, Becks," Short Gehry rumbled. "Saw this one go in with Amandine and come back without her, acting shifty. Ran when I called to her."

"I am not 'shifty,'" Faven said. The woman squeezed her wrists, making her gasp.

"Take it easy, Gehry." Becks pushed the visor up to reveal a sweaty face and wiped the back of their wrist across their forehead before putting the torch down. "Where's the cap'n?"

"Sere Steel's office, I think, the big room behind the bronze doors. Tagert's got Steel hostage and her guards—they're all dead. Amandine was fine when I left her, but—I'm sorry. I didn't know what to do. I could only think to run and find help."

"Ma Sere's guards are dead?" Gehry released her with an aghast intake of breath.

"Their throats were slit." Faven rubbed her wrists, turning to face Becks fully. "What do we do?"

Becks scratched their thumb along the side of their face hard enough to draw a red mark. "No one fucks with Ma Sere, and no one fucks with my cap'n. We go and we get ours back. You in, Gehry?"

"Aye," she said with a fierce grin. "Never liked Tagert."

"No one does," Becks said. "Now, Navi, I'm gonna need you to tell me everything you saw. Every single detail."

Faven gathered her wits, and explained what she'd seen to the best of her ability. No one had an answer for how Tagert had slain all the guards, but the glint of suspicion in Becks's eyes gave Faven's stomach a twist.

"All right," they said. "Here's how we're going to do this."

TWENTY-FOUR

Amandine

Amandine met Sere Steel's gaze and tried to glean some measure of information from the elder pirate's expression. All she found there was sour hate, directed at the man holding a knife to her throat. Amandine couldn't blame her. Put in the same position—her guards dead, her body held hostage—all she'd feel was hate, too.

So instead she watched Tagert, and tried to find anything there but his own anger, his hurt pride over having had his mark stolen out from under him. Sweat shined his skin, gave him a strange, febrile glow. Lightsick.

As far as she knew, lightsickness could make you bold, but it couldn't make you suicidal, and that's what this was. Because when it was all over—even if he walked away with his enemies dead and Faven in his clutches—the armada of Turtar Glas wouldn't forget, or forgive. They'd come for him. It was only a matter of time.

"Tagert," she said, keeping her voice light, but letting a touch of seriousness bleed through, "you have to know how this ends. Your only chance of having a life after this is walking away now, running as fast as you can, and hoping against the void that Ma Sere doesn't think you're worth the trouble to chase."

"You're wrong, Bitter. I've bigger allies than Sere." He raised his voice. "Come on out, now."

A woman taller than Tagert's ego materialized to the other side of Sere. Her long limbs were encased in a stiffly paneled coat dress, eyes the color of molten iron peering down at them all from within a face so narrow those cheekbones were liable to cut.

Cryst-scale flowed up the side of her neck, and in one gloved hand she held a whisper-thin stretch of a blade, long as her arm, dripping blood upon the floor. Where a pommel stone would rest, an armillary in miniature churned.

A Blademother. Amandine had heard tell of them on the battle-field during the Push, cryst-born who'd specialized in teleporting short distances to do their bloody work, but had never seen one in action before. Well, then. That explained Sere's guards.

"Tagert," Amandine said between clenched teeth, "what have you done?"

"They're waking." The fevered light in his eyes shone like silver coins at the bottom of a well. "They're waking and they're coming for us all and we can't win that fight, Bitter. We need them. Need the Choir."

Amandine recalled Faven's hypnotic voice whispering *wake* before the Bladeship's lightdrive went critical. Lightsickness. Had to be the common thread between the two.

The Blademother ignored this exchange and stepped down from Sere's dais, her clicking gait stilted. With a sinking gut Amandine realized that her feet had entirely gone to cryst-scale, forever frozen in deli-cate arches that made her appear strangely avian. She placed the slender tip of her bloodstained sword beneath Amandine's chin and lifted it.

"Where is Faven Sythe?"

That voice made her shiver. A wind through hollow reeds, hiss-ing down her spine.

"Never heard of her," Amandine said.

"Won't work," Tagert said to the Blademother. "I tol' you. Bitter won't break her word to save her own skin. But she'll do it for Ma Sere. Won't you, Bitter?"

Tagert pressed the knife deeper against Sere's throat, drawing a bloody smile that made Sere tense all over, straining against the back of her chair as if she could will her way through the wood and away from the knife.

"Fuck, Tagert, fine, I have her! Let Ma Sere walk."

"Drop your weapons first," he said.

The Blademother withdrew, seemingly bored with the antics of the humans in the room. Amandine shot a scowl at Tagert but began the slow process of stripping off the shotgun holster at her back, the pistols and stunners hidden about her hips and tucked up against the side of her torso, followed by a half dozen blades and even a couple sharp hairpins.

By the time it was done, a pile of metal gleamed on the floor between them. Tagert had lost track of the count of weapons— leaving her to keep one blade, secreted against the small of her back, where the thick material of her coat would hide the bulge.

"There." She tossed the hairpins onto the pile with a tinkle of metal. "Happy? Let Ma Sere go and I'll call for the navi. No one else has to die today."

"Bad news, Bitter," he said. "Now that I know the navi's here, I don't need either of you."

"If Sere Steel dies," Amandine told the Blademother, "you're never seeing Sythe again."

The Blademother tilted her head to the side, as if listening to a far-off sound, and didn't respond.

Sere clutched the arms of her chair so tightly her knuckles cracked. Tagert pressed the knife deeper into her throat. Amandine swore and kicked a shotgun up into her hands, pumped it, aimed for Tagert. There was no possible way she was going to be fast enough, but—

"There's no need for that," Faven said, crisp as morning frost, from the doorway.

Tagert smirked, but relaxed the pressure of the blade, and spoke to the Blademother. "There she is. Tol' you she was here, didn't I?"

Amandine half turned, keeping the shotgun aimed at Tagert, and saw Faven just in time to watch the blood drain from her face. Faven's lips went slack, mouth pouting open in an O of surprise, and it would have been comical, if Amandine didn't get the feeling that it meant they were all about to die.

"Choir Hatriel." Faven's voice lost its cold edge and became awed, almost childlike.

A Blademother and a member of the Choir. Neither of those ranks should have bothered with getting out of bed to collect a wayward navi, even if she was Spire-trained. Hatriel's scaled feet clicked across the floor as she approached Faven.

"Was this your pilot?"

Amandine had scarcely noticed, she'd been too surprised by the navi's arrival, but sure enough Captain Emmanuel stood beside Faven, looking rough around the edges. Scrapes and bruises peppered him, and his clothes had been twisted askew. He'd been in a fight that'd gone to the ground and ended up in a wrestling match he'd lost.

Quite probably that fight had been with the pirate standing behind him with a shotgun shoved into the small of his back. Tagert's crew—Amandine had never bothered to learn their names—were wiry and muscular and every one of them had skin wrinkled from light exposure, a pink to their cheeks that had nothing to do with blush. One of them had a similar weapon pressed into Faven's back, but the gun was for show. No one would kill Faven. She was too valuable.

That tableau didn't make any sense. Emmanuel had been locked up tight in the *Marquette*, and Becks had been there, hiding away the parts of the ship's hull that Amandine didn't want Sere's people to see when they came by with the cryst delivery later. Faven couldn't get past Becks, free Emmanuel, and get far enough away to be captured by Tagert's crew.

This was a plan.

One that had gone to shit, with the Blademother's arrival.

"Yes," Faven said at last, glancing sideways at Emmanuel as if even she'd forgotten the man's existence.

He fell to his knees at Hatriel's feet, blubbering apologies for his botched job. Amandine grimaced, knowing where this was going, and tried to catch Faven's eyes, but the navi had latched on to Hatriel like a lost duckling, unable to look away.

Hatriel parted Emmanuel's head from his shoulders, clean as you'd like. The head rolled to rest at Faven's feet, blank eyes staring.

The gentlest whisper could have knocked Faven over. Her hands shook, though she tried to hide them in her sleeves. If Hatriel noticed, she didn't care. With mechanical precision she relieved Tagert's crew members of their heads before they could even work up a good scream, then perched one clawlike hand on Faven's shoulder.

"You will follow."

Faven nodded jerkily.

"Hey!" Tagert bellowed, charging down from the dais. "Where do you think you're going? This isn't the deal! You can't kill my crew and fuck off without so much as touching the lightdrive you swore to fix, you thrice-fucked—"

Hatriel's blade alighted against his throat. Lifted his chin. "For your assistance, you will be paid with your life. Is that acceptable, or will you decline my offer?"

He swallowed hard. "Accepted."

"Then our business is concluded."

Hatriel turned to leave, taking Faven with her, naked blade dripping blood onto the floor in heavy *plat-plats*.

"Sythe," Amandine called out. The navi's head turned, but not far enough to look over her shoulder. "Someone tried to kill you. Don't forget that."

The Blademother slammed the doors behind them.

TWENTY-FIVE

Amandine

Tagert knew he was sunk the second the doors slammed shut in his face. He bellowed, rounding on Amandine with a wide, sloppy slash. Amandine twisted out of the way, then turned the shotgun around and cracked him over the skull with the butt hard enough to split skin.

Head injuries bled like no other. Crimson spurted from his scalp, washed down the side of his face as he staggered, swaying away from her, swiping out with his knife in an attempt to push her back. Amandine obliged. She had no desire to get close to Tagert Red.

"It's over, Tagert. Drop your weapon and maybe Ma Sere will let you keep your head."

"This is your fault," he growled. "You couldn't leave well enough alone, could you? Parading around all over the damn place with that fine ship of yours. Rubbing it in all our noses."

"What in the void are you on about?"

She could hear voices, low but insistent, beyond the door. The navis hadn't left yet. There wasn't much in the worlds that Amandine would risk her skin for, but she'd given the navi her word. Promised to keep her safe. Someone had tried to kill her, and letting her walk off with a Blademother seemed like a quick way to find out who exactly that had been. Of course, tangling with a Blademother seemed like a fine way to get killed herself.

Sometimes the world gave you nothing but shitty choices.

Tagert's voice was fast and wheedling. "I looked at the records. Poked around to see who'd left a functional ship out in the Clutch, who'd gone to make a score and hadn't come back, thinking I might find a ship so nice and quick and agile as yours abandoned in that grave-yard. I didn't find a thing. All we got for our trouble was lightsick."

"Your lack of research skills ain't my problem."

"Where did you get that ship?" he demanded, surging toward Amandine.

She took a startled step back, and her heel slipped in the blood of a fallen guard. Tagert grabbed her by the front of her coat and dragged her close, looming over her so that he could stare into her face, searching it. Amandine met that stare, the half-cocked smile she wore in every situation plastered on her face with such force that it looked more like a rictus grin.

Over Tagert's shoulder, Amandine caught a glimpse of Sere flowing into action. She'd tied a scarf around her neck to stanch the bleeding and pulled a sword from a sheath on the side of her chair. An elaborate weapon, meant to be ornamental, but blades didn't need to be plain to do damage.

Sere lined up to lunge. Amandine feinted toward Tagert with a downward stroke of her shotgun, forcing him to drop her to dodge directly into the path of Sere's blade. The steel burst through his side. Sere ripped it sideways, fountaining blood.

Tagert roared and swung around, slashing wildly, but Sere kicked out his knees and brought her blade down in a devastating arc toward his neck and, shit—Amandine was too close.

She twisted away, but the tip of Sere's blade found her anyway. Slashed a burning line from shoulder blade to shoulder blade, a shallow but searing smile.

Amandine staggered against a pillar, her breath coming in ragged gasps. Slick blood seeped through her clothes, her skin pinballing wildly between being too hot and too cold as her body struggled between shock and adrenaline. Every breath stretched the fiery agony in her back.

"You stabbed me!" Amandine blurted.

Sere flicked her blade to the side, knocking off droplets of blood, and huffed. "Cut. Not stabbed. Serves you right for all the trouble you've brought to my door. Black skies, Bitter. All this over a navi."

"How was I to know Tagert would lose his damn head?"

Sere kicked Tagert's disembodied head and sent it rolling to fetch up just short of Amandine's feet. "The feckless, void-headed, selfish piece of shit. I should have put him down decades ago."

Amandine pushed herself off the pillar and steadied her grip on the shotgun as she staggered for the doors. Faven might still be on the armada. She didn't like her chances against the Blademother, but—Sere stepped in front of her, blade poised and ready to strike.

"Where do you think you're going?"

"I told the navi I'd keep her safe, Ma Sere. My word is iron."

"She looked plenty safe to me."

"You heard me. Someone tried to kill her. If it's the Blademother—"

"If it is, the only thing you'll do is run off to die together. That what you want?"

Amandine grimaced. "No."

"Finally!" Sere threw her arms in the air. "Some sense. Sit. Talk to me. Who saw you come in with the navi?"

The only chair in the room was Sere's throne, and Amandine wasn't in bad enough shape to think for a second that her inglorious backside could grace that cushion without reprisal. She staggered her way to the dais, tried to find a step that wasn't spattered in someone else's blood, gave up, and sank down with a heavy sigh.

"Short Gehry and her crew. We came through the market, could have been seen by anyone and no one. Ain't no way to be sure."

"And the *Marquette*?"

"What of it?"

"Anyone see that ship of yours with a hole in its belly?"

There was a wary cast to Sere's voice that lifted Amandine's chin. The door was shut and there was no one about but the two of them and their collection of corpses, but still Amandine's lips pressed themselves flat. Held back.

"I need to know, honeyed girl. Were the black plates seen?"

There it was, right out in the open. A truth they hadn't spoken of in twenty-five long years. A truth they'd only danced around.

When Amandine had washed up on Turtar Glas with a half-functional ship and a set of wounds she couldn't explain, her old crew dead and her mind too fevered from lightsickness to make sense of anything, Sere had looked the other way, and not commented on the strange color of Amandine's salvaged ship.

Of the black cryst hull that encased it, and the lightdrive that wasn't shielded at all. A lightdrive that had, in fact, been installed in such a way that made it clear the original owners had no need to shield the drive.

Amandine had crashed onto Sere's shores in a cryst ship, stolen from the Clutch, convinced she could speak with the ship. That the ship cared for her. All Sere had done back then was patch her up, gotten her well, and by the time Amandine had gone back to the *Marquette* Sere had already hidden it away beneath the colorful cryst-glass expected of those who lived under the Choir of Stars. She'd even installed a containment caul for the lightdrive.

"No," Amandine said. "No one saw. We came in behind the crates you left on the dock and Becks has been out there ever since, welding it shut."

"Best be prayin' you're right, girl. Because if the navi tells the Blademother what that ship of yours is made of, you won't ever know peace."

Peace. Amandine wanted to laugh—she didn't know it now.

Hadn't since the day she'd pulled her laces tight and left Blackloach behind, a misty memory forever out of reach. Sere must have seen it in her face because a shadow passed behind her eyes, quickly driven away. She flicked her blade absently, then bent to wipe it clean on the back of Tagert's coat.

"Gather your people. Find out what really happened out there with the navi, then go to the *Stamping Bull* and salvage what you need, if it's got anything worth taking."

"Tagert's got more crew than who's dead on the floor here," Amandine said.

"He won't by the time my crew is done with them."

A small part of Amandine felt hollowed out. She hadn't liked Tagert, but she hadn't wanted him slaughtered at her feet. Hadn't wanted his crew cut down for his idiocy. She looked away. This wasn't Sere being cruel. This was Sere exacting justice.

"Aye, Ma Sere."

"And, Bitter?"

"Aye?"

"Make sure the *Marquette*'s stable enough to jump. I'll be moving the armada, lest that Blademother get any ideas and come back to stamp us out. If your ship's not ready, you'll be left behind."

Sere didn't look at her as she said those words. She'd turned away, a hand to her comm gem to indicate she was talking with Turtar Glas's inner crew. An old ache twisted beneath Amandine's breastbone.

When she'd first set out to seek a life of piracy, Amandine had intended to join Sere's crew. But she'd found Amber Jacq first, and everything that'd come after . . . Amandine had no doubt Sere would leave her in a heartbeat, if it meant the safety of the armada.

Amandine hefted herself up, wincing at the sting in her back, but she lengthened her stride. She was eager to wash her hair of the navigator and Choir politics and even the whisper of the Clutch. Foolish of her, to think she could tangle with such things and come out unscathed.

She should have left the navi to her fate, whatever it would have been, back on that Bladeship. Never should have gone chasing a ransom at all. Never should have reached out to grab a star, because Amandine knew better than most how deeply they could burn.

Sere gripped her arm as she walked past. Her weathered face was drawn.

"What is it?" Amandine asked.

"We've been drive-locked. Turtar Glas can't enter a starpath."

TWENTY-SIX

Faven

They were scarcely three steps through the grand, bronze-paneled doors when Hatriel's narrow, avian neck turned and she spat upon the kneeling body of a cryst-born man. Hatriel walked on as if the motion had been as simple as swatting a fly.

Faven could have walked the rest of her life with the specter of Hatriel's clawed hand guiding her steps, if it hadn't been for that foamy globule dripping down the corpse's cheek. She stopped, arrested, sudden clarity lancing through the fugue state she'd fallen into ever since Captain Emmanuel's eyes had stared up at her, dead and dull.

She tugged her sleeve over the heel of her palm and reached to clean the statue, but Hatriel yanked her away.

"They are traitors." Her lips screwed up tight with disgust, and Faven feared she might spit again. "Do not debase yourself by serving them. They deserve worse than eternity on their knees."

Faven could think of nothing to say that wouldn't land her in deeper trouble.

In her own silence, she found shame at last. It raised sickening curls of hot self-loathing to swirl through her veins and curdle her guts. Made her skin hot and her sweat feel rancid, sticky.

Hatriel scarcely seemed to notice. With one hand still gripping Faven tight, she held her bloodied blade point-down before her. The armillary at the end of its grip churned, the soft thrum of its miniature lightdrive making Faven's teeth ache. She blinked, and they'd left the honored hall of cryst-born behind and stood in the murky halls of a Bladeship.

Not just any Bladeship. Faven had never set foot on this ship before, but it must be Hatriel's private vessel. The overhead lights were kept low, cryst-glass mosaics of battlefields Faven could never hope to name painting myriad colors upon the floor.

Faven found her voice at last. "Did Gailliard send you?"

No answer.

"You didn't have to kill those people. They wouldn't have fought against you."

Hatriel's molten eyes lowered to Faven's blood-soaked slippers, and the footprints she'd trailed behind her on the floor. Her face was still as stone.

"This...tantrum...you are throwing is over. There will be no more talk of the Clutch. No more dealings with pirates. Those people are not dead because I killed them. They are dead because I was required to rescue you. Accept the consequences of your actions."

"I never asked for you to rescue me."

Slowly, Hatriel removed a thick cloth from one of her coat's many pockets and began to clean the length of her blade. She spoke without bothering to look at Faven, all focus on the care of her weapon. Her long white hair fell over her shoulder, hiding her face.

"You are alive because I promised your mother that I would keep you safe. The Choir would have deemed you a traitor, had I not intervened. You will spend tonight in the astarium, meditating upon what you have done. And tomorrow, when other members of the Choir arrive to assist me, you will join in weaving a path that unmakes Turtar Glas once and for all."

Faven's stomach fell and she struggled to keep her voice calm. "You would destroy all of them? Some may be worthy of death, but they are not all killers, Blademother. Most are merely thieves."

"I care not for the lives of thieves."

"And do you care not for people? At all? We are their children, though we've branched so far. Our progenitors were human flesh and blood, and they took the burden we inherited upon themselves to save humanity. That must *mean* something. We cannot blot them from existence because they irritate us."

"A few thousand dead pirates will do nothing to impact the human population, when they breed so quickly and easily."

"It's not about the number of them!" Faven had never raised her voice to Hatriel before. She could count on one hand the number of times she had raised it to those in authority, and most of those moments were born of calculation, not the passion that burned through her veins now. Not the disgust boiling up, demanding to be vomited free. "Do you think our progenitors were thinking of *numbers*? Scribbling cold calculations while they prayed for deliverance? They gave of themselves because they wanted to save family, friends, lovers—"

A snarl overtook Hatriel's face so vicious and quick that it startled Faven as surely as a slap across the face. "Humans know nothing of love. What they have is quick to kindle and faster to die. It is *easy*, and nothing worth devotion should ever be easy.

"They know not what it means to crack open the edifice of oneself along fissures grown deeper through long friendship. Know not what it is to find someone who draws you up to the surface of yourself after decades of waning, always waning. Could never understand what it means to burn brighter together upon the battlefield even as the scale takes deeper root because our flames are twin. Mirrors of each other."

Hatriel rounded on her, the blade forgotten in her hand.

"And then when it was over, when the battle was won and the

glory ours and all that should have been left was long years of burning together, another light called to her. Your light, Faven. It splintered her. Dimmed her faster than decades of scale growth, until our flames were no longer mirrored but warped away."

Faven hadn't known. The rawness of Hatriel's voice rocked her, the words cracking open half-forgotten memories—Hatriel, bringing her mother data drives full of recorded copies of her favorite books, long after her mother had lost the ability to turn paper pages. Hatriel, leaving pristine fruit bundled in soft blankets at their door. But never staying. Always leaving before Faven could even get to the door to open it, her stiff silhouette lurching away, pretending not to hear Faven call out a greeting.

That they'd worked together, Faven had known, but that was all. A distant story of her mother's past. Faven tried to imagine her mother wielding a blade, and couldn't.

"Mother never told me."

"Sariette. Her name was Sariette. And you never asked."

White-hot guilt speared through her, searing her thoughts, shortening her breath. She'd done what she had to do, hadn't she? She'd been a good daughter. She had. She'd locked up all her sour feelings and buried them deep. Made herself serene and kind and made certain that her mother had everything she'd needed toward the end—that was right, wasn't it?

It wasn't—it wasn't her fault the scale had progressed so quickly. It took everyone differently; the doctors had assured her of that over and over again.

The Blademother's tone reclaimed its cold detachment. "This is our true burden. Not the scale, not death, but the lessening of ourselves. An impossible brightness, and its loss. Humans cannot comprehend how exquisite that pain can be."

Faven found her voice at last. "Blademother, they know."

The rampart of Hatriel's stoicism cracked, and fell, an electric storm churning behind her eyes with such violence Faven feared she was about to forget her promise and cut Faven down then and there.

Hatriel gripped her arm and wrenched her around, marching her through the long halls of the ship, and threw her with such force into the astarium that Faven caught her toes on her robe. She stumbled, crashed to the floor, and gasped at the raw shock of pain scraping her palms, her knees.

"You will stay here, and meditate through the night on your true purpose."

"Hatriel," Faven called out. She stopped, but did not turn. "Thank you. For loving my mother."

"I wish Sariette hadn't wasted her life and her light to birth such an inconstant, flickering spark."

The door slid shut, the click of the lock louder than slamming the door could have been. Gathering herself was a slow affair. Alone in the low light of the astarium, her body felt distant, her limbs some other puppet's to be controlled with awkward strings.

How long since she'd had an injury worse than a stubbed toe or stubborn hangnail? Faven knelt in the center of the astarium. There was no velvet cushion for her here, and her armillary had been left behind in whatever drawer Amandine had locked it within. But those things were merely trappings. Useful, yes, but secondary to her nature.

She need only to close her eyes, and the world of flesh and blood and small agonies would wash away, her mind delivered unto the stars, which were her birthright.

Faven did not close her eyes.

She rested the backs of her hands on her scraped knees, palms up so that she could see the bruised-plum scratches, one hand partially obscured by the bandana Amandine had used to bind her wrist what felt like hours ago, now. Hatriel hadn't thrown her hard enough for the scratches to draw blood.

Faven was surprised to find that she wished she had.

She squeezed her hands. Folded the fingers down one by one to feel the sting in them, the ache so alien to her senses. Muted, still. The pain was distant. Her body was a shell of skin around the truth of the core of her and she squeezed harder, until the crescent smiles of her nails drew thin trickles of blood and her senses began to fizz with the sharpness in the sting.

The pain was a shivering, bright wave. Washing over her from her palms to lick up her arms, wrap itself around her and squeeze, warm, solid, and real. Faven breathed deeply, savoring, and nearly shouted in surprise as she inhaled the warm-spicy scent of Amandine's coat, wrapped around her still.

She startled, releasing her hands with a lurch, and felt ridiculous as she inspected the shallow cuts dripping red from her palms.

How Amandine would laugh at her. Digging into her own flesh just to feel. She removed a small first aid kit from the wall panels and cleaned herself up. It pleased her to find a splotch of a bloodstain on the edge of the bandana. A red tear, turning brown already.

Scale would come to those wounds, next. She wondered if she'd get to see herself scar, before the scale came. She'd never seen a cryst-born scar before.

Her purpose.

For all her talk of the vision of their ancestors, she couldn't deny that her own existence was an empty one. Every action she'd taken, every knee-jerk rebellion that had brought her here, in pursuit of Ulana, had been made without fear of real consequence. Perhaps, she mused, in hope of consequence.

She had wanted her mentor back. And while the thought of a conspiracy had its appeal, she'd only made it this far because Ulana had been taken from her, and she'd never had anything taken from her before.

You really don't know anything, do you?

She hadn't even known her mother had been in love.

Faven opened the compartment with the hard suits and stripped out the HUD glass stitched into the hood, then looped it around her ear and over one eye. It connected to the wider network, welcoming her to the Choir's familiar databases with a merry chime.

Rebellion. Cryst-born pirates. Where to begin? Faven sank back to her knees in the center of the room and keyed in: Sariette Sythe.

A stream of accolades, commendations. She hadn't been a Blademother, but oh, how she'd fought. A picture of her smiling, arm slung around a woman Faven didn't know, stared up at her out of the past. She wore the white uniform of the Choir's military, so seldom used, and even in a photo the glint in her eye was sharp, mischievous. Her chin tilted upward with a cockiness Faven had only glimpsed during their life together.

Tears clouded her vision. She brushed them aside.

Faven had always known, in a vague sort of way, that her mother must have been involved with the effort made against the rebellion. Evey member of that generation had been called to service in that short, brutal war, wherein a confederation of human planets had decided they could get along just fine without Choir oversight, and had been roundly routed for the assumption.

But knowing something and understanding it had always been two different things. She scrolled through articles, interviews, and felt like she was meeting her own mother for the first time.

Why had she never been told? Why had her mother hidden all of this away?

Faven thought she found her answer, in a clip from a video interview after the rebellion had been put down.

"What does peacetime mean to you?" the interviewer had asked.

Sariette had turned to the camera, face suffused with such radiance that it took Faven's breath away. "Safety, of course. In safety, we can grow together."

Safe. It was what she'd whispered of, toward the end. What she'd said to Faven every night, until she couldn't anymore.

Sleep safe, my little spark.

Her mother had been about Faven's age then, and she'd known precisely what she'd wanted. What did Faven want?

Truth? No, that was a far too trite and fragile thing. She pulled up the search once more and keyed in: Bitter Amandine.

Faven absorbed her recorded life in samples. Truncated news segments, articles, all painting the pirate as brazen and, inevitably, a menace to decent society. Of her life before becoming a pirate of Turtar Glas, there was no sign. A mention, once, of a name that might be her real one—Andielle Serville—but it was such a common name that there was no telling which Andielle had become Bitter Amandine.

There was an intimacy in the knowledge of her real name that surprised Faven. She imagined herself saying the words—what Amandine's face would look like. Surprise. Suspicion. That slight narrowing of the eyes that indicated she was both annoyed and impressed.

She coveted the name. Andielle. Rolled it over in her mouth and mind and buried it beneath her skin. Hardened the name into a seed and it didn't matter if it was ever Amandine's name or not—a seed is concentrated potential. An idea. A form to be replicated.

Not in the way of plants, sprouting deep roots and growing ever skyward, but a seed crystal. A shred of beryl to teach the mineral to grow straight and square. A shard of chocolate to temper the base, and teach it how to shine and snap. A sliver of someone who had been so bursting with the potential for change that they'd earned a new name altogether, and embodied it fully.

Faven craved that potentiate state. Wanted the seed of a name sewn under her skin to teach the rest of her to align with its shape.

She would need to change, for what came next.

Whatever she would become, she knew one thing down to the marrow of her being: She wouldn't let Turtar Glas be destroyed for the mistakes she alone had made.

TWENTY-SEVEN

Amandine

Thank the void for pirate dens, there was always someone willing to stitch up an injury without asking too many questions. Amandine had called Becks and had them gather her scattered ducklings, then took her time strolling back through the market after getting her wound treated.

Tension thickened the air. Word of Tagert's overdue demise had spread and already whispers were slipping through the cracks about a Blademother having stepped foot on the armada, though none had actually seen Hatriel in the flesh.

Some of the smaller ships were bailing, but as far as Amandine could tell, word of the locked drives hadn't gotten loose.

The rest were gearing for war.

Wouldn't be the first time Sere Steel had faced a Blademother, and Amandine comforted herself with the fact that it wasn't likely to be the last. Sere had been skirmishing with the Choir for longer than Turtar Glas had existed. She'd win through. She always did.

What worried Amandine was the collateral damage.

Because Sere didn't need to say the words outright for Amandine to know that she'd give her up, her and the *Marquette* both, if it meant saving the armada.

All she'd had to say was: *I might need some of that hull plating back.*

A simple enough request, unless you knew that the hull beneath that plating was void-black. A color never seen outside of the inner layers of the Clutch. A style of glass, it was said, that even the Choir of Stars found too difficult to work with.

Amandine felt her lips tug as she pressed them flat, chapped skin threatening to split. Denial was a fine thing. Could carry you far, if you clung to it tight enough. Could tell you that you'd lived a normal life, for a pirate. That your life was simple and straightforward and you didn't hear the whisper of an alien ship seep through your dreams. That you didn't notice Becks give you a side-eye whenever you let your hand linger too long on the body of the ship, sensing its mood. That such things were superstition. Old pirates' tales. Of course the captain spoke to her ship. She was the captain. That relationship was as old as human history.

Every step Amandine took closer to the *Marquette*, she felt the future she'd crafted for herself slip through her fingers. The hope of Blackloach, of handing the ship down to Becks or Kester or Tully someday, hanging up her captain's hat if not her shotgun, and retiring to a cottage in the mist where the whispers wouldn't find her.

Funny, that she'd ever let herself think that the *Marquette* would allow anyone else but Amandine to captain it.

The *Marquette* rested at the edge of the dock, Becks's plasma torch discarded by the breach in its side. Though it looked as quiet and dormant as any other ship waiting for its crew to return, each step closer felt like pushing through mud. Like the air was closing tight around her and soon she'd be encased in invisible amber, a fossil of another age left behind for some future variation of humanity to stumble across.

The doors yawned open for her, without her ordering them to do so.

She found her crew in the galley. Tully was still kitted out for a fight and bouncing on their toes while Becks stalked back and forth across the room, their hands clasped behind their back. Kester, bless her, managed to control her nervous energy and took up a wary post to Amandine's right, arms crossed, expression forcefully neutral.

"What in the void-crossed black just happened, Cap'n?" Becks asked.

Amandine scrubbed a hand down the side of her face. "Which part?"

"Best to start at the beginning, I think," Kester said.

She took a breath. Told them every detail starting from the moment she opened the doors to Sere's meeting room, and only paused when Becks stopped pacing to interrupt.

"Ma Sere stabbed you?" they asked.

"Cut," Amandine corrected.

"Cap'n—"

Amandine couldn't deal with their sympathy and held up a fist to silence them all. "I'm fine. That's not the important part."

They took the hint, falling silent, but both Becks and Tully went still after that, watching her warily. She couldn't blame them. Amandine took a breath.

"With the drives locked, we've no doubt that the Blademother will be back with reinforcements. Sere will fight. But if it comes down to it, her best bargaining chip may be the *Marquette* itself."

"What?" Tully sounded like a startled bird. "Why?"

"We all know this ship's...different." She rested her palm against the wall she leaned on. "I don't know what it is, or what it was for originally, but I found it in the Clutch and haven't stumbled across another ship like it. Ma Sere, she knows that. Saw the black hull and the drive when it was unshielded."

"Perhaps," Kester said, "it is time you tell us about the day you found it. In detail."

She'd known this was coming. You couldn't very well say your ship might be worth more to the Choir of Stars than the lives of every pirate in the armada without having to answer some questions. Still, part of her rebelled at digging up the past she wanted kept buried.

But Sere had, early on, taught her the importance of only taking on crew she could trust with her life. Looking at the three people she'd called family these past few years, she found it wasn't so hard to get the words out, after all.

"Amber Jacq got a tip-off about some high-value cargo the Choir was going to move through the Clutch. Didn't tell us what it was. I'm not sure if he knew himself, but he was jumpy about it. Excited, but nervous, too. Wouldn't let anyone see the starpath he'd been given, but that wasn't too unusual. You know how captains can be about their secret routes—and anyway, Jacq's crew was big. Not very gelled together.

"We got out there and were shot down. Not sure how, mind you, I was just an extra gunhand. Jacq got the ship down and when we came out, the Choir's guards were already there. I think our drive containment must have cracked in the crash, because we all started to get lightsick at that point. Jacq, he argued with the Choir."

Amandine crossed her arms. Shifted her weight. "I can't tell you what that argument was about. I don't know. But there was a kid there. Cryst-born. Something went wrong and Jacq went for him. I got between them." Amandine tapped her right shoulder, where the scar they'd all seen before was hidden under her shirt. "Got this for my trouble. The Choir whisked the kid away, and the lightsickness, it was getting bad at that point. Everyone was fighting and I just—ran, I guess. Felt this tug in my chest. Saw stars behind my eyes, you know? Usual stuff for light poisoning, but they looked like a map so I followed them. At the end I found a construct. Black cryst, square. Almost looked modular, with other cubes protruding off it. I went inside. When next I woke, I was in Ma Sere's med bay. She told me I'd gotten there in a ship she'd never seen the like of before. A cryst ship, plated in black. I figured the cube shape must have been a lightsick hallucination."

Tully's eyes were on the verge of popping out of their head. Becks's brow was cleaved down the middle, and they were stroking their chin, eyeing the walls all around them. Kester merely frowned.

"That's all you remember?" she asked.

"That's all," Amandine said.

Becks nodded to themself. "Always was something weird about the construction."

"What—what *is* it?" Tully asked.

"I don't know," Amandine said, and sighed. "The navi was on board and didn't twig to anything strange, as far as I know. She mentioned an unusual security system, though. A consciousness watching her while she meditated. She assumed it was shielding the lightdrive from navi interference. If she mentions that to the Blademother, there's no telling what she'll think."

"And what do you think, Captain?" Kester asked.

"With the drives locked, that Blademother is planning on coming back with bigger guns. Turtar Glas can't run and I won't be leaving it for the slaughter. But that's my fight. One I set down years ago, to be sure, but now it's come knocking I won't bar the door. But you all, you weren't part of the Push. And I know you never wanted a thing to do with the navi in the first place."

That last bit she said to Tully, who went about as red as a sunburned eel. "You heard that."

"I did." Amandine squeezed her crossed arms tighter. "Leaving's been on your minds, and I can't blame you overmuch. I haven't been the most forthright captain. If you don't want this fight, I've made a deal with Ma Sere. She's sent people to clean up Tagert's ship and refit the drive. Once it's set, it's yours if you want it. Take it and burn."

Becks whistled low. "What'd that deal cost you?"

Amandine smiled despite herself. "Too damn much." They glanced between one another, gazes asking silent questions. Amandine pushed off the wall. "I'll leave you to discuss it in private."

"Ain't no need for that, Cap'n," Becks said. "We're staying."

"You sure about that?" Amandine glanced sideways at Kester. "This isn't a fight we can talk our way out of. There will be blood."

"This ship is our home, and you are our captain. The matter is quite simple," Kester said.

Amandine blew out a long breath. "Right. Thank you. Now I gotta ask, that plan you cooked up with the navi and Gehry, it involve giving the navi her armillary back?"

"Nah," Becks said. "Kept that thing locked up tight. To get to the *Stamping Bull*, Tagert would have had to walk right past Gehry's ship. The navi was gonna trade her freedom for your life, and we were waiting to spring out and take her back."

"That's a terrible plan."

"We know," Tully said with a toothy grin, "but we were hoping that once things were in motion, you'd catch wind of what was up and come up with a better one."

Amandine laughed. "The faith you have in me."

"Speaking of," Becks said, "you got a plan for what's coming?"

"I was hoping the navi had her armillary back, so that we could track her movements. Without that..." Amandine sighed. "We're gonna have to dig in, and pray."

"What's a pirate even supposed to pray to?" Tully asked.

"Right now?" Amandine lifted her gaze to the ceiling, thinking of the pose Faven had struck in the cryst-born resting ground. "Best be prayin' Faven Sythe grows a backbone stiff enough to stand against a Blademother."

"I don't like those odds, Cap'n," Becks said.

"Funny," Amandine said. "I do."

TWENTY-EIGHT

Faven

The other navigators arrived cowled, their faces hidden in shadow. Even Faven had been given a long black cloak to obscure her form beneath. The oversized hood hid her eyes, but not the cryst-scale at the corner of her lips. She stood placid, arms folded within her sleeves, and hoped no one noticed her fidgeting with her borrowed armillary.

Gailliard was not among the fourteen who came to Hatriel's ship. Faven's heart thumped heavily as the airlock closed behind the last of them. There were many reasons for a member of the Choir to have stayed behind for this occasion, no matter how momentous. Gailliard's absence didn't have to mean anything.

Faven slid into place at the back of a line of seven, joining the solemn march to the astarium. Not every navigator Hatriel had called for was a member of the Choir. They were the finest weavers, regardless of status, Faven herself included. It would require an incredible show of skill to overwhelm the defenses of Turtar Glas and weave the whole of the armada a path into a star.

The working of so much death was both delicate and tedious.

Beside her walked Chryssa, and never had a woman looked more out of place in the sacred black robes. Her chin was lifted, brilliant hazel eyes soaking in every detail. So avid was her interest that she hadn't noticed her cowl slip back, revealing the stark gold of her long curls spilling haphazardly over her shoulder.

Faven leaned close and whispered, "Where's Gailliard?"

"Didn't you hear?" Chryssa tried to whisper, she really did, but she'd never been any good at it. Gossip was her favorite pastime, and excitement made her voice louder than Faven would like. She'd always gotten them in trouble back when they'd been at school, failing to whisper in the back of class. "He's missing. When your ship was declared lost, he commandeered a Bladeship and took off on his own. No one's heard from him since."

Faven's mouth sagged open. "What? No one at all? Where was he going?"

"*I* heard," Chryssa started to say, but the older navigator in front of her cut them both a look so sharp it dealt a fatal blow to the rest of that sentence.

Faven clutched her borrowed armillary tighter within her sleeve. Had it been guilt, and a desperation to save her that had driven him to run off? Or a different kind of guilt altogether—fear that his sabotage would be discovered?

Amandine certainly thought that Gailliard was the obvious choice for saboteur. Logically, Faven agreed with her. Gailliard had been the one to tell her about Ulana's ship's destruction, and had looked deeply shaken when she'd asserted that Ulana had never gone to Amiens at all. Still, Faven couldn't bring herself to see him setting her up for death. But then, he was Choir, and she was not. Those political games ran deeper than the oldest oceans.

Hatriel had prepared the astarium ahead of time with a projection of the dual lightdrives that dominated Turtar Glas, and all those who tied their systems into the greater whole while docked. Faven's breath caught in the back of her throat, seeing the intricate network play out in holographic space. The power shared between the two primary drives was a Möbius curl of light. A never-ending river of support, and safety, for all who might dare to call Turtar Glas home. What Sere Steel had built was truly beautiful.

Her peers murmured among themselves as they spread out to ring the room at equidistant points. Rubbing chins in thought. Pointing and leaning heads together. Faven ignored their conferring, her gaze locked on the burgundy sphere that hovered above all those delicate ships.

Tenebrae. The star at the heart of the Clutch. There were closer, more convenient stars to drop Turtar Glas into. Was Hatriel doing this to mock her?

The Blademother moved to the center of the display and lifted a hand so scaled it was clawlike to hover above the tangle of ships.

"The armada of Turtar Glas," she announced in that low, rasping hiss of a voice. Faven found herself wondering if scale had already begun to set in within her throat. "The two primary drives are the leisure yachts Sere Steel absconded with decades ago, and will be the primary focus of our efforts. As Tagert Red was foolish enough to bring me within the armada itself, I was close enough to lock the drives. They cannot be used by human hands, but that does not mean they are defenseless."

Appreciative murmurs all around.

"Navigator Sythe," Hatriel said, "were you made aware of any unusual methods of defense while in pirate hands?"

Her heartbeat grew syrupy slow as all those curious eyes turned to her. Watched. The drive of the *Marquette*, lurking in the corners of her mind. Amandine's obvious overreaction to the ship's security system activating. The instinct she couldn't explain—that the *Marquette*'s security was something else entirely. Something living.

Faven shook her head.

"Nothing unusual, Blademother. But I did not attempt to alter their drives."

Hatriel paused long enough that Faven began to fear that the question had been some sort of trap. That the Blademother had sensed something strange about the *Marquette* and had given Faven enough rope to hang herself with by asking the question.

But then she saw the downward curl of Hatriel's lip and realized that, no: Hatriel was only disgusted that Faven hadn't tried to fight back by damaging their drives. A kindling of anger smoked through her chest. Why should she have been expected to fight back? The Choir advised all kidnapped navigators to comply with their captors. To stay alive.

Faven was not her mother, fighting a war gone to dust decades ago. A snide remark balanced on her lips. She swallowed it down, lest Hatriel throw her from the room for insubordination. If she let her pride feed the smolder of her anger, then Turtar Glas was doomed.

With the armada's fate clutched tightly to her chest, it was no effort to keep her face impassive.

"Very well," Hatriel said at long last. "We will proceed as if there are traps, regardless."

"Surely a bunch of human pirates couldn't have come up with anything that would hurt us," Chryssa said.

"Underestimate them at your peril," Faven said flatly.

Hatriel tipped her head, slightly, to Faven. "Just so. Do not let your guard down under any circumstances. Our goal is a path between these drives"—Hatriel's hand swept over the armada's primary drives—"and Tenebrae. Let us begin."

As one, the navigators held their armillaries aloft, hovering the intricate devices above the palms of their hands. Faven's borrowed armillary floated above Amandine's bandana, still tied tight around her wrist. Hatriel's eyes flicked to it, then away. Faven found the Blademother's expression inscrutable.

Projections poured from the armillaries, filling the room with the delicate, interwoven lines of gravitational pulls, warp spillways, punch-through points. She saw through eyes both mortal and divine, the inner landscape of her meditations layered over the projections. Merging with them. Lifting her heart with sweet euphoria as her work merged with the others, and their craft flowed all around them in synchronous harmony.

Despite the ghoulish nature of the work, Faven found herself lost in it, reveling in the joy of a difficult task done well. Satisfaction filled the hollow of her spirit as they picked apart complex defense systems. Conferred without words—sharing the mind space of their work—suggesting, discarding, and adapting various paths at speeds faster than human thought.

The sparking of their neurons crunched numbers vaster than any computer could ever divine. This—this art was the purpose for which they'd been born, and working in concert with so many of her fellows bound them to her and she to them, an interweaving of lives and passions and brilliance—if any human were to look within the astarium, surely the strength of their light would blind them.

And at the height of this euphoria, when her skin shone with pearlescent sweat and her breath was shallow in her lungs, Faven felt watched.

She hadn't thought of herself by her own name in hours.

She missed a delicate merging of paths, jarring the weaving. The mistake was not unusual—they were talented, but they were not perfect—but fear pricked over her skin. Transformed the sweat of exertion into the sickly sweat of fear.

Had anyone else noticed that another mind watched their weaving?

Her mislaid work was discarded—the others would have heard it as a discordant note, while Faven's synesthesia twisted the path red in warning. It was fed back to her, and she worked it perfectly this time, laying the segment of the starpath back into the whole.

The path had taken shape. A tangle of golden threads woven through the air that only cryst-born eyes could parse. To weave a path into any part of the Clutch was dangerous. The debris field the cryst had left behind wasn't merely a shell of rubble—it comprised the chunks of stations and ships and unknowable structures tall as skyscrapers. Wider than moons. They demanded their own gravitational awareness from the frothing mass.

Even with sixteen navigators, sensing all potential crossed paths and pitfalls would have been impossible. But Turtar Glas didn't need to travel safely. It was meant to meet its end in the heart of Tenebrae.

A pathline made itself clear to her, soaked in indigo light, the color Faven's senses used to tell her a path was safe. She almost reached for it to incorporate it into the whole, but froze mid-gesture.

To weave that line into the greater working would transport Turtar Glas not into the star, but in orbit within the inner layers of the rubble. Not a safe path—there was no such thing in the Clutch—but one in which the pirates might survive.

Faven was surprised to remember that she had a body. She licked the tip of her tongue over her teeth and tasted the cool stone-and-glass flavor of cryst. Had her scale spread beneath the flesh around her lips already? She didn't feel any scraping against her teeth—but then, her teeth might have changed, too. She'd been steeped in so much light lately.

It was going to her head, making her see starpaths against her eyelids whenever she blinked. Making her feel the imposing but inquisitive presence of the *Marquette* watching her even within her own inner mindscape.

"Sythe," Hatriel said. "Is something wrong?"

A security system, Faven had thought.

"No, Blademother."

Her mouth tasted of iron filings. She ignored Hatriel's piercing stare. Committed herself to the work—she had to get this right, had to prove to them that she was no traitor, only heartsick with grief.

She was cryst-born and she was a god and she didn't care if the lives on Turtar Glas were lost.

Those weren't her thoughts.

Faven met Hatriel's molten stare at last, and was struck by the bitter sorrow haunting her features. It was almost sweet, in a way. Hatriel was trying to save Faven from herself. Keep her from crossing a line from which she could not return.

But she had already crossed that line in her heart.

The *Marquette*'s presence loomed larger in her mind. Pressed against her. Shadowed her. Let her shake free. Faven snatched up the safe pathline. Wrapped it around her wrist and fingers like a vine. A venomous snake. The motion wasn't unusual. They all saved scraps of their work in case they might be useful later.

She'd coiled it around the hand wrapped in Amandine's bandana.

Their work was nearly finished. A towering synthesis of time and space on dimensions that defied mortal eyes. It was beautiful. And it was the death of thousands.

They admired it in silence for a long moment, this shared work. Then Hatriel gestured, and they began the process of seating it into the prepared lightdrives.

This was the riskiest part. If they had missed a trap, then hours' worth of work could be destroyed. More than that, Faven had heard rumors of some navigators going mad when they tried to alter the drives of booby-trapped ships. Hearing voices for the rest of their lives.

That knowledge was fresh. She'd come across it just last night, researching Amandine and the rebellion. After all, a Spire navigator would never need to touch a potentially tampered-with drive. Why would she have ever needed to know?

Why would she have needed to know about gator traps?

About the severity of lightsickness?

About Sere Steel and her yachts?

About the rebellion, and those navigators who went to their end smiling?

The indigo pathline coiled tighter around her wrist, a promise to herself she was about to break, because the reality was that there was nothing she could do. She was one, and they were fifteen of the finest navigators the Spire had ever trained.

They'd notice. And when they did, their strength would overwhelm hers. Even if Hatriel didn't take her head on the spot—and her stomach flipped over at the memory, Emmanuel's captain's collar sagging off the dripping stump of his neck—she wouldn't have the fortitude to hold the change in place.

The *Marquette*'s awareness swelled within her, letting her glimpse a piece of its true nature within her mindscape—vast and powerful, dizzying in scope to even she, who was well versed in letting her mind wander between galaxies.

She didn't have the strength. But it did.

Faven welcomed it within.

Her senses crumbled, slipped through her fingers, as the *Marquette* saw through her eyes, and took control.

TWENTY-NINE

Amandine

Jump alarms shattered the still air of Turtar Glas. Amandine looked up from the portable shield she'd been installing at a likely bottleneck, and squinted against the glare of red light muddying the green glass above.

"We runnin'?" Tully called over the siren wail.

Sweat plastered a cowlick they could never quite tame to their forehead. They brushed it aside and it swung right back into place.

"Let me check." Amandine touched her comm gem and called Sere. "You get those drives unlocked?"

"No." Her voice was hammered flat. Shouts echoed in the background. Metal clanging.

"Then what—oh. Oh hells. Where are they moving us?"

"Tenebrae."

Amandine closed her eyes. They weren't even going to give them a chance to fight. "What do you need me to do?"

"I'm scuttling the two main drives. Then if they want us, the bastards will have to come down here and take us."

The trouble with being a captain, Amandine had always surmised, was that you knew too damn much. When she'd been just another gunhand in Amber Jacq's crew, he could have told her to scuttle a drive and she'd have hopped to the task with gusto. Blissfully unaware that it'd take two hours, working at the fastest possible pace, to get that thing safely unseated and away from the armada.

Sere was still talking. "Meet me in the *Claribel*'s engine bay. My crew's got this one covered, but I'll need extra hands down there."

"We'll be there." Amandine ended the call and explained to the others as she scooped up the tool bag she'd been using to install shields, then took off at a run for the engine bay.

"Cap'n." Becks panted a little but kept pace beside her. "This'll take hours."

"I know, I know, but it'll take them hours to weave the path, won't it?"

"The jump alarms are already blaring and Ma Sere has determined the destination." Kester's frown was soft, contemplative. "I think they must have already prepared the path."

"You got a better idea, I'd love to hear it."

The only other thing left for them to do was abandon Turtar Glas, and they knew that. Part of Amandine wished they would. That her crew would make a dash for the *Stamping Bull* and sail out of here fast as they could, joining all the other specks of ships lifting off from the armada's interwoven docks. If they ran, then at least they'd be safe.

But if Ma Sere was going down swinging, then so was Amandine. As they tore around a corner into the engine bay, she was heartened to see that the crew of the *Marquette* weren't the only ones to have a spine. Dozens of pirates poured down the halls, tools dangling from hands and belts. Amandine was warmed to spot Short Gehry and her crew among their number. Always nice to know you were right about a person being a good sod.

Amandine hadn't had a lot of wins in that department, lately.

The engine bay was a nonagon, similar to the nine-pointed star the cryst used to envision themselves in their art. In the center of the room, the lightdrive rose like an obelisk. The drive itself was a hexagonal podium of teal cryst-glass, tall enough to reach Amandine's shoulders. The containment wrapped it in double-walled glass, shielding the ship's human passengers from the lightdrive's deadly strength.

Sere stood at the starpath control console, the station that interfaced directly with the navigational energies of the drive. Amandine didn't like the look on her face. Beneath the expected bluster and fury, resignation lurked.

"Who taught you tadpoles to loosen bolts?" Sere bellowed. "A goddamn worm could work faster than this. Put your backs into it!"

Amandine lost track of her crew as she swung down to the housing floor to join the crush. The high-pitched whir of electric wrenches echoed all around her. No time to finesse the thing out— they were ripping off struts, yanking free supports and stabilizers.

The jump alarms began to pulse with a deep, thundering rhythm. Amandine looked up with the rest as the top of the drive pillar shimmered, the first hints of the golden threads of a starpath weaving into existence.

Her stomach sank. Not enough time.

"Work!" Sere roared from her podium.

The others scrambled to free the bolts, but Amandine was transfixed by those fine golden threads. She'd always thought, in the way of all brave souls, that when her death came for her, she'd fight it to the last. Funny how the real moment works out. Those golden threads were spelling her end and all she could do was stand there, wide-eyed, and watch her epitaph be written.

The first time Amandine had faced her own death she'd been lost to lightsickness. Had thought she could do something truly mad—like save herself. But now that she saw death coming in the clear light of day, all she could do was bear witness.

That's the only brave thing you can do, when you're small.

Amandine was no Sere Steel, no Blademother. Wasn't even on par with her old captain, Amber Jacq, who at least had a few hundred crew to his name.

Wasn't every day a scrub like her got to see a path being laid, but something about the spectacle felt off. Made her guts twist along with those shimmering lines.

The pathlines stretched. Unfolded and expanded beyond the base of the drive. As far as Amandine knew, that wasn't supposed to happen. The lines trembled—reached outward, piercing through the wall.

"Where are those going?" Sere demanded of no one in particular. "Get me visual."

Cryst-fans unfolded from the horseshoe desk arrayed before her, camera feeds trickling in. In the center of the armada, hovering in empty air below the vault of the green cryst-glass, was a figure.

Slight of frame and robed all in black, they could have been anyone. Amandine could have lied to herself until the day she walked into her own grave over who that person had been, if it weren't for her own bandana tied tight around the figure's outflung wrist.

Faven's face was hidden beneath the cowl of her hood, but her chest was lifted, as if a string connected her heart to the ceiling and she was dangling there, speared in place. The golden threads that had escaped the lightdrives tangled around both arms, shining shackles, and while she didn't move, Amandine could tell that she was struggling.

"Shoot her down." Sere's voice was grim as rusted iron.

"What?" Disbelief made the word loud, but not loud enough to draw Sere's attention. Amandine cut a look at Kester, who nodded and slipped off, though what the woman could do when Faven was floating in midair was anyone's guess.

Pirates abandoned wrenches for rifles and scrambled up the walkways. Amandine shouldered past them all to plant herself in front of Sere. The scramble for the exits slowed, gazes itching against Amandine's skin as they waited to see how this played out.

Wasn't a pirate in the verse who'd bend knee to Amandine over Sere, but sometimes, rarely, she thought—deep in her heart in the place she rarely let herself dwell—that Sere valued what she had to say. That Sere would bend to Amandine, if Amandine was truly right.

"You shoot her, you doom us all," Amandine said.

Sere held her stare as she reached out to take a rifle from a crew-member whose name Amandine didn't know. She didn't know any of Sere's crew. Made a point of it.

"That navi is fucking with my drives." Sere didn't raise her voice. She didn't need to. All the pirates there hung on every word.

"She's trying to *save* us."

"You got proof of that?"

Amandine's smile was small and sad. "No. I just have faith."

Something flickered across Sere's face. Shimmied up to the sur-face, and died. "Faith don't hunt."

Sere shouldered her aside, but Amandine gripped her arm tight. Sere was faster than she looked. Before Amandine could get her feet fully planted, the cold, round mouth of the barrel of Sere's pis-tol was pressed to her chest.

"I already stabbed you once, you think I won't shoot your ass?"

"Cut," Amandine corrected. The corner of Sere's lips twitched with an aborted smile. "And I gotta take the risk, because if I don't stop you, then we're all star food anyway."

A muscle in Sere's jaw jumped. This time, she raised her voice to carry. "What are you fools looking at? I gave you an order! Shoot the damn navi!"

Sere shoved her backward with such force that Amandine stum-bled into the horseshoe desk.

"Ma—" Amandine started to say, but the pirate queen had already turned away, dismissing her with her back.

Shit. What could she do? Even if she wanted to fight half of Tur-tar Glas—which she absolutely did not—there was no way to stop someone from sniping the navi. Faven was wide open.

The lightdrive hummed. Sere roared orders—Amandine wondered if anyone could hear them above the din of the drive. An inner light bloomed within its heart, aquamarine and shimmering. Amandine threw up an arm to shield her eyes against the stunning brightness.

A flash burned through her lids and something deep and vital groaned in the walls of the armada. The floor lurched, catwalks clattering against one another, and this was it—end of the road.

She still had her HUD glass on. In the corner of her eye, the *Marquette* pinged her with an urgent request to divest all the power stored in its drive—something only the captain could authorize. Amandine didn't know what in the void that was about and there was no time to ask.

She approved it. Let the *Marquette* burn everything it had, hoping that her ship would, even if it couldn't save the rest of them, save itself.

Amandine peeled her eyes open and gripped the edge of the desk, forcing herself to bear witness to what might very well be Faven's final moments. Her body jerked. Around the bandana-wrapped hand a writhing vine of indigo curled. Faven's fingers spread, and that curling vine split in twain, rushing down her arms to spread out through the golden pathlines and weave itself tight into them. The cryst-scale at the corner of her lips glowed to match the drives.

The indigo line plunged into the drive, and the high thrum shifted into a bone-jarring bass thunder that raced up the floor through the soles of her boots.

The drive flashed once more, but then the light faded, taking the golden pathlines and the jump alarms with it.

They'd jumped. But not into a star.

"Where are we?" Sere's bellow shook the eerie silence.

Amandine scrambled to switch one of the fan displays over to the local system. "We're—shit." Specks of rubble dotted the display, pieces large and small mottled with various shades of red to mark that their impact was imminent. "The Clutch." Amandine's voice was hoarse, but she raised it to be heard. "Inner layers, best I can tell."

The armada shuddered, small impacts denting their shields. Amandine met Sere's eyes, and the fear there was so raw it stole Amandine's breath.

But then it was gone, Sere's ironclad mask of professionalism back in place. "You!" She thrust a ring-encrusted finger at the nearest member of her crew. "Everything we've got into the shields—get the damn debris lasers humming." She swung around to point at Amandine. "Secure the fucking navi. We need her if we're ever going to get out of here."

"Aye." Amandine didn't bother to hide her smug grin, and received a scowl from Sere in return.

She turned back to the cryst-fans, double-checking Faven's location. The tension that'd held the navi taut as a wire had fled, and she'd sunk lower in the air than she had been at last glance. Amandine squinted. Was the navi unconscious? How did that even work, with her levitating trick? At least Kester should be there to catch her by now, if she fell.

A subtle shimmer slicked the air above the navi. Light warped along a thin line, sucked inward. Amandine's skin prickled—she'd seen that effect only once before.

The Blademother appeared in the air above Faven, sword drawn, body angled as viciously as her blade as she released her suspension and plunged. The blade burst through Faven's back, a bloody spike, and for the barest second, they hung together in the sky, the Blademother perched upon Faven's gored chest like a vulture.

Then they fell, and the cameras lost them.

"No." Amandine jerked back from the desk. "No fucking way."

Amandine ran. Sere was ahead of her, the crew that'd been rushing to ensure Faven's end now rushing to her defense. They pounded up the ramp out of the bay. Sweat slicked Amandine's back as she pushed herself to catch up, but they were already at the doors.

Impact alarms blared. The armada shuddered hard enough to knock Amandine to her knees. A thunderous crack tore through the air somewhere above, the terrible rush of water. Breach.

A shard of Turtar Glas's green cryst slammed into the floor outside the doors. Sere's people screamed. Stumbled backward.

"Run!" Amandine cupped her hands around her mouth and yelled for all she was worth.

They were already running. Falling. The newborn waterfall from the exterior hull rushed down the ramp, swept their feet. Sere staggered. Got a hand out to steady herself and hesitated, squinting at something beyond the door.

"Ma!" Amandine's voice cracked. Water rushed over her boots, but it was a weak tide by the time it reached her, sinking into systems long past designed to handle a surprise flood.

Sere turned, wrenched by her cry. Stacks of cargo strapped to shelves by the door sagged. Swayed drunkenly as a chunk of debris slammed into them. Sere ran.

She didn't make it.

THIRTY

Faven

Faven's blood tasted of iron, which didn't seem right. It bubbled in the back of her throat, hot and thick and suffocating—she couldn't breathe. Couldn't even lift her hands to clutch at her throat.

She lay in rubble, Hatriel perched upon her, the length of her blade sprouting bloody and bright from the center of her chest. Delicate droplets of crimson painted Hatriel's cheek in thin strokes.

The cryst-born bled red.

Faven had always known that. Didn't understand why the thought came to her then with the weight of realization. Didn't understand how she could still hurt so much more, as Hatriel dragged her blade free of Faven's chest with a sickening sucking sound that was terribly unfair, because it sounded like breathing, and she couldn't get anything past the blood in her throat.

"Do you know how long I searched?" Hatriel said. Had been saying. Maybe she had said more, but those were the first words to make it past the buzzing hum that filled Faven's ears.

"To find you here..." Hatriel's lip curled. Faven thought she might spit on her, but she swept her blade aside contemptuously instead, flicking free Faven's blood. "May Sariette forgive me, should our lights ever meet again."

Hatriel gazed down upon her, her figure swarmed with left-over visions of starpaths, and Faven knew somehow that she saw through Faven to the *Marquette*. To the ship that had granted her the strength to wrest control of the starpath from the others.

She couldn't speak. Couldn't even groan. Hatriel's eyes dulled as she waited, bored, for Faven to drown to death in her own blood.

There was a crackle, a flickering blue light in the air and Hatriel swore, limbs jerking. A flash of light—no, not light, white. A white suit. Kester.

Faven wanted to scream. Wanted to cry out that the pirate stood no chance against a Blademother. But their figures merged together, dark and light, until they seemed like nothing more than the clicking down of an old film reel, impressions pressed against her eyes while she faded into a quiet, sucking darkness.

Kester was beside her, kneeling. Her pristine white suit was stained rose red and she removed one silk glove with care, tucking it into her pocket.

"I am sorry," Kester said. "This will be painful."

Kester drew a blade and slashed the gleaming edge across her own palm.

She bled prisms.

She bled light.

Dying. Hallucinating. That's what must be happening as Kester's thick, nacreous blood flowed from her palm and puddled, cool as a spring breeze, into the gaping empty heat of Faven's chest.

When her breath finally returned to her, all she could do was scream.

THIRTY-ONE

Amandine

Amandine was on the floor and couldn't remember how she'd gotten there. She blinked gritty eyes, pushing herself up to her elbows, and flinched at the pounding in her head. Gingerly, she touched the aching spot and brought her fingertips away bloody. Great. A concussion. Just what she needed.

"Sere?" she croaked.

No answer.

Amandine swore and used the desk to drag herself the rest of the way to her feet. Dust motes muddied the air, and the scent of an electrical fire singed her nostrils.

Others were hauling themselves upright. Muttering under their breath. Asking questions that couldn't yet be answered. Amandine ignored them all and waved dust away from her face, turning toward the gangway.

The great shell of Turtar Glas had cracked. The armada's lights had darkened—broken or automatically downshifted to conserve power, she couldn't say—and cast the docks in shadows soaked through with the bloodied red of emergency strobes.

Breach sirens blared somewhere far away, muted by the thunderous rush of two newly birthed waterfalls disgorging death. The water only came up to the laces of her boots, the rest pouring off the sides of the docks or sinking down into spillways lining the drive's containment.

The wall of crates near the door had been smashed by a fallen beam, a twisted hunk of black metal thicker than Amandine's torso shattering supplies and people alike.

Sere's people. As Amandine sloshed through puddles of water dark with blood she wanted nothing more than to turn tail and bolt back into the *Marquette*, where reality wouldn't provide the evidence of what she knew to be true.

"Amandine," a soft voice said.

She followed Sere's rasp. Sank to her knees beside her and took her shaking hand. Bloody water stained her silver hair, her tanned face sunken and sallow. From the hips up, she appeared unharmed. The rest of her disappeared beneath the crush of fallen crates. Amandine lifted her, carefully, cradling the pirate queen's head in her lap so that she wouldn't lie in the spilled waters of her ruined kingdom.

"Hang on," Amandine said. "Help's coming."

Sere barked a short laugh. "Ain't enough help in the stars for this, girl."

"We'll get you two peg legs." Amandine tried to keep her voice light, even as it trembled. "You'll be a living cliché."

"Ah, Andielle. One of us has to learn to let go."

"Usually you call me Bitter when you're furious with me."

"Only one I'm furious with is myself." Sere sighed. A long, dragging rasp that Amandine feared would be her last. She rallied, if only a little, eyelids lowered to mere slits. "I'm sorry, girl. I should have let you go, all those years ago. Now you have to do it on your own."

"Ma, I don't—"

Sere grunted. "Never could be a real mother to you, could I? Thought you'd be better off without me, but then you went and crewed with Jacq—and by the time I found out, it was too late. You'd gone and gotten yourself killed."

"What? What are you talking about?"

"Go home, Andielle. You have to go home."

She frowned, searching Sere's face for some hint of what she meant, but her chest stilled with a soft rattle, the tension slackening from her muscles. Amandine stilled, too, her breath coming in slow, shallow drags until a burning ache of need filled her breastbone. A searing, living pain counter to the cooling emptiness in her arms.

Eventually, Becks touched her shoulder. "Cap'n. We need you."

Amandine's lips pulled back from her teeth in a sneer, a smothered shout. The captain didn't get to break down. Didn't get to sit on her knees in the mire and mourn when there was work to be done. When what Sere had built was bleeding out as surely as Sere had.

Gently, she brushed Sere's eyes closed and laid her back in the water, folding her arms over her chest. There was no moving that body, not yet. Amandine pushed to her feet and stood there a moment, unsteadily, letting her lungs fill completely at last.

"The navi?"

"Kester took her to the *Marquette*. She's unconscious but stable."

Still alive. Amandine closed her eyes briefly, knowing those few seconds of darkness were all the peace she'd get, for a while. "And the Blademother?"

"Dead."

"Good. Tell Kester to secure the ship. Don't let anyone know she's there. We're going to find Tully and organize emergency seals on those breaches and get the shields back up."

"And then?"

Amandine hated those words. *And then.* They implied she knew what was worth doing. That there was plan beneath it all, a logic to set the world to rights. Becks gave her a look that was equal parts hopeful and weary, and she knew what they wanted her to say, what she was supposed to say. Some grand gesture about rebuilding. Or a rousing screed about taking the fight to the Choir, show them what's what.

But Ma Sere's blood was soaking her socks and all Amandine could find within herself to say was "We'll see."

THIRTY-TWO

Amandine

Amandine dragged herself back to the *Marquette* only when the armada was as safe as it could get for the time being. They'd sealed the breaches and stabilized the meshed ships, getting the shields fully powered to protect the armada from further damage.

The pirates of Turtar Glas were scared. Furious. Half of them wanted to flee but didn't dare attempt to pilot their smaller ships out of the greater shielding of the armada. The other half were already jockeying for position, trying to fill the seat Sere had vacated while it was still warm. None of them dared to move definitively while the Clutch held them all.

Amandine let herself into the airlock of the *Marquette*. While her body cried out for rest, she had work yet to do. Rumors were already getting out about the navigator in Amandine's brig.

That Faven had saved them was both a fact Amandine couldn't prove, and one the pirates of Turtar Glas didn't want to hear. Navigators had thrown the armada into the Clutch, and in the seconds before, they'd all seen Faven.

And they'd all seen Amandine put her neck on the line to save Faven's life.

It was only a matter of time until people had a chance free from crises to think and showed up on her doorstep, braying for the navi's blood. They'd most likely keep her alive long enough to get themselves a path out, but even that was questionable. Fear kept common sense in short supply.

Amandine found Faven sound asleep in the med bay. She was breathing, her heart beating steadily. Amandine had to thump the diagnostic wand against the side of her hand a few times to get it working, but once she did, Faven's vitals all showed up as perfectly healthy in the wand's bland, crisp readout. Nothing eyebrow raising.

Except for the hole in her chest.

The blade had pierced Faven just below the collarbone, a little to the right of her spine. A bandage had been wrapped around her chest, though the darkness dampening the bandage wasn't blood but the clear fluid of wound gel. A starburst of cryst-scale radiated outward from the cratered center of the wound, spreading beyond the bandage.

Kester had mentioned filling it with wound gel, but the fact that she'd survived at all—let alone seemed relatively stable—felt surreal to Amandine. If she'd ever wanted proof that the navis weren't human, there it was. In the rise and fall of a chest that should be well on its way to rot, by now.

Twin vines of new scale marred both of the navi's arms. Twining down like snakes to wrap her wrists and slither over her fingers.

Amandine picked up Faven's bandana-wrapped hand and turned it over gently, testing the joints to be certain they still had some fluidity. Faven's skin pulled around the scale with the motion, but the joints didn't feel inhibited. The woman was a giant headache, but a fierce protective streak grabbed at Amandine, made her hot with an anger she couldn't place.

Faven threaded her fingers through Amandine's and squeezed.

Amandine startled, tried to pull back, but Faven clung on, and she didn't want to wrench her hand free for fear of tearing the skin around the scale. Faven's eyes fluttered open, slowly. She blinked a few times, but still they swam with headache-inducing constellations. Amandine turned her gaze away from that stare.

"Amandine." Faven's voice was soft. Dreamy. "You sent a star to save me."

"Kester's a lot of things," Amandine said, "but I don't think star ranks among them."

"She was shining." She pressed her free hand to her wound and took in a long, deep breath, seeming to savor the sensation before letting it out. Though her chest expanded enough to make Amandine wince in sympathy, she didn't seem to be in pain. Then she pushed herself up to sitting, despite Amandine's protests, using her grip on Amandine's hand for balance. "Is Kester all right?"

"A few scrapes, but nothing serious. Though that suit of hers isn't so starry-bright, now. Don't think the blood will ever wash out."

"I don't..." Again she pressed her free hand to her chest and breathed deeply. "I don't understand. I tried to tell her to run, that she'd never survive a battle with Hatriel."

"Kester's got a few more tricks up her sleeve than the average deck scrubber, and she knew what she was coming in to clash with. She used weave disrupters to stop the Blademother teleporting, and with Hatriel tired out from the weaving, it wasn't much trouble."

"Is that what she told you?"

"Should she have told me something else?"

Faven was an open book, her uncertainty written in bold strokes across her face. Amandine hooked a stool with her ankle and dragged it over, sitting with a soft grunt. Her own back bothered her more than being run through with a sword seemed to bother Faven, but she didn't mind the ache. It was the last thing Sere would ever give her.

"Tell me what happened," Amandine said. "From the beginning."

She was as surprised as she'd ever been when Faven complied. It was a meandering story, at first. Jittery with leftover fear and long, deep breaths the navi couldn't seem to stop herself from taking. By the end her breath had evened, and the hand Amandine held was warm as a coal, smoldering gently, instead of cold as marble.

"You thought Kester *bled* into you?" Amandine asked.

A dusky blush brought out the starkness of her freckles. "I was dying, and she was beautiful."

"Lot of beautiful things around, lately." Amandine cleared her throat and tried to slip her hand from Faven's, but the navi wouldn't let go. "How long do you think we've got? Before the navis figure out where we are and try the same stunt all over again."

"I don't know," Faven said. "In my trance I wove a lock into the drives that will take them time to undo. If they decide to teleport here, directly, then they can do so at any point. But of those on that ship, only Hatriel was a Blademother. The rest will hesitate to rush into a fight that not even she survived."

"You single-handedly managed to overpower fifteen Spire navis? How?"

"I didn't. But I think you know who did."

The *Marquette*'s request for power. Amandine's gaze drifted upward, tracing over ordinary walls and all the mundanity of human life cloistered within the ship's cryst-glass panes. The *Marquette* was her home, and it was her shadow, and sitting there in the low lights of the medical bay, she realized how rarely she looked at it.

She saw it, of course. Popped open its panels and fiddled with its wiring. Welded its wounds and smoothed its tuning. But whenever she placed her hand against it and sensed its moods, she averted her gaze, and couldn't quite say why.

"Maybe you can give me an answer. What is it? The *Marquette*."

That gave her pause. Faven tilted her head to the side, frowning. "You don't know?"

"No. I don't. The ship never saw fit to inhabit my thick skull."

"Why would it? There's nothing there for it to interface with."

"Really?" Amandine said dryly.

Faven gave her a slanted smile. "I mean that you're not cryst-born. Hatriel seemed to know what it was, or at least recognized something of it in me. But I can only tell you that the *Marquette* felt somehow...lesser than whatever it had been, before. I could sense its frustration. Its sadness. But it understood that the armada was in danger, and its desire to protect you all was so powerful I was washed away beneath it."

"That thing was inside your head, and you're telling me you haven't the foggiest idea?"

She shrugged one shoulder. "Believe me or not, your faith is irrelevant to the truth of the matter."

Amandine grunted in annoyance. "I should shoot you and drop you out the airlock."

Faven's smile turned coy. "You're still holding my hand."

Amandine rolled her eyes and let her hand go limp, willing Faven to let her go. To drop her hand so that she wouldn't have to twist free, but those small fingers clung on, their arms a rope between them.

Keeping their fingers interlocked, Faven swung her legs off the gurney. For having been unconscious a few minutes ago, she moved with sure, precise motions, and nothing about her appeared ill. She seemed hale. Strong. Her feet dropped to the floor and she stood, pressing close, tightening the space between them until Amandine had to stand and shimmy aside to avoid tangling her legs in the chair she'd vacated.

"What the void-crossed black do you think you're doing?" Amandine demanded.

"Choosing."

Amandine blew out an explosive breath. The feathery curls near Faven's temple rustled on that gust. "I'm grateful you saved our skin, Navi, I truly am. But choosing to come back doesn't mean you're not my prisoner. The armada's not a social club. They're going to want starpaths from you to get out of here, and if you don't oblige, it's my neck on the line." Amandine brushed her thumb over the scale on Faven's hand, unable to help herself. Faven's head tilted, and she lifted her star-spun gaze to Amandine's once more.

"You're not worried about yourself. You're feeling guilty about the toll the work will take on me."

Amandine straightened her spine. "Does it surprise you to learn I have a heart? It wasn't my intention to put you in a position where your disease progressed."

"Disease?" Faven scoffed. "Hardly. It is the natural state that the cryst-born return to." She considered Amandine for a long moment. "You don't know, do you? How we're born? Of course you wouldn't, it's not public information."

"I don't need the birds 'n' the bees talk from a navi," Amandine said. "I assure you, I'm well versed in the act."

Faven shook her head, the gemstones woven into her narrow braids clinking against one another as they slid over her shoulders. "Sex is meaningless in our genesis."

Amandine blinked. And blinked again.

"We are cryst-born, in every sense of the word. When a parent desires a child, they commune with the light that guides us all in deep meditation. If they are lucky, a shard forms." Faven's free hand drifted down and she pressed the tips of two fingers against Amandine's thigh, above her knee, then trailed them slowly up to rest the flat of her too-warm palm against the hard plane of Amandine's muscle. She tensed reflexively, and Faven's smile turned sly. Smug in a way that made her skin heat beneath that contact.

"It's a sliver, at first," Faven said, then spread her fingers out to grip her leg more firmly. "But it grows. And when it's of a viable size, it's excised. They place the shard in a birthing pillar to grow into the shape of a human child. We are cryst as infants, and moved to demineralization chambers to claim the flesh you see before you. From cryst we are born, and to cryst we return. It is no disease that claims us."

Amandine found it difficult to say anything intelligent with Faven's grip so surprisingly strong around her thigh. "You're telling me you're a rock."

Her chin lifted. "I am a concretion of divine light."

"All right. A very pretty rock."

Faven huffed, but her smile hadn't faded, and Amandine found she liked the rugged twist the scale gave to her lips. She took a steeling breath.

"Maybe that's the natural course for your kind," Amandine said, "but I can see it hurts. And whether it's meant to be or not, it's still your end coming faster. If I could get you out of this without leaving them all to die, I would."

"You're a very curious pirate, Bitter Amandine."

"You're pretty curious for a rock."

Faven leaned toward her, eyes sliding shut, and Amandine's palm slicked with sweat before she twisted her fingers free at last and ducked aside, putting space between them. The absence of Faven's hand left a cold spot on her thigh.

"Really?" Faven mused. She crossed her arms and leaned back, devastatingly haughty.

"Sorry, Navi." Amandine held her hands up, palms out, as a makeshift shield. "You're a prisoner, and I got rules."

"These scruples of yours are dreadfully annoying. I do not fear you, Amandine. Nor do I wish to seduce you to secure my escape. I wish to seduce you to secure my pleasure."

"Tempting. Truly. But ask me again when you're a free woman, and not before then."

Faven sniffed. "I've made my choice. I am free."

Amandine laughed. Right in her face. "Void, you—Faven. Sometimes I think you only hear half of what I say to you. You may have cut the Choir's leash, but you've only gone and hooked yourself to another. The pirates out there? They want your starpaths, and then they'll want your blood, because whether or not it's true, you're a symbol of the very thing that ripped their homes apart."

"You won't let them harm me." Faven spoke with the calm surety of someone insisting that space was black and water wet.

"And what, exactly, do you think I can do?"

"Sere Steel—"

"Is dead."

Her mouth hung open, and for the first time since their meeting Amandine saw real fear, real regret, crawl across her face and tangle up together. The bitter stain of resentment on Amandine's soul spread further. What luxury, to have lived so long without knowing how precarious your place in the worlds could be. How precious, to think you always had someone in high places ready to save your ass.

"Welcome to the real world, Sythe."

Amandine turned to leave. Faven grabbed her wrist. The damn woman had the gall to try to drag Amandine back, but she planted her feet, making her back rigid.

"Don't be stupid. You don't want to make this physical."

"I told you. I'm not afraid of you, Bitter Amandine."

Enough. She was frustrated and heartsick and wasn't going to let herself be yanked around by a Spire-raised whelp of a navi. If Faven wanted to enter her world, then Amandine would show her precisely what that meant.

"Funny," Amandine said. "You should be."

Amandine spun and stepped into Faven, pressing the side of her forearm against the navi's throat. She forced her to scramble backward until her back was against the wall. Fear widened her eyes as Amandine leaned over her, bracing one hand against the wall by the navi's head while she placed careful pressure on that velvet-dark skin and tipped her chin up until her neck strained. Faven's pulse pounded, her pupils wide, blackened pools.

"You said it yourself: Thirteen Blades don't mobilize for a ghost

story. And fuck me, but I should have listened, because Blade-
mothers don't descend from on high to collect wayward navis, either.
You want to find your mentor. Fine. But unlike you, I keep my ears
open, and it's struck me, Navi, how little you've said that name.

"From where I'm sitting, you're not looking for Ulana Valset.
You're looking for yourself, or some part of you that you think
you've lost. And I wouldn't mind that too much, I really wouldn't,
if you weren't so obviously lying to me about what you mean to the
Choir.

"You may have saved us in the end, but you still brought a
Blademother's wrath down on Turtar Glas. You got half the pirates
here looking at me sideways, got *my* own mentor killed." Amandine clenched her teeth. Took a breath. "You're not dead because
of those scruples you find so annoying, and not because I find your
precious blood too valuable to spill. Savvy?"

"Savvy," she rasped.

Amandine nodded and started to move away, but Faven clutched
her arm, holding her in place.

"Navi," Amandine said, "I don't know what the fuck you think
you're doing—"

Faven let out a strained laugh. A frantic, caged sound desperate
for escape. "You make me feel like flesh and blood when I've been
too long lost in the light."

Amandine lost all sense and kissed her. Faven gasped softly,
clutching Amandine's face to draw her deeper into an embrace that
was mingled soft, sweet lips and the cool, lithic scrape of cryst-scale.

If this went sideways, Amandine's crew would never let her hear
the end of it, but those protestations melted away under the firm
press of Faven's lips and the startled, delighted grunt that escaped
her. Far too soon, Amandine had to break away to suck down air,
and laughed when Faven scowled with annoyance and yanked her
back for more.

Amandine got an idea. She broke away once more, suffering

Faven's explosive huff of frustration, but before the navi could tell her off for chickening out again, she dropped her head to press a slow kiss against the starburst patch of scale below Faven's collarbone.

"How much of you is cryst?" Amandine murmured against her skin.

She tensed at first, then caught the sly spark in Amandine's upturned eyes and relaxed, letting her weight rest against the wall. Faven slid her fingers into Amandine's hair and tightened her grip. Then began, slowly, to push Amandine's head lower. "Why don't you take your time, and find out?"

THIRTY-THREE

Faven

Faven dreamed of inescapable grooves in the fabric of the universe. Of snapped constellation lines falling and spilling their stars into a ravening mouth from which there was no escape. The red-shifted light of terror rushed toward her, inexorable, until the Clutch itself filled the landscape of her dreams and in that otherplace it clenched, crushing star and universe alike.

She woke gasping in unfamiliar darkness, skin sheathed in sweat, limbs tangled in rough blankets. For one heart-stuttering breath she didn't know where she was, only that there was weight across her chest.

Amandine muttered in her sleep and shifted, withdrawing the pale stretch of her arm from Faven's chest. Her racing heart slowed, and she sank back into the twisted sheets, feeling silly and wrung-out. Just a dream.

A dream that threatened to slip back into her thoughts whenever she closed her eyes. Faven rolled carefully to her side, studying the sleeping woman beside her. Amandine's warm, slightly spicy scent lingered on the sheets. On Faven's skin. Grounding her in flesh and marrow, an anchor to the physical world.

Amandine had fallen asleep on her stomach, face turned away

from Faven, her mixture of thin braids and wavy tresses freed from her usual bandana to curl in the sweat on her shoulders and neck. Deep breaths lifted her back, the edges of the bandage that concealed Sere's cut straining with each heavy inhale.

Faven traced her fingers over the edges of that bandage, checking the seal—not being sentimental, she never would—and found the adhesive holding despite the exertion. A ridge of thick scar tissue drew a line up from the edge of the bandage. Faven followed it, finding it curve to the slope of her right shoulder, and stop.

The texture of the scar was rough beneath the tip of her finger, and she was surprised to find that the scar tissue beneath was thick and hardened, reminding her of cryst-scale.

"That was a long time ago," Amandine said.

Faven sucked in a startled breath but didn't withdraw her hand. "What happened?"

"Hmm." She yawned and shifted to face Faven, absently draping an arm over her waist as she propped her head up with her other hand. "My old captain wasn't as sweet as I am. I got between him and someone he wanted dead."

"Why risk yourself?"

Amandine shrugged, some of her bead-laden braids sliding forward over her shoulder. Faven picked one up, pinching the deep indigo bead between her fingers. Cryst-glass. Indigo had always felt warm to Faven. Safe.

"The target was a kid mixed up in a bad situation. Captain Jacq, he'd stopped seeing grey areas long before I crewed with him. But I didn't want that stain on my conscience."

"Why work for someone so cruel?"

She huffed softly, gaze dropping, and turned her head to place a kiss against the palm of the hand toying with her beads. "I was a kid myself."

"I'm sorry."

"Bah." She sniffed in negation and lifted her gaze once more, her usual mirthful glint overwhelming that flash of sorrow. "It was a long time ago. Why are you awake, goddess?" Amandine stroked one hand idly over the small of Faven's back. "I was certain I'd worn you out."

Faven was tempted, in the small huddle of their arms—her world narrowed down to the twin verdigris stars of Amandine's eyes—to tell the pirate of the terror that stalked her nightmares. Of the oblivion that consumed her dreams in the threat of rapidly approaching red. Her jaw tensed, holding back the words, and she lowered her lashes so that Amandine wouldn't see the regret that coiled through her.

"You'll have to try harder." Faven leaned toward the safe haven of lips and skin and sweat and an oblivion that was warm and gold and safe.

Amandine poked a finger into Faven's forehead, stopping her from claiming that release. "What was that?"

"What?"

"That . . . fear?" She squinted, as if trying to see through Faven to the starscapes that boiled through her every thought. "You didn't answer me. Why are you awake?"

Faven sighed, resigned to this saccharine exchange of heartache, and flopped onto her back, stretching her arms above her head. "I had a nightmare."

"Of?"

"A monster under my bed."

Amandine snorted and hooked one leg across Faven, leaving tingling sparks in the wake of her touch as she trailed her fingers over the soft curve of Faven's stomach. Faven reached for her, but Amandine snatched her wrists together in her other hand and held her arms in place above her head.

"Nice try." Amandine pressed a lingering kiss to the corner of Faven's lips, over her scale. "Tell me."

"What if I don't want to? Are you going to force all my secrets out of me, Bitter Amandine?"

"If you didn't want me asking, you would have lied about having a nightmare."

"Are you a pirate, or my therapist?"

"I'm..." The trailing hand stilled on Faven's stomach. "A friend."

"A friend," Faven said flatly.

Amandine's smirk was unbearably smug. "A very good one."

Faven bit her lip, struggling to find a way to put it into words. "Maybe it's best if I show you. May I have my armillary?"

She drew her head back, and a slight crease marred her forehead.

"I'm not going to dump you into a star," Faven said. "That'd be a waste."

Amandine laughed a little, but there was an edge to the sound. A subtle tension that wound through the muscles of the limbs draped over Faven.

"If you're planning to turn against me, please kill me now, because Becks will crow about me being an idiot for the rest of my life."

"I'll keep that in mind." Faven stole a kiss before Amandine peeled herself away.

The narrow bed was cold without her warmth, but Faven had zero complaints about the opportunity to watch her walk across the room and retrieve the weapon from a locked cabinet. The armillary warmed in Faven's grasp, familiar energies surging in anticipation, making her shiver.

"Are you cold?"

"Anything but."

Faven stood, letting the sheets fall away, while Amandine sat on the edge of the bed with her hands laced tightly together, a look in her eye like she wasn't sure if she should be expecting a fight. Faven could hardly blame her. She'd been less than predictable since their meeting. Better, perhaps, to put the pirate captain at ease before she shared her terror.

The armillary throbbed with inner light in the pelagic hues

of cryst-scale as Faven summoned to mind one of the practice starpaths all navigators must learn. Amandine leaned forward, entranced. The posture revealed a narrow tattoo. Thin black lines scrawled coordinates that flowed over the curve of Amandine's muscled bicep. Coordinates to a planet.

Its location filled her mind so swiftly and completely that it crowded out the tutorial starpath. It was a sleepy planet draped in thick grey clouds drifting in orbit around a distant, dying star. Faven closed her eyes and let that world and its system fill the workroom of her mind. After a few adjustments to the armillary, the tool hummed in sync with her mindscape.

It seemed almost eager, and far more responsive to her touch than it had ever been before. Faven spread her hands, letting the armillary float between her palms, the thrum of it pulsing against her skin. She opened her eyes.

The armillary projected the starscape in her mind onto the world around them. Amandine gasped, the bed squeaking as she jerked back from the vibrant planetarium she found herself within. Faven stood at the system's heart, its star a pendant resting on her breastbone, the planets and their moons spun out all around her, gleaming lines of gold tracing their orbital paths. A dwarf planet temporarily painted a charming freckle on Amandine's cheek.

Faven oriented herself within the space, then held out an arm and snatched the small, grey-draped planet in one hand, the holographic structure moving with her as she pushed it into the air between them.

Amandine's eyes widened. Then narrowed. She eased off the edge of the bed and padded closer to get a better look. "How did you . . . ?"

"I don't know its name. I saw it inked upon your skin."

Amandine covered the tattoo self-consciously with one hand. "It's Blackloach. A quiet backwater. That's all."

"Is it everything?"

"It's home." Her smile was wistful. Sad. She trailed her fingers through the illusion of that cloud-thick atmosphere and cupped her home world in the palm of her hand, cradling it like a delicate creature.

"Why did you leave?"

"Ah. That." Amandine frowned a moment, but with the tiny holo of the planet resting in her palm, her reservations seemed to wash away. "It was my grandfather's home. My father died fighting in the first rebellion, and my mother never came back, so my grandfather raised me there. He had a fishing cabin, out in the wilds. By the time I was old enough to help him, the rebellion was brewing again. I thought...I don't really know. I left to fight in the Push, the last upwelling before the rebellion was well and truly put down."

"You fought to unseat the Choir?"

Amandine looked up at her startled tone. "That surprises you? It seemed the only thing worth doing, at the time. Grandfather died while I was away, and when I returned to bury him, I realized I was a better fighter than a fisher. I'd heard rumors, during the war, of a veteran from the previous rebellion taking up piracy to fight back. I found a picture of her. Recognized her. So, when Captain Jacq came out my way recruiting, I was first in line."

"Do you mean—was Sere Steel your birth mother?"

"Ma Sere was Ma Sere," Amandine said. "My mother didn't come back from that war."

"Oh, Amandine. I'm so sorry. I didn't know, I..." Faven trailed off, feeling the flimsiness in those words. The strangeness of being on the other side of them, and knowing how little they helped but having nothing else worthwhile to say. Amandine's focus remained on the planet.

"I always thought I'd get back to the cabin, someday. Retire there."

Faven frowned at that, but the pirate had stiffened, and so she set the topic of Sere aside. She knew all too well how sometimes a distraction was the only thing keeping you going. "You still own the cabin?"

Amandine's smile twitched. "By the skin of my teeth. My share of our spoils goes to the ship, crew supplies, and the cabin, in that order. But Blackloach couldn't have been your nightmare."

"No," Faven admitted. "This is a demonstration. Of what it's like in my mind, when I'm envisioning a starpath."

Amandine looked up, craning her neck to better see the faraway stars represented in cinder-winks against the faux-darkness painted upon her ceiling. "It's beautiful."

Faven couldn't quite figure out why such a simple, flattering statement made a twist of sorrow tighten her heart. "It's a simplification, if I'm being honest. The armillary allows for focus, calculation, and storage. If I were, for example, to weave a path between your ship and Blackloach, I would first need to learn the signature of your lightdrive. As the *Marquette* and I are well acquainted"—attention tickled the back of her thoughts, the ship rousing to watch this display—"I would begin with the subspace connection."

She hovered a hand over the top of the armillary—palm flat, fingers straight as boards, as Ulana had taught her—and lifted her hand a few inches. A secondary plane appeared above the star system, a loose, mottled weave of light grey threads. Faven picked a path that looked likely, tested its beginning, and felt the *Marquette* thrum in anticipation. She snapped her fingers, uncurling a fan of calculations that crowded the air around her head.

The starpath to Blackloach practically begged to be woven, vectors and trajectories and velocities and punch-points all gleaming with a vibrant indigo in Faven's mind's eye that Amandine couldn't see, as the colors were her own special quirk, but screamed *safe* and *correct* to Faven.

"What are you doing?" Amandine asked.

"Weaving."

The armillary adjusted as she worked, storing viable pieces even as she pushed the rare bad turn aside with the flat of her hand to fizzle out into nothingness. It was effortless compared to untangling the twisted route Ulana had taken. That barbed path lingered in the back of her mind, threatening to overwhelm her work, but the starpath to Blackloach was as intuitive as breathing. As if that location had been stamped into her own skin.

By the time she was finished—quickly enough to have won her accolades back home—a fine mist of sweat beaded her skin, and her breath was hot and short. Amandine watched her with wide eyes.

"There," Faven said, breathless. Despite her wariness, Amandine closed the space between them and placed a hand on her arm, steadying her. "The path is done. Saved in my armillary for transfer into your lightdrive, when you're ready. Once placed, this ship will always be able to find its way to your home."

Amandine licked her lips, gaze drifting to the gauzy planet, then away again. "I can't take that as your payment. There's nothing on Blackloach. The crew will want a path that gets us somewhere we can use."

"Amandine." Faven picked up the planet and held it out to her. "It's a gift."

Instead of taking the planet, Amandine took her hand, sliding her fingers over the rough scale. "Your suffering is not a gift."

Faven kissed her, and when she pulled away, she brushed her lips against the corner of Amandine's mouth. "That weaving was a joy. I promise you, teaching such a simple path to your drive will cost me nothing. I caused you so much trouble—let me do this for you."

"Only if you're certain it won't advance the scale." While there was concern in Amandine's voice, her smile was impulsive—nearly giddy—and a delightful peachiness darkened her cheeks.

"I am." Faven let a low sigh slip free as she faced the armillary once more. "I can show you the type of starpath complicated enough to advance the scale. Once you see the difference, you'll understand."

"Which path?"

"My nightmare."

THIRTY-FOUR

Amandine

A twisted hellscape of metal and cryst-glass fractals filled the peaceful darkness where stars and planets had spun only moments before. Amandine struggled to convince her pounding heart that this was an illusion—nothing more—as the clenched fist of the Clutch filled the air.

Faven stood in the center, taking the place of the star Tenebrae. The graveyard wreckage of the cryst's remains swarmed her small frame. Broken ships, broken cities. Broken structures for which the humans who crawled through their remains held no frame of reference. The spaces between the shattered husks were slim, granting glimpses of Faven in their center. Amandine outstretched a hand to run her fingertips through a shard of construction larger than all of Votive City.

The outer and inner layers of the Clutch were void-black cryst-glass. Dark as the hidden hull of the *Marquette*. Unlucky, that shadowed glass was rumored to be.

When pirates braved the Clutch, it was only to slip behind the outer layer to the wreckage that lurked within. You did not take from the darkness, it was said, or the dark would take from you.

The pirates of Turtar Glas had mapped landmarks in that armored exterior. Found crevasses in which to slink between the precarious tugs of gravity within the maelstrom of so many massive structures. Amandine marked them in the swarm, and the secret ways known only to herself—she was certain the other pirates also had their own slip-throughs that they didn't share with Sere's collective. Those paths seemed like such minuscule things, in the face of all Faven held.

"Is this everything the Choir has mapped?" Amandine asked.

"Much of it," Faven said. "Turtar Glas is currently...". She skimmed through the mass of lines and marked a point in the inner layer. "Here. Lucky, that the *Marquette* helped me keep us away from Tenebrae's heart."

"Incredible," Amandine said with deep admiration.

"And do you often deliver threatening monologues to those you deem 'incredible'?" The wry twist in Faven's voice made Amandine snort.

"They're the only ones worth the time, because they might have it in 'em to listen." Amandine took a step, breaching the outer layer of coal-dark cryst. The prismatic rush of the inner layers stung her eyes, at first. Structures larger than any humanity had ever built flowed around her, and though they were intangible bits of light, they tickled her skin all the same.

"This was your nightmare?"

Faven's eyes glinted at her. Brief flickers through the churning of the Clutch. "Not precisely."

The navi outstretched her arms, palms flat, expanding the radius of the Clutch, and the blank spaces between the debris. Fine golden threads filled in those empty places, a tangled mass of glittering twine. Amandine examined the nearest snarl to drift past her. Those lines were the same bright gold that had appeared when Faven charted the course to Blackloach, but hopelessly crowded.

"This is why it's so difficult to path the ways through the Clutch," Amandine said.

"You're smarter than you look."

Amandine propped her fists on her hips and squinted at her through the swarm, but could only catch pieces of her expression in glimpses.

"Come closer," Faven ordered.

Despite this being nothing more than a holo, Amandine hesitated. No one who wanted to keep their skin and their sanity went deeper into the Clutch than skimming that first colorful layer. The one time they'd tried...Amandine rubbed the scar that wrapped over her right shoulder, and stepped deeper into Faven's nightmare. Through the prismatic inner core and into the dark inner shell hiding the Clutch's star—Tenebrae.

Though the density of structures thinned, the snarls of golden threads increased until Amandine felt as if she were choking on their nitid light. When she breached the inner shell and reached Faven, she understood.

Every single fine thread of light curved steadily inward until they pierced Faven's skin, giving her the illusion of being a puppet held taut on an infinity of strings.

"They're falling." Amandine plucked at a thread that terminated in the scale over Faven's breastbone.

"Every body that orbits another is forever falling into it."

Standing so close together, the heat of Faven's skin—warmed by her exertions with the armillary—brushed against Amandine's senses, their breath a mingling current nested together in the heart of a star. Amandine craned her neck, tracking the blackened shards that swam above them both, and the fine threads that bound them to their eventual destruction.

"One day it will all be gone," Amandine said. "I wonder what your Choir will do then, when it has no more cryst-glass to harvest."

"I daresay the whole thing will outlive us all."

"I don't think it's existential dread keeping you up at night, goddess."

Faven's lips twitched in something that might have been a sneer or a smile, Amandine couldn't tell. With the armillary hovering before her chest, Faven reached out into the mass. The slow spin of debris stopped. She flattened her palm and, muscles flexing, pushed the simulation around until she found the piece she desired.

She cupped her hands around the section and pulled them apart, increasing the scale. A labyrinth of threads crept between the pieces of the Clutch. Those threads snarled, frayed, broke. They jagged off at random to disappear into bloody red smears, and thinned away into nothing before picking up again. At the end of the path, nothing but emptiness.

"Your nightmare?" Amandine asked.

Faven's lips pursed in frustration. "The path my mentor wove before her disappearance."

Amandine traced the barbed mess with the tip of one finger. "It doesn't go anywhere."

"This is what the *Marquette* tried to help me understand, but I'm afraid its adjustments are beyond me, for now. Where the path ends is too cramped for a starpath, and . . . Wait. That can't be right."

"What is it?" Amandine asked.

"This is—this is wrong."

Faven's focus shifted entirely to the simulation caught between her hands. With the threads of that broken path reflected in her eyes like burst veins of gold and a frustrated tension in the navi's jaw, the back of Amandine's neck prickled, a primordial instinct whispering in her hindbrain—*run*.

Faven's head snapped up, tilted to the side, her otherworldly gaze piercing through the haze of the Clutch all around them to sweep the walls of the ship. The scale painting her body shimmered with a soft aquamarine glow.

"Did you feel that?" she asked.

"You're going to have to be more specific."

Faven shot her a sour look and started to speak, but her words dissolved into a startled grunt. The ship rocked, a concussive *whump* knocking them sideways. Amandine swore and stumbled, catching Faven before she fell.

The Clutch vanished, Faven's armillary clattering to the floor. Red warning lights pulsed around the edges of the room. Hull breach alarms blared.

Amandine made sure Faven was steady on her feet and whirled around, snatching the navi's robe—dress? What *was* that thing?—off the floor to toss at her before she sprinted to the intercom and hit the button with the side of her fist.

"Somebody better know what's happening."

"Breach, Cap'n," Becks said.

"The alarms are pretty clear on that point!" Amandine shouted over her shoulder as she tugged on her clothes.

Gehry's deep, rumbling voice came through the intercom, "We're here for the navi. Hand her over and there won't be any trouble."

"Blowing a hole in the hull I just patched sounds pretty fucking troublesome," Amandine called out. "The navi's still recovering. Or didn't you notice the Blademother ran her through?"

"If she's conscious, she can weave. We're not gonna sit around and wait for her colleagues to come back."

"Who says she's conscious?"

"C'mon, Bitter." Gehry sounded tired. "We can see she's prepping the *Marquette* to jump."

Amandine paused in shoving her foot in a boot and met Faven's wide eyes. *Are you?* Amandine mouthed. Faven shook her head vehemently, but her scale patches still had that soft glow. Amandine bit her lip, considering her options. She didn't like the look of any of them.

"She's not touching my drive."

"The void she isn't! There's only one navi in this armada, and that drive is revving to jump. Check the reports, Bitter. Knock her out, hand her over, and I won't breach your inner doors and slit your throat."

Amandine muted the all-ship channel and touched her comm gem.

"What's going on?" she demanded of her crew.

"She's right, Cap'n," Becks said. "Our drive is warming up."

"I have cameras on the docks," Kester cut in. "Gehry has five others arrayed for a fight, but they have yet to enter the breached airlock door."

"I can barricade the inner door," Tully said, "but I don't think it'll last long, and I'd rather not tangle with Gehry's people."

"Agreed," Amandine said. "Stall a second."

Amandine accessed the status of the *Marquette*'s drive from the screen inset on the wall, then half turned to pin Faven with a glare and thrust a finger at the display.

"You want to explain this?"

"It's not me." She was still shaking her head, jewel-braided hair clinking as she backed up until she pressed against the wall, palms flat on the bulkhead.

Amandine frowned. Faven's eyes were huge, golden spiderwebs stamped into the whites of them, a sheen of sweat on her skin that hadn't been there a moment ago. The glow of the cryst-scale brightened, seeming to pulse with the panting of her breath.

"Okay." Amandine took a sliding step toward her. "I know you don't mean to, goddess. I know. But you're the only navi in the armada, and someone's messing with my drive."

"It's not me," she insisted. Faven clutched the sides of her head in both hands, fingers tenting like spider's legs as she squeezed. "It's not. It's not."

Shit. Amandine spoke across comms. "Becks. You wanna tell me why our navi seems to be lightsick?"

"Uhhh." A crash of tools punctuated that statement. "So, you remember how I said our drive shielding would last a few more days? Yeah. Well. Revise that estimate. We've got a very small leak."

"That 'very' small leak has given us a very sick navi," Amandine whispered harshly as she shuffled closer to Faven.

"There are sedatives," Kester said, "in the top drawer of the med cart—two milliliters of the injector with the green label should do the trick."

"Copy that."

Amandine sidled up to the cart and palmed the correct injector. Faven's eyes were squeezed shut, her chest heaving, lips moving in silent litany.

"Faven," Amandine said gently as she crept closer. "I know you're not doing this on purpose. I understand. But we've got a crack in our drive shielding and it's gotten in your head. I'm going to give you something to calm down so we can get this under control, okay?"

"It's not me," she said. "It's not. It's not. *It's not.*"

Amandine grimaced. The navi had seemed fine until the breach hit. Maybe that leak had started after the impact. If so, they'd all be lightsick in a matter of minutes. But if she hadn't been messing with the drive before the breach, then why had Gehry attacked at all?

"Just breathe," she said. "I'm not going to let anyone hurt you. But I need you to breathe slowly, can you do that?"

Faven's head snapped up, empyreal eyes locking on to Amandine's with such intensity that she stiffened. There was nothing of the navi Amandine had come to know in that stare. It churned with the thorn-barbed starpath that haunted her nightmares, burst blood vessels filling in the snapped-off paths of gold.

"*Get out,*" she snarled.

The visualization of the Clutch burst into life all around her. It spread out to the expanded scale it had been in earlier, then contracted in the next breath to a tight fist, then out again, expanding and contracting with the drumbeat of the navi's heart.

Amandine lunged, lining up to plunge the sedative into the side of her neck. Faven's head fell back, her arms flung wide, and she vanished.

THIRTY-FIVE

Amandine

Amandine staggered into the place Faven had been standing and crashed against the wall, dropping the injector. She swore, ducked down to scoop the injector back up, but Faven had vanished—armillary and all.

Never should have given that cursed thing back to her.

Amandine stalked to the door and tore it open. Becks was running down the hall, sweat shimmering on their brow.

"Cap'n! Gehry's readying plasma cutters. I know you don't want to hand the navi to the mob, but—"

"Navi did a runner." Amandine shouldered past them, heading for the cockpit.

Becks jogged along beside her. "How?"

"I might have given her the armillary back."

"You—*what*?"

"Oh, calm down. At least it's still bugged. We can track her."

Becks made a small, strangled sound that was more than likely a denigration of her character, but Amandine chose to ignore it. She slid into the captain's seat and unfolded a cryst-fan, loading up their usual tracker program. Nothing pinged.

In fact, the serial number of the tracker she'd thought had been attached to Faven's armillary had never been checked out of their inventory.

Amandine looked over at Becks, who was sweating so much their clothes were beginning to wilt. "How is this possible?"

"How should I know?"

They were lying. The realization left her momentarily speechless. Becks was her right hand, trusted above all others. They could be cagey, sure, but she knew the way their head tilted away from whoever they were lying to. Knew they'd look anywhere but at another living soul when they were the slightest bit uncomfortable.

Becks's gaze was doing loop-de-loops over the dash.

"Becks," Amandine said slowly.

"Look." They pointed to the dash. "It loaded."

Reluctantly, Amandine looked. A map of the *Marquette*'s interior had appeared in the projection, the blip of a tracker light winking at her from the engine bay. The inventory database she'd set to the side of the screen showed the tracker had been checked out, now. Amandine wondered what she'd find, if she went and opened that storage crate.

"Must have been a delay in the system," Becks said.

"Must have" was all she could find to say. Her lips felt strangely numb, her head floating.

"Cap'n?"

Amandine pushed the external intercom button. Her voice was flat. "Gehry. If you ever trusted me, give me five minutes."

She stood before an answer came. Brushed a hand, out of habit, against the console to see if she could sense the ship's mood, but she needn't have bothered with the contact.

The *Marquette*'s mind was a palpable weight in the air, caressing Amandine's skin as she moved deeper into the ship. She knew that she should be frightened. That whatever the *Marquette* really was, it was probably dangerous. But Amandine had been riding around on the *Marquette* for decades, and while the ship occasionally felt prickly with annoyance, it'd never felt malevolent. A little lost, maybe. A little scared.

The *Marquette* had saved her, when her old crew's run on the Clutch had gone bad. It'd sung her out of danger, into its sheltering walls. Even if she'd been half-lost with lightsickness by the time she'd made it back to Turtar Glas, the ship hadn't known any better.

She supposed that all its previous passengers hadn't minded the exposed lightdrive.

Her boots echoed down halls that felt wider than usual. The proportions inside the *Marquette* had always been off, though she'd been too in love with the ship to admit it to herself. A little too tall, a little too wide. No one knew what the cryst had actually looked like. They'd left depictions behind, figures in stained glass, but they always rendered themselves as elaborate, nine-pointed stars, and so historians had assumed that they had an edict against self-representation in their art.

Amandine tried to imagine a living star floating through the halls, and couldn't.

Kester and Tully joined Becks, her crew trailing behind her shrouded in a silence so thick Amandine thought she might choke on it. Becks had known something was wrong about that tracker. It'd been written all over their face.

Was written in their silence, even now. A silence that was taut. Guilty. Expecting her to lash out and demand answers.

Her feet felt heavy, but she picked them up anyway. Made herself push into a run as she curved down the long ramp that led to the *Marquette*'s heart. She rarely came down here. Left most of the tinkering to Becks, and she'd told herself it was because they were her mechanic. It was their job. She didn't need to worry herself over the details.

But really, it was because every time she crossed that threshold she felt transported back to the Clutch. Heard the echoes of her crew dying all around her. Saw, in her mind's eye, the flash of a map that had led her to the *Marquette*. And how much that map had looked like a starpath.

The engine bay looked the same as any other ship's. A nonagon, similar to the nine-pointed star the cryst used to envision themselves in their art. In the center of the room, the obelisk of the lightdrive rose. Smaller than the primary drives of Turtar Glas, the hexagonal podium was tall enough to reach Amandine's shoulders. The containment wrapped it in double-walled glass, shielding the ship's human passengers from the lightdrive's deadly strength.

Faven hovered above the center of the drive. Her face was upturned, as if she could see straight through the ship's walls and into the vast blackness beyond.

"Faven," Amandine said gently, and when the woman didn't react, "*Marquette*."

Her head turned, slowly. Strange stars swirled through Faven's eyes. The twisting passages between time and space were beautiful, but the designs carried layers of meaning that Amandine could never hope to understand. A cold ache started up between her eyes the longer she gazed upon those stars, but she didn't look away. Couldn't.

Faven's face smiled, but it was the *Marquette* moving the muscles. The *Marquette* who spoke through her scale-bracketed lips. "I've long thought of what I would say to you, given the chance, but now I find only one thing matters—assurance to you that Faven consented to this."

"You'll forgive me for not believing you until you vacate that body and the navi can tell me herself. Because last I heard, she was telling you to get out of her head."

The *Marquette* nodded Faven's head in understanding, then turned alien eyes to the lightdrive. "There is so little of me left, now, that I cannot last like this. But in her weaving, she stumbled across a question she cannot answer. I will give her the means to find the truth she longs for."

"You can't do this." Tully stepped forward, cheeks ruddy. "You can't just—just use people like that! Get out of her!"

"Easy." She placed a hand on Tully's shoulder. Their skin was hot, muscles taut. They kept clenching and unclenching their fists. "Let it speak."

The *Marquette* attempted something that might have been a smile. "Thank you."

"Oh, this ain't a favor. Only reason I haven't knocked your lights out is because I don't know what it'll do to the navi. You got some grand secret to impart? Wonderful. Best start with explaining what the fuck you are and what you want, because while I'm grateful you helped save Turtar Glas, that goodwill strains the second you start possessing my crew."

"I am safety. It is my duty to protect them."

The *Marquette* lifted Faven's hand, hovering it above the shielding. The drive emitted a teal glow. It painted Faven's skin in murky waters, drew long shadows along her arm that made the fine lines of her body appear skeletal.

The *Marquette* slipped Faven's armillary from her sleeve. It unfolded, hovering above her open palm, the rings of cryst-glass and silvery metal shining as they spun. Those pieces that were purely cryst grew in new ways, sprouting extensions and pathways that unfurled, rearranging itself until it was as difficult to look at as Faven's eyes had been, twisted with strange geometries.

The golden lines of a new starpath being laid appeared above the lightdrive.

Jump alarms chimed.

"Don't you dare—"

A thin breath passed Faven's lips, her body canting forward, palm pressed hard against her breastbone. Slackness dragged her arms down, bowed her head. Amandine vaulted the safety rail, ignoring a grunt of protest from Becks, and was there when the navi fell, armillary clattering to the ground beside her, her weight solid and real and warm in Amandine's arms, though the stars printed in her eyes hinted at nothing from this reality.

"What did you do?" she asked. The alien light was already fading from Faven's eyes. The *Marquette*'s presence, previously a weight in the air, tactile and all-encompassing, receded, leaving Amandine breathless with a want she couldn't name.

The *Marquette* said, "Go home, Andielle."

The ship jumped.

THIRTY-SIX

Faven

Faven came back to herself nestled in the cradle of Amandine's arms. Her mind and body were a juiced lemon, stinging, electric, empty. A mournful wail howled through the empty halls of her mind—no, not just her mind. The *Marquette*'s light-leak alarms filled the engine bay with the cry of a poisoned ship.

"Can you stand?" Amandine asked.

Faven nodded, feeling silly and childish as Amandine set her carefully on her feet. She tottered, swaying with exhaustion. Amandine caught her arm and slung it over her shoulder without comment.

"Evacuate," Amandine ordered. She ducked down and scooped Faven's discarded armillary off the floor. It unfolded to reveal the beacon Gailliard had given her, a slim tracking device tucked away behind a gem.

Amandine froze a beat, her gaze stuck on that tracker. Faven wanted to tell her that it wasn't what she thought—that she hadn't used it to call the Blademother to them, she never would. But she was too drowsy to get the words out, and Amandine tucked the armillary into her waistband without comment.

The crew swore but swung into effortless motion, rattling off checklists as they rushed for the exits. The atmosphere outside—safe. The air pressure—perfect. High moisture, low microbes. Nothing outside the expected for humanity. With every tick of information, a grim certainty carved itself deeper into the grooves of Amandine's face.

She knew where they were.

"Don't bother with the suits," she announced. "Just get out."

"Cap'n," Becks said, "I can shut the drive down from the cockpit."

"No. If this ship loses power, all the doors lock to maintain pressure in case of a breach. You'll have four hours of air, tops, and won't be able to get out without powering up or taking the bloody doors apart, Becks."

"If we're going to repair the shielding, we need the light levels to dissipate, and that's not going to happen if the drive is powered on. There are backup hard suits in the cockpit to shield me from the light. I'll be fine."

Tully shifted from foot to foot. "You shouldn't stay here alone when the ship's like this, Becks. We—I mean—none of us should."

"Tully is correct," Kester said. "The ship is too unpredictable at the moment."

"Can it jump again?"

It took Faven a moment to realize that Amandine was addressing her directly. A fugue state still coated her mind like honey, thick and distorting her every sense. Even her fingers felt far away from her body, their tips numb.

"No, I don't believe so. I sense no more strength left within it."

"Good," Amandine said. "But staying behind is the captain's job." She started to shift Faven off her shoulder, but Becks pushed her back. Faven didn't enjoy being treated like a piece of luggage, but the crew of the *Marquette* were too wrapped up in their argument to pay her soft huff of annoyance any mind.

"We need you outside, Cap'n." Becks looked to Kester. "And don't you worry none. This ship and I, we're gonna come to an understanding. I won't be pushed around by a hunk of metal."

Kester frowned in response.

Amandine clasped hands with Becks. "Fine. But if it takes longer than four hours, I'm breaking the windscreen to get you air."

"Deal."

They stumbled out the airlock onto a plain so broad and endless it seemed to stretch on forever. Mist thick enough to hide the ground from view flowed over her feet, licking damp droplets against her bare ankles. Faven shivered, and Amandine held her closer.

Amandine touched her comm gem. "We're clear, Becks."

The *Marquette* quieted, the constant thrum of the engines dwindling away into nothing in concert with the exterior lights winking off one by one. Faven held her breath, and wasn't entirely certain why. The slow shuttering of the ship felt final in a way that rankled her senses.

With the crisis past, the crew of the *Marquette* turned to look at her with wide eyes and no small amount of suspicion, which was only fair. Faven herself couldn't begin to explain what had happened.

But it wasn't their wariness that worried her. No, what worried her was a new thread of tension between Amandine and her crew, a rigid readiness in Amandine's every movement.

"All right, Navi," Amandine said, and Faven could tell that she was trying to keep matters light, but the strain in her voice gave away her fear. "You got any idea what just happened?"

"I don't know. When the *Marquette* controlled me, I felt like I was dreaming...Floating beneath an endless sea. It was warm, and safe, but no matter how much I wanted to break through to the surface of myself, I couldn't find the way."

"Was it—" Amandine paused in the way of someone who knows what they have to say, but is afraid of what those words will do. "Was it living?"

"I don't believe so," Faven said. "But I can't be certain. It felt like a construct to me. Like the systems we navigators sometimes use to help us chart more complicated paths."

"A construct implies a builder."

"So it does."

The pirate gave her one of those long, searching looks that made her feel so exposed she tugged the neckline of her robe tighter closed. Amandine's warm sigh gusted against her face.

"You really don't know what it is, do you?"

"I wish that I did."

"Then I guess we'd better find out."

"Captain," Kester said, "what do you propose we do?"

Faven rubbed the memory of stars from her eyes, grounding herself in the physical world as best she could. Amandine's crew watched their captain expectantly. Waiting for orders. Waiting for Bitter Amandine to figure out what to do.

An emotion Faven didn't recognize tightened her throat. Weighted her stomach. Amandine's mother was dead, her community braying for her surrender, her ship very possibly possessed of an alien intelligence, but standing there with her chin tipped to the sky, she seemed, in that moment, more goddess than Faven ever had been.

"Right." Amandine summoned up a rakish smile that made Faven's heart ache. "Whatever the *Marquette* is, it's our only ride off this rock. We'll find Sythe a place to rest, then try to get in touch with the nearest shipyard for materials."

"Where are we?" Tully pushed to their toes as if a few extra inches would reveal more than the cloud-drenched sky.

"Blackloach," Amandine said.

"Amandine," Faven said carefully, "I don't think those coordinates on your arm lead to Blackloach."

"Don't be ridiculous. Where else would they go?"

"This is what I was trying to tell you, before the *Marquette* took me over. The path to those coordinates—it's identical to the path Ulana left behind."

THIRTY-SEVEN

Amandine

Amandine's crew looked at her like her head had spun all the way around. Even Faven seemed skeptical of her mental state, a downward slant to her lips that tugged her cryst-scale patch tight.

"Don't lie to me about this, Navi. You saw Blackloach. You put it in your hologram, and the *Marquette* moved that starpath into its drive before it jumped."

"I cannot explain the visualization, but I'm not lying. Perhaps..." Her nose wrinkled.

"What?"

"It's just that, I found that weaving remarkably easy. If the *Marquette* wanted to come here, then it could have distracted me from noticing the similarities at first through that euphoria—and through altering the visualization."

"No. No way." Amandine jerked her head side to side in negation. "I wouldn't get a tattoo of coordinates into the fucking Clutch."

"Are you certain?" Kester's unruffled voice chilled the brewing argument.

Amandine frowned, easing the navi's arm off her shoulders so that she could stand under her own strength, now that she seemed to have recovered her wits. Kester looked upward, her sharp eyes tracking the play of cloud cover. Amandine followed that glance, and her lungs briefly forgot how to do their duty.

Between the variegated patches of grey clouds, a black sky loomed. Not the endless expanse of a natural nighttime, sprinkled with stars. The churning, black cryst of the Clutch's interior layer dominated the thin spaces between the clouds. Endless, gnashing fractals of stations and ships and other structures Amandine couldn't begin to name crowded the firmament. Lights winked between the panes. Deadlights. Calling lost souls home.

"Thought you said Blackloach was your home world," Tully said warily.

"It was. It is." Amandine blinked, and blinked again, willing the next flutter of her lids to dash the scene before her from reality. No such luck.

"Maybe the navi got the starpath wrong?" Tully asked.

"I did not," Faven said with haughty indignity. She seemed on the verge of stamping a foot. "I told you, the paths are the same. Only a small section at the end varies—the part that I said doesn't make any sense."

Had the *Marquette* realized that Faven was about to make that discovery, and jumped them before she could reveal the deception? She swept that thought aside, then touched her sleeve over the tattoo of the coordinates.

"No. This is Blackloach. We're just getting lightsick, that's all. Gotta get farther from the ship. Let it pass."

Faven went ahead and stamped that foot. "This is *not*—"

Kester cleared her throat. "Perhaps we should survey the area and discover precisely where we are?"

"Yeah." Amandine shook off her stunned state. Her crew was marooned. The people of Turtar Glas were stuck light-years from home without a navi to help them get back. Gawping at an impossible sky wasn't going to solve either of those problems. "This way."

The mist limited visibility, making Amandine feel as if she were surrounded. Caught in a cage she couldn't quite define. She put one foot in front of the other and listened to the rasp of her own breath, to the crunch of scrub beneath her boots. Not the teeth-gnashing, grinding sound riding to her ears from farther away.

Just the wind. Just the wind and her foul mood and the chaos of the past few days playing tricks on her mind. Wasn't anything on Blackloach but fishing cabins and marshland. They were lightsick, or on their way to being so. Overtired and afraid, and the sky was the black of night obscured by clouds and nothing more.

Her grandfather's cabin reared up out of the mist. Lack of care showed in the broken, jagged teeth of the two front steps. In the weathering of the wooden walls, and the slump of a porch that had been too long left to the elements. A slow breath of relief hissed out of her, shoulders easing down from around her ears.

The green-painted door—chipped and dull, now—the porch posts she'd carved with her favorite constellations from the skies of other worlds, the black shutters pulled tight against the weather. All worn and sagging, with weeds pushing through the cracks in the walls. But hers. Faven had been mistaken. This wasn't the Clutch. This was home.

"Captain?" Kester asked.

Amandine ignored her and kept trudging onward. She'd feel better with four walls snug around her.

"Cap'n, wait!" Tully said.

The steps creaked as Amandine mounted them, and the door unlocked at the touch of her hand. A fan of dust washed away beneath the opening of the door. She wasn't quite certain what she'd expected. An infestation, maybe—rats or insects taking advantage of her long absence. She wouldn't have minded a squatter—it wasn't like she was making use of the place, and a pirate could hardly squawk about theft. But her cabin was in the middle of nowhere, and all she found was a stillness. A held-breath pause draped in the dust of long years.

"It's only two rooms," Amandine said over her shoulder, "but it'll give us a place to rest up and regroup."

Faven was looking at her like she was made of sand, and so much as a sneeze would see her crumble.

"What?" Amandine demanded.

Tully wouldn't look at her. It was Kester, adjusting her cuffs with a subtle twitch, who said, "Captain, where do you think you are right now?"

THIRTY-EIGHT

Amandine

The dust. The murky light. Amandine blinked, and turned, and the worn wood and creak of old floorboards altered with the turn of her head. Transformed into jagged planes of broken cryst-glass, the glacial groan of glass-on-glass, a shrieking and cracking that resonated deep within her. Even the tangle of scrub betrayed her senses, the crunch of dried grasses becoming the snap and grind of grit and debris.

Amandine pressed her hand over the tattooed coordinates. The light had gotten to her, sure, but her vision was clearing, now. This wasn't Blackloach. But neither did the navi make a mistake in her weaving. There was no running from it, not anymore. Amandine didn't need to check the starcharts to know that the coordinates on her arm would lead her here, and nowhere else.

Go home, Andielle.

She wondered how long Ma Sere had known what she kept buried. Known that Blackloach stopped being her only home the day her heart stopped out here, in the Clutch, under the blade of Captain Amber Jacq.

Stopped, and been started again, and in that revival a part of her had gotten tangled up in the Clutch. In the *Marquette*.

She wasn't ready for this. Didn't want to be. Wanted to turn tail and flee and find some other ship and fly far and fast where the shadows of her past couldn't reach her.

There was nowhere far enough.

"Cap'n?" Tully asked, voice tight with worry.

It didn't matter if she was ready. Amandine took a breath. Straightened her spine. Shook the memory of lightsickness from her eyes and focused. She'd escaped this nightmare once before. She'd do it again.

"Welcome to the *Black Celeste*," she said.

Tully sucked in a startled breath.

"This appears to be a planet," Kester said. Then, after a pause, "Albeit a small one."

"We shouldn't be here," Tully said in a voice so small it unsettled Amandine. They were usually first in line to explore anything unusual.

"We shouldn't," Kester said. "And so we must do our best to get out of here as quickly as possible."

"Right." Tully seemed to rally at that. They crouched down, brushing aside the mist to get a better look at the ground. They needn't have bothered. Amandine could have told them what it was. "Cryst-glass, looks like. They're shifting around. Grinding like tectonic plates. I'd wager that's where the noise is coming from."

"It's a construct," Faven said.

"Like the *Marquette*?" Amandine asked.

"I can't say for certain, but I think so." Her face pinched with concentration. "I can sense an awareness within it, slumbering."

"You mean that it's like a big cage, with a mind locked inside it?"

"Honestly, I have no idea. The *Marquette* is the only other thing I've ever sensed that was remotely similar, but its mind was never caged. This feels...chained, somehow."

"I don't like the sound of that," Amandine said.

"Neither do I," Kester said darkly.

Amandine knelt in the mist and sorted through the mound of rubble she'd thought was stairs. The planet was all black cryst, from what Amandine remembered, but the palm-sized shards were in the vibrant colors that humanity used in construction. She picked one up, running her thumb over the smooth pane, and wondered if she imagined the dried blood on its edge.

"Captain Jacq landed not far from here." Amandine dropped the shard and stood, brushing her hands off. "The lightdrive will be dead by now, but we might be able to repurpose its shielding."

"Are you sure that's a good idea, Captain?" Kester asked with uncharacteristic softness.

"You got a better plan?"

She shook her head. Too bad. Amandine would have preferred Kester had something else in mind. Affecting a confident swagger, Amandine led the way through the mists, preparing to rob the graves of those she'd left behind.

THIRTY-NINE

Faven

While Faven found the fact that the starpath that should have led to Blackloach had taken them deeper within the Clutch a fascinating puzzle to untangle, she kept that curiosity to herself as they trudged through the unending mist. Drawn onward by some internal compass Amandine alone seemed able to access.

They made a miserable party, with Amandine having fallen into a thoughtful, taut silence. Faven was tempted to prod at the pirate just to warm herself by the heat of her ire, but she refrained. While excitement welled within her for having finally made it to the *Black Celeste*, the others were tense. Frightened.

A sickly, hot sensation soured her stomach. Shame? She'd experienced it so little it was difficult to pin down; a wriggling, slithering emotion that shied away from close study. She thought of how happy she was to have made it here and, ah, yes—there it was again, stronger than ever.

The emotion had found her twice in a mere two days. Curious. Once, when Hatriel had chided her for failing to know her mother, and now—why? She'd gotten what she wanted at last. She was here, on the *Black Celeste*, her answers within reach. Wasn't this the path she had chosen for herself?

But in getting here, she'd hurt others she'd begun to care for.

Faven slipped on a patch of dusty debris. Amandine shot a hand out, catching her elbow, and steadied her. They shared a too-brief look, the pirate's eyes unreadable, and she glanced away once more, dropping Faven's arm to touch the coordinates on her skin. She'd been doing that a lot, since they'd set out.

"Watch your step." Amandine spoke to no one in particular. "The ground shifts."

"And rises." Faven pointed ahead, where broad, hexagonal pillars of cryst-glass speared through the sky, a staggered collection that reminded her poignantly of the spires of her home.

"We're close," Amandine said. "Be on your guard."

The pirates all touched their weapons, reassuring themselves of that killing weight. Amandine hadn't returned her armillary to her, but Faven was too exhausted to make use of it as a weapon regardless. Instead, she pulled herself straighter, tucked her hands into her sleeves, and tried to carry herself with some dignity, even if her robes were ragged.

Possibly Faven should have been afraid. She was stranded on an alien construct with a woman whose mental state was an open question. Despite all that, fear remained as far away from her as it had been when she'd schemed to wrest the starpath that would destroy Turtar Glas from the Choir's control.

The towering pillars drew near enough that they loomed above, vanishing into the thick cloud cover. Faven craned her neck, admiring their beauty.

"A light ahead," Kester said.

The pirates reacted as one, drawing weapons and dropping into ready stances as they crept forward. She felt...warm. Cozy, even, despite the clinging mist and relentless cloud cover.

Kester's spotted light was a starburst shimmering in the center of one of the pillars. The crew didn't quite relax, but they lowered their weapons. The pillars were wide enough around that all of them, linking hands, couldn't hope to half encircle one. Faven pressed a palm flat against the glass. A tingle tickled her palm, senses singing with warmth once again. The light within didn't seem to react to her presence, it stayed perfectly stationary, and yet Faven felt watched in the same way she had on the *Marquette*.

"I think there's fluid within the pillars," she said. "The light appears to be floating."

Amandine came to stand beside her and knocked on the glass with two knuckles. "Bioluminescent?"

"Possibly," Faven said with a small shrug. "Perhaps even a trick of the glass. It's difficult to say."

"As long as it's not hostile," Amandine said. Then, half under her breath, "You're not feeling lightsick?"

Faven's mind was still mired in the aftereffects of the *Marquette*'s takeover, making her feel slow-witted and plodding, but that was all. "Not that I can tell."

Amandine gave her a long, probing look that made Faven's cheeks heat with indignation—she was not a specimen to be *studied*.

"I assure you," Faven said briskly, "I am in control of my own faculties."

"Sure," Amandine said, returning her attention to the pillar. There seemed to be something more she wanted to say, her jaw flexing with half-formed words, but eventually she only let out a tired breath and shook her head.

"Cap'n, over here," Tully called out.

Amandine strode away, shotgun resting against her shoulder. Faven picked up her robes to better place her steps as she followed her captain's determined stride, and nearly bumped into her back when she stopped cold.

A museum piece of a ship had landed not far away. Landed and skidded, it looked like, as it'd pitched up against one of the pillars and cracked open its hull. A gangway reached down from an open airlock, the space within dark.

Corpses so old they'd become skeletons littered the ground before the ship. Amandine took a hesitant step forward, crouching beside a body shrouded in a russet-hued coat that had begun to come apart at the seams. She nudged it with the barrel of her shotgun, face blank as the bones rattled beneath the coat. A saber was still clutched in the dead man's hand. Absently, she touched the scar over her right shoulder.

"Amber Jacq," Faven said, then bit her lips shut when the crew collectively shot her a look.

"The very same." Amandine stood and spat on the remains of her old captain.

The grinding sound deepened, stealing whatever she would have said next. Amandine looked up, tracking the pillars that hemmed them in like trees, and frowned. Faven could have sworn the pillars had shifted position.

"Let's rob this grave and get out of here," Amandine said. "Wait here, Navi. If there's charge in that drive, I don't want you anywhere near it when we strip the shielding. Holler if something moves that's not supposed to."

The pirates entered the desolate ship, leaving Faven alone with the corpses of their colleagues. Such a strange thing, a battlefield. Faven skirted its perimeter, trying to make sense of the decomposed remains and reconstruct the final moments of the fight.

Mist obscured the ground, hiding away old bloodstains, but the bodies were substantial enough that she could make out the rough positions they'd been in when they'd fallen. A larger crew than Amandine's—twenty bodies were spread out behind Amber Jacq's position—they'd all been facing into the pillars. Toward the light.

Faven knelt beside the slain captain. His saber was light in her hand, and Faven had no doubt that it was Amandine's blood that had dried on the cutting edge. She ran her fingers over the tacky texture of the tarnished metal fittings around the grip. Swirls of metal intertwined with jewels and enamel—a much fancier weapon than any of Amandine's crew now carried. But then, Amber Jacq's style of piracy had been bolder—bloodier—than Amandine's. Perhaps he'd had a love of ornamentation.

Except that his coat was plain, threadbare long before decay had started its ruin, and his ship lacked the stained-glass scenes of bravado that the other pirates seemed to favor. The stains around the blade's grip, where the owner's fingers had long since decayed, were not in the correct position to line up with Captain Jacq's skeletal hand.

Faven stood, tipping the point of the blade toward the ground. A sigil capped the pommel, patterned with three concentric hexagons. Faven had never seen it before, but she recognized the source at once—the style of art and symbolism the Choir of Stars was prone to.

Someone had moved the blade from the hand of a dead Choir guard into Jacq's hand, and recently.

"I don't think this sword was yours," she said to the corpse.

She pried the sigil out of the pommel and tucked it into her pocket. With the tip of the blade she brushed mist aside, briefly revealing more of the ground. The glint of a white bone caught her eye. She swished more mist away, and found a skeletal hand reaching toward Jacq, the arm above it encased in brown leather.

Faven frowned, swiping at the mists. A right arm had been amputated from its owner at the shoulder joint, old blood staining the sleeve at the site of the injury. The rest of the corpse was missing—they must have gone somewhere else to die—and Faven wouldn't have thought much of it at all, if it weren't for the remains of a green bandana tied tight around the skeleton's hand.

A perfect match to the one tied around Faven's wrist.

She glanced to the derelict ship Amandine had disappeared within. Surely the disembodied arm wasn't the result of her injury. Amandine had both her arms still, and she couldn't have survived such a wound untreated.

Something familiar about the landscape drew Faven's attention, though she couldn't quite place the feeling. She thought she could sense a way *down*, but the mist obscured any such passage. She paced slowly in that direction, swiping the mist aside with broad slashes of the blade. It filled back in immediately, but cleared long enough for her to note a dingy white sleeve.

Faven knelt and felt along the sleeve. The fabric was smooth between her fingers, the form beneath firm as stone—not a skeleton, then.

She brushed mist aside and jerked her hand back with a soft hiss. The body had fallen against one of the pillars that the ship had bumped when it'd skidded to a stop. It was flat on its back, dead eyes staring straight up at nothing, and had transmuted to cryst, aquamarine scales enveloping it for all eternity. Its other arm, out-flung in the moment of its ending, had landed in a small puddle. The man had been a soldier in the Choir's employ, based on his uniform, but not of any division she recognized.

"What in the void do you think you're doing?" Amandine demanded.

"She has a weapon," Kester said.

Faven leapt to her feet and looked at the blade in surprise—she'd half forgotten its existence. She pitched the sword to the ground with a clatter.

"What happened here?" she asked.

"A disagreement." Amandine jerked her chin in the direction of the *Marquette*. "We got the shielding we need. We're leaving."

"These are Choir soldiers. We're deeper in the Clutch than even the Choir has mapped. What happened here?" Faven repeated. "What do you know?"

Amandine's chest heaved, eyes narrowing. Faven pulled herself up to her full height, despite her exhaustion, and narrowed her eyes right back at her. After a moment, Amandine let out a soft huff.

"I told you. I was young, and foolish, and when I realized Jacq wanted a kid dead, I got in the middle. The rest...I ran. I don't know."

"Was that child cryst-born?"

Amandine drew her head back. "How do you know that?"

"His name was Gailliard, I'm sure of it. The story I know is that his parent tried to sell him to pirates in the *outer* layers of the Clutch. This...doesn't make sense. How did Amber Jacq find this place? Why bring the boy here at all?"

"He got a transmission for the meeting. We showed up, didn't realize we were all getting lightsick, and when he tried to kill the kid, I intervened and then ran. The soldiers got the kid, I saw them usher him away, but I fled until I found the *Marquette*. That's all I know." Amandine's gaze had grown glazed, haunted, as if the mist that curled around their ankles had been slowly filling her up from within.

Gailliard himself couldn't talk about that day without flinching. How much worse, for Amandine, who hadn't been rescued, but had been forced to abscond with a ship and make her way home injured, unable to think clearly?

A new sensation stirred within Faven. Warm, a touch unpleasant. She pursed her lips and looked away from the captain, to the crystallized body lost beneath the mist.

"These pillars." Her voice was strangely detached to her own ears. "They appear to be filled with the mineralization fluid used to birth new navigators."

"What?"

The haze of the past cleared from Amandine's eyes. She was alert once more, striding through the mist, and paused when Faven held out an arm to motion for her to stay clear of the puddle. When Faven pointed, Amandine nodded and crouched down carefully, prodding at the body with the tip of a dagger she removed from her boot. It made a clear, ringing sound against the dead man's skin, like a bell.

"Correct me if I'm wrong here, but this fellow doesn't appear to be cryst-born, yet he's gone to the scale."

"You're correct," Faven said.

Amandine looked up, searching Faven's face for an answer she couldn't give her.

"It works on humans?"

"It shouldn't." Faven placed her hands on her hips and eyed the pillar with the glimmering light floating within—and didn't like the shape of the idea that took root in her mind.

"Navi, you look like someone just pissed on your grave."

"I won't have a grave," she said off-handedly, and was surprised at the depth of the frown that creased Amandine's face. "I have no proof. But I suspect... This amniotic fluid is far more potent than what the cryst-born use now." She gestured to the light within the pillars. "And does that not look familiar to you? Like the art the cryst left behind, depicting themselves?"

Amandine craned her neck around. Her face slackened. "You're kidding."

"I'm not."

"It's alive."

"It seems that way."

Amandine stood, slowly, tapping the flat of her dagger against her thigh, and took in the whole of the landscape once more. Thousands of birthing pillars stretched in all directions, countless as they were lost to the curve of the horizon. Many of those pillars held similar lights.

"The *Black Celeste* isn't a planet, or a ship," Amandine said, and glanced sideways at Faven for confirmation.

"It's a womb," Faven said. "A birthing ground for the cryst."

FORTY

Amandine

The trouble with being human was that, even if you found yourself stranded on the planet-sized womb of an alien species, you still had to deal with petty biological facts—like survival and finding some way to get off the womb before the owners noticed and decided you'd overstayed your welcome.

"Are the birthing pillars for the cryst-born usually that large?" Amandine asked as they trudged back to the *Marquette*.

"Not at all."

"I was afraid you'd say that."

Faven's face contorted with about a dozen different emotions before she settled on tired resignation. "Listen, Amandine, there's something you should know."

Amandine squinted at her. "There's a lot of things I'm guessing I should know, but that's usually a proclamation someone makes before they're about to say something mighty unpleasant."

"I don't know what it all means." She laid that out like she could circle the truth. Hem it in neat and tidy before revealing its ugliness. "But there are fewer and fewer cryst-born being born every year."

"How few are we talking?"

"None, this year."

"You're shittin' me."

"I'm not entirely certain what that would entail, but I speak the truth. My people, well…" It took her a minute to rally up the nerve. Amandine didn't hold the pause against her. It was a hard thing, letting your secrets all come bubbling to the surface. "Gail-liard told me that a research team had been sent to the Clutch to investigate methods to revitalize our fecundity. This fluid… I can't help but think they might be trying to repeat what our ancestors accomplished. Convert more humans into cryst-born."

"That the same man who put you on that sabotaged Bladeship?"

"And the child you saved."

That had a flavor of cyclicality to it that Amandine didn't much like. Felt like a rope around her neck, tying her back to the *Black Celeste* and whatever cursed experiments the navis got up to out here.

She thought of that tracker, never checked out of storage. Of Kester's words—*it is our duty to protect*—so closely mirroring the *Marquette*'s assertion that it was safety.

Thought all that, and shoved it back down in the dark of herself. She only had the mental bandwidth for one meltdown at a time.

"You think she's here somewhere?" Amandine asked. "Your mentor?"

"I do. And I'm sorry, I will help you get the *Marquette* in work-ing order so that you can leave if that's what you want, but I can't leave until I find her."

Faven looked so terribly solemn and regretful that Amandine laughed. "Don't be stupid."

"What does that mean?" An angry shade of plum darkened her cheeks.

"I left you behind once before, and you see the trouble it's caused me. Think I'm daft enough to do it again?"

Her smile was so bright and sudden that it startled Amandine.

That old cliché—she lit up—found new meaning when the woman grinning ear to ear at you was cryst-born, and quite literally shone from within, the scale at the corner of her lips pulsing with soft light. Amandine's chest tightened.

"C'mon," she grumbled. "Put that smile out before you blind me. We got work to do."

Kester and Tully had gone unusually quiet, both of them stomping along under the weight of the salvage strapped to their backs. Amandine glanced at them, frowning to herself. Stumbling across an alien birthing ground was the kind of thing that should have sent Tully into a tizzy of wild speculation. Their lips were sealed shut, eyes downcast.

"Do you have any idea who sent Amber Jacq the message with these coordinates?" Faven asked, voice bright—the woman liked a puzzle. It'd be charming, if said puzzle wasn't responsible for the death of her original crew and the peril of those present.

"Haven't a clue," Amandine said through short breaths—lightdrive shielding was heavier than she remembered. Or maybe Jacq's was so old it was a clunkier version. "The captain didn't exactly take his freshest hire into his confidences."

"Pity," Faven said with a small pout. "It would be good to know if the Black Celeste itself lured you here, or if the Choir had done so."

"How are either of those options good?"

"Well, it would tell us if the Black Celeste was likely to be hostile, to start with."

Amandine could have sworn that the shifting plates of glass beneath their feet took that statement as a chance to groan dramatically. She shot the ground a glare, which didn't do anything, but made her feel better.

"We're operating under the assumption that everything is hostile. Even my own cursed ship."

"Which you found here," Faven said.

Amandine didn't answer the implied questions that swirled on the end of that statement. She didn't know how to. Her memories of her time in the Clutch were hectic. A fever dream rendered incomprehensible by lightsickness and blood loss.

"Or maybe the ship found me," Amandine found herself saying, and wished she hadn't as Faven's eyes narrowed with calculation.

"The thought had occurred to me."

"Trouble is, Navi, that even if that ship sought out a person to get it out of the Clutch, it's clear it wanted to come back. We're in for a struggle, if we want to fly it back to help Turtar Glas once we're done here."

"I'm prepared for its tricks, now," she said with such casual confidence that Amandine almost laughed—but bit the sound off, lest she offend the navi.

"We'll see" was all Amandine would say.

Amandine sent her protesting crew out to patrol the perimeter and let herself back into the darkened halls of the *Marquette*, her HUD glass providing enough illumination to see by. She'd been tempted to leave the navi outside, too, in case she mucked up the shielding somehow and poisoned them all when she powered the ship back on, but she didn't want to let her out of her sight again.

"We're back," she said over comms. "Light levels look low enough in the engine bay, so I'm going to start patching the shielding. Kester and Tully are storing our extra salvage and sweeping the perimeter."

"Cap'n," Becks said, "wait a moment. I can be there in no time."

"Sit tight. I got it."

Becks grumbled at her, making her smile. She had no doubt they'd be out that door before Amandine finished the installation—if only to fuss over her work and tell her she'd done it all wrong, even if she hadn't.

She slung the canvas wrapping the shielding panes off her back and set it carefully on the ground beside the dormant drive, then retrieved a set of tools from a bulkhead storage compartment.

"May I help?" Faven asked.

Amandine eyed those muscular arms and nodded. "The shielding needs to be handled with care, even if it's busted. We might be able to use the scrap for patching later. I'm going to loosen these bolts—" She gestured to the set on one end of a long pane of the enclosure. "Then the ones on the other side. Once I'm done, I'll need you to help me ease it down flat without breaking it."

"I can do that." Faven rolled up her flowing sleeves and, by the virtue of some hidden button, pinned them in place, revealing the scale spreading over the backs of her hands and twining up her arms.

"Don't touch anything I don't tell you to touch."

They worked well together, peeling away the thin panes that shielded the drive. With each petal of cryst removed, Amandine ran her palm over the panes, frowning at their thinness—at the brittle *ting* when she tapped a nail against them. Becks had been underselling how worn-out they'd grown. These were practically gauze compared to the robust panes she'd scavenged.

She picked up one of the fresh panes, motioning for Faven to help her balance the long weight. The navi's face pinched when she touched it.

"Is the shielding meant to be cryst-glass?" she asked.

"It is," Amandine said. "The old stuff is barely recognizable as cryst, isn't it?"

Faven's lips parted, mouth sagging halfway open, and with a delicate grunt to clear her throat she said hesitantly, "Amandine. The panels we removed were never cryst at all."

Amandine looked up, startled, prepared to tell Faven she must be incorrect—they'd all be constantly lightsick, if the shielding wasn't cryst—and found Becks's shadow looming in the open doorway, a deep frown on their face that wiped away all her protests.

"I really wish you hadn't said that," Becks said.

FORTY-ONE

Amandine

Cheaping out on the shielding wasn't the action of the Becks Amandine knew. They were always harping on and on about how she needed to take better care of the ship—how they needed to focus their efforts on parts and retrofitting. A cold sensation slithered over in Amandine's belly and she eased the pane she'd been working on back to the ground, rising slowly into a tense, ready stance with the wrench gripped tight in one hand.

"Faven. Get behind me."

For once, she followed the order without question.

Becks frowned. "I'm not going to hurt the navi. You know that, Cap'n."

"The Becks I know wouldn't replace the drive shielding with plain glass, either. That you, *Marquette*? Did you find a way to get into my crew's minds now, too?"

They eased off the doorframe and moved into the room, stopping on the other side of the lightdrive when Amandine tightened her grip on the wrench in warning.

"You need to leave," Becks said.

"Leave? It's my own ship, and I won't be stranded on this thrice-cursed hunk of glass. Not again."

"You don't get it." Becks was breathing hard, now. Red blotched their cheeks. "You gotta get out, Cap'n, quick. The *Marquette*, it can't help it—it doesn't know any better anymore."

They looked likely to lose their lunch all over her floor. Amandine frowned, taking a hesitant step toward them. Faven made a soft sound of protest and grabbed the back of her coat, stopping her advance.

Their breathing smoothed. Their back straightened. The hairs on the back of Amandine's neck prickled as they looked around the engine bay with strangely doleful eyes.

"You know," they said, voice back to normal. "I've enjoyed you as my captain. We could have carried on until the end of your days together. I wanted to. I loved this...this freedom. But I've abandoned my duty for far too long. I ran away." They held out their hands, turning them over as they examined them. "I didn't know I could do that."

Amandine cracked her jaw. "Get out of Becks."

"I am not *in* anything."

"Amandine," Faven said, voice pitched with an incoming question that Amandine was certain she wasn't going to like, "how long ago was that shielding last replaced?"

"Hard to say," she admitted. "We've been patching it. Doing it in pieces."

"We?" Faven pressed.

Amandine let loose a ragged sigh, shoulders rounding. "Becks has. I don't—I don't understand. Why aren't we all raving mad? Why aren't we all *dead*?"

"Because I am whole, and capable of controlling my light levels."

"All this time you had me bleeding my pocketbook dry to fix something that didn't need fixing?"

"Amandine," Faven said sharply. "I don't believe that's pertinent at the moment."

But Faven didn't see the truth hiding beneath that question. Years spent patching and fixing and diverting every rare cent she had to keep their home safe, and it had always seemed to become critical whenever they were getting close to getting ahead.

Whenever she got a step closer to the money needed to see her set up back on Blackloach for the rest of her life.

She'd always known she wouldn't make it back, and that wasn't about the money. Blackloach was a dream. The kind you pin to the corkboard in your mind and orient yourself around, even though you know it's forever out of reach.

But she needed that. Needed something to strive for that wasn't something that could hurt if she never caught it.

"We didn't want you to go," Becks said, and the sadness in their voice almost broke her heart.

"You would have kept me caged on this ship forever?"

"Is it a cage if you don't know there are bars?"

"Yes," Amandine and Faven said in accidental unison.

Amandine glanced back at the navi, surprised by the vehemence in her voice. She rolled a shoulder, feigning nonchalance, but her fists were clenched tight.

"I'm sorry, Cap'n. I truly am. But it's time for you to leave."

Becks stepped closer. In Amandine's experience, people moving toward her with ill intent were usually set on violence, but she hesitated, tensing instead of reaching for the shotgun strapped across her back.

She didn't want to hurt Becks. The sad smile the *Marquette* gave her said the blasted ship knew as much—and was more than willing to use that hesitance against her.

Tully and Kester filtered into the room behind Becks, both faces drawn with concern as they took in the scene. Amandine's heart lifted, hoping they could restrain the mechanic without excess violence, then fell, as Kester's piercing gaze flicked to the disassembled lightdrive and she said, softly, "I see."

"What's goin' on, Cap'n?" Tully asked, their warm voice all quizzical innocence.

"The *Marquette*'s taken over Becks," Amandine said.

"Andielle," the *Marquette* said, frowning. "There's never been a Becks."

FORTY-TWO

Amandine

Amandine's first reaction—to laugh in their face—died on her lips at the somber, concerned look in Becks's eyes. Long ago, when Sere had finished nursing Amandine back to health after she'd washed up on Turtar Glas, Sere had told her: *You're on your own now, Amandine. A pirate without a crew is a poor one indeed. Take care, select your people, but also let them select you. Know their moods better than you know your own. A happy crew will throw themselves in the line of fire for you. A bored crew will throw you in the fire just to watch you burn.*

She hadn't wanted a crew. Not for a long time. The memory of Jacq's people being routed had been too fresh—the details smudged by lightsickness, but the screams and the blood and the bowel-shaking terror finding their way into her dreams most nights. She'd kept her thefts small, her world smaller. Had barely deigned to set foot off the ship, if she could help it, for fear of finding camaraderie that'd one day die as bloody as Jacq did and add its screams to the choir in her heart.

Becks hadn't given her much choice. They'd shown up on one of the rare days she'd put in at a dock and been discovered poking around her engine cones, telling her if she kept running the ship so hot she'd strip the enamel.

She should have kicked them out, but she'd been charmed by their gruff nature and amused by their desire to get away from the crummy little station they'd been living on. *Just to see something different*, they'd said.

Becks was her right hand. She knew them better than she knew herself, and the annoyed scrunch to their brow, their clear frustration with her slowness—that was Becks, and no other.

"How?" Amandine asked, when all other words failed her.

"You needed a crew to range wider, Cap'n, and I needed to collect more data."

"What *are* you?" Amandine demanded.

"I think I know," Faven said. Kester gave her a look that screamed threat, but the navi kept on talking, voice bright with the excitement of discovery. "You are the *Black Celeste*, are you not? This planet—the whole thing is a birthing ground, not just the pillars. The very plates of the ground can shift, change. Become what's needed. Amandine was dying, and your purpose is to preserve life, isn't it? So you budded off a ship to save her. Amandine." Faven clutched her arm. "You're the captain of the *Black Celeste*!"

Amandine winced. "Can't say I share your enthusiasm. Nothing good ever happens to the captains of ghost ships. Is what she said true?"

"I consider us more of a security system," Kester said. "But yes, that is close enough to true."

"So what now?" Amandine asked. "What happens next? You're home. You going to re-bond or whatever with the mothership and do what? Play midwife to a bunch of cryst?"

"Not exactly," Becks said. "It's like Kester said: We're a security system. We will secure the crèche for the birthing. And, I'm sorry to say, Cap'n, that humanity won't be invited. Your debt's come due."

"We did tell you to leave." Kester's voice was taut, thin sweat misting her neck. Holding herself back. Becks had the same look about them—strained, their hand braced against the lightdrive as if they could push themself back.

The greater mind of the *Black Celeste* was slipping under their skin. Exerting control. Filing away their individuality, and void-damn that thing for subverting what they worked so hard to earn for themselves.

"What debt?" she asked, scrambling for some way to slow this down. To stop it from escalating.

Kester said, "You survive by pillaging the corpses of our creators."

"Pillaging the *what*?" Tully squeaked.

Becks and Kester turned to them, startled.

Amandine didn't think Kester or Becks wanted to hurt her, but as a rule, Amandine responded to any variation of someone telling her that her debt was due with extreme prejudice. They were distracted. She'd never get a better opening.

"Let them go!" She swung the wrench with all her strength into the side of the lightdrive.

The thunderous snap of cryst cracking jerked Becks and Kester back around, but it was too late. The fluid in the drive burst forth, spraying Amandine's hand, and she had about a second to think—*oh, really?*—as her right hand and wrist stiffened, the skin itching and growing numb in waves as cryst-scale encased her hand, freezing it around the wrench, before Faven pulled her back.

There was a great deal of shouting then, from every party involved. Becks, standing closer to the burst drive than the rest, took the brunt of the assault. Their left side transmuted to gleaming cryst-scale. Kester threw up an arm, protecting her face from the splashes that made it around Becks, and hissed as she recoiled.

Amandine wanted to be sick. She hadn't thought—she'd just wanted to break the connection between the *Marquette* and her crew.

Becks roared. Amandine had never heard them make that sound

before, a guttural bellow that froze her in place. They lunged, eyes wide and red-ringed, one hand out like they were ready to wring Amandine's neck, and for once, she believed they'd go through with it.

Tully swept Becks's ankles and leapt over them, eyes bulging as they ran for the nearest exit. Amandine found her senses once more, whirling about to grab Faven by the arm and herd her through the twisting halls.

The three of them stumbled together out of the airlock and spun around, looking for any direction that seemed particularly promising, but it was the same as it had ever been—endless cryst-pane flooring, pillars, and clinging mist.

"The crash site," Faven panted, and thrust a finger that direction. "When you were in the ship, I thought I sensed—I don't know. A way down. A doorway."

"Do we want to go into the big spooky planet?" Tully demanded. "Don't tell me they don't have horror movies in the Spire, Navi. Never, ever go into the basement!"

"Unless you'd rather run in a random direction and hope for the best?" Faven countered.

Tully's lips twisted up. "Isn't that exactly what we're doing?"

Amandine pinched her temples with her good hand. "Crash site. The missing navis must be somewhere around here, and whatever weird shit they're doing, we need answers. I'm not leaving Kester and Becks to get mind-melded back into whatever the fuck this thing is. Turn your comms off. Until we can be certain they've been severed from the mothership, or whatever, we don't want them to track us."

"But it's—it's Kester and Becks, Cap'n! If we talked to them, if we all cool our heels and—"

"We just tried talking! They were sweating through their damn clothes struggling to maintain their autonomy! We go back there after this, they'd be in the right to take my head off."

"You didn't know—"

"I don't know anything, apparently! Shit." Amandine looked at her scaled hand, then away. Too much to deal with. Focus on what mattered. "We need a better idea of what's really going on here. Clear?"

Tully groaned dramatically but buttoned their lips at Amandine's slash of a glare. She didn't have time to come up with a better idea—anything that got them farther from the *Marquette* at the moment was a win, as far as she was concerned.

She needed space to think. To untangle what had happened, and what she was going to do about it, because as much as she loved Becks and Kester and the *Marquette* itself, she didn't know what it meant to love an illusion.

Didn't know if that illusion had ever been capable of loving her back.

FORTY-THREE

Faven

Faven didn't mean to stare at Amandine's frozen hand, but she couldn't help stealing glances. The crystallization fluid wasn't supposed to work on those who weren't cryst-born. Unless Faven had been sorely mistaken about Amandine's origins, the pirate was no such thing.

If it had been the more potent version in the pillars, then that might make some sense, but—Faven glanced at Amandine's cheek, where a droplet of the fluid had landed.

Her cheek was unmarred.

She kept thinking of that disembodied arm, reaching for Jacq. Of the bandana so obviously cousin to the one tied around her own wrist. It was possible that Amandine had loaned some other pirate one of her bandanas, but somehow Faven couldn't quite make herself believe that.

If it was Amandine's arm, what then? Such a wound would have been fatal without treatment. Faven recalled the fading vision she'd had of Kester pouring her own blood into Faven's wound, and doubted that it had been a hallucination.

They skidded to a halt near Amber Jacq's body. Amandine looked to Faven, brows up in silent question.

"A moment." Faven turned slowly, struggling to summon the inner world of starpath meditations, but her mind was too slippery, focus impossible. There was a way down, she was sure of it, but she couldn't find where that path began. "Do you still have my armillary? That may help."

Amandine stiffened, her hand dropping to the circular shape pressing against her coat at her waistband. Faven hadn't quite considered the depth of what she was asking until she saw the hesitation writ clear in every line of Amandine's wary stance.

Amandine's mother was dead. Those who'd been closest to her had betrayed her trust. She could scarcely trust her own mind—and here Faven was, unpredictable, still partially lightsick herself, asking for a weapon. A weapon with a tracker she hadn't yet had a chance to explain.

"The beacon you saw—that was to call Gailliard to my side, if I found myself in peril. I never used it, Amandine. I swear to you, I didn't know the Blademother could, or would, find me."

"Yeah." Amandine turned in the direction of the *Marquette*, a deep frown carving her face. "I was afraid it was something like that."

"I will return it to you once I've found my way," Faven added, voice soft.

Amandine's posture slackened, and she tugged the armillary from her belt. "Keep it."

Their fingers brushed as Faven took the armillary back, but Faven set aside that kindling warmth and spun the armillary to life, accessing the starpath Ulana had woven.

It had always been the end of the path that'd stymied her. The motions too minute, too tangled, making no sense at all in the context of ships and space and the endless, swallowing void. But some sense, perhaps, if reduced to the scale of people on the back of a ghost ship that had never been a ship at all, but a constructed world.

Faven pulled up that twisting mire and laid it over the landscape.

A startled laugh escaped her. Part of her hadn't really expected it to work, but the shining golden threads that had tied her heart in knots all this time revealed their purpose—conforming to the shifting ground, the towering pillars.

"The ending was never a starpath at all," Faven said, half to herself, but caught Amandine slide her an admiring smile.

"Let's see where this bread trail leads, then, shall we?" Amandine asked.

Tully squinted at it. "We're really gonna follow the suspicious glowing path into the metaphorical dark and unknown woods, aren't we?"

"Got a better idea?" Amandine asked.

Tully sighed heavily in answer, drawing a thin laugh out of Amandine and a clap on the shoulder. Faven found it remarkable how quickly the pirate could rally herself—but then, that was how she'd lived her life, wasn't it? Improvising every step of the way. Faven couldn't quite puzzle out why the thought made her melancholy, and decided to reexamine the sentiment later, when she was less exhausted.

It took all of Faven's concentration to follow that path. She led them past the field of battle and deep into the pillars until the ground began to slope downward, a ramp leading into a long, darkened hallway.

"Wait." Amandine touched her shoulder to stop her descent. "Tully, take my shotgun and go first."

"Excuse me?" Tully crossed their arms and huffed. "I didn't agree to this plan; why do I have to go first?"

Amandine's jaw cracked. "Because I've only got one hand free."

A strange sensation slithered over in Faven's stomach—pity, perhaps? No, she'd felt that often enough and could recognize it easily. Guilt, maybe? That one was unusual for her. Faven stole a glance at Amandine's face and found her expression awash with too many emotions for her to dissect any one of them. Catching her looking, Amandine smiled. Faven smiled back impulsively, and wondered why she'd done so, when her mood was far from pleased.

Faven guided Tully down the ramp and into a cavernous chamber. Rectangular in shape, it rose nearly four stories tall. The plates above their heads were semitransparent, letting in a little of the planet's light. Darker patches that might have been entryways pocked the walls above their heads.

"Look at this," Amandine said.

She swerved off the main path, approaching the shadow-draped walls. Mosaic scenes in shades of black, deepest violet, and indigo painted the wall in a long, narrow band. Faven touched her fingers to the rough texture, over an image of a birthing pillar.

Beside that scene was another depicting a human lifting their arms to the heavens, with one of the nine-pointed lights shining down on them from above. To the right, the same human, she suspected, only their arms were etched with the evidence of scale. Farther along, the human figure was placed within a birthing pillar. The scale that encased their body had grown. Stretched. Began to look like panes of cryst-glass, sheeting off of a scarcely recognizable humanoid form. Faven hissed and pulled back from the wall.

"You don't think . . . ?" She looked to Amandine, who had been following along with her. Amandine rubbed her scaled hand.

"I don't know what to think."

"Look." Faven gestured upward, where the same series of scenes repeated, only this time the human figure had been replaced with a bipedal species she didn't recognize.

Amandine flicked on a light from her HUD glass and shined it upward. The walls were covered in similar scenes, the place of a human taken by some other being in each. None were species Faven recognized.

"Does this look like . . . a life cycle to anyone else?" Amandine asked.

"It does." Faven ran her palm over the surface of the closest sequence, and light shimmered beneath her touch. "Look. There's another layer of data here."

"Where?" Amandine squinted, leaning closer in entirely the wrong spot.

"Ah. You can't see it. Give me a moment." She trailed her hands up the walls, craning her neck. "Each sequence is accompanied by a starpath. There are some phrases—words I can't read— but they're notated with the same symbols we use for designing starpaths. Every path, save the one above the sequence with the humans, is marked as—well. A dead end, more or less. 'Nothing of value remains' would be the accurate translation."

"I don't like the sound of that," Amandine said.

"It gets stranger." Faven pushed to her toes to better see. "There is a range of dates on each. The styling is old, but if I'm doing the calculation correctly, each covers precisely a thousand years. Humanity's sequence only shows the start date, no end."

"Let me guess. We're exactly a thousand years from that start date, now?"

"No." Faven frowned at the number, double- and triple-checking it as a lick of fear slithered cold down her spine. "Two thousand."

Tully whistled softly.

"Why do I get the feeling that's worse?" Amandine asked.

"I can't imagine it's good," Faven said.

"C'mon," Tully said. "We can't sit around and make guesses about a bunch of old art."

"Right," Amandine said, but she was having a hard time tearing her eyes away from the mosaics. "Lead on, goddess."

Ulana's map urged them onward, through the long chamber, into yet another space so large Faven couldn't see the edges clearly enough to define its shape. Hexagonal pillars twin to those they'd seen on the surface filled the room, in no particular pattern that

Faven could discern. These were all empty of the lights they'd seen above. Faven slipped the armillary back into her sleeve and approached one.

A set of stairs wrapped up the pillar—human construction added after the fact, she suspected—and she noted a thin division in the middle of the empty pillars, separating two kinds of fluid. All Faven could manage to say as she pressed her palm against the empty, bisected pillar was "I see."

"What is it?" Amandine peered over her shoulder.

"The pillars on the surface lacked this division." Faven pointed to the separation between chambers. "But these, without the lights, are birthing chambers for the cryst-born. We're drawing closer to my kin." Faven turned slowly, taking in the pillars, and found their number too great to count.

Amandine gestured to the dividing line. "Above is where the cryst-shard is placed to grow into the shape of a person, and then it descends into the bottom chamber to be demineralized into flesh, correct?"

"Yes," Faven said, and waited for the question she knew was coming, but didn't know how to answer.

"Can the fluid in the second chamber be used to fix my arm?" She held up her hand, still clutching the wrench.

"Perhaps," Faven said. "The demineralization fluid was tried on scale before, but it never worked after the birthing was complete. But you are ... The crystallization fluid is not supposed to work on those who aren't cryst-born."

"My arm disagrees." Amandine let out an explosive breath and turned away, as if unable to look at the pillar much longer. "Where does the path lead now?"

"This way." Faven gestured to the center aisle of the long chamber.

They carried on down the endless rows, Tully practically bouncing with nervous energy, Amandine stalking like a hunting cat, all her boisterous swagger ripped away. Faven found she had a curious urge to ask the pirate if she was okay—which was a ludicrous question. Of course she wasn't. Faven swallowed the words down and focused on following Ulana's path. Hours passed with only their footsteps and harsh breath echoing through the halls.

"We're nearing the end," Faven said, when the final threads of Ulana's starpath wound down to frayed slivers.

Ahead, the gentle thrum of machines broke the endless silence. A doorway stood open, yawning and bright, into a larger chamber. The soft murmur of voices joined the low sound of the machines. Indistinct, but harsh with the tenor of argument. She thought she could pick out the stern voice of Ulana, and smiled to herself.

Faven turned to Amandine, prepared to tell the pirate to wait while she went ahead to speak with her mentor, but the words died on her lips. Amandine's world had been upended, her dearest turned against her. There was no guarantee Faven's world wouldn't suffer the same fate.

Before meeting the pirate, Faven would have sauntered into that room without a second thought, assured of her safety. Now, she knew better.

"My kin are likely to be within," Faven said. "They will destroy you on sight, but they might speak with me. I'll go in first to cause a distraction and extract as much information as I can, but I need you to use the opportunity to discover the truth of what they're doing here. Whatever it may be."

"You want to go in alone?" Amandine shook her head. "Not a chance."

"Do you still not trust me? I won't betray your presence to my kin."

"It's not you sellin' me out I'm worried about. Someone tried to get you killed before you could make it here, and they're gonna be none too happy to find you knocking on their door. I don't know what's going on here, but I'm guessing your navis have something to do with why the *Marquette* said the crèche was calling it home for the birthing. We're staying together. That's nonnegotiable."

"I am not negotiating," Faven said.

Amandine tried to glare her into submission, she really did, but Faven didn't so much as blink. Eventually, Amandine sighed. "You realize your life has no value to those people, don't you? Won't be any skin off their noses to cut you down where you stand, if the mood strikes them."

"Yes," she said, and found herself smiling. "I'm looking forward to feeling true peril at last."

Tully grinned and clapped Faven on the back hard enough to make her gasp in surprise. "I'm starting to like you, Faven Sythe."

FORTY-FOUR

Amandine

Amandine felt a touch guilty about letting the navi stroll ahead to spring whatever trap awaited. But she found, strangely, that she did trust Faven Sythe. At least, she trusted her not to get herself killed in the next ten minutes or so, which was all she'd need to get into position.

When Faven was out of earshot, her slim profile disappearing into that wide-opened door, Tully leaned down to hiss-whisper, "You sure about this, Cap'n? The navi means well, but she hasn't exactly been reliable, has she? We should cut bait and bolt. I bet the Choir has ships around here somewhere, and what's a pirate good for, if not absconding with a ship?"

"Thought you said you liked her."

"I like her causing a distraction so that we can get outta here."

Amandine snorted. "We're not ditching the navi. I need answers about what's been happening here, and if she can get 'em for me, then that's what we're doing."

"You sure you want those answers?"

Did she? The question gave her pause, Tully's unusually solemn expression weighing down her thoughts. Tully had always struck her as the most resilient member of her crew—able to laugh their way through the biggest disasters. Maybe that hadn't been resilience. Maybe it was just carefully crafted denial.

Amandine could relate. Ever since the day she'd first landed in the Clutch, she'd spent her whole life avoiding coming back. Had tucked the events of that day carefully down in the dark recesses of her mind, where they could only escape to bother her in nightmares.

Every job they'd ever taken that'd brought them within spitting distance of the place had set her heart to thumping. Made her glance over her shoulder, waiting for the claws of her past to drag her back down. But here she was. Running willingly into the dark.

Easier to rip open the scars of your past for the sake of others. She hadn't even thought about what she was doing—had only thought that Kester and Becks needed help, and this was where she might find that help.

Maybe that instinct was what made her a good captain. Maybe it was what made her a good friend. Probably it was what was about to make her a dead woman.

"If there's a way to let Kester and Becks be themselves, I gotta find it."

"You think . . ." Tully swallowed. "You think they really can be their own selves again?"

"Sure," Amandine said. "They've been doing it all this while, haven't they?"

"Yeah." Tully's grin flashed back into place, as if nothing had happened. "They sure have."

"Come on." Amandine pointed to a wall visible through the open door, and a thin set of stairs that ran up the wall to join a catwalk network above. "We need to get eyes on the situation."

Amandine pressed a finger to her lips and led the way to the door, keeping her back flat against the wall. She urged her heart to slow its frantic thumping and strained to listen. Faven's soft steps drifted farther away.

Then, a voice she didn't know: "What are you doing here?"

"I've come to speak with Ulana Valset," Faven said with cold dignity.

There were a great deal of confused people talking all at once then, but no shouts of alarm. Amandine gestured for Tully to follow her and slipped into the room, heading for the stairs. They were partially obscured by one of the pillars. She found their construction firm, not letting out so much as a squeak, as she and Tully climbed high to the ceiling of the chamber. Choir engineering, she mused. Spared no expense.

This high up, the transparency of the plates above their heads became clearer, the mists on the planet occasionally darkening sections, like clouds across a sky. Amandine knelt beside Tully on a catwalk, peering down into the room.

Armed people in the livery of the Choir's internal guard had arrayed themselves between Faven and what seemed to be an area of the chamber set aside for terminals and other varieties of computers and monitoring equipment. The armed contingent was clearly at a loss regarding what they were supposed to do, as Faven demanded in increasingly exasperated tones to speak with her mentor. Curious, that there were no Blades to be seen.

The commotion was enough to draw the attention of those working at the terminals, heads lifting and turning Faven's direction. Scale marred some of those faces, and they wore robes similar in style to Faven's own. Tully tapped Amandine on the shoulder. She turned, following their point, and had to stifle a sharp intake of breath by shoving a hand over her mouth.

A woman transmuted to cryst-scale floated in the pillar closest to them. Her eyes were open, hands upstretched as if she'd been reaching for the surface, the unfurled banner of her robes flowing around her. There was a pinched look to the woman's face—frustration, perhaps, or confusion. Some of the scale on her arm had grown wider than her flesh should allow, extruded outward into the semblance of a pane of cryst-glass in miniature, just like the mosaics.

"That's not normal, is it?" Tully whispered.

Amandine shook her head and matched their whisper. "No. Faven said they all form like this, more or less, but I sincerely doubt they start out life fully grown and wearing clothes."

"Cap'n. Look."

Tully gestured to the other pillars. It took a moment for Amandine's eyes to adjust. The scaled bodies were teal, a similar shade to the fluid that enveloped them, and blended well. But not all of them had transmuted completely yet, and as Amandine examined the pillars one by one, she found glimpses of unmarred skin on many of the suspended navigators. Hundreds of pillars. Perhaps thousands. None of those carried the lights they'd found above.

"I think we found the missing navigators," Amandine whispered.

"Are they dead?"

"I don't think they're that lucky."

Tully muttered a soft curse under their breath. Something about the nearby woman's expression was familiar, though Amandine couldn't quite pin it down. She leaned closer, squinting through the gloom. Despite the pinched look frozen on the woman's face, there was something serene about her. Fine grooves traced swirling paths in her eyes, and her lips were parted, the muscles of her mouth tensed in such a way to indicate she'd been speaking when she'd finally lost her voice, if not her life.

Wake.

Amandine drew back, thinking she'd lost her mind at last, but it was only an echo of a memory, made all the more intense by this place. The woman had the same expression Faven had worn when the lightdrive of the Bladeship had gone critical. The same expression; the same geometries in the eyes.

There was a commotion among the navigators. A tall, silver-haired woman had risen from their midst and was striding purposefully toward Faven and the guards. Faven noticed her, and in a flash, her demeanor changed, eyes brightening, as she turned and held out her arms.

"Ulana!"

"Faven, sweet child." Ulana Valset took Faven's outstretched hands and leaned down to brush a kiss against her cheek. "You should not have come here."

Even from so far away, Amandine could see Faven's face fall. Could note the wary confusion settling into her stance, the tilt to her head that said that, no matter what was going on, she didn't understand why her mentor would not want her.

Amandine closed her eyes briefly and pressed her forehead against the cold metal railing. If Sere had been there, she'd have scruffed Amandine and carried her out, then shaken her until her teeth cracked together for being a fool.

The thought made her smile. Amandine rallied and pointed to another set of stairs leading down near the navigators. "We're going to have to get closer, because I don't think this is going to be the joyous reunion Faven was hoping for."

Tully's brows crowded up their forehead. "Just us? There're dozens of them."

"Don't worry, Tully." Amandine winked. "I've got one more trick up someone else's sleeve."

FORTY-FIVE

Faven

Faven released Ulana and, as she'd done countless times before, slid her hands within her sleeves. While she let Ulana see confusion on her face, she wrapped her fingers around one of the arms of her armillary and pressed the button on her locator beacon.

Gailliard had given the beacon to her before she'd allowed herself to be taken away to the Clutch, with the understanding that—when all seemed lost—she was to trigger it, and the micro lightdrive of her armillary would transmit her location to Gailliard. While she couldn't be certain who had sabotaged her Bladeship, she was certain that the coldness in her mentor's expression foretold nothing short of impending disaster.

In the corner of her eye, a golden light winked. Faven turned to that light and didn't understand what she was seeing. Not at first.

A man floated in the center of a pillar. His soft grey robes spread around him, face upturned in gentle repose. Not all of his skin had gone to scale, not yet, but patches of clear skin were few. His robes had twisted askew, revealing the fault line of a scar racing over his back, and the cryst-scale that followed it.

A scar twin to the one on Amandine's back.

The comm gem in his ear flashed. Faven's incoming call, never to be answered. She approached. Pressed her palm flat against the pillar.

"Gailliard."

Ulana stood beside her, hands folded solemnly. "He came here looking for you, when you vanished."

"I thought…" *I thought he'd tried to have me killed. I thought he'd forsaken everything we ever were to each other.* "The Clutch was his living nightmare."

"I'm told he took a Bladeship," Ulana said. "Against the advice of the Choir, when he heard your ship had been lost en route."

"He must have been so scared."

"He was."

Faven touched the small sigil hidden away in her pocket and understood part, if not all, of what had happened. Gailliard had come here searching for her, and whether he'd remembered what had happened to him before, or realized it upon his arrival, he'd moved the blade from the hand of a Choir guard into the skeletal grip of Amber Jacq. Trying to force what he thought was true onto the scene. Faven wondered if it had worked. If he'd managed to make himself believe that it was Jacq who had wielded that blade against him, and not his own people.

How easy it would have been, all those years ago, to twist the story around, when those involved were lightsick.

One thing Faven was very, very certain of now was that a navigator—even a child—was more valuable to a pirate alive than dead. A pirate wouldn't kill a cryst-born child. But a member of the Choir might, if that child had been a threat to their power. Amber Jacq had no reason to strike out at Gailliard. Perhaps he'd even been trying to save the boy. Faven smiled a little, at that. The possibility would ease Amandine's heart.

"And yet Gailliard came here anyway," Faven said. "To save me." She removed the sword's sigil and placed it in Ulana's outstretched hand. Her mentor, her mother figure, the woman she'd trusted with her heart and the development of her mind smiled upon it with a tinge of sadness. "From you."

"I'd hoped it wouldn't come to this." Ulana closed her fist around the sigil. "Easier if you had been lost with your ship. Though I must say, I was proud to hear that you had survived."

A swirl of pride, like foul smoke, bloomed within her. Faven squashed it. Of course her ship had been sabotaged in the same way as Ulana's. Ulana had been covering her tracks both times.

"But you left a trail for me to follow. I thought—I thought you needed *help*."

"Help? From you?" The cruel chime of Ulana's laugh hooked burrs into her heart. "A talented weaver you may be, but you have ever lacked the fortitude for difficult work."

"Lacked the—" Her cheeks burned. "I am here! I unwound the path you thought you'd hidden and survived your death trap. I—" Faven held out one cryst-vined arm. "I survived a Blademother's strike and wrested control of a starpath from a council of sixteen. I jumped all of Turtar Glas into the inner rings of the Clutch without proper preparation and kept it whole. You will not treat me like a child."

Ulana took her hand, examining the twisting vine pattern of cryst-scale. A lavender film covered one of her eyes. "Fascinating. Your scale is rife with light."

"What does that *mean*." Faven stopped just short of throwing her arms up in exasperation.

"I suppose there's no harm in freeing you from your ignorance. A reward, then, for having made it this far." Ulana spoke while examining Faven's new patches of scale. Her mentor reached for Faven's other hand, and she gave it freely, biting her lip to keep from comment as Ulana untied the bandana and let it fall to the ground. Ulana's tongue had always been looser when her mind was occupied.

"Well?" Faven prompted.

"We are cryst," she said. "And not some watered-down offshoot, but the real thing, and we always have been."

Faven swallowed but kept her voice in the mildly curious tone she used during Ulana's lessons. "Why lie?"

"I can't say for certain—I wasn't there when the decision was made. Useful cover, I expect. If humanity ever discovered what we were, they might fight against us. This way, they feel indebted to our ancestors. Perhaps they even have a sense of kinship with us."

Faven wondered if Ulana had ever noticed that humanity had been finding plenty of ways to fight back all this time, but kept the thought to herself. "Then why do we look so much like them?"

"As elders, we cryst are beings of immense size and ponderous thought. We are slow to move, to think. But when we're younger, we are capable of transmuting ourselves to flesh. In that state, we rule those lesser lives. We give them our gifts and in return we use our time in skin to make plans to protect our elders, and our species, into the far future."

Faven had the disorienting sensation that she'd had a piece of her life she'd never known she was missing handed back to her. Felt the truth of those words slot into place, connecting her more solidly with her own flesh and scale, and at the distant periphery of her mind, she felt the *Marquette* once more.

Watching. Gently curious. She could sense its wound, a terrible shattering, but more than that its regret. A despair older and deeper than its scuffle with Amandine could account for. It didn't know what to do and it was so, so afraid.

Faven recalled the art she'd studied, as a student. Abstract and ancient, but always a light came, and a light left. And with this seismic shift in her perspective, she knew.

Nothing of value remains.

"The cryst killed them, didn't they? All those civilizations in the mosaics. When they were done taking what they wanted, when they'd learned all they could and the time came for them to grow into their elder form, they wiped them out."

Ulana looked at her then, and she thought she glimpsed real

sorrow in the lowering of her brows. "That was true. In the old ways, when the cryst are finished with a species, we leave no trace behind lest that civilization find a way to track us down. It was kinder, in many ways. We are their gods, and when we leave, we leave nothing but despair."

"And now?"

"When our flesh wears out its welcome, we return to the crèche. Here, the cryst-scale grows. Burgeons into the twisting structures you think of as the remnants of cryst technology."

Faven swallowed, gaze tracking up, to the hexagonal ceiling. To the floor her dirty slippers had trodden over. "We build our ships and stations out of the corpses of our elders?"

"They are not corpses yet."

"They're *alive* when you reforge them to house us?"

"Of course. Without the light of their lives suffusing the glass, the material cannot shield softer bodies from the everyday radiation of the universe. But do not worry so, dear. Your elders are not awake. The Choir sings them a lullaby so that they won't awaken and then continue their life cycle as they have always done. This"— Ulana gestured to the pillars around them, letting her gaze linger on the floating figures—"is a distasteful, but necessary, measure. The elders must rest, or they will move on, and humanity will fall."

"And you?" A traitorous strain rattled her voice. She filled her lungs, feeling the scale of her chest wound stretch, and pressed on. "Will you join them when your time comes?"

Ulana gave her the contemptuous look of a teacher who's just discovered her pupil wasn't paying attention. "Of course. It's only sleeping."

Faven found it hard to believe that those forced into slumber for centuries would consider it only sleeping, but she tamped her anger down. Hammered all she was feeling flat as nails. Or, tried to. She found caging her emotions more difficult than it'd ever been, and could almost feel Amandine laughing good-naturedly at her for this delayed realization. "And my mother? Does she sleep, or sing?"

276 MEGAN E. O'KEEFE

"She sleeps. Only those in the pillars sing, and they, I'm sorry to say, must have some awareness to complete their task. But we do try to make it gentle for them. They are my students, after all. The ones whose minds I deemed suited to submission."

"They're—" Faven's voice rose, and Ulana cut her a sharp look. The second she lost her temper Ulana would grow bored with this exchange. She reached desperately for logic. "But we are dying out, Ulana. Our numbers dwindle every year while you gather more to sing your lullaby. If they lose us all to the lullaby, then humanity will be just as doomed as if the elders awakened."

"You misunderstand me." Ulana tapped a nail against Faven's scale, listening with a tilted head to the soft ting. "I care not for humanity's survival. I wish to keep the elders from awakening so that they will not destroy *us* when they move on. Our elders will not be forgiving, should they wake and realize what has been done to them."

"But we aren't the ones who forced them to slumber in the first place!"

Ulana looked up from Faven's scale at last. "Just because something isn't your fault, dear child, doesn't mean it isn't your problem. The elders must sleep, or this civilization will fall."

"There must be another way than this." Faven gestured forcefully to the endless pillars of her unconscious kin, but her gaze caught on Gailliard, and she found she couldn't look away. "Oh," she said softly.

"I see you understand. Other methods were tried, I promise you that. Gailliard was intentionally born here. We had hoped that a child, raised for the purpose and naive of the outside world, might sing a more persuasive lullaby so that we could lessen the number of those required for the choir. A disaster, I'm afraid. He nearly woke them all."

Faven began to laugh. A low, gravelly sound from deep within her belly. Ulana turned to her, surprise on her face. Faven took a breath, flicking a mirthful tear off her cheek. "Oh, Ulana. Gailliard woke more than you can possibly imagine."

FORTY-SIX

Amandine

Amandine was close enough to Faven that she could make out the dark circles under her eyes, the spread of cryst-scale over the backs of her hands. It was hard to think of such a small person as something that could grow into an intergalactic spaceship. But, then, Faven had never been human, and Amandine had only been fooling herself to think of the navigator in human terms.

Ulana had the look of someone who was deeply disappointed in the actions of a recalcitrant child, and her shoulders rounded with a muted sigh. "Do you think I don't know where you've been hiding? I can taste it on you."

That was high on the list of the creepiest things Amandine had ever heard another soul say, but before she could fully process it, Ulana had raised her hand above the back of Faven's, and the line of scale there began to change.

It surged upward, the aquamarine scales growing into a long, curving plane of glass that extended, clawlike, from the back of Faven's hand.

She cried out, dropping to her knees, and Amandine had taken a step before she realized it, Tully's hand a firm anchor.

"Plan first," Tully whispered sharply.

It galled that they were right, but luckily—for once—Ulana seemed to have finished her twisted demonstration.

"The light of the black cryst is so rich that even being near it has infused your scale with its potentiate state. Fascinating," Ulana mused, then turned to the guards. "I am finished. Send her to her rest."

Faven surged upward from her knees and slashed her new talon viciously across Ulana's face. Amandine's mouth sagged open with surprise as a spray of brilliant blood arced through the air. Ulana rocked back a few steps and brought her hands up to cover her wound. Not a fighter's reaction. Good to know.

"Guards!" Ulana roared.

"You're dooming us all!" Faven shouted as the guards swarmed her.

Ulana spat blood. "Stupid girl. Do you think we haven't weathered a birthing before? I will take as many as I must to soothe the crèche, and when it's over, I'll scrap your bodies and free splinters of your light to return to be birthed again."

Faven swore with such foul eloquence that Amandine was impressed. The guards wrestled her toward one of the unoccupied pillars. Ulana didn't seem inclined to do Amandine any favors by getting distracted in the next few minutes.

"What should we do?" Tully whispered.

"We're going to have to save the goddess."

Tully wrinkled their nose. "Tall order. Got a plan?"

"One, but it's terrible." Amandine gave them a toothy grin.

Tully grinned right back at her. Of all the members of her crew to be pinned down with, at least Tully was the most fun.

"Listen, Tully...If this goes sideways, I want you to turn tail. Bolt back to the *Marquette*, and tell Kester what we've just learned."

Their face fell. "What if the *Black Celeste* is still controllin' her?"

Amandine put a hand on their shoulder and held their eyes. "I think they might listen to you."

Tully seemed on the verge of saying something, but eventually they merely nodded, forcing a smile. Amandine took a breath, straightened her torn and bloodstained coat, and plastered on her best we're-all-friends-here smile.

With her cryst-scale hand in her pocket, she strolled out into the middle of the gathering, whistling a bawdy tune. She paused a few dozen strides away from Ulana and her guards when they noticed her approach.

"Bitter Amandine," Ulana said, amused. The slash along her face was already sealing, cryst-scale flowing over the top edge of the wound while blood dripped down her chin to stain those pretty robes. "I wondered how Faven had managed to come here on her own. I see now that she did not. It is your ship, then, that escaped the *Black Celeste* all those years ago?"

"You'd be amazed at the breadth of what Sythe came here with," Amandine said.

Ulana gave her a warm smile that was far too charming. Murderous assholes should be sneering and cruel, in Amandine's estimation. Not sweet-faced and kindly. "Curious as I might be, I have no interest in speaking with pirates. Your presence is not welcome here."

Amandine *tsked*, and caught Faven's eye, speaking directly to her. "I think you might want to talk to this pirate, Navigator Valset. After all, I've got one more nasty trick up my sleeve."

Amandine didn't see Ulana's reaction, so focused was she on Faven's flash of confusion, then the determined narrowing of the navigator's eyes when she noticed Amandine shift her scale-encased hand in her pocket.

Faven let loose the highest-pitched howl Amandine had ever heard and arched her back, throwing her body into convulsions. The guards panicked, dropping one of her arms, and in that moment she ripped the armillary from her sleeve and tossed it as hard as she could.

It hit the ground with a clatter, skidded across the floor with a soft hiss until Amandine stopped its wild slide with a light press of her boot. The guards got Faven back under control. Ulana whipped around to scowl at Amandine, a strand of hair falling from her perfect bun.

"I'm beginning to find your presence most irritating," Ulana said.

"Ah, Valset." Amandine scooped the armillary off the floor in her good hand. "I'm going to have to ask you politely to stop your bullshit. Let Sythe go, stand down your guards, and we'll talk this out without a fight."

"I have no interest in parlaying with you, pirate. You will not be spared."

"It's not your clemency I'm counting on." Amandine smiled slowly into her puckered face. "You've got your cronies, that's true. I've got one caught navi and my own two bits of wit to rely on. Doesn't look pretty, I grant you that, but you're missing one very important piece."

Amandine brushed her fingertips against the armillary, willing it to access the starpath that had brought them to the *Black Celeste*.

It was there, waiting, warm to the touch, the cryst-gems in the metal winking up at her. If what Ulana had said was true, those gems were pieces of the cryst in their final stage of development. Bone and sinew. She hoped whoever had been chopped up for parts to make the armillary would forgive her, because she was about to use it to wreck their nursery.

She held the armillary out before her. Despite the gleam of the cryst-gems, it looked like a dead, limp thing. Not quite folded, but not opened, either. The concentric rings sagged, not a hint of a holo between their metal arms.

Ulana sniffed and brushed Amandine off with a quick shake of her head. "Only the cryst can make use of weaving technology."

"We've been a long time living cheek by jowl, Navi. You still sure about that?"

A sour frown flickered across her face. Amandine knew that look. Ulana saw humanity as a curiosity to be enjoyed. A museum piece placed under glass to dance for her entertainment. And now she was baffled and irritated to find her toys were talking back.

Amandine had been performing one way or another her whole life. That's what it was, to be a pirate. You swaggered and you postured and you made damn sure everyone believed you were the biggest bad in the room, if you wanted to be the one walking out again. Amandine didn't have much of anything to back up her bravado with. Didn't even have use of her shotgun at the moment.

What she did have was a hand turned to cryst and an armada of pissed-off pirates on her heels.

Amandine pitched the armillary into the air as effortlessly as Faven ever had and was satisfied to hear those cryst fuckheads gasp as it unfurled and burst to life with the holo of the starpath that led into the *Black Celeste*. Before it could fall, she tugged her cryst-scale hand from her pocket and held it under the armillary.

It hovered in place, as two like magnets. Amandine had watched Faven fiddle with the thing closely enough that it took her no time at all to figure out how to make it transmit that path to the primary drives of Turtar Glas and, by extension, all the pirates who were currently combing through that drive, trying to figure out a way out of the Clutch. Then she opened a video call. Used codes she'd pilfered from Sere ages ago to push it through to all of Turtar Glas.

"Here I am, lovelies," she drawled. "Come and get me."

Something groaned, high in the cavernous ceiling. Amandine lifted her gaze to find the hazy shadows of hundreds of ships pouring into the atmosphere of the *Black Celeste*.

"What have you done?" Ulana demanded.

Amandine smiled up at those angry, swarming shadows. "Consorted with pirates."

FORTY-SEVEN

Amandine

Someone in the armada got the bright idea to fire their rail gun through the ceiling. While Amandine generally approved of that kind of behavior, she found it nettlesome when the hexagonal plates above her head shattered, sending potentially skull-crushing debris raining down upon the miserable gathering below.

Chaos erupted. Ulana shouted something that was probably an order to attack, based on the amount of gunfire screeching from her people. Perfect. Amandine tucked the armillary back into her waistband and sprinted away from the center of the room, ducking down to take shelter beside Tully as another chunk of cryst-glass slammed into the floor nearby.

"Excellent plan, Cap'n, but now you've got two factions here who want you dead."

"Chaos is a virtue," Amandine said, singsongy in the way she always was when the panic was rising up out of the swamp she kept it buried in. "But what I'm really counting on is that the armada is going to want the cryst dead more than they want me dead. At least, for the time being."

"And what are you going to do?"

"Oh, you know. Save the goddess, free Becks, Kester, and the

Marquette from the *Black Celeste*'s mind control. Your usual evening activities."

"That's not a plan, that's a wish list." Tully squinted at her. "And it's lunchtime."

"I don't think that's my biggest obstacle at the moment." Amandine squeezed Tully's arm. "I need you to bug out. Try to find whatever ship Gailliard came here on and get it online for us, because if this goes sideways, then we're going to need the universe's fastest exit."

Tully threw a longing glance at the chaos of the fight raging throughout the room. "But I'm your only backup."

Amandine shot them a look. "Tully, my lovely, if the situation gets hot enough that I require backup in a fight, neither one of us is making it out of here."

"I know. But it'd be unfriendly of me to rush off without offering to heroically stay behind." Tully hesitated, and that was all that was needed to reveal the fear hiding behind their devil-may-care facade. They passed the shotgun back to her. "I think you might need this more than me."

"Not sure I can fire it."

"Not sure you need two hands to bash someone over the head, Cap'n."

Amandine tossed her head back and laughed, then pushed the shotgun back into Tully's hands before giving them an encouraging shove. "Go on. Get our exit ready. I've got a goddess to save and a mind-meld to shut down."

"Clear skies, Cap'n."

Amandine nodded, forcing a smile around the ill-timed knot in her throat. Tully grinned a little, a lopsided expression, and winked before disappearing into the forest of pillars.

Right. All she had to do now was rescue a goddess from the top of a highly visible pillar in the middle of a combat zone.

"Bloody woman," Amandine said as she ducked down and scurried closer to the pillar she'd last seen Faven near.

Short Gehry had been first through the hole in the ceiling, setting down her sleek fighter with a screeching of glass and bodies as she slammed the ship belly-down onto debris and navigators alike. Amandine wrinkled her nose at that—Gehry had always been too heavy on the trigger for her tastes—but she could hardly complain. She'd called them here to fight, after all.

Faven's captors were making slow but steady progress and had dragged her up a set of stairs to the top of a pillar. She thrashed like a feral cat and stomped down on the instep of one of them hard enough that they reeled away from her. Amandine sprinted for all she was worth, not caring who heard or saw her, as Faven tried to shove her other captor away.

No survival skills, in that navi. The soldier swore and, having had enough of her nonsense, pushed her into the open mouth of the pillar. Faven cried out, her voice stolen by the mineralization fluid rushing over her.

Amandine barreled into the guards. She slammed her ever-present wrench into the back of one's head and shouldered into the chest of the other, knocking him from the platform. She dropped to her knees, holding out her cryst-coated hand—the wrench gave her extra reach—and Faven strained for her hand, but missed, and sank within the fluid.

Amandine blinked a few times. She'd only been a step behind. That really should have worked. The navi's head stubbornly refused to reemerge from the fluid. Amandine closed her eyes a moment, resigned.

The navis in the pillars weren't completely scaled. It took time. Faven would fall beneath the sedative and join the chorus of the sleeping navigators, lending her strength to making the elder cryst sleep.

When this was all over, she could be plucked out and probably wouldn't be that far gone to the scale. Except that Amandine had no way of knowing that for certain. And, really, how was she going to fix any of this without the navi's help?

"I'm an idiot," Amandine muttered to herself as she stripped off her coat and tossed it aside. "A soft-hearted fool of a woman."

An explosion rocked the stairs. Her feet went out from under her, and Amandine threw out her good hand to grasp the narrow metal handrail as the stairs groaned, leaning away from the pillar to which they'd been anchored. Metal tore, loud enough to drown out Amandine's swearing, as something heavy and vital in the ceiling gave way and slammed to the ground, shivering the stairs.

A fallen ceiling strut had bashed through a nearby catwalk, splitting it in two, and while it swung wildly it didn't appear to be in danger of toppling at any second, unlike the stairs. Cursing her luck and her birth and every damn decision that'd led her to this point, Amandine swung herself away from the careening stairs and slammed into a section of the swaying catwalk, hooking her scale-encased arm around its railing.

Panting, she dragged herself up and flopped over onto her back to lay there a moment, breathing, getting her wits back about her. She didn't need to look to know that the thunderous crash that filled the room had come from the stairs collapsing.

"Bitter!" Short Gehry called out, far too close for comfort.

Amandine's arms were shaking, but she hauled herself to her feet. She gripped the cable that suspended the walkway in one hand to steady herself, and prayed the contraption would hold a little longer.

Gehry stood on the other piece of the split-in-two catwalk, steadying herself in a similar manner with the cables, but she had the advantage of carrying a shotgun in her other hand. Amandine wanted to curl her scale-encased fingers into a fist, but naturally, they didn't get the message.

"Gehry, my lovely," Amandine said, all smiles. "Going to shoot me while I'm unarmed?"

"Sorry, Bitter." Gehry got her footing stable. Lifted the shotgun. Braced it. "But you know how it is. We were tight. If I show mercy, I'm on the chop next." Her voice was rough. "Why'd you have to go and protect that fuckin' navi over the armada, anyway?"

"Wasn't one over the other," Amandine called back. She braced her legs, pretended to stumble a bit, but was really pushing the catwalk. Making it swing higher. Farther. Closer to the open mouth of the pillar on the upswing. "It wasn't her that jumped us, Gehry. Not really."

Gehry's gaze flicked pointedly to Amandine's scaled arm. "Was it you?"

"No! Even if I could, do you really believe I'd leave Turtar Glas in the middle of the Clutch?"

Part of her had hoped, she supposed, that Gehry would realize the ridiculousness of that question. That there shouldn't be any doubt in Gehry's mind—or in the minds of all the pirates of the armada—that Bitter Amandine wouldn't put the armada in danger intentionally. Wouldn't risk breaking what Ma Sere had built.

But Gehry, the damn woman, broke her heart. Gave her a taut, sad slash of a smile, and took aim. "I gave you your five minutes, Bitter. You took it and ran."

Amandine swore, pushed the swaying catwalk for one last swing, and really hoping Gehry's aim was as bad as her judgment of Amandine's character, she leapt. Should she close her eyes? Would it matter? Amandine took a deep breath, and dove.

It was difficult to say what, exactly, Amandine had expected when diving face-first into a vat of fluid designed to force the cryst into a lightsick trance and mineralize their bodies to be extruded later for construction materials. She'd half expected herself to turn straight to stone, or be sedated like the cryst, or otherwise instantly die. If Amandine were being honest with herself, she'd always assumed she'd get herself killed someday by doing something reckless on behalf of a pretty face.

Said pretty face was a few feet below her and sinking fast. Faven's eyes had closed, her body limp with unconsciousness, her arms upraised. Amandine caught a glimpse of her hand, and the clawed pane of glass extending from the knuckles.

She tried not to think about that. Or the fact that every nerve in her body felt like it was being used as a current. The skin around her arm and shoulder tingled and itched and burned—she purposefully ignored these changes.

Amandine kicked, driving herself deeper, and caught Faven's cool, rough hand at last. She held the navi tight and, against all reason and sense, dove deeper. She really, really hoped she'd heard Faven correctly when she'd talked about cryst birthing chambers.

She hit the bottom, fumbled stiff fingers along an emergency release, but the mechanism wouldn't slide. With her arms full of navi, she didn't have many options, so she drew her scaled hand back and swung the wrench down, hard as she could, into the divider. The mechanism cracked. Her fingers cracked, too, and maybe one or two went missing along with the wrench, but she kept on pounding on it until it gave way.

They were sucked down into a chamber built for a child. Amandine smashed them against the bottom pane, lungs burning as the mechanism tried to seal off and start pumping the mineralization fluid out.

Amandine had a moment of calm in which she could contemplate how bad of an idea this was before the bottom opened, spilling them into another chamber of fluid that washed over her like a cold drink on a hot summer day. Her chest burned and her jaw ached from the effort of holding her breath as she hit the bottom, fumbled along the floor, brushing aside bits of shed scale, and worked the last mechanism.

It sucked them both down. Amandine flattened herself against Faven once more, making them as small as she possibly could. The second airlock slammed shut and started siphoning liquid away. When she had a pocket of air within which to breathe, Amandine gasped—but the air was stale and vile, making her choke, and all she saw was black fuzziness behind her eyes before the bottom opened, and they were dumped unceremoniously onto the floor.

Amandine grunted, and was relieved to find she had enough mobility to roll off Faven and flop onto her back. What was left of her scaled hand clinked against the floor. They were in a room below the one with the navis, the sealed ends of the pillars that filled the above chamber pockmarking the ceiling.

Faven groaned softly. Amandine forced herself to roll back to her side and help the navi sit up to cough various fluids onto the floor. When she was recovered enough to speak, she pushed wet hair from her face and looked up at Amandine with wide eyes.

"Amandine, your hand—"

Amandine pressed her good hand over Faven's mouth. "I don't want to know. Are you all right?"

"I might be better off than you," she said with a thin smile.

Amandine looked her up and down, tracking the patches of new scale that she could see—there was no telling what had transformed beneath her robes—and forced herself to smile back. "I doubt that."

"Your ship," Faven said, voice growing clipped and fast as reality reasserted itself. "I believe the *Marquette* was accidentally awoken by Gailliard when he tried to wake our elders."

"I know." Amandine pushed to her feet and took Faven's hand, dragging her upright. "Or, at least, I figured most of that out. Come on. We have to get out of here. Tully is getting us a ship, but I don't even know where we are."

"Leave?" Faven asked. "I can't leave my kin in that monstrous trance. I have to destroy it all."

"Navi," Amandine said, "the pirates of Turtar Glas are currently busy doing most of that work for you. If we're lucky, they'll break enough to shut the whole thing down and the *Marquette* will lose its connection to the *Black Celeste*. But in the meantime, we don't want to get caught in the cross fire."

"That's your plan?" Faven scoffed. "Destructive you pirates

may be, but they cannot undo what has been done to my kin and elders."

Amandine grunted with exasperation. "It's not a plan. I'm winging it, here. And please tell me I didn't just save your ass for you to turn around and side with the jerks who want to wipe out humanity so that they can move on to greener pastures."

"Don't be ridiculous." Faven shook her robes, wringing out the sodden fabric.

"Then what's your plan?"

"Plan? I thought you pirates were fond of 'winging it.'"

"But you don't consort with pirates, do you, goddess?"

Faven narrowed her eyes in challenge, and despite everything, the upturned lift of her chin and squared-off shoulders made Amandine's pulse surge.

"Very well, pirate. I have developed something that I might be inclined to call an idea."

Amandine crossed her arms and looked the dripping-wet navi up and down. "An idea."

"A good one."

"I'm listening."

"I'm going wake the sleeping navigators."

FORTY-EIGHT

Faven

Faven watched Amandine's jaw tense with mild fascination. A muscle in her cheek twitched and the tendons along the sides of her neck stood out starkly against her skin. A patch of scale now ran over Amandine's shoulder, disappearing beneath the curve of her shirt collar, and Faven caught herself letting her gaze linger a beat too long before she peeled her attention away.

"And how, pray tell, are you going to do that?" Amandine asked at last.

"When I was sedated, I joined them in their trance. I had no choice. I knew what was happening, I wanted to do anything but add my voice to their chorus, but the pull was too strong. If I were to make myself lightsick outside of the sedative, I could join in their song—and change it. Add the voice I wanted to add, the discordant clash, and wake them all."

"You want to make yourself lightsick." Her tone was highly skeptical. One brow arched even higher still. "What happens if you get so lightsick you don't know what you're doing or, voids—what if you're successful? What happens, Navi, when they all wake up? Your elders will wake, too. The very ground we're standing on will wake, and how kindly do you think it will take to having been vivisected and lived within all these long centuries? We can't even know if they'll be *sane*. I wouldn't be after a day of living like that—who knows how much your elders can withstand?"

Amandine's voice was fast and clipped and—scared, Faven realized with a start. The Amandine Faven had come to know would never run when others were in need of help, but this was too big for her. The scope beyond her ability to accurately understand, and under that weight, her gusto burned away. Faven thought she might be seeing her as she'd been the first time she'd ever come to the Clutch, and almost lost her life. Young and raw. Trying to do what was right, but not knowing what that was, or even believing that she could.

"The *Marquette* is scared," Faven said.

That rocked her, shattered the building panic, and her spine straightened, a wary glint in her eye as she regarded Faven. "You talked to it?"

"No, but I could feel it. The song suppresses more than the elders, Amandine. Gailliard's cry broke their rest, for a little while, so that the *Black Celeste* woke up enough to send up a distress signal. That's what Captain Jacq was responding to. There was never any deal, that's why he was so cagey about it all. He received the *Black Celeste*'s distress signal and told you all he had a deal out here, but how could he possibly? The Choir never would have drawn him here."

Amandine scoffed. "You can't know that."

"I do. I looked at that battlefield and—it's the only thing that makes sense. If we had the time, I'd make you check the logs of Jacq's crashed ship myself, but we don't. Your captain answered the *Black Celeste*'s cry for help, but he didn't know what he was facing, and in the aftermath of that battle the *Black Celeste* budded off a ship to save you. But the *Marquette* is tired, and wounded, and this time it needs you to save it."

"I don't know *how*."

"We wake them all."

Amandine's lip curled. "And possibly destroy everything."

Faven pointed to the pillars surrounding them. "Look at where we are."

The pirate clearly did not want to follow Faven's direction. She scowled, and after a drawn-out moment of staring each other down, she finally relented and let her gaze track slowly around the room. Hundreds of pillars. All empty, it seemed, from down here in the dark where new cryst were meant to be born. But above, they were anything but empty.

"How many?" Faven asked. "How many is it going to take, do you think, to keep up that song? How many are you comfortable sacrificing to keep the elders at rest? I was in there, Amandine. I know what the trance is like. It's not sleep, for the singing. I was aware, but I was numb, and though my heart cried out against it, I could do nothing but sing what was compelled of me. How many are you willing to leave to that fate?"

Amandine sighed, low and slow, and let her arms uncross. "Not even one."

Faven felt something warm kindle in her breast that had nothing at all to do with attraction or momentary indulgences. Something like hope.

FORTY-NINE

Amandine

The trouble with Faven's plan was that it wasn't one. She was all bright ideas and big concepts, but when it came to the nuts and bolts of getting something done, the navi rolled a delicate shoulder and said not to worry, they'd find a way.

Amandine liked a plan. She liked, most of all, the moment when a plan went to shit and the adrenaline-surge of knowing she was on her own, improvising to stay alive, or free, or any combination thereof. She got a little jumpy, however, when improvising about the fate of the entire human species.

"You need access to a lightdrive if you're going to get yourself lightsick," Amandine said. "And I don't think the pirates of the armada fighting above are keen to let you anywhere near their ships, so we're going to have to steal one."

"Pirate one," Faven corrected, with a dash too much gusto.

"Your hunger for the adventures of my profession is inspiring, Navi, but when it's pirate-to-pirate, we're stealing like grease-slick thieves. Not that I got any honor among pirates left to maintain, mind you, but you should know what we're dealing with. Regardless, I've got an easier way to get us access to a lightdrive."

"Oh?" Faven's brows lifted.

Amandine pulled Faven's armillary from her waistband and held it out, gesturing grandly to the miniature drive at its core. "Ta-da."

Faven laughed, but the sound was exhausted. "I need a controlled source. One I can get away from, once I'm finished."

"I think I can take the trinket away when you're done," Amandine said.

"Except that you'll be lightsick, too."

"Oh," Amandine said. "Damn."

Faven took the armillary back regardless, and this time, when their fingers brushed, she let the touch linger. "The *Marquette* claimed to be able to control its levels of light exposure."

"No. That bloody ship took you over without asking once before, and there's no telling what it will do now that it's back on the *Black Celeste* proper. Kester and Becks—" Her voice caught. She cleared it. "They weren't themselves. We can't get anywhere near them until we're sure we've freed their minds, because I'm not—I'm not risking another fight with them. I can't."

"Amandine," Faven said gently. "Do you really think that the *Marquette* means you harm? It could have let you die here, once, but it didn't. And that was while it was still fully a part of the *Black Celeste*."

"You saw how Kester and Becks were fighting to keep it out. They told us to run."

"And the *Marquette* told us it was safety," Faven said. "This place...It's overwhelming. The *Marquette* lost itself, for a little while. It's meant to keep the cryst safe, and it didn't know what to do with us. But I think it might have learned a desire to keep more than just the cryst safe, too. And I think it learned that from you."

It is our duty to protect.

Amandine pinched her temples. "I don't know what to think."

"I do." Faven placed her hand on Amandine's scaled shoulder. "They don't need to be freed, Amandine. You already did that. Now, you have to face what that means. They're scared, and they're hiding, and I'd bet everything that, despite it all—they're waiting for their captain to tell them what to do."

Amandine closed her eyes lightly for a moment, then grudgingly pulled her HUD glass from her pocket. She fitted the piece over her ear and slung the glass around to cover one eye. "It's funny. Things got so confused I damn near forgot the first real lesson Ma Sere ever taught me, but you remembered."

"What's that?" Faven asked.

"Trust your crew." Amandine put the call through to Kester.

"Bitter." Kester's smooth, unflappable voice tightened Amandine's chest. "How unexpected."

"Kester, my lovely, I need a ride."

"I am aware of your location, and the chaos above. You've brought war to the sanctum it is my directive to protect. Why would I help you?"

"Because we're on the same side now, as a matter of fact."

"Are we." It wasn't quite a question, her voice was perfectly flat, but Amandine thought she caught a hint of curiosity.

"The navi and I, we think her people have been done wrong. It's time to release them from their slumber, and Sythe's willing to do the work. We just need an unshielded lightdrive."

"How convenient," Kester said dryly.

Amandine smiled, recognizing her friend's tone breaking through the Marquette's deadened monotone. "Isn't it just. Pick me up in seven? I'll wear my best leathers."

"Aye, Captain," Kester said with far less sarcasm than expected.

With the Marquette's lightdrive busted, it had to fly to them with its sublight engines, slipping under the battle raging above. Which didn't prove to be much of a problem, as the ship assured Amandine that it knew the way. The Marquette knew the Black Celeste down to the bolts.

Faven stood side by side with her as the Marquette appeared in the distance. It came to a restful landing despite the gaping hole in the side of the ship throwing off its maneuverability. Amandine supposed that since the ship itself was flying now, it had more finesse than she'd ever had on those controls, and felt a pang of jealousy.

Kester exited. The lithe woman wore her usual stark white suit, hair slicked back and no weapon that Amandine could see on her person, though Kester was better at hiding weapons than Amandine had ever been at using them. Her gelid eyes flicked over the sodden huddle of Amandine and the navi, and her lips twitched with something that might have been a smile, on another face.

"Bitter." Kester stopped a few short strides away. "Sythe. This had better be worth my time. You may have noticed that I have a lightdrive in need of extensive repairs."

Faven opened her mouth, but Amandine gave her a slight shake of the head, urging her to bite her tongue for the time being.

"I've been trying to figure something out," Amandine said conversationally, and pressed on when Kester's face creased with annoyance. "Which one of you is the real you, I mean. The real *Marquette*. And I know what you're thinking—you're all the real you. I get that. I do. But I figured there had to be a kernel of a real personality hiding in one of you, you know? Like a split-personality three-card monte. Pick a person. One's the ace."

"If you've brought me here to ramble on, Bitter, then—"

"The obvious pick is the *Marquette* itself." Amandine spoke over her, smiling warm as starshine into Kester's scowl. "Once you were speaking through Faven, the mask came off, eh? But I'm not so sure. I think that, once those three cards are dealt, when we flip them over, we'll find an ace under each of them."

Kester turned and began to walk away.

"You're a security system, Kester." Amandine raised her voice to be heard but didn't shout. Tried to keep it gentle. Kind. One friend pushing another to see the damage done to themselves that they hadn't yet acknowledged. "One with a lot of weapons. One that's had to kill. But you don't want to kill anymore, do you? Don't want any more blood on your hands, even if it's in self-defense.

"Especially not the blood of a child. It was Gailliard, wasn't it? The kid your directives wanted you to kill. He made a hell of a racket and brought fighting to your sanctuary. But you couldn't do it anymore. You fled. With me."

Kester stopped walking. Tipped her head to one side.

"And Becks. Well, that's easy. You were getting annoyed with me, weren't you? I wasn't taking good enough care of the ship— going to strip out the enamel—and so you, well, it's your job to protect, isn't it? And you can't do that if you're not secure yourself."

"And Tully." Kester's shoulders tightened. Amandine nodded to herself. "Tully has always been a kid at heart, really. Curious about the world. But they got a little too independent, and don't even know what they are, anymore.

"You didn't expect yourself to have so much life dwelling within you—that wasn't part of your directive, was it? To bud off a piece of yourself just to have fun?"

Kester refused to answer.

"Faven said that she sensed you were diminished. Somehow less than you were, when you got in her head, but I don't think that's quite right. The mind left dwelling in the *Marquette* itself is fractured, sure. I get that. It portioned itself out to make you ancillaries.

"But I think it was telling the truth, when it said it would have continued on flying with me until I'd crumbled to dust if Faven hadn't shown up and tipped you off that something wasn't right here on the *Black Celeste*. Let you know that the charges you left behind weren't safe."

Kester didn't so much as twitch a muscle.

"And then there's me," Amandine said. Kester turned at last, mouth open in protest, but Amandine kept talking. "I don't mean that I'm you, *Marquette*. Not entirely. Part of me is, though, isn't it? How dead was I, when I tripped over your doorstep?"

"Amandine..." Faven started to say, but trailed off as she shook her head and waited for Kester to answer.

Kester's lips twitched, but she canted her head aside before Amandine could read her expression. "How did you know?"

"I saw the battlefield. Then Gailliard's scar, with the cryst-scale following along it like a seam." Amandine rolled her scarred shoulder. "There's no way that blade didn't go through me. Took off my arm at the shoulder, didn't it? You know, I always wondered. I found you, sure, but even if I could remember the coordinates to Turtar Glas, your lightdrive didn't have the starpath or the docking permissions. You shouldn't have been able to take me there."

"You were delirious with blood loss," Kester said. "And thought the *Marquette* was your own ship. You entered the coordinates for Turtar Glas and collapsed onto my lightdrive. You . . . you just wanted to go home. I gave a piece of myself to you. To save you. Then I wove the path myself."

"Thank you," Amandine said, and smiled at the slight widening of Kester's eyes. "That's how it all got mixed up, didn't it? My home and yours. Blackloach. The *Black Celeste*. They blurred together, in my mind, and when I put those coordinates on my arm after I was well enough to walk again, Ma Serè must have looked at them and thought—well. Thought I was like you, though she didn't have words for it. Thought I was a thing born of the Clutch. That's why she told me to go home.

"But I'm not. I'm just a woman, Kester, and I need your help. Not to save me—but to save all these people here. The cryst-born in stasis, the elders in their slumber, and humanity, too, if we can manage it."

Kester straightened her collar, and Amandine smiled to herself, recognizing the motion as a tic of hers before she'd indulge in whatever absurd plan Amandine had come up with.

"My directive is the defense of the Clutch and the newly born cryst."

"Sure." Amandine held up her scaled hand. "But I think it's safe to say those waters are muddied now, aren't they? Human or cryst, it makes no difference to me. I need them all alive to keep on plundering the starry skies."

Kester barked a short, startled laugh. "You intend to continue pirating if you survive this?"

"Don't you?"

Kester studied her for a long time. "Kester was never real. I am the *Marquette*. Your crew doesn't exist."

"Maybe that was true to start, but it's not anymore. You've segmented yourself so much that what's left in the *Marquette* is just intention, now. The desire to protect the cryst children. But there aren't any. Because the sleeping elders can't fade away to be reborn, and those being raised in the Spire are outside your reach. All save one. Gailliard was born here, and cried out, and that woke you up at last, but everything that happened after…

"Your segments are more than pieces. More than playactors. Kester and Becks and Tully—and the *Marquette*. You're my crew. My family."

Kester drew her head back, lips pressing together until they turned bloodless. "I am a construct."

"You're my friend. Makes no difference to me what your body's made of."

Kester considered this for a moment so long that Amandine thought she'd miscalculated, and they were all going to die after all.

"Very well," Kester said, and her slantwise smile slashed her face at last. "What is your plan, Captain?"

Amandine grinned. "Oh, you're going to hate every second of it."

FIFTY

Faven

While Faven had pushed Amandine to face the truth of the *Marquette*, she wasn't entirely certain that Amandine's ready acceptance that her crew was composed of the fragmented mind of her ship was emotionally healthy. Ultimately, she decided that she was in no position to raise any protest. Perhaps the pirate was rubbing off on her, but Faven had to admit that her own plan was nearly as reckless.

She followed Kester and a once more swaggering Amandine back into the damaged engine bay of the *Marquette*, and studiously averted her eyes when Amandine's confident stride missed a step at the sight of Becks, fully consumed in cryst-scale.

"Are they...?" Amandine trailed off.

"That vessel is lost to me," Kester said. "After you left, I tried... It was too late."

"Can you do it again?"

"I could," Kester said. "But they wouldn't be the same."

"No. I suppose they wouldn't." Amandine brushed the back of her knuckles down Becks's scaled cheek, her smile trembling. "Clear skies, Becks."

"They tried to kill you," Faven said.

"Wasn't even the first time." Amandine paused. "But maybe the first time they'd meant to finish the deed."

"Tully tried to warn them that staying with the *Marquette* so soon after its return to the *Black Celeste* was dangerous, but they were..." Kester frowned at the figure, struggling to find the words. "Always more adherent to protocol."

Amandine laughed, voice thick. "Yeah. I guess they were. Always ragging on me about the wear in our shielding—" Amandine's eyes narrowed. "Which we didn't need."

Kester shrugged. "We were aware that most ships required shielding. The need was a convenient cover for moments when the *Marquette* itself was overstrained and unable to contain its light."

"Speaking of," Amandine said, "how are you feeling, Navi?"

"Lightheaded," Faven admitted.

Amandine gave her a flat look.

"That was not a pun."

"Sure," Amandine said in such a way that Faven couldn't help but smile.

"Kester," Faven said, "I presume you can't wake the sleeping cryst yourself, or you would have done so already."

"That is correct, Navigator. I am a construct budded off from the *Marquette* itself, neither human nor cryst. To speak with all those sleeping is beyond me."

She nodded, having feared as much. "Is it within your strength to help me find my way, should the sleepers' lullaby overwhelm me?"

"I will do my best, Navigator."

Faven thought Kester might have smiled then, but the expression was too fast—a blur—but then, most of the world was beginning to blur. She blinked, and the world smudged at the corners of her eyes, fine threads of gold superimposing themselves in a lightning-bright flash. Her heart beat faster, the sense memory of sinking beneath the mineralization fluid threatening to send her fleeing in panic, but she breathed deeply and caught the earthy scent of Amandine's skin nearby.

Her heart rate slowed. Faven entered trances similar to being lightsick all the time. She knew this feeling. The skin-prickling thrum of unknown forces, of power within her grasp, making each breath sharp.

The armillary was in her hand, though she couldn't recall having drawn it. She let her vision soften, seeing through the chaotic clutter of the engine room to the greater chamber beyond the ship. To all the thousands of lights—of minuscule stars—held in suspension.

Faven unfolded the armillary, subconsciously mapping the location of each, a tangled web of interlinked minds whispering the same cloying dream. *Rest. Sleep.* It threatened to drag her under. To wash her beneath a tide of somnambulistic bliss.

It would be so very easy to let herself go. To slip into slumber and join the multitudes in peace. To be safe and cared for, tucked away with nothing but long rest to ease the aching of her scale-afflicted joints. The comforts of life in the Spire, everlasting.

Safe. Her mother's most cherished wish within her grasp.

The small part of Faven that forever wanted to pull the tiger's tail almost laughed at this persuasion. Faven did not want the Spire's gems and silks. She did not want to come to gentle stillness by the Rosette Pond and watch the gleamfish swim for all eternity.

The song of sleep was discordant within her heart, jarring, and Faven found it no trouble at all to push against it—to cry out for all those sleeping to wake.

There was no answer to her cry, at first. A ripple, perhaps, on the surface of a pond, spreading out from Faven's position. Her cry buffeted all those glittering minds held in the webs between them. Then faded into nothingness. They slept on.

Faven clenched her jaw. She cried out, in mind and heart, again and again—*wake, wake, wake!*—and still the navigators slept on, their dreams singing of their rest. It was as if there was some kind of barrier, pushing back any thought not of the choir itself.

What hope did she have of success? Gailliard, though a child, had been trained to interface with all those minds at once, and still he could only wake the *Marquette*.

Faven recalled with sudden clarity the moment Amandine had saved her from the exploding Bladeship. When she'd been lost in lightsickness, and whispered in concert with the *Marquette*—*wake*.

The *Marquette*'s cry, passed through her lips, had been an attempt to wake the elder slumbering within the lightdrive of the Bladeship. A desperate plea for it to rise and save itself, before it was too late.

It hadn't worked, but that had been the *Marquette*'s voice. A construct, by its own admission, without the ability to be heard by the cryst through the caul of their slumber. Faven had no such limitations. She was cryst, whether or not she had fully accepted the fact, and while her kin were gripped in chorus, the elder cryst were only listening to their lullaby, not singing it themselves.

She needed to plead with those who were already primed to listen.

Faven brushed her fingertips over her armillary, feeling out the dimmer lights in the web. The ones fading to time, or long slumber. The ones that, when she had been in Ulana's classroom, would have been brushed off as inconsequential in their weaving.

Faven cried out once more, calling with every scrap of strength she had for the sleeping elders to wake. Calling directly to them.

This time, they heard her.

She heard their first awakenings as the ringing of a bell—a crystal-clear sound that reverberated against her bones. Faven's teeth jarred, the armillary fell from her hands with a clatter. A shadow rose in her mindscape. Massive. Eldritch. A twisting fractal of glass and metal and light so vast it overwhelmed her senses, and she knew, with gut-wrenching certainty, that this was only one of the elders rising.

She had never felt truly small before.

But such was the strength of her plea that it pushed even Faven out of her trance. Amandine held her, keeping her upright as she bent over to heave in long breaths.

"Did it work?" Amandine asked.

Somewhere, everywhere, a deep and grinding sound filled the air. Thousands of birthing pillar mechanisms working all at once.

FIFTY-ONE

Amandine

Faven was shaking as Amandine led her out of the *Marquette*, and so she kept her arm around the navi, steadying her every step. Her eyes were fever-bright, and she was blinking far too often while hugging her arms against her chest to keep from scratching herself raw. Lightsickness was a real bastard like that. It'd take time to fade.

Back in the birthing chamber, what had been a cold, sterile room full of nothing but the sounds of their bickering was now full of the groans of the disgorged. The scent of the demineralization fluid was heavy on the air, acrid and oily, coating the back of Amandine's throat with every breath.

Some of the cryst-born had been in their chambers for years and were completely gone over to scale despite passing through the demineralization bath. Amandine recalled Faven's warning that the demineralization fluid didn't work after a navigator's initial birthing, and hoped they'd be all right. They wouldn't all be. She knew that. Birthing a new world always came with loss, but she allowed herself the luxury of that hope all the same.

"Faven," a small, rasping voice said.

The navi spun on her heel and took off at a sprint, dropping to her knees alongside one of the freed navigators. Amandine shared a look with Kester, who merely shrugged. They followed to find Faven holding the stiffened hand of a young man half gone to cryst. His remaining eye swiveled, alighting upon Amandine.

"We meet here again," he said, voice slow and soft with exhaustion. "Thank you, Bitter Amandine. For saving my life."

Amandine brushed her fingertips over the exposed ridge of her scar, now stiff with scale, and bowed her head to the young man. "Gailliard, is it? I got one question that needs answering, if you want to make tangible your thanks. I know how I got out that day, but how did you?"

"Faven's mother," he said, and squeezed Faven's hand. "When Captain Jacq arrived and the fighting broke out, she whisked me away to her Bladeship and brought me to the Spire. I'd forgotten, until I saw Captain Jacq's body there."

"She never told me," Faven said.

He smiled thinly with what lips he could move. "She wanted me to forget that day. To be a normal child of the Spire. I don't know if it was the right thing, to pretend none of this had happened, but... I was happy, for so very long, thanks to her." Whatever he would have said next was lost to the rising moans of the freshly released navigators. Faven looked up, surveying the countless pillars, and her face fell.

"What do we do?" Faven asked, voice thready and high from strain. "There are so many."

"I don't know." Amandine cast her a sidelong glance. "This was your plan."

"You said it wasn't a plan."

"I'm still convinced of that."

"Captain." Kester gestured up, toward the ceiling.

A ceiling that was splitting open. Sliding open like a camera lens yawning wide. Above, the pirates of Turtar Glas swarmed. They'd been harrying Ulana's people, but now they swirled in a formation

Amandine didn't recognize. A perfect spiral, like a maelstrom, and they flew so close to one another that Amandine was certain no human mind was piloting those ships. Faven pressed the heel of her palm to her forehead, wincing.

"What is it?" Amandine asked.

"They're...joyous," Faven said.

"The *Black Celeste* believes this is a normal birthing," Kester said.

Kester's gaze tracked up, to the ceiling of the room above the birthing chamber, the planet's ground. Another aperture was shuddering open, wider than the hole the rail gun had punched through. The mist of the planet seeped within, curling between the massing swarm of ships. People fell over the edge of both openings. Their cries followed them for so very long until they smashed against the floor. Amandine looked away, focusing instead on the swarm of pirate ships.

"What will those ships do?" Amandine asked.

"I cannot say," Kester said. "In the past the newborn cryst would enter the atmosphere to nourish themselves in its tides before braving the vacuum of space. Those ships are under the direction of the *Black Celeste*'s protocols, now. Once they are deemed well enough to leave the crèche, I don't know what will happen. It's likely they'll never be deemed well enough to leave, as they are merely pieces of elders welded together."

"The *Black Celeste*'s protocols? This whole planet—the birthing process—it's an automated system?"

"It is," Kester said. "The cryst have no parent but that which they made for themselves."

"No," Faven said softly. "No...That's not true."

Amandine frowned at her. "What is it?"

Her chin was upturned, eyes churning with stars, and there was a slight part to her lips where her breath slipped unobtrusively in and out. She seemed to have forgotten that she was still holding her injured friend's hand.

"Nothing of value remains," she said, half to herself, and touched the corner of her lips where the scale had grown. "But that doesn't mean that we don't take something of value with us, when we leave. We've done this before...All of this. The *Black Celeste* doesn't feel human, nor fully cryst, to me. Its mind is...It's something else. It's something the cryst consumed and transformed long before humanity."

"We are a construct," Kester said. "Neither human nor cryst by definition. That is what you're sensing."

"Maybe, but...No. You're something else. Something older. That the cryst found, and changed for their purpose. They only told you that you were constructed to suit them because that's how they view all the things they consume."

Kester's weight shifted. "I know nothing of this."

Faven scarcely seemed to hear her. "If I could make it understand..."

Faven released Gailliard and knelt, pressing her palms and her forehead against the floor. Her eyes slipped shut, her breaths slowed. Amandine was very close to picking up the navi and hauling her out of there, but the twin apertures slowed in their widening. The fervent swirl of the ships above calmed.

"Wait," Faven said. And then, when the ships paused in their swarming and the apertures stopped: "Listen."

The subtle shifting of the hexagonal plates that'd been constant since their arrival stopped. The air thickened, a held-breath tension that prickled the back of Amandine's neck. She felt watched, and exposed, and had a sudden desire to sprint back into the *Marquette* so that she could wipe her boots off before setting foot on those plates once more.

The *Black Celeste* stilled. And listened.

EPILOGUE

Faven

Faven Sythe told humanity two lies on the day she was elevated to Grand Hierarch of the Choir. The first was the easy, expected lie. That the Choir of Stars had had no knowledge of the actions of a small subset of its rogue members, and had begun the brutal process of culling out the rot before it spread.

That rot had spread centuries ago. But the worlds were in turmoil, the people waking up to the truth of their reality—that they dwelled within the bones of their gods—and to know that their governing body had betrayed their trust from the start would be to upend everything.

Sometimes, Faven wondered if throwing the entire system to the gnashing teeth of a fearful human species would have been the right thing to do. But that would only lead to more strife, more pain, and Faven had no desire to refight a war that had been decided centuries past. Humanity would be the last species the cryst ever attempted to consume.

It was, in the end, a small lie. One of the many that papered over the cracks in Faven's society. That allowed the people to move forward, instead of being frozen by fear.

Unrest bubbled, and fell. The Choir tore itself apart from within while presenting an austere, smiling face to the people—*Do not worry, we are at peace. We talk with our elders. We know what we are doing.*

The biggest lie of all, the last. But not the second lie Faven told.

No. The quiet lie, the insidious lie, the one so natural and quick you could blink and miss it, was that Faven Sythe was happy to serve.

It was not until speaking those words on a balcony of the Spire, her image projected to all those under the governance of the Choir of Stars, that she knew them to be false. Her heart rebelled, and the vitality she'd found rise up within her during her time with Bitter Amandine paled and withered, as she swore to stay put and mend the things that had been broken.

At first it was not so stifling. There were the elders to commune with, and the *Black Celeste* itself to find accord with. And while doing so took days and weeks and would take lifetimes yet, she came to understand her elders. That, while they'd been fractured to build humanity's ships and stations, their light remained whole, and they did not hurt. Did not feel pain in the way a human thought of pain at all.

Many of the elders agreed to stay, to shelter their strange human symbiotes. But some, upon awakening, decided to let their light fade away at last. The people on those ships and stations had to be rehoused. Infrastructure rebuilt. Faven's mind was a rigid landscape of logistics, crystalline in its clarity, and day by day the vibrancy she'd found to her moods when chasing down the Clutch began to fade.

Until, a year later, she received a letter.

Dear Grand Hierarch Sythe,

I would like to commission a starpath between the Vigil and Orvieto Station. We have a shipment of quartz wine, and I hear they're in need.

Most reverent regards, oh holiest, et cetera, et cetera,
                                                    Your Captain

The Grand Hierarch of the Choir of Stars did not lower herself to mete out mere starpath commissions. Neither did the Grand Hierarch lower herself to answer questions from her guards as she bade them stay behind, tugged a grey cloak over her shoulders, and rode a travel censer down to the docks.

Faven found her way to the Broken Mast, and though her face was hooded, the bartender took one look at her, sighed, and said, "This way."

She was led to a smaller room than the first time. Or perhaps it only seemed smaller because the woman who sat across the table from her filled it with her presence. Amandine lounged against a curved bench seat, her arm thrown up along the back, her battered cryst-scale hand shining in the low light. She wore her brown leathers, gems sparkling in the twisting braids that spilled down around the bandana that kept them out of her eyes.

Those eyes sparked when Faven slipped through the door, and skimmed over her grey-cloaked body before coming back up to rest on Faven's own. The air was warm and rich with the scents of spice and rum and well-worn wood, and as Faven sank onto the bench across from Amandine, the knots in her back began to unwind.

"Grand Hierarch." Amandine's tone was grandiose with mockery. "I thought you didn't consort with pirates."

"I have found, after careful study, that there's no one else I'd rather consort with."

Her lips twitched, a slow slanting, and she pushed a mug across the table. Faven picked it up, savoring the cool condensation as she ran it between her hands. "I thought you poured for your crew first."

"I do. You came when your captain called."

"I shall always come when you call, Amandine."

She rucked up one brow. "I'd like to put that to the test."

Faven blushed, and Amandine laughed, and the final knots in

her back unwound, letting her take a full breath for the first time in months. "What is it you need, oh Captain?"

"A great many things," she drawled, and took a deep drink. "But at the present, I was wondering if you might want to go on a little adventure."

Faven coughed delicately over her drink. "I am Grand Hierarch. I cannot run off."

"Can't you?"

Faven contemplated that for a long moment. The Choir was stable. Inroads had been made with the elders. If the system she had created was properly balanced, the absence of one person should not strain it overmuch.

It is my pleasure to serve the people of the Choir.

She winced and tried to cover the motion with a sip. "What are you planning?"

"There's an elder in the outskirts of the Huguet system. Wants to give its glass to Turtar Glas, but some corp bastards have dibs on salvage in the sector and are likely to scrap the whole thing before the armada can get to it."

"How do you know the elder wishes to give its glass to the armada?" Faven asked. Only the cryst could communicate with their elders, as far as she knew, but the coy twist of Amandine's lips told her otherwise.

"The *Marquette*," Faven said.

"Maybe. Maybe I'm just silver-tongued." She stretched along the back of the bench, emphasizing her frozen hand. Faven's brows lifted.

"I see. And you require a navigator to get you to the elder before this corporation, and I'm the only one you know."

"Faven. I don't need *a* navi. I need you."

All the gentle teasing had left her voice. Her smile lost its edge and became a soft, warm thing Faven had only ever seen in their shared dark. Faven's chest ached, a pang of longing so sharp it briefly constricted her breath, scudded her thoughts to the winds.

"Tell me," Faven said. "Did you ever find Blackloach again? The real place?"

"I did," Amandine said, head tilted in question.

"And did you decide to retire after all?"

"I think..." Amandine traced a fingertip around the rim of her cup, watching Faven from beneath half-mast lids. "...It's going to be a long, long time before I retire."

Faven turned her head, and though she saw only a pebbled wall, she was looking up the city, to the Spire, and the seat of her power. The laurels upon which she might rest.

"I think," she said, "that it will be a very long time before I retire, too."

Amandine held out her hand. "What say you, then, Navigator Sythe? Will you help me steal a god?"

ACKNOWLEDGMENTS

This book started out life as an unplanned National Novel Writing Month draft back in 2020. For those who've read the Devoured Worlds trilogy, you may know that I started that series in 2020 and wrote all three of those books back-to-back, carrying over into 2021. I was so deep into that world that I hadn't planned on starting anything new for NaNoWriMo, as it's called, but by the time November—when the event takes place—rolled around, I was waiting for beta reader feedback on *The Blighted Stars* and somewhat at a standstill.

I can't say where the original idea for *The Two Lies of Faven Sythe* came from, precisely. I had a vague sort of idea for a Gráinne Ní Mháille–like figure, and while Bitter Amandine ended up quite far away from the genuine article, I think the old pirate queen would still approve.

That November this story became a creative respite for me. I had a great deal of fun writing about Faven, Amandine, and the worlds they inhabit. I hope their story was able to extend you a little joy, and a little peace, too.

Thank you first and always to my husband, Joey Hewitt, for his endless support. To my beta readers Tina Gower, Andrea Stewart, Anthea Sharp, and Thomas K. Carpenter for your invaluable insights. And to my dear friends Marina Lostetter, Laura Blackwell, Laura Davy, David Dalglish, and Essa Hansen, who listened while I rambled endlessly about this project.

Thank you, too, to those writers' groups that have sent strength to my sword arm and offered community: the Isle, the Bunker, and naturally, the crew of the good ship MurderCabin.

A special thanks to the minds behind the avatars of the *FFXIV* characters Fruity Snacks, Beans Mcgee, and D'zinhla Rhee for allowing me to name the wardens after your characters. I hope their inclusion made you smile.

Thank you to my publishing team, Brit Hvide, Angelica Chong, Nick Burnham, Bryn A. McDonald, Kelley Frodel, Crystal Shelley, Raquel Brown, Ellen Wright, Emily Byron, Anna Jackson, Angela Man, Eric Arroyo, and Six Red Marbles & Jouve India. And of course to all the wonderful booksellers and librarians who helped this story get into readers' hands.

A huge thank you to my agents Chris Lotts and Sam Morgan, and everyone at the Lotts Agency, for their tireless support.

And of course, thank *you*, dear readers, for choosing to spend your time letting me tell you a story.

extras

orbit-books.co.uk

about the author

Megan E. O'Keefe was raised among journalists and, as soon as she was able, joined them by crafting a newsletter that chronicled the daily adventures of the local cat population. She has worked in both arts management and graphic design, and has won Writers of the Future and the David Gemmell Morningstar Award. Megan lives in the Bay Area of California.

Find out more about Megan E. O'Keefe and other Orbit authors by registering for the free monthly newsletter at orbit-books.co.uk.

if you enjoyed

THE TWO LIES OF FAVEN SYTHE

look out for

THESE BURNING STARS

The Kindom trilogy: Book One

by

Bethany Jacobs

Jun Ironway, hacker, con artist and only occasional thief, has got her hands on a piece of contraband that could set her up for life: evidence that implicates the powerful Nightfoot family in a planet-wide genocide seventy-five years ago. The Nightfoots control the precious sevite that fuels interplanetary travel through three star systems. And someone is sure to pay handsomely for anything that could break their hold.

Of course, anything valuable is also dangerous. The Kindom, the ruling power of the three star systems, is inextricably tied up in the Nightfoots' monopoly – and they can't afford to let Jun expose the truth. They task two of their most brutal clerics with hunting her down: preternaturally stoic Chono, and brilliant hothead Esek, who also happens to be the heir to the Nightfoot empire.

But Chono and Esek are haunted in turn by a figure from their shared past, known only as Six. What Six truly wants is anyone's guess. And the closer they get to finding Jun, the surer Chono is that Six is manipulating them all – and that they are heading for a bloody confrontation that no one will survive unscathed.

If you enjoyed

THE TWO LIES OF FAVEN SYTHE

look out for

THESE BURNING STARS

The Kindom Trilogy: Book One

by

Bethany Jacobs

CHAPTER ONE

1643

YEAR OF THE LETTING

Kinschool of Principes
Loez Continent
The Planet Ma'kess

H er ship alighted on the tarmac with engines snarling, hot air
billowing out from beneath the thrusters. The hatch opened
with a hiss and she disembarked to the stench of the jump gate that
had so recently spit her into Ma'kess's orbit—a smell like piss and
ozone.

Underfoot, blast burns scorched the ground, signatures from ships
that had been coming and going for three hundred years. The township

of Principes would have no cause for so much activity, if it weren't for the kinschool that loomed ahead.

She was hungry. A little annoyed. There was a marble of nausea lodged in the base of her throat, a leftover effect of being flung from one star system to another in the space of two minutes. This part of Ma'kess was cold and wet, and she disliked the monotonous sable plains flowing away from the tarmac. She disliked the filmy dampness in the air. If the kinschool master had brought her here for nothing, she would make him regret it.

The school itself was all stone and mortar and austerity. Somber-looking effigies stared down at her from the parapet of the second-story roof: the Six Gods, assembled like jurors. She looked over her shoulder at her trio of novitiates, huddled close to one another, watchful. Birds of prey in common brown. By contrast, she was quite resplendent in her red-gold coat, the ends swishing around her ankles as she started toward the open gates. She was a cleric of the Kindom, a holy woman, a member of the Righteous Hand. In this school were many students who longed to be clerics and saw her as the pinnacle of their own aspirations. But she doubted any had the potential to match her.

Already the kinschool master had appeared. They met in the small courtyard under the awning of the entryway, his excitement and eagerness instantly apparent. He bowed over his hands a degree lower than necessary, a simpering flattery. In these star systems, power resided in the Hands of the Kindom, and it resided in the First Families. She was both.

"Thank you for the honor of your presence, Burning One."

She made a quick blessing over him, rote, and they walked together into the school. The novitiates trailed behind, silent as the statues that guarded the walls of the receiving hall. It had all looked bigger when she graduated seven years ago.

As if reading her mind, the kinschool master said, "It seems a life-time since you were my student."

She chuckled, which he was welcome to take as friendly, or mocking. They walked down a hallway lined with portraiture of the most famous students and masters in the school's history: Aver Paiye, Khen Sikhen Khen, Luto Moonback. All painted. No holograms. Indeed, outside the tech aptitude classrooms, casting technology was little-to-be-seen in this school. Not fifty miles away, her family's factories produced the very sevite fuel that made jump travel and casting possible, yet here the masters lit their halls with torches and sent messages to each other via couriers. As if training the future Hands was too holy a mission to tolerate basic conveniences.

The master said, "I hope your return pleases you?"

She wondered what they'd done with her own watercolor portrait. She recalled looking very smug in it, which, to be fair, was not an uncommon condition for her.

"I was on Teros when I got your message. Anywhere is better than that garbage rock."

The master smiled timidly. "Of course. Teros is an unpleasant planet. Ma'kess is the planet of your heart. And the most beautiful of all!" He sounded like a tourist pamphlet, extolling the virtues of the many planets that populated the Treble star systems. She grunted. He asked, "Was your trip pleasant?"

"Hardly any reentry disturbance. Didn't even vomit during the jump."

They both laughed, him a little nervously. They walked down a narrow flight of steps and turned onto the landing of a wider staircase of deep blue marble. She paused and went to the banister, gazing down at the room below.

Six children stood in a line, each as rigid as the staves they held at their sides. They couldn't have been older than ten or eleven. They were dressed identically, in tunics and leggings, and their heads were shaved. They knew she was there, but they did not look up at her. Staring straight ahead, they put all their discipline on display, and she observed them like a butcher at a meat market.

"Fourth-years," she remarked, noticing the appliqués on their chests. They were slender and elfin looking, even the bigger ones. No giants in this cohort. A pity.

"I promise you, Sa, you won't be disappointed."

She started down the staircase, brisk and cheerful, ignoring the students. They had no names, no gendermarks—and no humanity as far as their teachers were concerned. They were called by numbers, given "it" for a pronoun. She herself was called Three, once. Just another object, honed for a purpose. Legally, Treble children had the right to gender themselves as soon as they discovered what fit. But *these* children would have to wait until they graduated. Only then could they take genders and names. Only then would they have their own identities.

At the foot of the staircase, she made a sound at her novitiates. They didn't follow her farther, taking sentry on the last step. On the combat floor, she gloried in the familiar smells of wood and stone and sweat. Her hard-soled boots *clacked* pleasingly as she took a slow circle about the room, gazing up at the magnificent mural on the ceiling, of the Six Gods at war. A brilliant golden light fell upon them, emanating from the sunlike symbol of the Godfire—their parent god, their essence, and the core of the Treble's faith.

She wandered around the room, brushing past the students as if they were scenery. The anticipation in the room ratcheted, the six students trying hard not to move. When she did finally look at them, it was with a quick twist of her neck, eyes locking on with predatory precision. All but one flinched, and she smiled. She brought her hand out from where it had been resting on the hilt of her bloodletter dagger, and saw several of them glance at the weapon. A weapon ordinarily reserved for cloaksaan.

This was just one of the things that must make her extraordinary to the students. Her family name being another. Her youth, of course. And she was very beautiful. Clerics deeply valued beauty, which pleased gods and people alike. *Her* beauty was like the Godfire itself, consuming and hypnotic and deadly.

Add to this the thing she represented: not just the Clerisy itself, in all its holy power, but the future the students might have. When they finished their schooling (*if* they finished their schooling), they would be one step closer to a position like hers. They would have power and prestige and choice—to adopt gendermarks, to take their family names again or create new ones. But *so much* lay between them and that future. Six more years of school and then five years as a novitiate. (Not everyone could do it in three, like her.) If all that went right, they'd receive an appointment to one of the three Hands of the Kindom. But only if they worked hard. Only if they survived.

Only if they were extraordinary.

"Tell me," she said to them all. "What is the mission of the Kindom?"

They answered in chorus: "Peace, under the Kindom. Unity, in the Treble."

"Good." She looked each one over carefully, observed their proudly clasped staves. Though "staves" was a stretch. The long poles in their hands were made from a heavy-duty foam composite. Strong enough to bruise, even to break skin—but not bones. The schools, after all, were responsible for a precious commodity. This cheapened the drama of the upcoming performance, but she was determined to enjoy herself anyway.

"And what are the three pillars of the Kindom?" she asked.

"Righteousness! Cleverness! Brutality!"

She hummed approval. Righteousness for the Clerisy. Cleverness for the Secretaries. Brutality for the Cloaksaan. The three Hands. In other parts of the school, students were studying the righteous God-texts of their history and faith, or they were perfecting the clever arts of economy and law. But these students, these little fourth-years, were here to be brutal.

She gave the kinschool master a curt nod. His eyes lit up and he turned to the students like a conductor to his orchestra. With theatrical aplomb, he clapped once.

It seemed impossible that the six students could look any smarter, but they managed it, brandishing their staves with stolid expressions. She searched for cracks in the facades, for shadows and tremors. She saw several. They were so young, and it was to be expected in front of someone like her. Only one of them was a perfect statue. Her eyes flicked over this one for a moment longer than the others.

The master barked, "One!"

Immediately, five of the children turned on the sixth, staves sweeping into offense like dancers taking position, and then—oh, what a dance it was! The first blow was like a *clap* against One's shoulder; the second, a heavy *thwack* on its thigh. It fought back hard—it had to, swinging its stave in furious arcs and trying like hell not to be pushed too far off-balance. She watched its face, how the sweat broke out, how the eyes narrowed, and its upper teeth came down on its lip to keep from crying out when one of the children struck it again, hard, on the hip. That sound was particularly good, a *crack* that made it stumble and lose position. The five children gave no quarter, and then there was a fifth blow, and a sixth, and—

"Done!" boomed the master.

Instantly, all six children dropped back into line, staves at rest beside them. The first child was breathing heavily. Someone had got it in the mouth, and there was blood, but it didn't cry.

The master waited a few seconds, pure showmanship, and said, "Two!"

The dance began again, five students turning against the other. This was an old game, with simple rules. Esek had played it many times herself, when she was Three. The attack went on until either offense or defense landed six blows. It was impressive if the attacked child scored a hit at all, and yet as she watched the progressing bouts, the second and fourth students both made their marks before losing the round. The children were merciless with one another, crowding their victim in, jabbing and kicking and swinging without reprieve. Her lip curled back in raw delight. These students were as vicious as desert foxes.

But by the time the fifth student lost its round, they were getting sloppy. They were bruised, bleeding, tired. Only the sixth remained to defend itself, and everything would be slower and less controlled now. No more soldierly discipline, no more pristine choreography. Just tired children brawling. Yet she was no less interested, because the sixth student was the one with no fissures in its mask of calm. Even more interestingly, this one had been the least aggressive in the preceding fights. It joined in, yes, but she wasn't sure it ever landed a body blow. It was not timid so much as . . . restrained. Like a leashed dog.

When the master said, "Six," something changed in the room.

She couldn't miss the strange note in the master's voice—of pleasure and expectation. The children, despite their obvious fatigue, snapped to attention like rabbits scenting a predator. They didn't rush at Six as they had rushed at one another. No, suddenly, they moved into a half-circle formation, approaching this last target with an unmistakable caution. Their gazes sharpened and they gripped their staves tighter than before, as if expecting to be disarmed. The sweat and blood stood out on their faces, and one of them quickly wiped a streak away, as if this would be its only chance to clear its eyes.

And Six? The one who commanded this sudden tension, this careful advance? It stood a moment, taking them all in at once, stare like a razor's edge. And then, it flew.

She could think of no other word for it. It was like a whirling storm, and its stave was a lightning strike. No defensive stance for this one—it went after the nearest student with a brutal spinning kick that knocked it on its ass, then it whipped its body to the left and cracked its stave against a different student's shoulder, and finished with a jab to yet another's carelessly exposed shin. All of this happened before the five attackers even had their wits about them, and for a moment she thought they would throw their weapons down, cower, and retreat before this superior fighter.

Instead, they charged.

It was like watching a wave that had gone out to sea suddenly surge upon the shore. They didn't fight as individuals, but as one corralling force, spreading out and pressing in. They drove Six back and back and back—against the wall. For the first time, they struck it, hard, in the ribs, and a moment later they got it again, across the jaw. The sound sent a thrill down her spine, made her fingers clench in hungry eagerness for a stave of her own. She watched the sixth fighter's jaw flush with blood and the promise of bruising, but it didn't falter. It swept its stave in an arc, creating an opening. It struck one of them in the chest, then another in the side, and a third in the thigh—six blows altogether. The students staggered, their offense broken, their wave disintegrating on the sixth student's immovable shore.

She glanced at their master, waiting for him to announce the conclusion of the match, and its decisive victor. To her great interest, he did no such thing, nor did the children seem to expect he would. They recovered, and charged.

Was the sixth fighter surprised? Did it feel the sting of its master's betrayal? Not that she could tell. That face was a stony glower of intent, and those eyes were smart and ruthless.

The other fights had been quick, dirty, over in less than a minute. This last fight went on and on, and each second made her pulse race. The exhaustion she'd seen in the students before gave way to an almost frenzied energy. How else could they hold their ground against Six? They parried and dodged and swung in increasingly desperate bursts, but through it all the sixth kept *hitting* them. Gods! It was relentless. Even when the other students started to catch up (strikes to the hip, to the wrist, to the thigh) it *kept going*. The room was full of ragged gasping, but when she listened for Six's breath, it was controlled. Loud, but steady, and its eyes never lost their militant focus.

In the feverish minutes of the fight, it landed eighteen strikes (she counted; she couldn't help counting) before finally one of the others got in a sixth blow, a lucky cuff across its already bruised mouth.

The master called, "Done!"

The children practically dropped where they stood, their stave arms falling limply at their sides, their relief as palpable as the sweat in the air. They got obediently back in line, and as they did, she noticed that one of them met Six's eye. A tiny grin passed between them, conspiratorial, childlike, before they were stoic again.

She could see the master's satisfied smile. She had of course not known *why* he asked her to come to Principes. A new statue in her honor, perhaps? Or a business opportunity that would benefit her family's sevite industry? Maybe one of the eighth-years, close to graduating, had particular promise? No, in the end, it was none of that. He'd brought her here for a fourth-year. He'd brought her here so he could show off his shining star. She herself left school years earlier than any student in Principes's history, a mere fifteen when she became a novitiate. Clearly the master wanted to break her record. To have this student noticed by her, recruited by her as an eleven-year-old—what a feather that would be, in the master's cap.

She looked at him directly, absorbing his smug expression.

"Did its parents put you up to that?" she asked, voice like a razor blade.

The smugness bled from his face. He grew pale and cleared his throat. "It has no parents."

Interesting. The Kindom was generally very good about making sure orphans were rehomed. Who had sponsored the child's admission to a kinschool? Such things weren't cheap.

The master said, clearly hoping to absolve himself, "After you, it's the most promising student I have ever seen. Its intelligence, its casting skills, its—"

She chuckled, cutting him off.

"Many students are impressive in the beginning. In my fourth year, I wasn't the star. And the one who was the star, that year? What happened to it? Why, I don't even think it graduated. Fourth year is far too early to know anything about a student."

She said these things as if the sixth student hadn't filled her with visceral excitement. As if she didn't see, vast as the Black Ocean itself, what it might become. Then she noticed that the master had said nothing. No acquiescence. No apology, either, which surprised her.

"What aren't you telling me?" she asked.

He cleared his throat again, and said, very lowly, "Its family name was Alanye."

Her brows shot up. She glanced back at the child, who was not making eye contact. At this distance, it couldn't have heard the master's words.

"Really?" she asked.

"Yes. A secretary adopted it after its father died. The secretary sent it here."

She continued staring at the child. Watching it fight was exhilarating, but knowing its origins made her giddy. This was delicious.

"Does it know?"

The master barely shook his head no. She *hmmed* a bright sound of pleasure.

Turning from him, she strode toward the child, shaking open her knee-length coat. When she was still several feet away from it, she crooked a finger.

"Come here, little fish. Let me have a look at you."

The fourth-year moved forward until it was a foot away, gazing up, up, into her face. She looked it over more carefully than before. Aside from their own natural appearance, students weren't allowed any distinguishing characteristics, and sometimes it was hard to tell them apart. She took in the details, looked for signs of the child's famous ancestor, Lucos Alanye: a man who started with nothing, acquired a mining fleet, and blew up a moon to stop anyone else from taking its riches. The sheer pettiness of it! He was the most notorious mass murderer in Treble history. She hadn't known he *had* descendants. With a flick of her wrist, she cast an image of Alanye to her ocular screen, comparing the ancestor to the descendant. Inconclusive.

The child remained utterly calm. Her own novitiates weren't always so calm.

"So, you are Six. That is a very holy designation, you know." It said nothing, and she asked it cheerfully, "Tell me: Who is the Sixth God?"

This was an old riddle from the Godtexts, one with no answer. A person from Ma'kess would claim the god Makala. A person from Quietus would say Capamame. Katishsaan favored Kata, and so on, each planet giving primacy to its own god. Asking the question was just a way to figure out where a person's loyalty or origins lay. This student looked Katish to her, but maybe it would claim a different loyalty?

Then it said, "There is no Sixth God, Sa. Only the Godfire."

She tilted her head curiously. So, it claimed no loyalty, no planet of origin. Only a devotion to the Kindom, for whom the Godfire held primacy. How...strategic.

She ignored its answer, asking, "Do you know who I am?"

The silence in the room seemed to deepen, as if some great invisible creature had sucked in its breath.

"Yes, Burning One. You are Esek Nightfoot."

She saw the other children from the corner of her eye, looking tense and excited.

She nodded. "Yes." And bent closer to it. "I come from a very important family," she said, as if it didn't know. "That's a big responsibility. Perhaps you know what it's like?"

For the first time, it showed emotion—a slight widening of the eyes. Almost instantly, its expression resolved back into blankness.

"The master says you don't know who you are...Is that true, little fish?"

"We don't have names, Sa."

She grinned. "You are very disciplined. From all accounts, so was Lucos Alanye."

Its throat moved, a tiny swallow. It knew *exactly* what family it came from. The kinschool master was a fool.

"Do you know," Esek said, "all the First Families of the Treble are required to give of their children to the Kindom? One from each generation must become a Hand. My matriarch selected me from my generation. It seems fate has selected you from yours."

There was a fierceness in its eyes that said it liked this idea very much—though, of course, the Alanyes were not a First Family. Lucos himself was nothing more than an upstart and opportunist, a resource-raping traitor, a genocider. Esek half admired him.

"Your family did mine a great service," she said.

It looked wary now, a little confused. She nodded. "Yes, my family controls the sevite factories. And do you know who are the laborers that keep our factories going?"

This time it ventured an answer, so quiet its voice barely registered, "The Jeveni, Sa."

"Yes! The Jeveni." Esek smiled, as if the Jeveni were kings and not refugees. "And if Lucos Alanye had never destroyed their moon world, the Jeveni would not need my family to employ them, would they? And then, who would run the factories? So you see it is all very well, coming from the bloodline of a butcher. All our evils give something back."

The student looked at her with that same wariness. She changed the subject.

"What do you think of your performance today?"

Its face hardened. "The fight had no honor, Sa."

Esek's brows lifted. They were conversing in Ma'kessi, the language of the planet Ma'kess. But just then, the student had used a Teron word for "honor." One that more accurately translated to "bragging rights." Perhaps the student was from the planet Teros? Or perhaps it had a precise attitude toward language—always the best word for the best circumstance.

"You struck your attackers eighteen times. Is there no honor in that?"

"I lost. Honor is for winning."

"But the master cheated you."

The invisible creature in the room drew in its breath again. Behind her she could *feel* the master's quickening pulse. Esek's smile brightened, but Six looked apprehensive. Its compatriots were glancing uneasily at one another, discipline fractured.

She said, "Beyond these walls, out in the world, people don't have to tell you if you've won. You know it for yourself, and you make other people know it. If I were you, and the master tried to cheat me out of my win, I'd kill him for it."

The tension ratcheted so high that she could taste it, thick and cloying. Six's eyes widened. Before anything could get out of hand, Esek laughed.

"Of course, if *you* tried to kill the master, he would decapitate you before you'd even lifted your little stave off the ground, wouldn't he?"

It was like lacerating a boil. The hot tightness under the skin released, and if there was a foul smell left over, well . . . that was worth it.

"Tell me, Six," she carried on, "what do you want most of all?"

It answered immediately, confidence surging with the return to script, "To go unnoticed, Sa."

She'd thought so. These were the words of the Cloaksaan. The master wouldn't be parading its best student under her nose like a bitch in heat if the bitch didn't want to be a cloaksaan—those deadly officers of the Kindom's Brutal Hand, those military masterminds and shadow-like assassins, who made peace possible in the Treble through their ruthlessness. Esek had only ever taken cloaksaan novitiates. It was an idiosyncrasy of hers. Most clerics trained clerics and most secretaries trained secretaries, but Cleric Nightfoot trained cloaksaan.

"You held back in the first five fights," she remarked.

The child offered no excuses. Did she imagine defiance in its eyes?

"That's all right. That was smart. You conserved your strength for the fight that mattered. Your teachers might tell you it was cowardly, but cloaksaan don't have to be brave. They have to be smart. They have to win. Right?"

Six nodded.

"Would you like to be my novitiate someday, little fish?" asked Esek gently.

It showed no overt excitement. But its voice was vehement. "Yes, Burning One."

She considered it for long moments, looking over its body, its muscles and form, like it was a racehorse she might like to sponsor. It knew what she would see, and she felt its hope. Her smile spread like taffy, and she said simply, "No."

She might as well have struck it. Its shock broke over her like a wave. Seeing that it could feel was important; unlike some Hands, she didn't relish an emotionless novitiate.

"I won't take you. More than that, I'm going to tell the other Hands not to take you."

The child's stunned expression nearly made her laugh, but she chose for once to be serious, watching it for the next move. Its mouth opened and closed. Clearly it wanted to speak but knew it had no right. She gave it a little nod of permission, eager to hear what it would say. It glanced toward its master, then spoke in a voice so soft, no one would hear.

"Burning One...I am not my ancestor. I am—loyal. I am Kindom in my heart."

She hummed and nodded. "Yes, I can see that. But haven't we established? My family owes your ancestor a debt, for the Jeveni, and I don't care if you're like him or not. The fact is, I find you very impressive. Just as your master does, and your schoolkin do. I imagine everyone finds you impressive, little fish. But that's of no use to me. I require something different."

Esek watched with interest as it struggled to maintain its composure. She wondered if it would cry, or lose its temper, or drop into traumatized blankness. When none of these things happened, but it only stood there with its throat bobbing, she dropped a lifeline.

"When you are ready, you must come directly to me."

Its throat stilled. She'd startled it again.

"You must come and tell me that you want to be my novitiate. Don't go to my people, or the other Hands. Don't announce yourself. Come to me unawares, without invitation."

It looked at her in despairing confusion. "Burning One, you're surrounded by novitiates. If I come to you without permission, your people will kill me."

She nodded. "That's right. They'll never let you through without my leave. What's worse, I probably won't even remember you exist. Don't feel bad. I never remember any of the little fish I visit in the schools. Why should I, with so many things to occupy me? No, in a couple of days, you'll slip my mind. And if, in a few years, some strange young person newly gendered and named tries to come before me and ask to be my novitiate, well! Even if you get through my people, I may kill you myself." A long pause stretched between them, before she added, "Unless..."

It was exhilarating, to whip the child from one end to the other with the power of a single word. Its eyes lit up. It didn't even breathe, waiting for her to name her condition. She leaned closer still, until their faces were only inches apart, and she whispered in a voice only it could hear, "You must do something *extraordinary*." She breathed the word into its soul, and it flowed there hot and powerful as the Godfire. "You must do something I have never seen before. Something memorable, and shocking, and *brutal*. Something that will make me pause before I kill you. I have no idea what it is. I have no idea what I'll *want* when that day comes. But if you do it, then I will make you my novitiate. Your ancestry won't matter. Your past won't matter. This moment won't matter. You will have everything you deserve: all the honor a life can bring. And you will earn it at my side."

The child stared at her, caught in the terrible power of the silence she let hang between them. And then, like a fishersaan cutting a line, she drew back. Her voice was a normal volume again, and she shrugged.

"It's not a great offer, I'll grant you. Probably you'll die. If you choose not to come to me, I won't hold it against you. I won't remember you, after all. There are other, excellent careers in the Kindom. You don't have to be a Hand to do good work. Someone as talented as you could be a marshal or guardsaan. The master says you're good at casting. You could be an archivist! But whatever you decide, I wish you luck, little fish." She pinned it with her mocking stare. "Now swim away."

It blinked, released from the spell. After a moment of wretched bewilderment, it dropped back into place beside its schoolkin, who looked most shocked of all; one was crying silently. She whirled around, each click of her boots on the stone floor like a gunshot. The gold threads in her coat caught the light until she shimmered like a flame.

She locked eyes with the master, whose friendliness had evaporated in these tense minutes. He was now marshaling forty years of training into a blank expression, but Esek sensed the cold terror in him. No one in his life had seen him this frightened before, and the shame of it, of all these little fourth-years witnessing it, would torture him.

Esek moved as if she would go right past him, but paused at the last moment. They were parallel, arms brushing, and she heard his minuscule gasp. Perhaps he expected the plunge of the bloodletter? As a Hand of the Kindom, she had every right to kill him if she judged his actions unrighteous. Still, knowing he was afraid of it happening was its own reward—and she didn't feel like dealing with the aftermath today. Instead, she studied the master's face. He was staring straight forward, as well trained as the students, and just as vulnerable.

"Graduate it to the eighth-years."

The master's temple ticked. "You've already determined that no Hand will make it their novitiate. It has no future here."

Esek chuckled, amazed at the brazenness of this master. "Let it decide on its own. Personally, I think this one will find its way. Or has your confidence in it proved so fickle?" The master was silent, and this time Esek's voice was a threatening purr. "What about your confidence in *me*, Master? I am your window to the glory and wisdom of the Godfire. Don't you believe in the power of the Clerisy?" She drew out the final word, clicking the *C* with malevolent humor.

The master nodded shortly. "Of course, Sa. I will do as you say."

Esek smiled at him. She patted his shoulder, enjoying the flinch he couldn't control. She was preparing to murmur some new ridicule into his ear, when a voice interrupted them.

"Burning One."

She looked toward the marble staircase, where her novitiates still stood. They had been there all this time, invisible until she had need.

"Yes?" Esek asked. "What is it?"

"You have a message from Alisiana Nightfoot. The matriarch requests your presence at Verdant."

Esek clucked her tongue. "No rest for a Nightfoot." She swept past the master without farewells. She heard his barely discernible exhale of relief, and then the trio of novitiates were behind her, following her up the stairs. They retraced their steps to the school gates and the tarmac, where her docked warcrow awaited them. As they went, she called over her shoulder, "Send word to the Cloaksaan that they should visit the master. I think his tenure has run its course."

Who is the Sixth God, to your mind?
Fecund Makala or Kata wise?
Is it wily Terotonteris?
Or else Sajeven, warm and barren?
Is it the devouring Som?
Or Capamame, of gentle songs?
Beware you love them more than me,
For my eye perceives everything.

A Record of the Gods, 1:1–8. Godtexts, pre-Treble

Enter the monthly
Orbit sweepstakes at
www.orbitloot.com

With a different prize every month,
from advance copies of books by
your favourite authors to exclusive
merchandise packs,
we think you'll find something
you love.

facebook.com/OrbitBooksUK
@orbitbooks_uk
@OrbitBooks
orbit-books.co.uk